As Bramble moved down the solid rock face with her saddlebags over her shoulder, she could feel Acton's bones shift and slide with each step.

The movement unsettled her as nothing in her life had ever done. She had tried to pack them tightly but they shook loose, as though Acton was determined in death, as he had been in life, not to be trammelled. As though at every step he tapped her on the back, saying, "Remember me?"

It was bad enough to bear her grief for him; to bear his bones as well, to be a packhorse for his remains, was too much. She wanted to be rid of them. Wanted fiercely to see him again, even as a ghost, and also wanted fiercely not to see him as a ghost, pale and insubstantial. She thought it was a good thing the gods were driving her, because if it had been up to her she was not sure whether she would have brought him back.

But she would complete her task and stop Saker. Kill him, too, if the gods were kind. And then, only then, could she stop and consider what Obsidian Lake had done to her, and who she might be afterwards.

So if Lady Death tried to stop her, too bad for the Lady.

Praise for *Blood Ties*

"With magic, murder, adventure, and mystery, *Blood Ties* is an exciting beginning to a brand-new fantasy epic." —*scifichick.com*

BY PAMELA FREEMAN

The Castings Trilogy

Blood Ties
Deep Water
Full Circle

FULL CIRCLE

The Castings Trilogy
Book Three

PAMELA FREEMAN

www.orbitbooks.net

New York   London

Orbit
Hachette Book Group
237 Park Avenue, New York, NY 10017
www.HachetteBookGroup.com

First North American Orbit edition: November 2009
Originally published in paperback by Hachette Australia, 2009

Orbit is an imprint of Hachette Book Group, Inc. The Orbit name and logo are trademarks of Little, Brown Book Group Limited.

Library of Congress Control Number: 2009934728

ISBN: 9780316035620

10 9 8 7 6 5 4 3 2 1

Printed in the United States of America

To Stephen and Robert

ICE KING'S
COUNTRY

Cliffhaven

Hidden
Valley

Spritford

Death Pass

Sharp River

WESTERN
MOUNTAINS
DOMAIN

Whitehaven

SOUTH
DOMAIN

FAR SOUTH
DOMAIN

Turvite

WIND CITIES

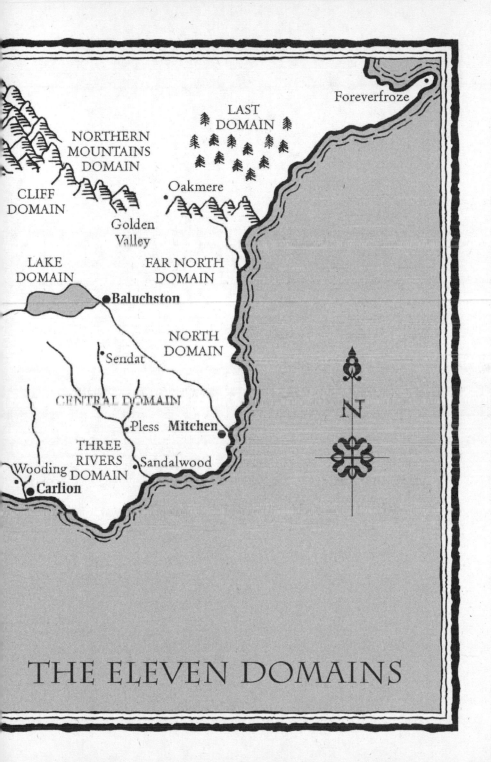

Foreverfroze

LAST
DOMAIN

NORTHERN
MOUNTAINS
DOMAIN

Oakmere

CLIFF
DOMAIN

Golden
Valley

LAKE
DOMAIN

FAR NORTH
DOMAIN

●Baluchston

NORTH
DOMAIN

●Sendat

CENTRAL DOMAIN

●Pless **Mitchen**

THREE
RIVERS
DOMAIN

Sandalwood

Wooding

Carlion

N

THE ELEVEN DOMAINS

FULL CIRCLE

BRAMBLE

I'M SENDING a rope down!" Medric said. "There's nothing to hitch it to here, so don't pull on it until I'm braced and I give you the word."

"All right," said Bramble. She was lucky, she supposed, that she had come down into the caves with Medric, an experienced miner, but part of her wished he would let her stay down here at the bottom of this shaft, alone in the middle of a mountain with Acton's bones, until she too had died and her flesh had sifted into dust.

"Ready?" Medric called.

Bramble adjusted the rope under her armpits and clasped her arms around the fragile bundle of Acton's bones. She pushed down all feeling. She didn't have time for grief, or love, or anything but revenge. Saker the enchanter was going to come to grief himself, and she would be there to destroy him. For her sister Maryrose. For all the innocents killed by Saker's ghost army.

"Ready," she said.

"Now!"

She began to climb, bracing herself against the shaft wall with her feet as Medric hauled from above. The rope cut her, but she was making steady progress when Medric yelled something from above and the world came tumbling down.

Dirt and small rocks hit her face first, blinding her, and then Medric's heavy body slid down the shaft, slamming them both to the ground, with rubble and pebbles cascading after them, covering the candle stub and plunging them into darkness.

They lay gasping for a long moment before Bramble could move.

"Everlasting dark!" Medric swore, his voice shaky. "The edge just gave way."

Somehow, it made Bramble grin. Gods and powers, delvers and hunters from the Great Forest, all had conspired to get her here to find these bones, and now a simple accident could undo it all. She rather liked

1

that, liked the feeling of being, for the moment, free from destiny and instruction. No one had foreseen this, as far as she knew. That meant she could react as she liked and do as she pleased in response.

So she laughed.

"Bramble!" Medric reproved, much as her mother used to.

"Well, it could have been worse," she said. "You're not really hurt, are you?"

She sat up and felt both the jacket full of bones and herself for injuries. Scrapes, bruises (gods, lots of bruises!), and a swelling above one ear—although it seemed very large for something that had just happened, so it may have been a legacy from her first fall down the shaft.

Medric searched around in the rubble until he found the tinderbox, then fished a spare candle out of his belt pouch and lit it. She *was* lucky that Medric had proved so steadfast. She wouldn't have blamed him if he had run away when the delvers came and pushed her down this shaft.

"Always carry a few," he said, although earlier he had intimated that they would run out of light if they didn't turn back soon. He really didn't like being underground, Bramble thought, with a flicker of worry. They weren't likely to get out of here anytime soon.

"Will your friend go for help?"

"Fursey?" Medric shook his head, sending dust flying out of his hair like gold in the candlelight. "He left after the delvers came. Doesn't even know we're down here." His voice was dark with abandonment; he'd hoped that Fursey would stay with him, Bramble thought.

She ignored his sigh; they didn't have time to worry about love affairs gone wrong, no matter how strange the beloved or how deep the hurt. "So we'll have to find another way out."

"I might be able to climb out," Medric said doubtfully, but when they examined the shaft they found it was clogged with rubble, and with her saddlebags, which had slid down the shaft with Medric. Bramble dislodged them, sending gravel spinning off, and emptied out everything in them: spare clothes, hairbrush, boot ties, rags, salt were all moved to one bag, leaving the other empty, ready. Almost empty. At the bottom, where she had put it before leaving Gorham's farm, months ago, was the red scarf she had won when she became the Kill Reborn. It was the only colour in this dark world, and she let it stay where it was, not sure if she were being sentimental or prudent. It was tangled with the brooch Ash had given her. She had tucked it in there when they left Obsidian Lake.

She left the brooch and scarf and put Acton's bones in on top of them. The leg bones didn't fit, and she had to suppress a feeling of panic that she had to leave them behind. She placed them carefully on a low rock, feeling both solemn and silly; they looked ridiculous, like pickings from a giant's plate, but they were Acton's, and she couldn't just throw them away.

Medric tried pulling a few rocks out from the shaft, but more just shifted down into their place. "There's been a big rockfall," he said, in a far more confident tone, the voice of the miner. "No getting out that way, not without a gang of men working from above."

"So," Bramble said, turning and staring into the dark. "We go exploring."

They were standing under a low roof in a flat-bottomed area which sloped gently down to their left and rose more steeply to their right, where the roof became too low for them to walk. There was only one way to go.

"Just as well it's heading the right way," Bramble said.

"Everything gets turned around underground," Medric said warningly. "Don't depend on your sense of direction down here."

"But—" Bramble always knew where she was, and that sense seemed to be working fine. She pointed down the slope and slightly to the right. "The mine entrance is that way."

Medric looked sceptical. "No choice either way," he said. "We follow the river bed."

"What?"

"This would have been a river course, one time," he explained as he led the way down, candle held high. "That's why the walls are so smooth."

Bramble hitched Acton's bones over her shoulder more comfortably, and reached out to touch the wall with the other hand. It was smoother than she'd expected. "So if we follow it down, we find water?" she suggested.

"If we're lucky. If it doesn't narrow too much, or if there's been no rockfalls, or if the land hasn't shifted since the river flowed—which it probably has, which is why the course is dry now." He turned to look seriously at her, his hazel eyes reflecting the spark of candlelight. "We'll be lucky if we get out alive."

Bramble smiled. At least this was *real*—not god-given dreams or time shifting beneath her feet. And it distracted her from thoughts of Acton, which she wasn't ready to face. She thumped Medric on the shoulder and saw him wince as she hit a bruise. "I'm hard to kill," she said. "Let's go."

They went carefully but as fast as they dared, not knowing how long they'd be down here. The candles wouldn't last forever. They followed the old river, ignoring narrower side passages, even though some of them sloped upwards, because in the larger course there was a faint stream of air across their faces.

"Follow the air," Medric said, as though it was the one rule of life, Bramble thought, and maybe it was, in a mine.

Medric settled down into a plodding careful state. He looked at the floor, mostly, leaving it to Bramble to look ahead. She realised that this shutting off was how he had managed to survive the long years of mining.

The old river bed was leading them gradually astray, further down, further north. Bramble reckoned they had passed the mine entrance some time back, and they were now much deeper than when they had started, but she was encouraged by the fresh air which still blew gently in their faces. It had to come from somewhere.

They reached a section where the passage closed in, so they had to crouch, and then slither along. Medric started breathing more heavily. He was a big man, and it was a tight fit.

"I'll go up ahead," Bramble said, "and see if it widens out."

He nodded thankfully and backed out to where he could sit up, his hands shaking. Bramble left the candle with him and went backwards on her stomach, feeling with her toes. The passage narrowed until she could only just move, and she felt a sudden spurt of panic. The walls seemed to press down upon her, the dark she had found soothing only a few minutes before was now full of death, the earth itself a grave where she would be pinned, helpless, forever...

4

She set the fear aside, but it gave her more sympathy for Medric. If he felt like this all the time, he was being heroic just for not screaming. With an effort of will, she kept moving.

As if to reward her, the toe of her boot, sliding carefully backwards, fell into empty air. A ledge, dropping off. How far down? She bent her leg up and found that at the edge her toe couldn't reach the upper wall. The passage widened just before the drop—perhaps enough to let her sit up and turn around. She snaked sideways so that she wouldn't be hanging half-off and half-on the ledge and edged carefully down.

She could feel the air moving more freely around her head and shoulders as she came closer to the drop, and cautiously sat up, bumping her head just a little. She could sit crouched over easily enough, and she could sense a huge empty space in front of her, full of sound ... whispering, plinking, rushing ...

"It opens up," she called back to Medric, "but come carefully—there's a drop on the other side." She sat and listened hard as her voice echoed out and round. Other noises, too. Water and air, air and water ...

Medric came face first, pushing the candle in front of him. That's not going to do much good in a place this size, Bramble thought, but she took it from him and raised it high as he shuffled closer and sat up, more hunched than she but a safer distance from the drop.

The tiny light from the candle was caught, reflected, from a million places, a million drops of water. They were at the top of what must have once been a short waterfall, at the edge of a cavern so large that every sound they made was taken and echoed and echoed again.

There was just enough light to see boulders and arches of rock, icicles and ant hills of rock reaching down and up from ceiling and floor, joining in places into pillars. The cave—the cavern—stretched up in places so high that no light reached. It seemed to reach up into the dark of the night sky, so Bramble felt surprised not to see any stars.

"There are no wonders like the wonders of the dark," Medric said quietly. Bramble suspected that was something Fursey had once said to him, but whoever said it was right. The echoes of Medric's voice climbed and soared and flew back to them in high cascades of sound.

"Wonders ..." the echoes said, and, "Dark ..."

The echoes were surrounded and supported by another sound.

5

Everywhere, from the icicles of rock and from points on the cavern's roof, the tiny drops of water fell, onto rock or into shallow pools. Each small *plop* or splat was magnified and transmuted into a thin, ceaseless, mourning cry. The rocks were weeping, and this was the sound of their tears.

The falling water caught the candlelight and sent sparks of it back to them, so that they were caught in a small pool of dazzle, of rainbow glimpses and fleeting lines of light.

"You know where we are, don't you?" Medric said. "These are the Weeping Caverns. The home of Lady Death herself. We'll never get out."

ASH

LIKE HARP music, the sound of the river rippled far below them. It sounded calm, now. Soothing, as though it had never leapt high, never threatened. The old man smiled, his long white hair casting a shining circle around his head in the firelight. Ash was aware of the other men, his father included, standing in the shadows of the cave, but he couldn't bring himself to look at them. Desperately, he stared into the old man's intense blue eyes.

"She calls you," the man said. "She calls your name. Close your eyes. Listen."

Bewildered, hoping that he was not beyond acceptance, that the human face which had reflected back at him from the pool did not mean that he was worthless, Ash closed his eyes. He had so hoped to find his true shape when he climbed down to meet the River. Every other Traveller man did so, after all. Why should he be different? Did he *have* no true shape? No animal spirit deep in his soul which the River could call out? What did that make him?

Ash shuddered with a combination of grief and horror at the thought and felt the old man pat his back in comfort. .

"Listen," he said gently. "She will speak to you."

The river was growing louder. Ash concentrated. He had heard the River speak only minutes ago, when he stood in her waters and asked permission to drink. She had laughed, and granted it. Now there were no words, only sounds, like music, like the music he carried in his head, day after day.

The music built in his mind, speaking of emotion deeper than thought, deeper than words, stronger than time. Love was only a small part of it, on the edges. Desire ran through it, but was not the centre. He strained, listening harder, and felt it slip away.

"Be still," the old man said.

The hand on Ash's back was warm and reassuring. He let out a long breath, forcing his muscles to loosen, and found the centre of the music, the rhythm that controlled everything. *Welcome*, it said. *Belong*.

He began to cry. He had yearned towards homecoming when he lived with Doronit, hoping past sense that she could give it to him. He had seen belonging like this and envied it, watching Mabry and Elva hold their baby, his namesake. He had dreamt of returning to the Road with his parents as a stonecaster, earning a place with them as he had not been able to do as a musician. Each dream had withered, sending him back to the Road, and finally pushing him here. Perhaps he had been Travelling towards the River all his life.

Yes, said the music. *All your life*.

Ash raised his face to the old man, who was smiling.

"She has been waiting for you for a long, long time, child," he said, as he had said once before. "And so have I."

Ash found his voice with difficulty. "Who are you?" he whispered.

"I am the Prowman."

It was a term Ash knew from old river songs—the Prowman stood at the front of the boat and signalled to the steersman which direction to take, to avoid the rapids and treacherous currents. He found the name reassuring.

Ash's father, Rowan, came forward hesitantly. His head was a badger's; each of the men there wore his true nature in the form of an animal, revealed to them through the power of the River. The sweat on his naked skin reflected the torchlight in slabs of gold and red.

Rowan put a hand gently on Ash's shoulder. The dark badger eyes searched his. And then Rowan let Ash go, turned to the other men and lifted his arms high in a gesture of victory. He howled triumph and the other men joined in, dancing and shouting, the animal screams and yowls echoing off the cave walls until Ash was nearly deafened. It was a terrible sound: harsh, cacophonous, wonderful. It lifted him up into a kind of exaltation. He still didn't understand what had happened, or why he had not been given his true shape like the other men; but he did understand that they accepted him, honoured him, just as he was. The moment was over too soon. Rowan and the other men ran off into the darkness which led to another cave. Some of them carried torches, the flames and smoke flickering behind them as they ran.

They left one torch behind, stuck in a crevice in the rock wall. The dark closed in around, making the cave seem even bigger, the echoes sharper. Ash was aware of his wet feet and calves, suddenly cold where the River had splashed him as he climbed.

The Prowman walked behind one of the boulders near the passage and came back with a blanket and pack. He threw the blanket to Ash, who hesitated. All the other men were naked, except for the Prowman, who wore leggings and a tunic.

"Am I...allowed?"

The old man shrugged, the beads at the end of his long braids clicking softly. "Animals go naked," he said. "We are not animals."

"What are we?"

The Prowman gestured to the floor and they sat, cross-legged, Ash pulling the blanket around himself. The pack held food: cooked chicken, bread, apples, dried pear. Ash fell on it thankfully. He hadn't eaten in three days.

"Slowly," the Prowman said. "Or you'll just throw it all up again."

It was good advice, but it was hard to follow. Ash forced himself to start with the bread and chewed it thoroughly instead of wolfing it down.

"What are we...Well, that's a little hard to say," the Prowman said, smiling. "We are...Hers. I can tell you some things about yourself, although I do not know you. You are a musician."

Ash shook his head vigorously, glad his mouth was full of bread so he didn't have to say the disappointing words out loud.

"No?" The Prowman paused, surprised. "You *don't* make up music?"

Ash stilled, his hand over the chicken. *Did* he make up music? The moment seemed to stretch for hours.

"In my head," he said finally. "Only in my head."

"Ah, well, that's where all music starts."

"But I can't sing!" Ash said. "Or play anything."

"The River doesn't care about that. She wants what's inside you, not what you do outside."

"What? What's inside me?"

"The thing that makes the music, that *thinks* the music. The centre of you. It's why She chose me, why She chose you."

"Chose us to do what?"

For the first time, the Prowman seemed unsure. "Different things. Be Her voice, for one. Be Her eyes in the world, Her...life, Her..."

"Her lover, you said," Ash prompted. He wasn't sure how he felt about that, except intensely curious.

"Mmm...you'll find out about that in time, although it won't be what you expect."

"Nothing ever is!" Ash exclaimed, tired of being told only part of things, tired of always being at the beginning of understanding. Enough of this mysticism. He had a job to do. "I need to learn the secret songs."

The Prowman shook his head, and Ash jumped to his feet, infuriated. "Don't tell me there's *another* shagging test!"

"No, no, don't worry," the Prowman said, laughing sympathetically. "You don't need to learn the songs because when you need them, She will give them to you. How do you think the men learnt them in the first place? She gave them to me, and I gave them to the men. She will be your teacher, lad, when the time comes."

But Ash had a better idea.

"*You* can sing them!" It was a relief, to hand over the responsibility to someone he was sure could fulfil it. But the Prowman put up a hand in refusal.

"No. This is your job. Your time to be active in the world. I have had my time, and it was more than enough." There was a note of sorrow, of loss, of relinquishment, in his voice. "So there is nothing to keep you here," the Prowman went on. "Go where you need to go, and She will be there waiting for you."

"Sanctuary," Ash said without thinking. "I have to go to Sanctuary."

The Prowman's face became shadowed; tears stood in his eyes. With their bright blue clouded, he looked very old, the torchlight showing hundreds of wrinkles, his hands browned with age spots, his hair snow white.

"Sanctuary," he whispered. "That is a name I have not heard in a very long time." He looked up, tears disappearing. "Why do you go to Sanctuary?"

Ash hesitated, overwhelmed by how much he had to explain.

"To raise the ghost of Acton," he said simply. "So that Acton can lay this army of ghosts to rest."

The Prowman went very still.

"Acton," he said. "She did not tell me that. I wonder why." He sat for a long moment and then stood up, as supple as a young boy. "If you go to raise Acton's ghost, lad, I think you will need me with you."

Relief washed over Ash. "You'll come with us?"

"I will take you the River's way."

LEOF

A T NOON the enchanter had sent the wind wraiths away and the ghosts moved off to the south, and Leof, Alston, Hodge and Horst followed them on Thegan's orders. The other troops had returned with Thegan to Sendat after the ghosts had routed them at Bonhill, but there was just a chance that a small group of horsemen could pick off the enchanter from a distance.

"Take any chance you have," Thegan had said. "At any cost."

Leof nodded. "The other reports say that the ghosts faded at sunset or sunrise," he reminded Thegan. "We might get our chance then."

Thegan clapped him on the shoulder in a parody of his usual comradeship. It was a show for the men watching, and Leof was glad that Thegan could still make a show. He had never seen his lord angry like this, not even when Bramble had defied him and escaped.

Now the four warlord's men followed as the ghost army, frustrated by the solid doors and shuttered windows of Bonhill, headed out into the countryside, looking for easier prey. Horst strung his bow, the short bow he kept for using on horseback.

"My lord," he said to Leof, indicating the enchanter and the bow.

During the battle, the wind wraiths had plucked their arrows out of the air and they had lost their best chance to take the enchanter. If the wraiths stayed away now, Leof knew they might have a chance. "Yes," he replied. "Anytime you get a clear shot, take him."

But as they rode, slowly, always at a distance, they could see that the wraiths were hovering far overhead. The enchanter probably couldn't see them, but they were ready to protect him.

Leof turned to Alston. "If we can charge them suddenly, Horst might get a shot away. He only needs one."

He expected Horst to preen at the praise, but the man just nodded. Something was worrying Horst, more than the ghosts. He had arrived back from the Last Domain only just in time to come south with Thegan,

12

but without Sully, who had been killed in an ambush in the Golden Valley. Another problem for Thegan to deal with, but not one Leof could think about now.

Perhaps Horst was missing his friend. He kept glancing at the sky and wiping his hands on his breeches. Well, wind wraiths were enough to make anyone nervous. Gods knew they made Leof jittery enough.

"Do you know this country, Alston?" Leof asked. He knew it well himself, from riding chases all over it.

Alston nodded. "Aye, my lord, a little."

"The road goes between a small hill and a stream, up ahead, about a mile away. Once they pass the hill, we can come after them fast and catch them up on the other side. If we come in fast enough, the wind wraiths may be taken by surprise. It might give us a chance."

Nodding, Alston considered it.

"We should close up the gap, maybe," he ventured, and Leof agreed.

"But slowly, and gently. Don't alarm the wraiths."

Hodge and Horst both shivered at the thought, then exchanged embarrassed glances. Horst set his face in a scowl, as though preparing himself for the worst.

They urged the horses to a faster walk and gradually, as the ghosts and the enchanter strode on, unheeding, they closed the gap little by little. The wraiths seemed unaware of them, but Leof didn't hold out much hope. As soon as they moved in, the wraiths would swoop to protect the enchanter. He wondered if he should give Horst his own horse Arrow to ride — she was by far the fastest, and would get him closest to the ghosts. But she wasn't used to her rider shooting as he rode, and Horst's bay was. He would just have to take care not to get in Horst's line of fire.

Ahead, the last of the ghosts disappeared as the road bent behind the hill. "Draw weapons. Horst, ready bow. Now!" Leof ordered.

They spurred their horses, Arrow getting away first, but the others catching up fast as Leof held her back a little. Horst took the lead, arrow nocked and bow held down, reins between his teeth. His horse knew what was expected of her, and she gave it: a steady pace, like a regular drum beat, so that Horst could loose the arrow at precisely the right moment in her gait.

As they rounded the hill, Horst was just in the lead.

"Spread out!" Leof commanded, and he and Alston took point either side of Horst while Hodge brought up the rear, his own bow out and ready.

The ghosts turned at the sound of their hoof beats, but they were too far from the horsemen to interfere. Horst was almost within bow shot. The enchanter turned.

"Wait, wait, not too soon," Leof called.

Horst took aim and the enchanter put up a futile hand to ward him away. As the arrow left the bow the ghosts moved in front of the enchanter, but too late.

Then, in the split second before the arrow reached him, the wraiths dived between, snatching the arrow from the air, screaming. They turned towards Horst, claws out, teeth bared, and lunged.

"Fire again!" Leof commanded, but Horst screamed, too, and turned the terrified horse, kicking her away. The other horses were also panicking, and the ghosts had closed in around the enchanter. They had lost their chance. Bitterness in his mouth, Leof shouted, "Back! Back!" and they turned their horses and took off after Horst, who was well down the road, his bay galloping faster than ever before.

The wraiths nipped and scratched at them as they went, scoring the horses' rumps and scratching long furrows in their scalps. It was terrifying. The wraiths' shrieking seemed to sap all the strength from Leof's muscles, but he was bolstered by fury, and he rounded on them and shouted, "We are in settled lands and there has been no betrayal. Begone!"

They were the words his father had taught him, to banish wind wraiths. The words had worked for a long, long time, part of the compact between the spirits and humans, which had been established so long ago that its beginning had passed out of memory. The spirits—water, wind, fire, forest, earth—were free to hunt in wilderness but forbidden to attack humans in settled lands. Unless a human betrayed one of their own to the wraiths, as humans sometimes did. But that did no harm to the compact itself. Without the compact, the wraiths could feast on body and soul right across the Domains, with nothing to stop them. They were even harder to fight than ghosts. Without the compact every stream would be full of water sprites, every wind a carrier of death, every step into a wood a step into peril…

Leof wasn't sure the compact still held, and the thought that it might have broken irrevocably was frightening. But the wraiths hovered behind him and screamed disappointment, their claws dripping blood. Arrow would not be held. She pulled her head around and made off after the other horses, the herd instinct taking over.

Leof let them run half a mile or so before he called them in. The horses' sides were lathered and their eyes still showed too much white. He had to let them rest and drink before following the enchanter again. For all the good that would do, he thought.

The stream was close to the road here, and Hodge walked the horses for a few minutes to cool them down, then watered them. He was shaking, still.

"Horst," Leof said. "Come."

He took Horst aside. The man wouldn't look him in the eyes. Like Hodge, he was still shaking, but Leof suspected it was with shame as much as with the aftermath of fear.

"You did not follow my order, Horst." Leof kept his voice deliberately calm.

"I'm sorry, my lord! Please—please don't tell my lord Thegan."

Leof considered that. Could he blame this man for panicking in the face of those deadly claws and teeth? A human enemy was one thing, but a foe who could eat your soul was something very different. Thegan, on the other hand, would blame him and punish him. And Horst was Thegan's man. He worshipped his lord. A hard word from Thegan was enough to cause anguish—real punishment, real shame, would be unbearable.

They needed every archer they could get, if they were to have any chance at this enchanter. There would be opportunities in the next battle. Horst was the best they had.

"There will be another time," Leof said slowly, "when we may confront the enchanter again, *with* his wraiths, and only an archer can save us."

"It won't happen again, my lord. I swear it. I swear it."

There was something else here, something Horst wasn't saying, something that accounted for the panic. Leof took a guess. "You've met wind wraiths before."

15

Horst looked astounded "Aye, my lord," he mumbled. "They almost killed me."

"And now you have faced them again. Tell me honestly, Horst, if I needed you to face them one more time, could you?"

Horst stared at the ground for a long moment, then looked up and deliberately met Leof's eyes, as a common soldier rarely did to an officer. "I could," he said firmly.

"Then I think Lord Thegan may not need to know any more than that the wind wraiths stopped our attack."

Horst's face was flooded with relief. "Thank you, my lord."

"Don't let us down, Horst."

"I'd die first," Horst promised.

Leof slapped him on the shoulder. "I'd prefer you didn't. We have need of you."

They remounted and took the road again, watching with beating hearts for the first sign of wind wraiths in the sky above them. Where there were wind wraiths, they would find the enchanter.

The horses were rested and their wounds staunched, but they didn't like being asked to go back down the road towards the spot where they had been so terrified. Hodge's black gelding dug in his hooves and refused to move.

"We might do better on foot," Leof said. "The horses won't face the wraiths without bolting."

Hodge cleared his throat the way sergeants do when officers are about to make a big mistake.

"Well, sergeant?" Leof asked.

"Without the horses, we'd've been dead back there. Sir." Hodge said it simply, and he was right, of course.

"Very well, then. Our aim is to keep them in sight until sunset, when the enchanter will be without his army, at least, and we may have a chance to waylay him without the wraiths seeing us."

They nodded together, Alston, Hodge and Horst. Good men. Experienced, level headed. Leof wondered if they would all make it back home, but shoved the thought away, down where it belonged, in the well of shadows that every soldier avoided thinking about.

"We'll go across country, then," Leof said. "Skirt the hill and find him on the other side."

The black gelding—Canker, a bad name for a horse, Leof thought—was happy enough to take to the fields and the other horses followed Arrow eagerly.

By mid-afternoon they had traced a big circle around the hill and made their way back to the road. But there was no sign of the enchanter.

"A hand canter until we have them in sight," Leof ordered. "Horst, you lead. Keep an eye out for signs they've left the road."

It was a strange journey. The sun was shining brightly, the breeze was warm, Leof could hear thrushes in the hedgerows and grasshoppers shrilling. A beautiful day, and a lovely ride. But behind them lay death and before them terror. It was as though they rode in a bubble of safety that might be popped at any moment. He shook his head to clear it. It had been a long night and longer morning, and he was much too tired. He should eat something, although he felt at the moment as though he'd never again be hungry. He dug some dried grapes out of his belt pouch and chewed on them stolidly, the sweetness making him thirsty, so he drank. The others were doing the same, he noted, except Horst, who had no attention to spare from the dust of the road.

They should have caught up with the enchanter quickly enough, despite their long detour, but the road stretched on and they came eventually to the next village, Feathers Dale, which lay so quiet and orderly under the sun that Leof knew immediately that the ghosts had not come this far.

"We've missed them," he said, turning Arrow. She moved reluctantly, smelling water and stables and hay in the town somewhere. "Come on, lass," he encouraged her, and they went back again to investigate more thoroughly.

It turned out the ghosts had left the road just after the hill where they had tried to ambush the enchanter. They'd wasted more than an hour and a half. Hodge swore, and Leof felt like joining him. "Let's go," he said instead, taking Arrow through a gate into a field. The ghosts had left the gate open, and he made sure Alston closed it again behind them. For some reason, that carelessness with the gate made him angry, angrier even than during the battle.

He was suddenly sure that this enchanter had never worked with his hands, never sweated in a field to get the hay in as he had, next to his father and brothers and all the inhabitants of their town, as just about every person in a warlord's domain had at one time or another. Bringing in the hay, harvesting the grain or the grapes or the fruit or the beans, these were a part of life, one of the patterns of life which brought people together in comradeship and common purpose.

Up until this moment, he had feared the enchanter's scheme, but he had not thought about the man himself. Now he was filled with hatred. Contempt. This man was a destroyer of lives and he deserved to be destroyed in return.

The trail was clear enough, and they followed as fast as the horses could bear. Arrow was tiring badly, after her great run from Carlion the day before, and the others, not as fit as she, were in much the same case. The wounds the wraiths had made weren't deep but the horses had bled enough to weaken them.

The country here was a series of dales and small hills, fields separated by coppices of beech and birch and ash, the trees for spears and chairs and trugs and charcoal. Settled country, with farms regularly spaced. Peaceful.

Cantering down a gentle hill towards a farmhouse, they heard screams. Dying screams, familiar to them all from many battles. They urged the horses forward, Leof feeling sick, because what could they do to protect these people? Nothing. Nothing except try to get them inside and barricaded.

"Hunda!" they heard someone scream. "Run!"

A young man came skittering out of the farmyard, a ghost close behind, two wind wraiths sailed down from the heights and swept across his path. Perhaps it was fear that made him stop in his tracks and watch them as they sailed up again into the sky and disappeared, but it gave the ghost behind him time to catch up and bring down his scythe. The youth fell, fair hair darkening with blood.

"There they are!" Alston shouted.

18

The ghosts were outside a barn, arguing with the enchanter, it seemed. There were three bodies already on the ground, but no wind wraiths, thank the gods. The ghosts looked up as the horsemen approached, and the leader, the short one with beaded hair, hefted Leof's own sword and grinned at them. But the enchanter pulled him away, speaking urgently, and the ghosts, reluctantly, followed him out of the farmyard, running.

"See to the wounded," Leof told Hodge, and he kicked Arrow forward to her best pace. He rode into the pack of ghosts, Arrow following her battle training, kicking out behind her to stop pursuers, allowing Leof precious seconds to swoop on the enchanter and drag him across the saddlebow.

He almost made it. Would have made it, despite the ghosts. But the wraiths descended from where they had been perched, unseen, on the far side of the barn roof, and flapped and clawed and spat and dragged the enchanter back into the air with them. He looked almost despairing as he vanished into the sky.

Leof pulled Arrow away as the ghost leader aimed a huge blow at her neck. He blocked it with his borrowed sword and slashed down at the man's head. The blow cut right through his neck. The head didn't fall, as a living man's would have, but he reeled and swayed and gave Leof enough time to back Arrow and turn her.

The other wraiths, he realised, were attacking his men. "Back!" Leof shouted. "He's gone. Get back!"

Then the ghosts had run after their enchanter and the wraiths flew away, and they were left, the four of them, looking at the bodies, the youth, an older woman and two young girls barely out of childhood, whose blood gleamed darkly in the sun.

HUNDA'S STORY

IN THE end, we are animals, and all we can touch is flesh. Our spirits are imprisoned in clay, and every day, every night, we yearn to break free. I know you have—surely you've had the flying dream? The swimming dream? The one where you're soaring, weightless, swooping and gliding and shifting on a thought, on a prayer...

We've all had those dreams, which are the yearning of our spirits.

I think this world is punishment. My da says that if we are noble and good in this life, we will be reborn, but I think he's got it wrong. I think if we are good enough we are *not* reborn, at least, not as humans. Not as heavy flesh.

We are animals. That's why they eat us, because they know us for what we are.

The first time I saw one, I was three summers old. Maybe four. We were down at the stream, Hengi and Caela and me, where we weren't supposed to be on our own, because of them. Hengi was showing off, the way he always does, dipping his toe into the water, trying to prove that he was braver than anyone else.

"Come and get me!" he yelled. "I'm not afraid of you!"

It came. It snatched for his toe but he jerked back as it came up at him from the green depths, and it missed. I could hear it hiss with annoyance, even from under the water. Hengi and Caela scrambled away from the bank and ran screaming to the cottage, but I stayed, staring, and it stared back at me. She stared. It was a girl, no doubt.

The stonecasters say that there are moments when your life shifts its path, when what you do, what you decide, changes everything from then on. So. That was my moment. If I'd run, I wouldn't have seen her clearly.

I wouldn't have seen that she was beautiful. And young. Not a child, like me, but not old like my mam. More like Ethelin, Caela's big sister. Her eyes were green and long, and they were green all the way, with no

20

whites to them. They gleamed like a cat's. She looked at me, and smiled. Beckoned.

I wasn't stupid, not even at four. I shook my head and kept my feet planted firmly on the ground. But I didn't run. And then...then she started to sing.

There are no words for it. If you haven't heard it, I can't recreate it. No human could. It went too high for a human voice, and too low as well. It was like a dozen voices singing, but it was only one. It was water and laughter and silver in the sun...It called to all the parts of me that were *not* animal. It filled my chest with hot tight longing because it spoke of everything I could never have — spirit, pure and simple, flying free of flesh, free of earth, free of death.

I didn't think those things then. Not at four. But I felt them. Cried for them. Sank down on my haunches and wept silently, until my mam and the other adults came running to beat the waters and shout until she went away.

They made sure we didn't go anywhere near the stream after that. I crept down, sometimes, but she was never there, even when I stuck my toe in the water and shouted, "Come and get me!"

I heard her singing in my dreams, but what good was that? It wasn't her I wanted, it was the freedom I heard in her song.

SAKER

THE DARKNESS covered Saker like a shield. His army was somewhere behind him and would have faded by now, with the sunlight. The wind wraiths had deposited him next to an old mill and sped back into the air on his order, so he was safe and concealed, where no one would look for a great enchanter.

And yet... He drank from the millrace, relieved himself against the cracked wall of the mill, went back to the loft and wondered why he felt so... alone. He had always been alone, since the day the warlord's men had killed his family, his whole village. Even when he lived with Freite, the enchanter who had trained him, he had been alone. It was no different now.

But today the ghosts had protected him, defended him, drawn around him. Without that defence, he felt vulnerable. Saker frowned. There had to be a way to enable the ghosts to stay after the sun shifted. It seemed that he could call them up for a day, or for a night, but no longer. Sunset or sunrise drew them back into death, into the darkness before rebirth, and he had to summon them all over again the next time he needed them.

At least the wind wraiths had gone.

"You may not stay near me," he had said to them when they let him down from that horrifying flight. "The Warlord's men will see you, and after dark I am vulnerable."

"Do not fear, human," one of the wraiths had replied. "We will protect you."

Saker shook his head. "You cannot protect me against an army of archers, and that is what they will bring against me if they find me. I will summon you when I next have need of you."

"And we will feast!" the wraiths shrieked.

"You will feast," Saker confirmed, close to vomiting at the thought of them eating the spirits as well as the bodies of their victims. "But now you must go."

"We will watch from a distance," the wraith said. "And be ready when you need us, master."

They had streamed up into the sky, laughing and screaming.

Lying in the dark of the mill, Saker felt very small and too young, somehow, for his task. Perhaps he should raise his father's ghost. Call him: Alder, son of Crane. Let his own blood flow to call his father back, give Alder strength so that Saker could lean into his embrace...

But he was too weak. He had lost a lot of blood already, raising the ghost army to defend himself against the warlord. And he knew, if he were honest, that his father would rather plan the next battle than fold him in his arms.

His father would be right, Saker knew. He had to plan.

Turvite was his goal. He wanted to take the city that Acton had despoiled. But that day's futile battering on the solid doors and walls of Bonhill had shown him that taking a city would be a long, long fight. And he could not allow himself to be unprotected each night. It would only take one assassin and the whole great scheme of reclamation and revenge would be over.

He had to find a way to keep the ghosts alive. Until their work was finished.

ASH

"YOU CAN'T come the River's way," Ash said.

"How will I get to the meeting place?" Flax asked, caught between surprise and uncertainty.

"My father will take you there," Ash said. He had made the plan as soon as the Prowman had explained that the two of them would have to go alone. Rowan would take Flax to meet Ash's mother, Swallow, and then journey together to Sanctuary. It would mean that Ash wouldn't have to see that first meeting, his mother's delight at Flax's voice, their first song together... Ash wondered if he was grasping at the Prowman's offer so eagerly just to escape that.

But no. If there were a faster way to Sanctuary, he had to take it. He looked around the clearing where the other men, restored to their normal human selves, were dressing and eating, laughing as they did so. Not demons any more, but singers and musicians, discussing their craft. Ash caught snatches of melody as one man—Skink, the leader—pulled a pipe from his pocket and began to play. A dawn song, greeting the day, the same one Flax had sung to him in Golden Valley.

A bass voice picked up the words and a tenor joined in, not Flax, an older man, without Flax's purity of sound but with a richer timbre. Ash and Flax both paused to listen.

Up jumps the sun in the early, early morning
The early, early morning
The early dawn of day
Up wings the lark in the early light of dawning
The early light of dawning
When gold replaces grey

The voices supported each other and echoed richly from the cliffs. When they had finished they began discussing the song, the best

24

instruments to use, the timing, all the daylight talk of the Deep. With the night gone, the Deep was almost ordinary. Not quite. The high red-streaked sandstone walls which enclosed them were always a reminder of the need for secrecy, the need for silence about what happened here. It had taken them days to reach it, and the way had been dangerous, but Rowan would guide Flax back.

"Take the horses," Ash said to Flax. "For all our sakes, get them back to Bramble safely!"

Flax grinned at that, but seemed uncertain still. "Are you sure I can't come with you?"

Ash was reminded of his promise to Zel, to look after Flax as if he were his own brer. It made him feel guilty, but he reasoned that if Flax *were* his own brother, he would do exactly the same thing — entrust him to his parents.

"My father wants you to meet my mother. She's a singer like you, you know — better than you!" He was deliberately provocative to get Flax bristling, but instead the youngster's face lit up.

"She'll teach me? Certain sure?"

"Certain sure," Ash confirmed, a sour taste in his mouth. Teach him and rejoice. He pushed the thought away, all thoughts away except the miraculous one that the River was waiting for, and wanting, *him*. Not Flax or his father or any other in these long, long years. Him. He was overtaken by a sense of his father's vulnerability, out there in the world which contained murderous ghosts and unknown terrors. "And — look after my father, too."

Flax nodded, as though he'd been given a task by the gods. He would have to do something about that hero worship, Ash thought as Skink handed him some fresh-cooked fish. He ate hungrily without tasting the food and walked over to Rowan.

"Sanctuary," Rowan said musingly as he approached. "I know it. A cursed place, they say it is. There's a song…"

"Yes," Ash said, surprising himself by finding a need to be gentle with his father, who was not accustomed to fighting or fearing or struggling with anything except a difficult melody. "I know the song. But it is just a meeting place. Get there as soon as you can."

Rowan nodded and embraced him, and it was only as Ash raced into the cave to meet the Prowman that he realised it was the first time he had given his father a direct order. Yet it had seemed so natural. This was his craft, it seemed—action.

He said as much to the Prowman as they made their way back to the inner cave, where Ash had climbed down only the night before.

"Action and music," the old man agreed. "That is our craft, to meld the two." He grinned. "And, I'm afraid, to do as we are told. We are followers, boy, not leaders."

Ash digested that. It struck a sour note, but he knew it was true. He had always followed: his parents, Doronit, Martine, Safred. Even Bramble, half-conscious, had made the decisions. And now the River.

"If you are to survive Her," the Prowman said, "you must know yourself."

Filled with a sudden impatience, Ash snapped, "That's the sort of thing old men say."

The Prowman laughed. "Aye, that's so! That is so indeed. Well, lad, perhaps you know yourself too well already. Perhaps what you need is to lose yourself in Her instead."

Ash grinned, sure suddenly that he could speak his mind as freely as he liked. Somehow, he was at ease with the Prowman as he had never been at ease with anyone before. "Enigmatic," he teased. "Very like an old sage from the stories."

The old man smiled and flicked him on the shoulder with the back of his hand, as boys do to each other. "Race you to the water," he said.

Together they ran through to the caverns where the green stars on the walls never faded, following the winding, crooked path, laughing as they went, and as they came to the final cave, the final cliff, and Ash slowed, the Prowman called back over his shoulder, "Trust Her!" and leapt out high over the rushing water.

As he disappeared from sight, Ash took a deep breath, full of sudden joy and sudden fear, and leapt after him.

There was music.

He couldn't recognise the instrument, and that frightened him, but the River's voice soothed him with wordless harmonies. *Home*, She said, *Belonging*, and he was calm.

But not still. Ash was rushing, rushing past rock walls, rushing through openings surely too small for his body, spinning and splashing and sliding. As fear left him and he let the music fill him instead, he was equally full of joy and something he'd never known before...but the feeling, like the instrument, had no name, because it was outside human experience. It was not happiness, or joy, or satisfaction. It was all of those.

A sense of purpose—of *being* the purpose, rather than fulfilling one.

A sense of power.

Liberation.

Speed.

Deep, deep calm and stability, hidden in the middle of the rushing, as water, swung in a bucket quickly over one's head, stays firm in the centre and cannot fall.

He was the water, the bucket, the swinging arm. The centre which moved.

He was the River's way.

BRAMBLE

BRAMBLE DIDN'T believe they were in the Weeping Caverns. There were too many stories about them—the entrance was supposed to move, certainly, but it was always on the surface. This was just a large cave with water in it. She looked over at Medric, "So, if no one can get out, how did the stories get told?"

He had no answer for that, but his hands shook as they slowly climbed down the rock wall to the floor of the cavern.

As she moved down the solid rock face with her saddlebags over her shoulder, she could feel Acton's bones shift and slide with each step. The movement unsettled her as nothing in her life had ever done. She had tried to pack them tightly but they shook loose, as though Acton was determined in death, as he had been in life, not to be trammelled. As though at every step he tapped her on the back, saying, "Remember me?"

It was bad enough to bear her grief for him; to bear his bones as well, to be a packhorse for his remains, was too much. She wanted to be rid of them. Wanted fiercely to see him again, even as a ghost, and also wanted fiercely not to see him as a ghost, pale and insubstantial. She thought it was a good thing the gods were driving her, because if it had been up to her she was not sure whether she would have brought him back.

But she would complete her task and stop Saker. Kill him, too, if the gods were kind. And then, only then, could she stop and consider what Obsidian Lake had done to her, and who she might be afterwards.

So if Lady Death tried to stop her, too bad for the Lady.

They reached the cavern floor with legs and arms shaking, and collapsed on a damp rock. When they had recovered they drank water from one of the clear pools, water that tasted of nothing except, faintly, chalk.

"Follow the air," Medric said again, and the air seemed to be curving around the high wall to their left, so that was the way they walked, picking their steps between shallow pools and small spires of rock, past pillars and grotesque shapes that looked, again and again, as though a hunched human figure had been turned to stone by the endlessly dripping water. Yet it was beautiful. There were wings of rock, and towers and colours that glowed in the candlelight: cream and ochre and orange and green. And everywhere, the murmuring sigh of water and air.

"Who brings light into the darkness?" a voice boomed from above them. "Who disturbs this holy place?" The echoes took the words and grew them into an accusation, a promise of punishment, a death knell.

"Oh, Swith!" Medric whispered, but Bramble peered further ahead, holding the light high, although her heart was beating fast. This was one of those times, she thought, when other people feared, but she had never been on good terms with fear and she wasn't planning to start now.

"Who wants to know?" she demanded.

"Oh, hells, Bramble, you might at least squeal!" It was Ash's voice, coming from a platform of rock to their right.

Bramble laughed, as she felt the gods smile in her head and leave her to stream towards Ash. He was staring at her with a broad grin, looking fitter and happier than when she had last seen him.

"I don't squeal," she said. "How did you get here?"

He shrugged as he walked to the edge to help them climb up. "The same way you did," he said casually. "Enchantment."

She nodded and let it go. If he wanted to tell her more, he would. She handed the candle to Medric and surprised herself by embracing Ash. "This is Medric," she said, stepping back. "He was a miner—helped me find the place I had to go."

Medric stared at Ash. "Like scaring people, do you?" he asked.

"It was a fair question," Ash replied absently, "I couldn't see who you were." He turned and waved someone forward from the gloom.

Medric held the candle higher to reveal an old man walking towards them, making no sound.

Bramble felt a slight shock—he was dressed the way Acton's people had dressed a thousand years ago: leggings and tunic, long hair with beaded braids in the front, sheepskin boots with the fleece still inside. All that was missing was a beard.

He reached the circle of candlelight and smiled at them. "Greetings," he said. "We are well met, it seems."

A wave of cold went over her and she began to shake. She knew that voice. Surely she knew it, would know it to her grave.

"This is the Prowman," Ash said to her. "Prowman, this is Bramble."

The old man's eyes were puzzled as she stood there in silence. She swallowed the lump in her throat and forced herself to talk, although there were tears gathering in her eyes and her legs were still shaking. She had to force herself not to embrace him, not to throw herself at him as she would have at Maryrose, or her grandfather. He didn't know her, after all.

"He was a prowman once," she said. "But his shipmates called him Baluch."

Bramble stared into blue, blue eyes. Eyes that she remembered as clearly as she remembered Maryrose. Those eyes were bright with interest and she could almost, almost hear the music that was no doubt going on behind them. Some kind of pipe music, she'd be willing to bet, high and trilling. She was finding it hard to catch her breath.

Ash was standing very still, paler even than usual, as though he were looking at a puzzle that suddenly made sense but had an answer he didn't like. "You're *Baluch?*" he asked.

The old man nodded, slowly, his face carefully blank.

Baluch.

Here. A thousand years later. Still here. Bramble was overwhelmed by a cascade of memories: Baluch as a toddler, reproving Acton; Baluch as a young boy, a lad, a young man, a man full grown... Baluch whooping with laughter as Acton's boat went over the rapids. Baluch shouting with rage as his sword cut through his enemies. Baluch standing by the edge of the White River, saying, "There's something up north that calls me..."

"The Lake," Bramble said, clutching at the only possible explanation so her head would stop swimming. "The Lake transported you in time."

Baluch's eyes were alive with curiosity and a kind of pleasure, as though he enjoyed having someone know him.

"Often," he said. "I come by my wrinkles honestly, but I've earned them in a dozen different times, whenever She had need of me. I've skipped from time to time like a stone over water. But how did you know me?"

Trying to work out how to explain made her legs, finally, give out from under her. She sank down onto a rock, knees trembling.

"Thank the local gods," she said eventually. "They showed me your face." Which was true enough, even if it was woefully incomplete. But how could she explain Obsidian Lake and her own, very different, travels in time? Baluch smiled as though some of what she was thinking showed in her eyes and she smiled back, a rush of pleasure swamping her. Someone else who remembered... It was a kind of homecoming, to look into Baluch's blue eyes, as she had when she was Ragni, or even the girl on the mountain.

"Who is he?" Medric asked her softly, while Baluch went to talk quietly to Ash. Ash stood straight and disapproving, but listened.

Whatever Baluch said didn't convince him. He shook his head, and Baluch slapped his own thigh, his voice growing louder. "I've spent my whole life protecting the Lake People, from attack after attack!" he said. "Ask her!"

He paused for a moment, and waited. Finally, Ash nodded, but his face was still troubled. Bramble could understand that. Baluch was, after all, implicated in everything Acton had done. It wasn't easy to face your enemy and realise he wasn't a monster, after all.

Baluch clapped Ash on the shoulder, a gesture he and Acton had used often to each other. It made Bramble's heart clench.

"Baluch. You know — from the old stories, Acton's friend," she said to Medric.

"Donkey dung!" Medric exclaimed. "He's dead!"

"Apparently not."

It was a bit much to take, she supposed, for someone whose life had until yesterday been as solidly sensible as a life could be. But he was the man who had fallen in love with Fursey, so he *could* cope with oddity if he chose. He'd just have to. The trick was to keep him busy. And they should all be busy, because if Ash were here and she were here... "I have the bones," she called to Ash. A trembling began in her gut at the thought of what they were about to do, but she ignored it and got up, forcing her knees to stay firm. "Do you have the songs?"

Ash hesitated, looking to Baluch, any remnants of hostility vanishing into a need for guidance.

"There are songs," Ash said slowly. "But they don't seem to be enough...in themselves."

"When Tern the enchanter raised the ghosts of Turvite against Acton, she used her own blood," Bramble said. "She sang the song and then cut herself and scattered the blood on the corpses."

Ash raised his eyebrows. "That's not in the old story. It just says she raised the ghosts of Turvite to fight Acton, and failed, then jumped off the cliff."

"Her name was Tern?" Baluch said. "I remember her. But as Ash said, she failed."

"She failed to give them fighting strength," Bramble corrected him. "But she raised the ghosts well enough, which is what we want to do."

She knelt and took off her jacket, spreading it out on a flat piece of ground, and then slid her hand to the very bottom of one saddlebag and pulled out the red scarf. It was the symbol of rebirth, and perhaps it would help, now, to bring him back. She spread it on her jacket.

Her heart faltered. Stuck to the scarf, in the folds, were hairs. Horse hairs, from the roan. She had brushed them off her own clothes too often to mistake them. Gently, she brushed them together into a small pile. There were only a few, but it was as though the roan were with her, encouraging her.

Unpacking the bones was next. She slid her fingers gently over the curve of his skull, a secret caress, and the only one she'd ever have. Enough. She drew out the bones as though they were just anyone's, and laid them on the scarf, placing the skull over the roan's hair, to keep it safe. It was the first time she'd looked at the bones closely in the light, even in the poor candle glow. They seemed ridiculously small.

"I had to leaves the leg bones behind," she said, almost in apology to Acton. "I couldn't fit them."

Baluch crouched next to the scarf and put his hand out to touch the skull. His hand shook. "Acton," he whispered.

But of course there was no answer. Bramble turned aside. She knew too much of what Baluch was feeling, and it unsettled her. She wondered how much he had changed, living his life in snatches, moving from time to time for a thousand years at the whim of the Lake. His smile hadn't changed, or his eyes. Or that voice.

Ash was staring at the bones like a rabbit stares at a weasel, eyes wide and stuck.

"*Ash*," Bramble said sharply. He blinked and turned to her in relief. "Sing," she said.

"I'm not sure..." He looked at Baluch and lowered his voice. "She's given me a kind of pattern of song, but not the words and not the exact melody."

Baluch nodded. "There are some songs which must be sung new each time. You will have to find your own version of what she has given you."

Bramble wondered if "she" were the Lake, but the men clearly weren't going to say. Fair enough. She had secrets of her own.

Ash fished his belt knife out of its sheath and held it a little uncertainly, and began to sing.

The first notes, harsh as rock grating on stone, startled Bramble and made her deeply uneasy. She'd heard this sound before, when Safred tried to heal Cael. It was the sound of power, which should have been reassuring given what they were trying to do, yet it wasn't. It just felt wrong.

Ash seemed to feel that, too, because after a moment he fell silent, shaking his head. "It's not right," he said.

"That song felt old to me," Baluch said mildly. "I think you have to make it new." His head tilted to one side as though he were listening to something, someone, else. "You have to make it *yours*," he added.

Ash nodded, and knelt down beside the bones. He put his hand out, hesitating, over the skull, then slid it sideways and rested his palm on the curve of the collarbone. "Acton," he said quietly.

Bramble remembered something and dug quickly in the bottom of the other bag for Acton's brooch. She had always meant to give it back to Ash at some point. This seemed like a good time—it might help him as it had helped her.

She knelt beside him and put the brooch down next to Acton's skull. Baluch gasped. His grandfather had made it, Bramble remembered. Eric the Foreigner had made it for the chieftain Harald to give to his wife, who had given it in turn to her daughter Asa, Acton's mother. And Asa had given it to Acton. Acton's murderer, Asgarn, had ripped it from Acton's cloak as he lay dying and given it to his accomplice, Red, the traitor. And from there, who knew whose hands it had passed through before it came to Ash? A thousand years of ownership. This brooch had come to their time by the long road, as though it had walked slowly through the undergrowth of a forest, while Baluch had, as it were, jumped from tree to tree.

Bramble weighed the brooch in her hand as if it should have grown heavier with each year. She placed it on the scarf, next to Acton's skull.

"I give this back to you," she said, not sure if she were talking to Ash or to Acton.

Ash nodded gratefully and put his other hand on the brooch, shivering slightly as his fingers touched the cold metal. "Acton, I call you back from the darkness beyond death," he said, and began to sing in the voice of the healer.

His first notes faltered, but when Baluch came forward and placed a hand on his shoulder his voice gained strength, the notes and the words building, gathering power and authority.

It felt irresistible. The words were unfamiliar to her, although she caught echoes of the languages that Gris and Asa and Hawk had spoken. The notes were not really a melody — they seemed more like half a conversation, a chant rather than a song.

Ash began to shake, but he gripped the knife in his hand more surely and raised it, then brought his other hand off the brooch and held it ready over the bones. It trembled slightly, although Bramble couldn't tell if that was from fright or from the passage of power through him.

Ash brought the knife down on his palm, and blood flicked out over the bones.

Bramble held her breath, feeling shaky. Ash's voice climbed to a climax and stopped on a high note that brought the echoes ringing and ringing after it. She was staring at the bones so hard her eyes started to burn.

Nothing happened.

The blood trickled down over the skull and dripped into the empty eye sockets. A small, slightly mad, part of Bramble's mind was concerned about getting blood stains on the scarf; she was thinking about anything, bloodstains, washing, the cold of the stone floor through her thin boots, anything rather than face the possibility that everything they had done had been for nothing. That she would never see him again.

Ash sighed and sat back, his face carefully blank.

There was a long silence.

"So," Medric said, "is that it?"

"It was not complete," Baluch said gently.

Bramble was reminded of Tern on the cliffs of Turvite, and her own sense that what was missing from Tern's spell was feeling, some emotion apart from the desire for revenge. "You have to really want him back," she said, her voice trembling a little. She breathed in deeply, controlling it. "And you don't, do you?"

"Of course I do!" Ash said. "We need him."

"But you hate him," she said. Ash stared at her and Baluch stared at him, as though surprised at the idea.

"Of course I hate him," Ash said impatiently. "He invaded my country and massacred my people."

"No, no, that's not how it happened!" Baluch protested.

"Yes it was," Bramble said. She wasn't minded to let Baluch paint Acton in rosy colours, no matter how much she loved him.

"You weren't there—" Baluch started.

"Really?" Bramble said. "I have two words for you, Baluch son of Eric who never took part in massacres. River Bluff."

Baluch fell silent, staring at her as if she were the Well of Secrets herself. Bramble felt a quick flash of sympathy for Safred. That look made her feel not fully human.

"There *were* massacres," Bramble said quietly. "Whole towns, killed or dispossessed. He wanted T'vit, didn't he, and he did whatever it took to get it. So don't tell me Ash doesn't have reason to hate him. Anyone with Traveller blood has reason to hate him."

"Including you?" Baluch asked.

"I have reason," Bramble said. "And none of that matters. What matters is how to get him back."

"The problem is," Ash said, "I think it needs a memory in the middle of it, or a true longing, and I don't have either."

35

"I could help," Baluch said, "but it might upset the song to have two singers."

"I'll do it," Bramble said.

"You?" Baluch gazed at her in astonishment. "You remember Acton?"

It was too much, suddenly. "Better than you," she hissed. "You let him go off to that meeting with Asgarn while you went to your precious Lake, didn't you? You let him go off to be killed!"

"Asgarn..." Baluch breathed, his eyes hardening. "I knew. I *knew* it was him, but I could never prove it. Never even find the body."

"Enough!" Ash said firmly. "We can discuss the past later. Right now we have a job to do." He turned to Bramble. "Prepare your memory," he said gently. He had gained in authority, somehow, since she'd last seen him.

She knew it would need more than memory. It needed the longing he had spoken of. Gods knew she had that, but she would have to share it with Ash for the spell to work. She turned aside for a moment, her face burning. How much was she prepared to give to stop Saker? All her certainties were gone, all her defences were down. Now it seemed her privacy and dignity had to be sacrificed too.

Maryrose, she thought. This is for you.

She turned back, her face calm again, and joined hands with Ash, her other hand resting on the familiar curve of the brooch, Asa's brooch, Acton's brooch. Red's, after he had thrust the knife into Acton's back. That memory brought the rush of feeling that she needed, they all needed, to bring him back: longing, regret...love. Ash felt it sweep through her and he gulped in surprise, then started singing, a little faster, a little more urgently than before, the harsh notes rising and rising, words a bit different, rhythm altered so that it matched her breathing as she thought of him, remembered him, *needed* him as the heart needs blood, as the loom needs thread, to be whole.

And this time, it was her hand that Ash slashed, her blood that spilled over his pale, pale bones. She welcomed the pain because it was easier to bear than the loss of him, easier to think about than the emptiness which he had filled. Memories of his life flooded her, and it was as though she were him as well as Baluch, as well as Asa, seeing the world through his eyes briefly as she had seen it through theirs: climbing the mountain to find Friede, she was both Baluch and Acton; guiding the boat down the river to Turvite, she was both steersman and prowman, both exulting; fighting the people of River Bluff, she wielded two swords, and both killed... Standing on the mountain, watching him climb to his death, she was him, too, looking at a dark-haired wild-looking girl, feeling his heart leap...

Come back from beyond death, she willed into the darkness. We have need of you. Come back. *I* have need of you.

She could feel something happening, and hear something, too, a whisper without body, a bodiless chant without words, a high whine. It made her feel sick, and suddenly she thought, this is unnatural. Wrong. The gods had deserted her, as though they wanted nothing to do with it, although they had sent her here for just this moment.

She heard Medric gasp suddenly and Baluch's breath hissed out, but she could not look up from the bones where gently, hesitantly, a mist was gathering.

Her breath was hard to find. At the edge of her vision shapes twisted, pale shadows of writhing bodies. She willed herself not to look at them and concentrated on Acton, Acton. Come, I have need of you.

Ash pulled her back, still singing, but she kept hold of the brooch as he guided her to her feet so she could see more, back a few steps until their legs knocked against a rock pillar and they stood and stared at the ghost standing before them, white and clear as a sculpture in ice. There were no shapes in the darkness now, no twisting forms, no sense of wrongness. Just him.

MARTINE

TRINE WAS housed in a small hold that opened up directly to the deck.

"Fish hold," the shipmaster had said, and it smelled like it. Trine hadn't settled easily, but it was much better than trying to get her below decks. Half of the hold was covered over to give her shelter from rain and sun, but she could get her nose up into the open air and move around on her tether a little.

"Look. That's my Aunty Rumer," Zel said blankly, staring up at the rigging where a dark-haired woman flipped open a sail and let it drop free. "Or maybe Rawnie." She blinked, as if trying to make her eyes see better. "They're twins."

Trine snorted and tried to shy as the sail bellowed, but Zel held her firmly and patted her, taking the excuse to look away from the rigging and attend to the horse.

"Don't give her too much freedom," the shipmaster told her. "If the swell gets up, we'll have to lash her down and she won't like that, so keep her close tied."

Zel had frowned but seen the sense to it, and they'd loaded Trine first and let her get used to her quarters well before they set sail. Martine and Zel had kept her company. She was beginning, Martine thought, to accept them as inadequate substitutes for Bramble. As the ship left the dock, Zel began rebinding Trine's forefoot with a padded bandage, designed to stop her being bruised in bad weather, and she was carefully not looking up.

"Nice for you, to meet family," Martine said lightly, but she wondered. Zel's face was bemused, as though she wasn't quite sure what she should be feeling. She certainly wasn't feeling anything uncomplicated like pleasure at meeting family.

Then, when was family ever uncomplicated? Martine mused on her own four aunties, all dead, who were as fine a mixture of love, interference, exasperation and pride as any niece could have had. She

38

wondered how she'd feel if she'd encountered them unexpectedly, in those years she'd been on the Road before they'd all been killed by the Ice King's men. Somehow she thought there was more in Zel's eyes than the ambivalence an independent girl might feel about kin.

"Your mam's sisters?" Martine asked politely. "Or your da's?"

"Mam's," Zel said, her lips tucking back as soon as she said the word, as if she wanted to unsay it.

Yes, there it was. Something about Zel's mam. Martine's Sight nudged her, but she didn't need it to know that Zel and her mam had had a difficult time of it together. Perhaps seeing these aunties brought back bad memories. But later she saw Zel eating her supper with two women as alike as two hen's eggs, and the three of them were laughing.

They sailed into Mitchen in the early morning, on a grey day with a chill wind. Unlike Turvite, the Mitchenites had built right up to the edge of their headlands, so coming into harbour meant passing below houses and shops, aware of people out early in the streets pointing to them, calling out, running down to the docks, clutching their money pouches.

"No ships in port," Arvid said, looking worried.

By the time the sailors were tying up at the big dock, a crowd was pushing its way to the ship. Mostly men, but some women carrying babies or leading children by the hand. There were no dark heads among them, or none Martine could see. She wondered if all the Travellers of Mitchen had taken shelter somewhere. She hoped so — with news of the massacre at Carlion clearly spreading across the country, it wouldn't be long before someone decided all Travellers were somehow responsible.

The shipmaster called, "Don't put the gangplank out!"

Rumer and Rawnie, who were holding it, laid it down. The sailors on the mooring ropes let out a little slack, so that the people on the dock couldn't touch the ship.

"Captain! Captain! I can pay, all the way to the Wind Cities!"

"Take my children if you won't take me!"

They shouted and pleaded with her, becoming more agitated, until the shipmaster held up her hands for quiet. Gradually, they fell silent, their upturned faces a mixture of anxiety and hope.

"We are not going to the Wind Cities," she shouted. "We're going to Turvite."

They started shouting again: "You're mad! You're fools! The ghost'll go there, sure as fire burns! They love ghosts in Turvite!"

The shipmaster just stood there and gradually, one by one, the crowd dispersed, turning back home with heavy treads and slumped shoulders.

The only one who stayed was an old, grizzled sailor who said, "I'd rather be where they know how to deal with ghosts," and spat over the side of the dock to mark his words.

"Fair enough," the shipmaster said, and threw him a rope to climb up. "We might need an extra steersman," she added to Arvid. "The waters around Turvite are liable to be rough, this time of year, when the current changes."

The harbour master emerged from his house and organised the unloading of the cargo and the restocking of the boat's larders and water barrels.

Safred was first off the gangplank, sitting down thankfully on a crate. "When my stomach settles down, I might even be able to eat something," she said, half-laughing.

Apple and the other two merchants started heading for town. "Don't know what kind of bargain we're going to make," she called back to Arvid from the deck. "Frightened people hold on hard to their purses."

But she seemed cheerful enough, her blond hair swinging in its single long plait. She looked younger than she had at the Plantation, Martine thought. Probably comes of not having to look after anyone, or cook any meals. Or wear the big, heavy jackets you needed in the Last Domain. Martine herself felt much freer now they were far enough south that she could pack away her felt coat.

Arvid came up behind Martine and put his hands on her waist. A squirm of pleasure went right through her. She bit back a smile.

"Not going into town?" he asked.

"I'm thinking about it," she replied. "Times of trouble, a stonecaster can make good money. But by the same stone, a stonecaster can get into a lot of trouble if the answers aren't to everyone's liking."

"So stay with me," he breathed. "I have no duties here at all. It's Apple and her friends who do the bargaining. I just turn up for the celebration meal afterwards, so our customers can brag about having dinner with the warlord."

Martine sniffed. "Not much to brag about."

"Not from where I sit," he agreed, nuzzling her ear. The hot breath melted her.

"Oh, all right," she said, feigning reluctance. "I suppose I don't have anything else to do right now."

Laughing, he pulled her by the hand down the companionway and into his cabin. As they tumbled onto the bunk, she could hear Trine's hooves clunking down the gangplank, with Zel's footfalls in between. So they were all right, and she could concentrate on Arvid.

They didn't come out until it was night.

On deck, Safred and Cael were having a late supper: "Just something light," Safred said. "My stomach isn't quite settled yet." There were more sailors on board than she had expected—didn't sailors just disappear off to the inns and brothels when a ship was in port?

Rumer and Rawnie were having a cha with Zel in Trine's hold while she curried the mare down. Martine asked them.

"Everything's locked up," they said. "Brothel's open, but the inn's not letting strangers drink. Only place we could get an ale was a Traveller's hut, out on the edges, and that wasn't the best place to drink for two women. Lot of young'uns, full of beer and piss and thinking they're cock of the dunghill. And *they* wouldn't serve blondies, so most of the crew can't get a drink anywhere. Might as well be here."

Martine and Arvid moved to the side and looked at the town. Shuttered up tight; no one on the streets. Martine had been to Mitchen many times before, and it was a town, like Turvite, that enjoyed its summer nights. This quiet readiness disturbed her greatly.

"Have we heard from Apple and the others?" she asked the shipmaster.

"No, but I wouldn't worry. We've made this trip a dozen times before. The merchants always stay late."

"But they usually call for me to come to the dinner," Arvid said, looking worried. "Holly, Beetle, on duty, now!"

His guards had been playing dice aft. They threw down the cup and sprang up, running to Arvid's side.

"We're going to check on the merchants," Arvid said. "Stay close."

"I'd better come," Safred said, her eyes wide in the darkness, glinting in the light from the lantern hung on the mainmast. "You might have need of me."

The guards checked their weapons and settled their uniforms into place, then followed Arvid down the gangplank. "They'll be at the Moot Hall, most likely," he said.

Safred went after them, and Martine followed. Arvid glanced back and saw her, and opened his mouth to order her back on board. She could see the moment he realised he had no right to give her orders — particularly in a free town! — and closed his mouth with some chagrin.

She smiled grimly. So. He didn't like that. Serve him right for falling for an outsider.

His guards had moved into formation around them, hands on swords even though it was illegal in a free town for warlords' men to use weapons. Martine found herself glad of them, and reflected that it didn't take much for even a Traveller to range herself with the stronger party when danger threatened. If danger threatened.

Her Sight was showing her nothing. But many distressing things happened without Sight warning her. It was only when the gods thought that the event was important that Sight intervened.

Walking through the silent town was unnerving, like a dream that was about to turn into a nightmare.

It was a relief to hear some noises coming from the centre, near the Moot Hall: voices, singing, shouting. They quickened their pace.

Men's voices, singing snatches of a drunken song: "Kill 'em all, kill 'em all!" they roared. It was the chorus of one of the best-known songs about Acton. She expected to find a mob of burly blonds and red-heads sitting on the steps of the hall, swinging their tankards.

They rounded the corner to the central square. There were no market stalls left here; they'd all been packed away, and the eating houses were closed, as was the Moot Hall.

There were no people, either. The only sign of life was that the lanterns on the walls next to the Moot Hall doors had been smashed and were dripping oil down the bricks.

The singing continued, from a road that led up and out of town.

Arvid hesitated. "We should ask at the hall," he said.

Then the singing stopped and became shouting, and the sounds of crashing and splintering wood.

They ran, Holly and the other guards taking the lead, but Arvid not far behind. Safred and Martine kept pace. Martine's heart was thudding hard.

The shouting was getting louder.

"That's right, you bastards, hide behind your bars and shutters! We're going to get you all!"

"Thass it, you tell 'em, Bass!"

"Scared of *us*, now, aren't you? Where's your bloody Acton now, eh? Our people are comin' back and you can't stop us!"

"Look, Bass, lookee 'ere."

"Show 'em how we can fight, Bass!"

"Take that, blondie!"

A woman screamed.

It was only a few more paces. They could see figures struggling, hear them gasping, panting.

Holly drew her sword as she ran and the others copied her, Arvid included.

Martine tried to sort it out in the meagre light leaking from between the shutters of the surrounding buildings. Four men, five, six...two women. One of them was screeching and trying to pull two fighting men apart. The other hit her attacker as he brought both hands down on her head. Was one of them Apple?

"Break them apart," Arvid ordered, and Holly leapt into the struggling group and pulled one back, throwing him towards another guard, who hit him and pushed him down to sit groggily, holding his head.

Arvid went in after Holly, ramming one tall figure with his shoulder, using the hilt of his sword under the man's chin. He crumpled on the spot. The other guards were equally efficient, pulling the combatants away one by one until there were six separate men instead of a fight, and two women, one of them still swearing and the other lying still, legs sprawled.

Martine went to her, making room for Safred by her side. It was Apple, her blue eyes half-open, her knife lying in one slack hand.

"Too late," Safred said sadly. She turned immediately to lay her hands on another man who had a wound from Apple's knife. He was the only other one seriously hurt. Safred began to sing, the harsh song, the healing song.

Martine shivered and her eyes filled with tears as she closed Apple's eyes and straightened her clothes. She thought of Snow, Apple's son, waiting for her to come home, and her heart clenched, her mind inevitably going to her own daughter, Elva, and how she would feel in the same situation.

Arvid crouched beside her. "Drunken thugs," he said bitterly. "Travellers, attacking anyone who came along."

"Because they could," Martine said. "For once, people were afraid of them."

She turned and confronted the man who had killed Apple. Safred had finished. Martine looked at him. She could see him clearly, now her eyes had adjusted to the light. No more than twenty, probably, and not too bright. A life spent looking at the ground instead of in people's eyes, in case they hit you or dragged you off to the warlord for insolence. A life spent being hated, or despised, or overlooked. She should be filled with compassion for someone like this, who had been so warped by the hatred of Acton's people.

She spat in his face.

"You have become just like them," she said. "You've let them win."

Then she turned and walked away, back to the ship, and didn't look to see if anyone followed.

BRAMBLE

ASH'S SONG ended and he cleared his throat, staring at Acton. Bramble had forgotten, again, that he was so big. Baluch and Ash were tall men, and Medric was solidly muscled, but he dwarfed all of them, or seemed to.

Baluch moved towards him, and Medric followed, his mouth open in wonder at a childhood hero standing right there in front of him. Ash stood next to her, glaring, bristling with hatred now that he confronted his people's enemy. All Acton had to do was stand there, Bramble thought, and he created followers and enemies just like that; his whole life had been the same. Even Baluch had put loyalty over friendship—he would have obeyed Acton's orders, she was sure, even if it had meant both their deaths. Had Acton ever known anyone who wasn't either follower or enemy?

As the ghosts of Turvite had been when Tern raised them, he seemed a little confused at first, and looked around, blinking. His gaze passed over Medric, Baluch, Ash, and came to her. And then he smiled. Her heart turned over, because it was the smile he had given her on the hillside, in the one moment where he and she had been alive in the same place at the same time, a smile of promise, of complicity, of mischief and delight. It broke her heart, but she couldn't help smiling back even while she lifted her chin and squared her shoulders. Curse him. She might not be his enemy any more, but she'd walk into the cold hell on her own two feet before she'd be his follower, before she'd let him cozen her the way he'd cozened the girl on the mountain. No matter how much she loved him.

Acton took a step towards her and she braced herself, unsure why. He was a ghost. He couldn't touch, or talk, or . . . She looked at Ash. "You can make them talk, can't you?"

Ash nodded and moved in front of Acton. "Speak," he said.

Acton's face was clear, even in the dim light, as though he had merely been dusted with flour and the real man, hearty and hale, was waiting underneath the pale covering. It made her want to weep.

"You can talk, now," she said, wondering what he'd say.

"Am I dead, then?" Acton asked in the language of the past. She understood the words, after so long hearing them, but he spoke in the healer's voice, the prophet's voice, rock on grating stone. Soul-destroying. Bramble trembled with revulsion and anger. This was not *fair*!

Acton was startled by the sound, too, and closed his mouth firmly. He raised his hands apologetically and smiled at her, inviting her to understand his silence. But she hadn't gone through all this to not be able to talk to him.

"Ash," she said. "Make him talk in his own voice."

Ash looked at her with pity in his eyes. "I can't. From the grave, all speak alike."

It was a great disappointment, but she would have to deal with it. Acton was looking at Baluch, puzzlement all over his face.

Baluch came forward, moving quietly, like a man in a sick room, and stood in front of him. "You've been dead a very long time," he said gently, in the language they shared.

"Bal?" Acton said. His incredulity showed only in his face; the voice stayed as it was, stone. Baluch winced at the sound, and then nodded. Acton grinned, looking him up and down in a mime of astonishment at how old he was, teasing.

Baluch smiled back, the boy he had been showing clearly through the wrinkles. "At least I got to be old," he said. "They all thought you'd been killed by a jealous husband somewhere. Why else would you ride out alone, but to some secret meeting with a lover?"

Acton shook his head. "Not a lover."

"Bramble says it was Asgarn."

Acton turned to her. She could see his lips make the motions of saying her name, but he didn't say it out loud, and she was thankful for that. She didn't want to hear her name in that terrible voice. But he spoke anyway, looking puzzled.

"By the way Baluch looks it's been, what—sixty years or so? But you're young."

"A thousand years," she said.

He blinked. "Swith the Strong! How—"

He looked at her with an assessing gaze, as he'd look at a stranger, as he'd looked at Tern the enchanter on the headland outside Turvite. He mistrusted her. She had appeared just before his death and here she was a thousand years later, unchanged. Of course he mistrusted her. But the look hurt.

She felt herself empty out, as though her ribs were a hollow ring around nothingness. If she let herself feel it, she would break apart, bones clattering onto the weeping rocks. She would not show him weakness. He shielded weakness from harm, he took responsibility for the weak, and she would rather he mistrusted her than have him feel paternal.

"There's a lot to explain," she said briskly. "But we can talk as we go. We have to get to Sanctuary." She began to pack his bones back into the saddlebags. The roan's hairs were stuck to Acton's skull with her blood. That seemed fitting, somehow, and she left them there, turning the skull inward so the hairs wouldn't rub off. She felt, irrationally, that the roan would keep Acton safe, somehow.

"Wait," he said, gazing at the bones in sudden understanding. "You raised my ghost?" He looked at Baluch, at Ash, at Medric. "Why?"

"We don't have time for this." Bramble said. "We'll explain on the way."

"Really?" Ash asked dryly. "And do you know how to get out?"

"You got in," she said. "Don't you know the way?"

"The way we came, you can't travel," Baluch said.

Bramble pulled shut the drawstring on the bag and closed the flap. The scarf had absorbed the blood and was dry, although the spots on her jacket were still wet. It was only her blood, not his; she put on her jacket and slung the bags over her shoulder.

"I suspect," she said, "that what guided you here knows the way."

Baluch and Ash exchanged an unreadable look, and then she saw Baluch's eyes go unfocused, the way the Well of Secrets looked when she communed with the gods.

"Aye," Baluch said slowly. "We will be guided."

He had carefully avoided saying who would be guiding them, but Bramble would be willing to bet it was the Lake, somehow reaching out. "Glad she's on our side," she said. Ash and Baluch looked startled, and she laughed.

She knew the others didn't think it was funny, but she didn't care.

Grief and loss were walking beside her wearing the face of a man a thousand years dead. The only way she could cope was to laugh. Then Acton grinned at her, his eyes lighting with shared amusement at Baluch's discomfiture, and the clench of muscles around her heart eased a little. She wasn't so foolish as to think he'd come to love her—*could* ghosts love? She knew that what she felt, she felt alone. But perhaps they could be comrades, at least.

Then she stumbled a little on the broken ground and Acton instinctively put out a hand to support her elbow.

She expected his hand to pass through her, but instead she came up with a jolt. He was solid. The cold of the burial caves washed over her, crept up her arm from where he touched her and chilled her heart, but he was solid, like the enchanter's ghosts. He had touched her.

Ash looked astonished.

Acton let go of her slowly, staring at his own hand. He hadn't expected this, either. "So…" he said, and his hand went to where his sword should have hung. But he hadn't taken it to that meeting with Asgarn a thousand years ago. He moved to draw his belt knife instead, but it had fallen to the floor of the cave when Red had knifed him. He looked at Baluch. "I'll need weapons."

Baluch smiled, slowly, and stepped forward to clasp forearms with Acton. They stared into each other's eyes for a moment, smiles growing. "We'll find you a sword. You can take my knife until then."

He handed over his belt knife.

Acton flipped it in the air and caught it again by the blade, a boy's trick, then tucked it into the sheath on his belt.

"We didn't bring you back to fight," Bramble said, as angry as she had ever been at any warlord. Why was fighting the first thing he always thought of? She knew the answer to that—had lived through battle after battle with him—but he had *died*. Hadn't that changed anything in him?

Acton looked at her, and his surprise turned into that intense gaze that he used when something important was happening. Bramble wondered what was in her face to make him look like that, but it didn't matter. She had to explain, and she had to do it well. She couldn't let Acton leave these caves thinking that another fight would solve things.

"We brought you back because we have need of you. A thousand years have passed, and the land you invaded is now known as the Eleven Domains." His language was easy for her, it had become part of her mind, part of her heart, as familiar as her mother's voice. "Asgarn set up the warlord system that he described to you, using your name to justify it. The original inhabitants of this land were massacred and dispossessed..."

He listened intently, the commander taking a briefing from an officer, assessing everything she said, looking occasionally to Baluch for a confirming nod. He was not looking at her as a young woman any more, which was a different kind of grief, and one she had not expected.

As they followed Baluch through dark and echoing caverns, across pools and over cracks that pierced the heart of the earth, while water dripped like a reminder of time passing, she painted a history of blood and division and oppression, painted it as vividly as she could, so that he would understand what he had done, what he had allowed to happen. So that he would want to help.

She knew exactly what to say, because she knew his weaknesses, knew his strengths, his dreams and his nightmares. It felt a little like betraying him, to use her knowledge of him this way. But it would have been a greater betrayal—of him, as well as Maryrose—not to.

"So we need your help," she said at last, stopping for a moment to stare him right in the eyes. Not a follower, not an enemy. An ally, perhaps.

"You will have it," he said. The echoes took his voice and amplified it, so that it became a god's voice, Swith's voice, booming from the walls and the roof, high above.

She couldn't avoid suspecting that he said it mostly to please Baluch; he had been fascinated by the story of the Domains but not shocked by her tales of endless battles. That had been his life, after all—death didn't change who he had been, who he was.

"Whatever I can do," he went on, "I will do." The echoes answered, "I will do, will do, will do..." and she knew he would stand by that oath.

"Then the next task," Bramble said, "is to find Saker."

FLAX

WATCHING ROWAN try to ride was even funnier than watching Ash. At least Ash was fit and strong—Rowan was wiry with the endurance built up by decades of walking the Road, but he had very little strength in his shoulders or arms. When Mud decided to go one way and Rowan wanted him to go differently, the man had no chance.

Flax grabbed the reins from him. "I'll lead you," he said, pushing down his amusement.

Rowan dropped his head, his face reddening. "Not so good at this, am I?"

"You'd not expect me to play the flute right first try, would you?" Flax said cheerfully. "Riding's just as complicated."

Rowan's eyebrows lifted and he settled back more comfortably in his saddle while he thought it through. That reassured Mud, and he followed Flax and Cam willingly enough as they made their way along the flat-bottomed valley that led back to Gabriston.

The other singers and musicians had left before them, one by one, slipping off into the darkness with a simple, "Wind at your back"—the Travellers' 'bye.

The horses needed light to pick their way out along the rocky defiles that surrounded the Deep, so he and Rowan had waited until dawn, Rowan sitting on a rock playing the flute while Flax had curried and groomed both horses and made sure they were fit to travel. Each to his own trade, he supposed, and all of a part with this strange time in the Deep, where he had been very much the apprentice. A youngling, just learning the first notes of a new song, that's what he had been.

He shivered as he saw the canyon opening up before them and the long slit of daylight widen to show the valley beyond. He had to put away all thoughts of the Deep, now, all the memories of the River, her water flowing over his skin like silk and blood, all thoughts of the fires in the caverns where the demons had taught him mysteries. A surge of excitement went through him and he felt tinglingly alive. He was truly becoming a man! He had been Zel's little brer for so long, following along after her, doing what he was told. But this was beyond her, forbidden to her, and no matter what she said, he was coming here again next year, to learn more. To become a man like Ash. A man who had no fear, not even of warlords and their men.

He turned in the saddle to smile at Ash's father, who had skills of a different sort to teach him. He was excited—to think that Ash's mother was the legendary Swallow! He had heard about her so often, from other musicians on the Road: her voice, her skill, her dedication. If anyone could teach him what he still needed to know about singing, it was her.

"When we get to Gabriston," he said to Rowan, "we'll have to earn some silver."

Rowan shook his head. "No, not so close. Never that close to the Deep, coming or going. Swallow's at Baluchston. We'll head straight there."

"The canyons change," he added. "Every year is different. I just follow the sun."

Following the sun, they found their way to a path up the cliff, which would skirt around Gabriston and take them on a secondary road to Baluchston.

"Now we are back to country I know," Rowan said, climbing down from Mud with difficulty. He would be sore the next day.

"Make sure you stretch your legs t'night," Flax said. "Or you won't be walking tomorrow."

Rowan grimaced and stared up the cliff, looking at Mud with doubt.

"I'll lead," Flax said, grinning. Cam was happy to be led, Mud was happy to follow Cam.

The climb was stiff but Flax found himself oddly happy. He had always wanted his life to be exciting, and since meeting Ash, it had been. Great things at stake—life and death, the future of the world. He began to sing without even thinking about it, as he often did, a wedding song from the South Domain.

A new day, a new day
Seed and fruit,

Fruit and seed
A *new life, a new life*
Tree and root
Root and tree.
Growing, growing, growing…

Rowan smiled. "Thinking of settling down?"

Flax laughed, too pleased with himself to even be embarrassed, and they climbed in companionable silence.

The road was deserted all afternoon. In the fields, the grapes were untended. They were not ripe, but there should have been workers out, checking for bugs and weeds. It was odd. Unchancy. As the day went on they both became increasingly nervous. The horses picked up on their anxiety and began to sidle and shy at blown leaves. Rowan had no hope of controlling Mud, so they dismounted and began walking along the empty track.

"Usually like this?" Flax asked.

Rowan shook his head. "No. No. There are usually Travellers, farmers, workers. There's a village up ahead. Let's go quietly, eh?"

"Let's mount up," Flax said. Rowan looked at him and Flax shrugged. "Just in case."

The village was busy, at least. This was where everyone had gone—they were barricading their houses and the inn, nailing shutters closed, dragging barrels of water indoors, carrying food from sheds and barns into the houses. They had clearly heard news of the enchanter and his ghosts.

No one paid them any attention at first, beyond a quick look to make sure it wasn't the warlord's men. Then one of the women, a skinny red-head with big hands, who was rolling a barrel towards one of the cottages, looked at them more closely.

"Traveller!" she shouted. All over the village heads swivelled, and the hands that were nailing and sawing hefted their tools.

"Go!" Flax said, kicking Cam into a trot and looking back to make sure Rowan had heard.

Rowan wasn't quick enough. A burly man in a butcher's leather apron had grabbed Mud's bridle and was trying to pull Rowan out of the saddle. Rowan kicked at his head, and the man fell back a moment, but came on again. Mud was spooked and lashing out with his back hooves. Flax reined Cam in, unsure of what to do.

The other villagers were gathering, staying away from Mud's hooves but preparing to rush in. Some of them ran towards Flax and for a moment he was gripped by the desire to run — to urge Cam into a gallop and race away, as he and Ash had raced from the warlord's man in Golden Valley. He could hear Zel's voice in his head, screaming, *Get out of there!*

But Rowan...

Ash would never leave Rowan behind, even if Rowan were a stranger. Look how he'd rushed to save Bramble. Ash would *act*, even if it meant risking his own life.

Flax pulled Cam's head around and kicked her back towards the struggling group. They almost had Rowan out of the saddle, and then there would be no chance for him if they did. Flax noticed a boy with a hoe watching, dancing from foot to foot with excitement. He leant down and grabbed it, then used it to beat aside two women who were screeching and grabbing at Mud's head.

Cam didn't like it. Her ears were flat on her head and the whites of her eyes were showing. She wanted to shy away, but he used every bit of skill he had to force her ahead, towards Rowan. "Come on, girl, come on, take the bastards down!" he called, and the sound of his voice steadied her.

He put a foot in the face of the butcher and poked the hoe into the stomach of another man, who wrenched it out of his hands. Just as well, he thought — time to clear a path out of here. He whistled the signal Gorham taught all his horses that meant "Run! Follow me!" — praying to all the gods that Bramble had taught her horses the same way.

He whirled Cam and set her straight at the woman who had called out. She didn't believe he would ride her down at first, standing there grinning and waving a knife — a carving knife, big enough to disembowel Cam if she got in the right blow. Flax yelled, screamed as he picked up pace, no words, just anger and hate making a sound to raise the dead. The woman's face changed as he came towards her. He knew he was moving fast, but to him everything seemed to move slowly. She'll be dead if she don't move, he thought, screaming, and the red-head jumped out of the way just in time.

Mud followed immediately. They left the village at a gallop, with a thrown axe whistling past Rowan's ear, clattering on the ground under Cam's heels. She kicked backwards and kept going, Flax urging her on. He had stopped screaming, his throat raw. He wouldn't be able to sing for a while.

"Dark-haired bastards!" the red-head yelled after them. "Don't bother running! We'll get the shagging lot of you!"

As though they understood her words, the horses increased their pace, Mud coming up level with Cam. They rode at a good pace for another half mile, until they were sure no one in the village had a horse to follow them on, then slowed.

"Walk them," Flax said. "Let them cool down and catch their breath. We may need them again later."

"Gods of field and stream!" Rowan gasped. "They would have killed us."

"Reckon they know the enchanter are a Traveller," Flax said grimly. "Have you got a hat?"

Rowan bit his lip; Flax could see he didn't like the idea of pretending to be one of Acton's people. But he wasn't a fool. He fished a knitted cap out of his backpack and slid it on, covering his hair and ears. Odd in full summer, but by the time someone started to wonder about that they would be gone.

Flax wished it were winter: the long summer twilight seemed to make them more conspicuous. So much for his cheerful mood of the morning.

"I know another way," Rowan said. "It's longer, but it avoids most of the towns between here and Baluchston."

"You've convinced me!" Flax said, trying to sound encouraging. Ash was depending on him to look after Rowan, but it was more of a responsibility than he had realised. The older man looked very tired, and he squirmed in the saddle, making Mud roll his eyes back and flatten his ears. Flax clucked reassuringly at him and he settled down.

"We should travel at night," Rowan said.

"Certain sure. And find a place to spell the horses."

It was a long time before they came to the small path that led off to the left, towards Baluchston. The track was rocky under the horses' hooves, and Cam picked up a stone. Flax noticed almost immediately and dug it out, but she still went lame for a while, slowing them to the point where Flax wanted to scream—in his highest register—in frustration.

They stopped to rest themselves and the horses at a tiny clearing where deer were drinking from a rill. The hinds startled away, bounding off into the shadows.

Flax realised with satisfaction that it was almost dark. "An hour," he said, loosening Cam's girth and motioning Rowan to do the same for Mud. "We'll give them an hour."

"I could use more than that," Rowan said, sitting on a flat rock at the water's edge. He looked up at Flax seriously. "Thank you, lad. I'd have been hacked to pieces if you hadn't come back for me."

Flax grinned at him, feeling buoyed up and as strong as an ox. All right, they were in the wilderness with everyone's hand raised against them, but it was still better than trailing around behind Zel from inn to inn, singing to clods who wouldn't know a true note from a pig's fart. And he had taken action when danger threatened. Like Ash.

"Have a drink," he said. "There's a long night ahead of us."

MARTINE

T HE SHANTYMAN was singing as they brought up the anchor.

> *Lady Death will ring her knell*
> *Heave away*
> *Haul away*
> *And call us all to the coldest hell*
> *Raise the anchor, maties!*

Martine stood at the stern and watched the huge anchor, wood bounded by iron, slide slowly up out of the dark green water, dripping weed.

The Last Domain cargo having been finally off-loaded and paid for, and Trine well exercised by Zel while that was done, they were catching an evening tide out of the small harbour, back onto the open sea. Without Apple. The men who had attacked her had been taken by the Moot staff, and would be tried and punished. The two merchants who had come with her were riding back north.

"Didn't have no Travellers there to start with," one had said. "May not be no ghosts there, either."

Martine was full of foreboding, but her Sight couldn't tell her about what. No matter what happened, the next few weeks were unlikely to go well. People would die; the dead would walk; not even the gods knew what the outcome would be. Perhaps her jitters were no more than that; or perhaps, since Safred didn't seem to share them, they were more personal. Perhaps this new-found joy with Arvid was doomed to end when they reached Turvite.

Perversely, that thought cheered her. If all she had to worry about was a love affair gone wrong, she was in good shape.

On the thought, Arvid appeared from below decks and joined her. "Safred's sick again. Cael's tending her."

"Never take a seer over water," Martine said lightly.

"*You* don't get sick."

She ignored the implication. "Cael's not well himself."

"No." Arvid's face darkened with worry and he pushed a hand through his light brown hair. "He's worse."

"If Safred can't heal him, and the ship's healer can't..."

"Cast the stones again for him," Arvid said.

It was worth a try. She sat cross legged on the bare warm deck and pulled out of her belt the square of blue linen she used to cast on, and spread it on the deck. She spat in her hand and held it out to Arvid. He spat in his and clasped hands. The familiar ritual calmed her, reminded her of who she was. Not Arvid's bed mate, but a stonecaster, Sighted and strong.

"Ask your question," she said.

"Why can't Cael be cured?" Arvid asked.

Her right hand went into the pouch and the stones leapt to her fingers, the ones she needed seeming almost to stick, as they always did. She brought them out and cast them across the linen, her head bent to watch their fall, her ears ready.

"Death," she said, a catch in her voice, because she liked Cael. "Destiny. Sacrifice." She reached out to turn the other two over. Although she recognised each of her stones no matter which way they lay, they spoke to her only when they were face up, and other stonecasters she knew had told her that it was the same for them. "Time, and Memory, both hidden."

"Dragon's fart!" Arvid said angrily. It was so unexpected she just gaped at him, and he was puzzled for a moment. "It's a northern saying," he said. "I just meant—well, it's clear, isn't it, even to me?"

Martine bent her head over the stones and listened. They spoke quietly but surely. Lady Death was coming for Cael, and coming soon, but there was a reason for it, not just blind malignant chance. She said so to Arvid.

"And that's comforting, is it?" he said, staring at the stones. "I'd hoped to give Safred better news."

Martine felt that pang that all stonecasters knew. They were only the heralds, the messengers, but somehow they felt responsible for the bad

57

news they delivered—and certainly, customers tended to act as though they were. It irritated Martine when the questioners stared at her with anger and suspicion, but when they didn't she felt even more culpable. Like with Ranny of Highmark. She was still unsure if she'd made the right choice there. It had seemed right, to deny Ranny the knowledge the stones had given her of the time and date of her death. But had she the right to censor the stones? She didn't know.

She felt so young, all her old certainties dissipated. Who was she to withhold information from anyone? She sighed and packed the stones away in her pouch, folded her casting cloth. When they reached Turvite she'd find Ranny and tell her what she wanted to know.

Then Arvid touched her hand and smiled tentatively at her. He was unsure, too, even after a week of sharing a bed, and that gave her more confidence. She smiled back, touching his cheek lightly, and he lit up from within, glowing with desire and what she had to suspect was love. Oh, gods. How could she love a warlord?

Cael came up on deck not long after, while Arvid was aft talking to the captain. He was sweating and pale, a bad combination, and he sat next to her at the bow heavily, turning his face into the wind with relief. Zel followed him like a shadow and sat at his feet, her face serious.

"I'm dying," he said conversationally.

He wasn't asking for reassurance, so there was nothing to say except the truth. Zel sat perfectly still, waiting for Martine's response.

"Yes," she said. "I think you are."

A shiver ran through Zel and her face twisted, fighting tears, but Cael nodded and simply sat for a time.

"Why, do you think?" he asked. "Why won't it heal?"

She had puzzled over that many times, with few answers. "It may be because your wound was given...somewhere else, some other time. May be it can only be healed then, too."

He frowned, thinking back to the stream in the Great Forest which had seemingly taken him to somewhere else, to be attacked and wounded. "So I have to go back to the stream? But we each went to a different place."

58

"No," Martine said, sure of this at least. "A different time."

"So there's no guarantee that I'd go to the time I needed. And I'd have to take Saffie back too, back to where those...things are."

"I think so."

He shook his head with decision. "Not a chance."

"No."

It was a fine day and they sat for a while, enjoying the sunshine and the breeze. Zel pulled out some tiny balls and juggled for a while, keeping in practice.

Cael's eyes seemed to look at a different horizon, somewhere in the past. "I had a family, you know," he said. "We were Valuers, born and bred. Sage, my wife, she died of a fever when Safred was two. We had two girls, March and Nim. They married. There were three little ones: a girl and two boys. Linnet, Birch and Eagle. Nim was so excited when she saw an eagle from the birthing chamber—she thought it meant he would be something great in the world."

"What happened?" Martine asked, as gently as she could.

"Safred's father, the warlord, came looking for her. I took Saffie to safety, so he couldn't take her and use her as a warlord's weapon. He killed them, one by one, until someone in the village told him where we had gone."

Martine was plunged into deep empathy and old grief. Her village, too, had been killed off; everyone she loved, gone, except the young Elva, because Martine had taken her on the road. She sent a prayer to the gods for Elva's safety.

There were tears on Zel's cheeks. She turned her head away and scrubbed at them with the back of her hand, then went on juggling.

"They should have told straight away," he said with old anger. "When it came down to it, they didn't believe in Valuing after all—her life, my life, was no more important than theirs. But it's hard to believe that where she's concerned. And she'd helped so many of them. Healed so many...They loved her."

"And she escaped," Zel said, still not looking at him.

"Aye. The delvers rescued her." He paused, staring at his hands. "I'll be glad to see Sage and March and Nim again. If they've waited for me."

The lump in Martine's throat was so hard she couldn't talk.

"You're lucky that your dead love you," Zel said, then pushed herself up, hard, and tucked the balls in her pocket as she walked away, her eyes resolutely turned up, to find her aunties in the rigging.

"That one carries a lot of grief, still, even after Safred helped her," Cael said sadly.

"Everyone carries grief," Martine said, "if they live long enough."

Memories of her own dead came back to her: Elva's parents, Cob and Lark, her own parents, her aunties and uncles, cousins, grammers and granfers. Everyone in the two villages was related, one way or another.

The Ice King's men had come on them so unexpectedly, early, very early in the season...too early, you would have thought, for them to have made it over the snow-choked mountains.

Once again she remembered her girlhood vision of the villages being attacked. Not by the Ice King, but by the warlord and his men. That was crazy, though. Why would the warlord have attacked his own people? The thought came, inevitably: they weren't *his* people. Dark-haired villagers were never his people. But why would he have done it? She searched her memory more closely, trying to piece together the separate parts of the vision. It was so long ago, she'd only been fifteen...She had seen a young officer leading, not the warlord himself. Not even the warlord's heir, Masry. She hadn't known this officer, but he had definitely been in charge.

She rubbed at her side, where an old scar still sometimes ached. She owed that scar to Alder, the village voice at Cliffhaven, who had beaten her for telling about that vision, for raising a false alarm. Yet it had seemed so clear, so true to that young self. The danger had seemed...so real.

Oh, what was the point? False visions happened sometimes, particularly to the young. And sometimes the Sight couched itself in riddles, leading you astray, even though, looking back, the meaning was clear.

It didn't matter now, anyway. No matter who had attacked Cliffhaven, it was a long time ago and over and done with.

She touched Cael on the back of his hand. He was too warm to the touch. "I'll make you a tisane to bring down the fever," she said.

He nodded heavily. "Aye. But don't let Saffie know. She worries too much as it is."

Rumer and Rawnie dropped down out of the rigging and draped an arm each over Zel, laughing about something.

"Family," Cael said, and sighed.

RAWNIE'S STORY

I ALWAYS WANTED to be beautiful, like my little sister Osyth. She had that Traveller kind of beauty, dark and elegant and lithe. Well, we was lithe enough, my twin Rumer and me, but that was because we was tumblers and worked hard at it. She were—oh, I don't know. Her eyes was big and her nose were straight and there were just something about her that made men look.

Rumer and me, we was ordinary, as ordinary as Travellers can be in the Domains. Not ill-featured nor even so plain, but ordinary. Osyth stood out like a dark moon. After she married that Gorham (and he worshipped the ground she walked on, that were clear), me and Rumer took to the Road alone, and had a good time of it. Osyth said we'd be short of silver within a month, and she were near enough right, for neither of us had the knack of keeping money. Sweet in, sweet out, we thought, and if we had to shag for our shelter more often than we'd like, well, everything has a price. It was a bad summer, too, that year, the worst I remember, and there was no silver to be had for tumbling, not even tumbling in someone's bed.

So we decided to head north, where the weather is different and the year might not have been so bad. And since we was heading north, we thought we'd go see our mam, in Foreverfroze. She were a fisher, our mam, like one of the Seal Mother's people, and she loved the clean colours of the ice and the sea and the sky, white and blue and green and grey. Fishing was her passion, I reckon, and Da came a cold second to it.

She's a funny one, my mam. I mean, look at the names she gave us: Osyth and Rumer and Rawnie. Whoever heard of Traveller girls with names like those? But Mam never did think much of tradition, and Da thought that whatever Mam did was right. We talked about her and him, in the nights after a tumbling performance, but we could never seem to understand her right. Guess we never will.

I think we was a bit kin-hungry without Osyth, and maybe a bit mother-hungry too, cause Osyth used to boss us around just like Mam and it felt a bit rootless, somehow, not to have anyone telling us what to do.

We got up to Foreverfroze at the end of summer, which wasn't so smart, maybe, but it let us spend the winter with Mam and Da, helping to salt down the fish the women had brought back and helping Da weave the sweet-grass baskets the men traded down south. And Mam filled the long nights with stories about the fisherwomen and their freedom and prosperity. It sounded good enough, all right.

The next spring Mam said, "Come out and try it for yourselves," and she got us berths on her ship, the *Flying Spray*, as a hooking and gutting team. All the fishers are women on those ships, and they work in partnerships, one woman hooking the fish and flipping it back to deck, the other gutting it and rebaiting the hook.

Well, we tried it and we didn't like it, although Rumer and I could work like one body when we wanted to, and the rhythm of hooking and gutting the fish was easy enough for us to learn. But it was boring, boring as walking a long road between high walls, and before three days were out we was up on the rigging with the sailors, laughing as we raced each other to the topsails.

They marvelled at us, but it weren't hard for professional tumblers to keep balance, even on a swaying rope fathoms above the deck and the icy sea.

So that's how we found our passion, Rumer and me, the passion of high places and wide horizons, of swell and spray and sea and sail. Of always moving, even in port. Of always seeing new things, good things and bad. Of taking your home with you wherever you go, so that you are always where you belong.

Now there's lots of stories about the fishing women, about what they get up to on those ships, alone for months without men except for a few of the sailors. I notice those stories are always told by men.

Oh, there were a couple of teams shared more than their bed space, but mostly fishers are too tired to even think about shagging—sleep is precious and hard won when the fish are biting, and when they're not the fishers are more likely to snipe at each other than throw kisses. And put a lot of women together in one place, you get them all having their monthlies at the same time—that's a recipe for arguments and tears and friendships broken and made up again; oh, Rumer and me, we stayed way up in the rigging those days.

We've always liked sweet young men, Rumer and I, and on the *Flying Spray* we learnt to like sweet older men, too. There was always a few men sailors 'cause there are things that need pure strength on any ship and men are best for that, no question. Takes three women to hold the steerboard against a current, and one strong man does a better job. So we had some men to choose from.

Unlike most of the women, we didn't have men to go home to, so we were popular. No complications, see? We didn't have to give up any pleasures, except food. You can get good and tired of fish stew.

But for all that, it was a fine life and we loved it. Mam too. And Da seemed happy enough with his men friends, working and looking after the childer in the winter. He started making comments about needing grandchildren to look after, but we was in no hurry, Rumer and me. It would mean a full year on land, and we was still in the early stages of the passion, where even a day away seems too long.

And then... You can't trust the gods. Not for long.

We was on the *Cormorant* three days out from Foreverfroze, when the storm come up out of a clear sky.

The sea were on a nice even swell, we had a good following wind—but not so much to make her dig her nose in, which that ship was prone to do, like many two-masters that came out of Mitchen's yards. The sun were shining. The gulls that was following us didn't even notice anything, though usually they're more weather-wise than we humans.

Then, *whoomp*! A huge clap of wind, like a hand sweeping across the surface of the sea and hitting us broadside. The ship reeled and staggered, but thank the gods we hadn't caught much in those three days so she were still riding light. She righted herself with an effort we could all feel.

There was a pause. We was all shouting. The ship owner were also the steersman, and she went dead pale and called to bring down the sheets, but it were too late. The wind hit us before the riggers had cleared the first crossbar.

And the sky stayed clear. Clear as poverty soup, that sky, but wind screeching down on us and tearing the rigging apart, pushing every hand that wasn't lashed to her post right across the deck to the steerboard side. Me and my twin clung to a bollard and each other and the wind whipped tears up in our eyes like we was mourning each other already.

Wind wraiths, I thought. Can't be nothing else.

And I worked my mouth, trying to bring up spit, because the story goes that if you're of Traveller blood whistling will tame them, but you can't whistle with a mouth dust dry with fear, so most folks never get to test if it's true.

Then they came.

They're hard to describe, and I can't do it, but they was only half in the world, it seemed, and half somewhere else. And they laughed.

The wind dropped as they hovered, just above the poop deck, and the master came to meet them. She passed us as she went and avoided our eyes, and that was bad, I knew.

They hailed her in screeching voices. "Master!" they said. "We have found you."

She worked her mouth for enough spit to form an answer. She didn't want to say anything, it looked like, but she had to. "You have found us."

The spirits sent up a triumphant laugh, a howl more like, that sent cold down into my marrow bones.

"Present your sacrifice," one of the spirits said.

And the master turned her head and looked at us.

Pity in her eyes.

We looked around, wildly, but the others was turning away from us, ashamed, crying or stony-faced, and we knew we was dead as we stood.

We'd heard the stories. In the dead watch, by a crescent moon, sailors love to tell the wind wraith stories. About the compact, made no one knows how long ago, where the wind wraiths and the humans made a deal—if the spirits found a ship in the wide wastes of the ocean, they could take a single soul but the ship and the rest of the crew had to be left safe.

It was a good deal for the shipowner, for the sailors, for the fishers. For everyone except the one they threw to the spirits. The newest sailor on board.

"Last on, first off," the master said. I will say she was sorrowing as she said it, but she meant it, nonetheless. "Which of you was last on?"

"Me," Rumer said.

"Me," I said in the same moment.

The master were taken fair aback. Even the spirits looked confused. I didn't look at Rumer, and she didn't look at me. Nothing to say. But we gripped hands tight, like just before a performance, or afterwards, when we was taking our bows.

"Both..." the wind wraith said in a voice half venom and half hiss.

"No! I was last on." The voice had come from the hooking deck below us. We spun around and there was Mam, laying down her rod like it were made of ruby, nodding to her partner and the other fishers, climbing up the companionway from the hooking deck to stand beside us.

"Not true," Rumer and I said together, with one voice.

"True enough," Mam said. She didn't look at us, after one quick glance that were full of warning, like she used to look at us when we was half-grown, after she'd told us to do something we didn't want to. We knew that look, right enough. It meant, "Do as you're told or suffer the consequences."

My guts was churning and I were sweating like a smith. I didn't know what to want. What to hope for. Seemed to me it would be easier to die than see either Rumer or Mam taken, but maybe they felt the same.

The master looked helplessly from Mam to us, and we all looked stonily back at her.

"We have to give one," she said. "But only one."

"*Three* have volunteered," the spirit said, swooping closer, mouth agape.

That seemed to strengthen the master. "*One* was agreed to. Do you break the compact?"

It seemed disturbed by that idea, and slid away from her, higher up, and hung next to its companions. "No," it wailed. "One. One is enough."

"Well, then," Mam said. "Here I am."

"No!" we shouted, but the master and Mam locked gazes for a moment, and the master nodded.

The spirits stooped at Mam, and dragged her from the deck. I felt them swipe by me, their flesh like cold cloth dragging on my skin, and then they launched into the sky, dragging Mam with them, screeching and shrieking with triumph. We tried to pull her back, Rumer and me, grabbing onto her feet, but they was too strong, strong like the sea, unstoppable, and they ripped her away from us and left us sprawling on the deck.

She turned her head back to see us, but by then she were too far up for us to see into her eyes. But she didn't scream, our mam. She didn't give them any fear to play with. She didn't give them anything except herself.

And in a heartbeat, two, three, they were gone across the wide, level sea, and we was left fallen on the deck under a calm blue sky, with a steady following wind bringing us the sound of gulls.

We just sailed on and all we was left with was questions, and too much imagining about where they took her to, and what they did when they got there.

We had nightmares every night, after.

And yet, it's like she answered a question for us that we'd never of dared to ask, and that's left a sweetness as well as a pain behind.

For Rumer to offer to die instead of me, well, that's easy to understand. She's my twin. Of course we'd die for each other. And maybe others would say, well, she were your mother, of course she'd die for you. But I tell you, it came as a shock to both of us. It weren't something I'd have ever predicted. Tell the truth, I don't think even a stonecaster could've predicted it.

What I want to know is, what did the master see in Mam's eyes that made her nod? 'Cause I don't think we ever seen it, and when I wish, that's what I wish for: to see those eyes and see if it were love that made her a sacrifice. Or something else.

LEOF

THEY LEFT the farmyard and quartered as much ground as they could, but it was useless. The gods only knew where the wraiths had flown to with their enchanter. And at dusk, if things went as they had in Spritford and Carlion, the ghosts themselves would fade.

An hour before sunset, Leof ordered his men to turn around and head for Sendat. Wearily, they turned the horses' heads towards home. It was a measure of the quality of these three men, Leof thought, that even after all the unsettling events of the day, they unerringly turned towards the fort at Sendat. It was one of the first things his own father had taught him—always know where you are, always know where you can retreat to if necessary, so that in the heat of battle you are not disoriented, so that if you need to run you don't run the wrong way.

Although he'd always followed that advice, today was the first time he had really needed it. Today was the first time Thegan had ever retreated. Leof considered how livid his lord was going to be when they returned empty-handed. They made the trip in silence, and he suspected that the others were considering the same thing, and wondering how Thegan would greet them. Leof was heart-sick that he wasn't returning with the enchanter—Thegan had risked his own life to save his, back at Bonhill, and the only way he could repay that was to deal with the enchanter. He had failed, and it weighed on him as nothing ever had. His lord would be angry, and rightfully so.

But when he walked into the hall at Sendat just after the evening meal had ended, Thegan took one look at his face and, although his mouth tightened, he waved Leof into his workroom calmly. At Thegan's signal, Sorn rose and followed them. Leof felt his heart lift and clench at the same time. Seeing her was a blessing from the gods, but also a danger, with Thegan watching.

"No luck?" his lord asked.

"We found him, followed him. Tried to take him down by bow,

but the wraiths intervened. Then we found him and the ghosts in a farm—they'd killed the people there—and I rode in to grab him, almost had him, but the wraiths dragged him up into the sky and we don't know where they took him. We searched, but they could be anywhere. Out of the Domain, maybe." He shrugged, suddenly bone weary.

Thegan listened closely, and Leof knew that later, tomorrow maybe, his commander would take him through it all again, in detail, looking for any weakness they could exploit.

"Enough, now," he said. "Eat and rest. Tomorrow we take action."

It was comforting to realise that Thegan had already devised a strategy; but alarming, too. Any action they took was likely to be desperate.

"There is food," Sorn said, her voice soft. "Come and eat."

In a dream he followed her back into the noise and movement of the hall. He really was very tired. It seemed impossible that it was only two days ago that he had left her here to go to Carlion. With a shock, he remembered the white-haired man, the Lake's ambassador. His warnings had made the trip to Carlion necessary. The Lake seemed the least of their problems, now, and with a surge of relief Leof realised that it was, indeed, the least of their problems. Thegan was unlikely to move against Baluchston anytime soon. That was one thing he could stop worrying about. He wondered when he had started being someone who worried.

Sorn signalled to a maid and as if by enchantment food appeared in front of him. Good, solid food: soup, sausages, bread. Comforting food. He set to, relying on Sorn to make sure that Alston and the others would also be fed. He could always rely on her. For a moment his gaze rested on her as she spoke to one of the serving maids, her head bent to listen to the girl's answer. She was as calm as always, and watching her he could almost believe that the world outside was safe. Then he realised he was staring and looked down at his plate.

He slept like the dead. Better than he deserved. Better than the dead were sleeping, around here.

The next morning Thegan called him to his office.

"Take Alston and fortify the old barn," he said. "Use our own masons, not the Travellers. Make sure it's secure." He paused, weighing his words. "We are building a prison. I want it watertight."

Leof was speechless for a moment, looking at Thegan from across the warlord's desk. "You think the ghosts can be imprisoned?" It was an intriguing idea.

"No, no. How would we get them here? No." He seemed to come to some decision, and moved around his desk, resting his thigh against it so that he looked casual. Leof could tell that he was anything but relaxed.

"To save Sendat, we will need hostages," Thegan said. Leof had no idea what he meant.

Thegan nodded at the papers on his desk. "I compiled reports while I was in Carlion. The ghosts ignored some people and killed others. Not a single Traveller was killed. Not one. And when I questioned the survivors, it was the same story. A Traveller grandmother, a Traveller great-grandfather. Some of them had never heard of Travellers in the family, but that's not surprising. Families hush it up. But most knew it was somewhere in their bloodline. Far back at times, but there."

Leof slowly absorbed the information. He felt as though his head were full of horsehair, like a cushion. It had always been likely that the enchanter was a Traveller — like the first enchanter who tried to make ghosts solid, in Turvite. But this was proof. "He's making the ghosts kill — for Travellers, you think?"

"I think he wants to take back what Acton took and he is protecting his own people."

"The ghosts don't kill their own," Leof said slowly.

"Exactly. And more than that — they *will* not kill their own, or all his work is for nothing. Which is why we need hostages."

Leof nodded, understanding. It was purely logical; he ignored a feeling of dismay. Time to trust his lord. Thegan had proved, yesterday, that Leof could trust him, even to the risk of his own life.

"So — set Alston to fortify the barn, and then you and Gard will take a detail to collect every Traveller within a day's ride of Sendat. Explain to Alston so he can prepare here."

"My lord, what if they will not come?"

Thegan smiled sourly. "They'll come all right. Once people know

70

that the ghosts spare the Travellers, this will be the only safe place in the Domain for them. And that's what you will offer them, Leof—safety. Safety from their neighbours behind the strong walls of the warlord's fort." He paused, weighing his words. "I will not let this enchanter destroy life in the Domains. I will crush him one way or the other. I swear it."

Leof left, wondering how he had come to a place where he questioned his lord's orders. But Thegan was right. The news about Travellers and ghosts would get around, no doubt, spurred by Thegan's own questions, if by nothing else, and then he shivered. No Traveller would be safe. He was doing them a favour by offering shelter. And if the ghosts really did respect the lives of their own, then the Travellers and Sendat would survive. It was the only way. The only choice they had.

But as he explained the plan to Alston and saw the ready acceptance in his eyes, he was troubled. If the ghosts did not respect Traveller lives, what then? Were they all to be slaughtered, their own people and the Travellers alike? If the ghosts overwhelmed their defences—well, then, he would die. The road was long only if you were lucky. The thought made him oddly cheerful and he whistled as he went to the stables to find Thistle.

BRAMBLE

THEY WALKED through the dark, following Baluch, with only Medric's small candle to light their way. They were using one candle at a time, not knowing how long it would take them to reach the surface.

Ash motioned Bramble away from the others and they walked together. "You must keep the bones with you at all times," he said. "We can find another singer, if we have to, but you are the key."

The ghosts Ash and Martine had seen at Spritford had faded at sunset. If Acton faded too... She pushed down her grief at the thought. They would have to raise him again, that was all.

"I'm rather glad I can't raise him on my own," she said. It would be both a temptation and a torment, to be able to call him to her.

"The way you feel about him, I thought you'd want to be able to." His voice was accusing.

She flushed. "He's not as bad as history paints him."

"He's the enemy of our people."

"I'm from both, remember?" she replied. "I've come to realise that I have no enemies but the warlords. And no matter what the stories say, he didn't start the warlord system."

That gave him pause. "So he's not a killer?"

Her step faltered a little. "Aye," she said. "He's a killer." The words sent a pain straight through her chest. "But so are we."

Ash flinched at that, and said nothing for a while. His hand went to his belt, as though to reassure himself, and Bramble noticed a pouch hanging there, the type stonecasters used.

"Are you a caster now as well?" she asked him.

Ash nodded. "I can cast." But his tone was doubtful.

She left it at that and they walked companionably until they were in a dry, smooth area of the caves, a round pocket in the middle of a long corridor of stone. The air was fresh, and they knew they were getting closer to the surface, because there was a narrow crack letting in a tiny lozenge of light. It glowed in the darkness and left afterimages on her eyes.

Medric blew out his candle. Their eyes were so adjusted to the dark that the cave seemed like bright daylight.

"Let's take a break," Ash suggested.

Bramble went over to the crack and looked up; the slender chimney seemed to go up forever. Her sense of time was unsettled in here, but still it seemed she could feel the sun setting. Would Acton fade at sunset? The thought made her shiver. She wouldn't look at him. Better to turn around and have him gone than watch him fade away. Then he came to stand beside her, making all the hairs on her arms stand up. She didn't know if that was because he was a ghost, or because he was...him.

"What would you see, if you stood on top of this hill?" Acton asked.

Bramble shrugged. "Farms, villages, towns—as far as the horizon and beyond."

"So much..." he said, wonderingly. "We've built a great country!"

"Out of the blood of my people," Ash reminded him.

Acton turned, and the last red light of sunset caught him, gilding him so that for a moment Bramble could see the man he had been, hale and rosy. She strangled something like a sob, and felt irritated with herself. She had to take control of these ridiculous surges of emotion.

"Aye," Acton said. "You are right. It was badly done. By me, by others." He paused, choosing his words, and Baluch paused too, a curious look on his face, as though he were remembering old and difficult times. "We tried for peace. But we were betrayed by your people."

"You murdering bastard!" Ash snarled. He somehow looked larger, as though rage had swollen him. Medric moved behind Acton, not understanding Acton's words but aware of conflict, and immediately taking his side. It enraged Ash further. "You can't excuse massacres with a lie about betrayal."

Bramble moved to Ash's side, sensing his approval, as though she were ranging herself on the side of right. "He's telling the truth, Ash," she said. Startled, he whirled to face her, a protest on his lips. She held up her hand. "Oh, yes, he's a killer, he's a murdering bastard all right,

73

he invaded, all of that. But it's true he tried to do it peacefully and the original inhabitants massacred his kin."

Ash stood silent, his breath rasping.

Baluch came forward and laid a hand on his arm. "True," he said quietly. "Acton's mother, my sweetheart, all our friends...butchered by the dark haired ones. Our girls raped and degraded. Our home burnt."

"Hawk," Bramble said. "The leader's name was Hawk. It was his steading."

Fumbling with the shards of everything he had ever believed, Ash latched on to that. He knew that name. "Hawk? Hawksted? Like in 'The Distant Hills'?"

The words of the song, the tune, slid back into Bramble's mind, and the pieces fell into place. She realised that she had even heard the tune forming in Baluch's head, as he had looked down at the corpse of Friede's killer, but she hadn't recognised it then. "For Friede?" she asked Baluch. " 'The Distant Hills'was for Friede?"

"*You* wrote that?" Ash looked awe-struck, as thought he had met a god.

Baluch's mouth firmed and he turned away. Bramble felt cold. Shaky. Baluch had written "The Distant Hills." She had known that song all her life; she had known it before it was written. The thought unsettled her. Time whirled in her head.

Ash was staring at the ground, his face confused and wondering.

"You know too much," Baluch said, staring at bare wall.

"Aye," Bramble said. "I do."

"You were right," Baluch said at last, in her own language. "I went to the Lake just before Acton's death. The calling was so strong...I intended to be back before the Moot, before Acton went to Hawksted, but I didn't understand, then, about how She takes time. It was thirty years, that first time. She brought me forwards to where the Lake People were being attacked for the first time. I...advised on their defence. Asgarn was an old man, then. I killed him without knowing who he was. She only told me afterwards. I felt...It was a bad moment, finding out I'd killed someone I'd fought with."

"So you avenged Acton without knowing it," Bramble said. Baluch laughed bitterly.

"Do you think She knew he had killed Acton?" she asked.

"The Lake? I doubt it."

Bramble looked at Acton, finally, needing to see his reaction, although it seemed like a weakness in her that she needed it. In the moments when Baluch had claimed her attention, the sun had set, but Acton was still there, still staring at them with concern, not understanding. She felt a surge of relief.

"He doesn't fade..." Bramble said. She didn't know if she were glad or not. Ash looked up, his face set, giving nothing more away, but she was sure there was turmoil in his mind. Gods knew, there was turmoil in hers. The past, the present, the future were too mixed for peace of mind.

"He should have faded," Ash said. "If it's the same spell."

"Who knows?" Baluch mused. "It may be different in some small way..."

"Who cares?" Bramble said, and Acton smiled at her tone, although he hadn't understood their words.

"We can stay the night here," Ash said, in the old language.

"I will guard you," Acton said immediately. Ash looked irritated, resenting the easy way Acton took over. A lifetime of giving other people orders—the habit lasted even beyond the grave, Bramble thought. But it was sensible to leave the watch to him. He didn't need to sleep.

Ash avoided Baluch's eyes as he lay down next to Bramble. "Even if they did kill Acton's people, did that excuse him going on to murder thousands of innocent people?" he muttered to her.

She paused, as though she didn't want to answer. "No," she said. "There was no excuse for killing the men of Turvite, or all the people of River Bluff. No excuse. But Hawksted—what would you have done if your parents and all your friends had been betrayed, massacred, by a stranger?" Ash didn't answer, just sat with his shoulders hunched. "Pray you'll never have to find out." She turned her back on him and settled down, her head on the bag that contained Acton's bones. It had taken living all of Acton's life for her to understand him even a little. Poor Ash—all his certainties were being challenged in a single day.

Baluch, instead of resting, had moved aside to talk to Acton.

"Teach him our language," she called to Baluch. "He's going to need

75

it." She sighed, watching them. They had a lot of information to share. A lot of memories. She felt a pang of resentment—she knew so much, shared so many of those memories, but had no right to them...and no chance of making new ones with him, not in this life.

The shock of the dead voice woke her fully. "Well then, Bramble the beautiful, the resolute," Acton said. "Who are you, then? And how do you know so much about me and mine?" He was sitting beside her, Baluch was asleep next to Ash.

He was not charming her, not trying to seduce her into following him. He just wanted to know. So she told him about Obsidian Lake, and he listened, and although his brows knit a time or two, he didn't interrupt.

"Just how much did you see?" he asked cautiously.

"Wili, for example?" she mocked. He flinched, but a smile tugged the side of his mouth as though he laughed at himself. She smiled involuntarily. For the first time she thought about his reaction, were she to betray her love for him. Apart from risking her own dignity, it wouldn't be fair to him, to burden him in an instant with a love that had taken all his life to form, which he couldn't possibly return. "I didn't see enough to make you blush," she said. "Or me either." Which was stretching the truth.

His mouth twisted wryly. "Good," he said. "I wouldn't mind making you blush, but not that way."

He said it so easily, she was sure it was a habit left over from before the grave, like the habit of command. Always, wherever he'd gone, he'd charmed his way into beds and into hearts. It was nothing to do with her personally. Nothing to make her heart leap. But her heart beat faster anyway. At least she had the satisfaction of knowing he would have desired her, if they'd met for more than a moment. Would have acted on the desire.

She tore her thoughts off that path as he cocked an eyebrow at her, laughing at her so easily, with such an invitation to share his amusement, that she melted into laughter and then into something else entirely. He reached out towards her face, but she flinched back. She never wanted to feel that bone deep chill again.

He froze, chagrin on his face, and brought down his hand. "I forgot," he said. He seemed to brood for a moment, then looked up at her. "But on the mountainside? You were really there, weren't you? Not a vision?"

She told him about the hunter, and the journey to the place where she could find his bones.

"You looked so... wild, like a spirit from the forest," he said. She wasn't sure if it were reminiscence or mistrust.

"I'd been living like one for months," she said.

He grinned. "You smiled and then you frowned, and I thought—Oh, that one won't ever be tamed!"

It was a compliment. It seemed the strangest thing yet, to hear the words that had haunted her for so long transformed in his mouth into something good. "So a demon once told me," she said lightly, passing it off.

"Now that's a story I'd like to hear!"

She shook her head, remembering the rest of the demon's prophecy, which had been proven with such a twisting truth: *Born wild and died wild...No one will ever tame thee, woman, and thou wilt love no man never.* She never would, because the only one she'd ever loved was a ghost, not a man.

"I need sleep," she said brusquely. "Even if you don't."

His mouth twisted again, but not in amusement this time. "Aye," he said. "Sleep. I will guard you."

Because of the grating voice of the dead, she couldn't tell if his tone was protective or resentful. She thought his pale shadow beside her would keep her awake, but she dropped into sleep as a stone into a well, and did not dream.

FLAX

"WE'LL BE safe in Baluchston," Rowan said.

Flax grimaced and stared forward, down the long, winding, overgrown track that led north and west, eventually.

"Are you sure? They're Acton's people, even if they do live with the Lake."

Rowan smiled. "The Lake is more than water, lad, remember? She will keep us safe. She always has kept her people safe."

"I thought that were only the Lake people themselves, the ones that set their roots down there."

"Old blood is known," Rowan sang, in a light, clear tenor.

Flax turned more towards him in excitement. "I don't know that song," he said. He hadn't thought about that—the chance to learn new songs. With luck, whole new cycles of songs…His heart lifted and he smiled. "Teach me," he said.

A shadow went over Rowan's face as though the words brought back a difficult memory, but he fished out a little pipe—the sort of thing shepherds whittled while they watched their flocks—and began to play a simple melody. It sounded old. Flax hummed along as Rowan repeated the refrain.

"One of the oldest we have," Rowan said. "From before the land-taken. I'll teach you the new words, the translation, first, and then the old words, so you'll know what you're singing."

"Does Ash know many of the old songs?" Flax asked.

"Aye," Rowan said. "He knows them all, now."

They camped for the night in a tiny, tight space under two big willows—one for them and one for the animals. Once they were settled and he had groomed the horses, Flax crept out and foraged in a nearby field of oats for horse feed, trying to take a little from each row so that the farmer wouldn't raise the alarm in the morning. He had been brought up to buy, not steal, but that didn't worry him. We's owed a little fodder, he thought, after all that stravaging.

He came back with his arms full, and Mud and Cam nosed at him eagerly, so that he almost dropped it all. He carefully divided his booty into two equal piles, and then stood between them so that Mud, who ate faster than Cam, wouldn't steal her portion too.

"They need more than grass, if we're going to keep riding each day," he explained when Rowan asked. "These are just ripe—they're early, but it's protected down here in the valley and that far slope's a sun trap."

Rowan was a good campfire cook, even with the meagre rations they had left. After they'd eaten, he pulled a fishing line from his pack and baited the hook with the last bit of cheese, then edged out over the stream on a willow root and tied the line off.

"Never know your luck," he said.

The River might have been looking after them, because there was a nice sized pike on the hook the next morning, and pike weren't known for liking cheese.

Rowan built a small, almost smokeless fire and cooked it quickly, dousing the embers straight afterwards. It was delicious, even without salt, which they'd run out of the day before. Flax could have eaten two more.

The day that followed was one of constant tension and boredom. Keeping a lookout became Flax's obsession. Sweat trickled down his back, and he had to remember to relax his hands so that Cam wouldn't get nervous. The memory of that axe whistling through the air past their ears, the memory of the hate in the red-head's face came rushing back, over and over again, every time he heard a noise or saw a distant figure across the fields.

Nothing happened when he did. There was no shout of "Traveller!". At this distance, they looked respectable, as people did on horseback. Flax raised his hand genially as they passed, and no one even looked twice at them.

By the time Baluchston rose up across the water he was exhausted. He hoped that Rowan was right about the Lake protecting them, because he didn't think he could.

They caught the ferry across the narrow end of the Lake, and they were the only passengers. The ferry man looked sharply at them, but said nothing except to name the fare. Rowan handed over some coppers and they led the horses onto the flat-bottomed boat. There were ferries of many different sizes, depending on what had to be taken across; they had boarded the large one, which could take horses and wagons and dogs.

Flax expected Mud and Cam to be nervous, but although they snuffled at the side of the ferry, they stood calmly, as though they were used to boats. He wondered just where Bramble had been, and what she had done there.

There was a man waiting for the ferry on the other side; a man with a tight mouth, greying hair and a wonderfully decorated tan leather belt cinching in his spreading waist. Flax eyed it enviously.

Rowan noticed his glance, and smiled. "My friend likes your work, Reed. He's a singer, like Swallow," he said, looking over at Flax. "Reed's the leatherworker in these parts."

Flax blushed a little. He wasn't greedy, but the belt was truly beautiful, covered with intricate scrollwork, and it was nice to be distracted by something attractive after the last few days. He said so, a little defensively, and Reed laughed, the lines around his mouth loosening.

"My shop's in the main square," he said. "I'll give you a discount, same as I give Rowan, if you'll give me a song."

"One of Reed's belts'll last you a lifetime," the ferryman confirmed.

"I wish I could," Flax said honestly. The idea of doing something as simple as shopping appealed to him greatly.

As Reed climbed in the ferry they waved goodbye and walked towards the town square. Flax had been more reassured by the conversation than he would have believed.

Baluchston was a normal free town, it seemed. People in the streets, maybe more with dark hair than was usual, all of them busy about their daily tasks. A few glances came their way; each time, Flax tensed.

"Calm down, lad," Rowan said. "We're safe here."

Rowan led the way straight to a small cottage on the outskirts, near the road that wound south towards Sendat. It belonged to Swallow's cousin, the man Skink who had been with them in the Deep. Swallow always stayed there when Rowan was away.

And there was Swallow, laying clothes out to dry on the lavender bushes along one side of the cottage. Would she take him as a pupil?

80

He could feel his stomach trying to climb up his throat with nerves, and his mouth was dry. She looked him up and down, a question in her eyes, not moving to greet Rowan until the question had been answered.

"This is Flax, a singer for you to train," Rowan said, and he looked around as if to check whether anyone was listening.

She noticed, and then walked over to Rowan and kissed him. It were an act, put on for whoever were watching, Flax thought, and yet it weren't an act. She loved him. Had missed him. But she went through the motions of greeting her man with her eyes watchful and her mind alert.

As they passed through the door into the main room of the cottage—kitchen, eating and sitting room combined—Rowan whispered, "Ash sent him."

Swallow's steps halted for a moment, a tiny heartbeat while her hands tightened to white knuckles at her side, and then she loosened her fingers and kept going as if she hadn't heard.

"I'll take the horses round the back," he said, wanting to leave them to their hellos in private. "Best to get them out of sight."

"There's a shed," Swallow replied. Even in those few words, Flax could hear the flexibility and control of her voice. The muscles along her cheeks and jaw were strong, and she carried her shoulders well back, to keep her breath clear. She was aware of him assessing her and smiled, amused. "Get on with you," she said. "Do your tasks and come back here for food."

"Aye, my lady," he said, half mocking and half serious, and she took it as he intended, with a smile, so that he left the house with a jaunty step, feeling welcomed.

Over supper of cheese melted on toast with salted fish for flavour, Rowan told Swallow a carefully edited account of what had happened. It was hard to leave out the Deep and the River, but Flax realised that he—that all Traveller men—had lots of practice at it. Years. The story was disturbing enough, likewise that her son was about to raise the dead.

"Those songs are forbidden!" Swallow said, her voice sharp.

"For a reason," Rowan agreed mildly. "Time to set that reason aside when the need arises."

SAKER

SAKER RAN his hand through the stones in his pouch, feeling their familiar tingle and click.

He knew that casting the stones for himself was a fool's task, but he had nowhere else to turn for counsel. If only his father could talk! But although he could bring his father back, solid and real, he could not give him a voice.

Right now, he had several problems.

They knew what he looked like, and they would be searching for him.

His army needed weapons—and tools, particularly steel axes, to hack their way into the houses where the invaders cowered away from them.

The ghosts faded. That was his main problem.

He knew where to get the weapons he needed—Sendat, the warlord's fort. All reports said that Thegan had been stockpiling weapons and goods against a war with the Lake People. If the ghosts could take the fort, they would have all the weapons they needed.

But reports also said that Thegan had strengthened the town's defences. It might take longer than a day or a night to storm the fort to defeat him. And if the ghosts faded in the middle of that—the siege could stretch on for days, months even, with his army attacking by day and the fortifications being rebuilt at night. He would win, eventually, but...each night he would be left defenceless, in the middle of the warlord's territory.

This whole great enterprise rested on his shoulders, and he must *not* let himself be killed. He told himself he wasn't afraid.

His first task was to make the ghosts perpetual. He did not need to cast the stones after all. The decision made him more cheerful. This was a matter of skill.

He tucked his pouch into his belt and sat with his back against the mill loft wall. He was tired of this hiding place. Tired of hiding. If he could just craft a spell to give the ghosts continuance...

Somehow the ghosts were tied to the sun's rhythms, but how? The only thing they were tied to was his blood.

The blood dried out... The ghosts faded exactly at sunset or sunrise. But blood... Was *that* tied to the sun; or to time?

He couldn't work out how.

As the day waned, he set himself to remember everything his teacher, Freite, had said about blood spells. To remember every time she had used one.

The memories were unpleasant, and made him shake. But he forced himself on, remembering day by day, night by night, every time Freite had raised that black stone knife and used his blood, or a cat's blood, or someone else's... those were the worst memories. One made him stagger outside to puke. He had puked back then, too, when he'd seen what she was doing to an old man she'd bought from a Wind Cities trader, a slave who couldn't work any more. The man wasn't even drugged, as they usually were, so his eyes were wide open, pleading with Saker to intervene. To save him. She put those eyes out with her bare hands, and when he vomited, she laughed at him, said he was weak.

"We are power itself, boy," she hissed. "Blood is breath, pain is strength, death is the wind in our sails."

"Other people's death," he muttered.

"Well, ours wouldn't be much use, would it!" She cuffed him on the back of the head so that his ears rang. "You remember, boy. Death is the wind in our sails."

Then she brought the knife down across the old man's throat, and he felt the surge of power go through her.

Was that what his ghosts needed? Other people's blood?

Saker was filled with excitement. Was it, could it be, that simple? There was always blood on the battlefield. If that was all, it would have worked already. There must be another ingredient...

He washed his mouth out and sat back down to sift through his memories once again. This time, he would control his gorge. And he would find the missing piece.

LEOF

THEY STARTED in Sendat, and that was easy. Leof simply sent messengers to the town to announce that Lord Thegan wanted all Travellers to report to the fort. He knew that the Travellers would assume that the warlord was putting restrictions on their movements, as had often happened in the past, that they would be forbidden to enter towns, for example, or forced to pay extra taxes. They would grumble among themselves, but they would come, and Alston would put them in the barn when they did, to wait for Thegan. The masons and carpenters who were working on the fortifications would join them. Minus their tools.

He had the harder job of collecting people from the outlying villages.

"Don't you worry, sir, it'll be just like requisitioning horses," Hodge said comfortably, as their squad rode down the hill from the fort. The first Travellers were walking up the road, and stood aside to let them pass, bowing and bobbing their heads in respect. Leof nodded his thanks to them and raised a hand in greeting to a family with a small boy who stared openly at the horses. The father, who had been moving to cuff the boy for disrespect, stared at Leof instead, doubt and gratitude warring on his face. It was curiously disturbing. What had he expected? Reprisal against the boy for staring? What treatment did these people get from warlords' men usually?

"People aren't horses, sergeants."

Hodge looked sceptical. "Some may as well be, sir."

Leof let it pass. They were facing a huge job. "I want scouts on messenger horses sent to the outlying villages to find our people," he said. "Then small squads—four men should be plenty—to go out and bring them in. They should bring their goods, too, and any food they have. No sense us feeding them if they can feed themselves."

Hodge nodded. "What if they won't come?"

"My lord Thegan is sure they will," Leof said, but he had private doubts. "I'll ride out with the first squad. There are reports of Travellers in Pigeonvale. We'll start there."

Pigeonvale was half an hour's ride away. The weather was threatening rain, and Leof wondered if they'd be able to get the hay in safely this year. There was never a good time to go to battle, but the weeks between spring sowing and the hay harvest were best—the oath men could concentrate on their duties instead of worrying about their families being left hungry over winter.

A mile out of the village, Hodge, who was riding at point, put up a hand to signal a stop where the road widened into a camping place near a stream. There was a small tent there next to the ashes of last night's fire, and a handcart, the kind Travellers often used.

"Gather them in, sergeant," Leof said.

Hodge nodded to one of the oath men and he dismounted and went over to the tent. He was a young one, green as grass, and only in this detail because he was good with horses. Scarf, they called him, because he always wore a brown scarf around his neck. The men joked that his mother had knitted it for him to keep her darling safe from fever, but he said it was a gift from his sweetheart. Leof smiled, remembering the look on his face as he'd said it—a mixture of pride and embarrassment.

Scarf called out, "Ho, Travellers!" in a voice meant to sound full and stern, but which came out squeaky with nerves. He flushed and bent down to the tent opening, shouting, "Out here now!" to cover his discomfiture.

Then he went still and turned, retching into the stream, vomit and tears mingling on his face. Leof jumped down from Thistle and strode to the tent. He didn't want to know what was in there, but had to.

Two bodies, a man and a woman, in their mid-years by the beginnings of grey in their hair. Stabbed, throats cut. A terrible smell from where their bowels had loosened as they died. The flies were all over their staring eyes. But nothing had been taken—all their meagre belongings were around them, cooking pots, tinderbox, food...This was murder, not banditry.

He felt a cold anger take him over, and motioned Hodge to come and look.

Turning away from the tent, the sergeant's face was unreadable, but he went over to Scarf and patted him on the shoulders. The man had stopped vomiting and was washing his face in the stream.

"Come," Leof said. "Let us talk to the people of Pigeonvale."

"We can't just leave them there." Scarf said, pointing to the tent.

Hodge looked at him pityingly. "Lad, they're dead. No harm's going to come to them now. We'll get a burial detail out here from the village."

Scarf climbed back on his horse with unsteady legs. The other men clustered around him, keen to find out what had been in the tent and telling them gave him back a little of his dignity.

"Ride on," Leof said.

Pigeonvale was shuttered and barricaded. They rode into the market square—an open space more dirt than grass, which barely deserved the name of square—and immediately people came flooding out of their houses, clamouring for help. There were only twenty or so—it was a small, poor village.

"My lord, my lord, are they coming, the ghosts?" a man called.

"We got rid of the Travellers, lord. The ghosts are a plot of those dark-haired bastards," a woman yelled.

Leof held up a hand for silence. "You got rid of the Travellers?"

"Aye, my lord," the woman said proudly. "When we heard from Lord Thegan's man that the ghosts were sparing Travellers, we killed them!"

"Stuck 'em like pigs," another man said. "They didn't even fight."

Leof felt ice travel through his veins. Thegan had seeded this. Deliberately. Knowing that murders would result. Used the information to get the rumours started so that Travellers would be under threat and come to the fort willingly. To save himself time, and trouble. And it would, the cold trained officer's part of his mind confirmed. It would make things much easier.

"My lord Thegan's man told you that?" he asked.

"Aye, my lord, one of his own officers."

"My lord Wil, it was," an older man said. "Him what comes from over Bonhill way."

"You did wrong," Leof said. "My lord does not wish Travellers killed." He was amazed that he could keep his voice steady. "Lord Thegan wishes all Travellers to come to the fort at Sendat, where they will be safe."

The older man grinned. "Ah, that's right. My lord Thegan wants to do the job himself, eh? Well, there's a few left. Cherry and her boys have shut themselves in and we couldn't get to them, and there's a farmhand over at Esher's place with a head as dark as night on him, though he swears he's one of us."

"Aye, and that woman down near Barleydale," a young woman said eagerly. "She's a red-head, but she's got dark eyes, and you know there's always Traveller blood with dark eyes. She's got two girls, too."

"Take a list down, sergeant," Leof said, and he rode away, no longer able to listen. He had studied old battles, old campaigns. Humans would sacrifice anyone, especially strangers, to save their own. Nothing more ruthless existed than a man—or woman—with children to protect and someone weak to kill.

And he knew, too, the fury that rose against the victim precisely because he was weak. Leof had felt it himself, in battle, when an enemy couldn't protect himself. When fighting turned to slaughter anger filled you, made you implacable, as though the enemy's weakness was an insult. He had never understood that, but he had felt it, and now he recognised it in the eyes of these people. They hated the Travellers even more than they had yesterday, because they had been easy to kill.

"Cherry and her boys" turned out to be the local candlemaker, living in a respectable house on the outskirts of the village. The house, like all the others, was shuttered and barred.

Hodge banged on the door and shouted, "Warlord's men, mistress! Here to take you and your boys to safety at the warlord's fort."

There was a scuffling behind the door and then a woman's voice: "Why would the warlord protect *us*?"

A good question, Leof thought bleakly.

"You pay your taxes, don't you?" Hodge asked. "Warlords don't like people who pay taxes being killed off."

Leof frowned at that, but the cynicism of the answer was reassuring to the woman, and she opened the door slowly, her three boys craning to see from behind her.

"Gather up whatever food you've got, and some blankets and clothes, too," Hodge said. "We won't wait long."

His impatience also reassured her. She nodded and vanished into the house, calling out instructions to the boys, and reappeared a few minutes later with bundles and bags, while the eldest boy, about twelve years, trundled a handcart around from the back yard where the candles were made. The handcart had a couple of dozen candles in the bottom, and the woman looked shyly up at Leof.

"It may be the lady would like some extra candles?" she asked.

He smiled warmly at her. "I'm sure she would, with so many people coming to the fort. That was well thought of."

Cherry bobbed her head and dumped the food and blankets on top of the candles, more cheerful now she felt that she wasn't going empty-handed. That she could prove her respectability.

Leof suspected that the respectable and the not-so-respectable would be lumped together in Thegan's mind. "Let's go, sergeant," he said, and they rode off to "near Barleyvale" where the red-headed woman lived with her family.

It went on like that all day.

They came across the remnants of other massacres: a family of four cut down on the road and left on the verge for the crows; an old man garotted in a parody of a warlord's execution, and hung up from a tree as the warlord hung criminals in the gibbet; a house that had been fired and still stank of burnt meat. Scarf puked each time, and Leof found himself feeling grateful to the boy for expressing simple human revulsion, as he could not, being the officer.

He had to remain in control of himself, although his anger rose higher as the day went on and they heard more reports about "my lord's officer" spreading the news about the ghosts sparing Traveller lives.

His own messengers did their job thoroughly. By the end of the day as soon as they rode into a town the inhabitants were ready, either with a group of stony-faced Travellers surrounded by guards with pitchforks and scythes, or with directions to where the "black-haired bastards" had barricaded themselves in. At least the messengers had stopped the slaughter. But across the Domain, Leof estimated, hundreds would have been killed.

They turned for home at noon with a band of about sixty Travellers, a mixture of small families and singles, most with handcarts or backpacks full of food and clothing.

"To Sendat, sergeant," Leof ordered, and he rode at the back of the group so the dust from Thistle's hooves wouldn't get in their eyes. It was a long boring ride, and it gave him far too much time to think about Thegan, and Wil, and what was going to happen to the Travellers when they reached the fort.

But what could he do? There was nowhere else to take them, and they were definitely not safe where they were. At least in the fort they had a chance. He lashed himself with blame. He should have killed the enchanter when he had the chance, before Thegan's troops arrived in Bonhill, when it was just him and the enchanter up on the hill. If he had borrowed a bow from the town, he could have shot him without even the wind wraiths being alerted. If he had been quicker in the farmyard he could have slit his throat before the wraiths rescued him.

Unbidden, the image of Sorn's face rose in his mind, smiling at him, and he felt comforted. She would not blame him, and she would tell him not to blame himself. But although he kept his face calm, as befitted an officer, he felt that he wanted to ride home crying like a baby.

They arrived back at Sendat late, in the dark, long after the evening meal. Leof left the settling of the Travellers in the barn to Alston and Hodge, and went straight to Thegan's workroom.

"Leof," Thegan greeted him. "Good. How many did you bring in?"

"Sixty-two," Leof said, walking into the warlord's workroom. He stood looking straight at Thegan, unsure what to say. "There were massacres," he managed finally. "Murders. All over the Domain."

Thegan nodded. "Yes."

That was all. But it wasn't enough.

"Wil spread the news about the ghosts protecting Travellers."

Thegan was looking at him strangely, a small smile curling the corners of his mouth. "On my orders," he confirmed, and he sat back in his chair, waiting for Leof's response.

"Why, my lord?"

"Difficult times call for difficult measures," he said. "Of course it would be better if we didn't have to take this action. On the other hand, the Travellers have always been a weakness in the Domain's defence. And in the future, they would have been a weakness in the defence of Actonsland."

Actonsland. The united country Thegan was trying to create. With him as its overlord. He was still planning for the long term—and wasn't that what you wanted in a warlord? Someone who thought ahead, who took pains to ensure the future of his people?

"You think they would join the enchanter?" Leof asked, feeling deflated. Thegan was as logical as always.

"Of course they will, as soon as they understand what he's trying to do. The young men, at the very least. The hot heads. The kind who end up in the gibbet."

He smiled, not the miraculous smile, nor the one that invited you to join his select group of friends, but a kind smile, the sort of smile Leof might have given Scarf.

Leof was so tired that he couldn't think properly.

"You did your duty," Thegan said, absently, as he looked back at the map spread out on his table. "Now go and eat, and rest. There will be more to do tomorrow."

Leof was almost persuaded that Thegan had done what he had to do—the right thing, the reasonable thing—and then he walked back into the hall, looking for food, as he had been ordered, and saw Sorn.

She was standing at the door to the kitchen, her little dog Fortune hiding in her skirts as he always did. She was discussing something with the cook. She looked up and he was shocked by how drawn her face looked, how pale. Her eyes were desperate.

He went towards her without thinking, but halfway across the room he realised how fast he was walking, and slowed so that the men and serving girls gathered around the tables wouldn't notice. He had been ordered to get food. He was following orders, he told himself. But his heart was beating uncomfortably fast and he was angry at whatever, whoever, had put that fear into her eyes.

"My lady," he said, and bowed, as etiquette demanded.

She bowed back, eyes down. "My lord Leof." She looked up to the cook. "My lord is hungry. Get him food."

"Yes, my lady," the man said, and he raced back to the kitchen, leaving them, for the moment, in a pocket of silence.

"Are you all right?" he asked. It was breaking their rule of never saying anything personal in public, but he had to know what had brought that look of grief, of anger, he wasn't sure what it was.

"Is it true?" she asked in a low voice. "Is it true that my lord sent Wil out to spread a rumour that the ghosts protect Travellers?"

"Not a rumour. The truth."

She looked up sharply and met his eyes. "And that makes it all right? To connive at the murder of innocents?"

It was as though she had turned a picture the right side up, so that he could see it all clearly, recognise his lord's scheme for what it was. "No," he replied. "That does not make it all right. But for now, the Travellers are safer here."

"We must make sure they stay safe," she said, low and insistent.

He nodded.

They stood, quietly, until the cook returned with a tray of food, pretending to the world, even to each other, that they had not just committed themselves to treachery—he against his sworn lord, she against her husband.

BRAMBLE

WHEN THEY woke, the world had changed around them. Instead of a small cave in a long passage, they were in one of the huge caverns, water dripping from the walls, pillars of rock forming on roof and floor, the friendly little lozenge of light nowhere to be seen. Next to them, a dark river flowed silently, its quiet ripples threatening in the flickering candlelight. It disappeared between a high, thin crack in the wall.

On the river's banks were strange shapes in rock: a huge bird, wings outspread, a winter tree, perfect but only as high as Bramble's chest, an old woman hunched over a fire. Others looked more monstrous, like water sprites or wild boars, tusks shining. The sound of water trickling, slapping gently at its banks, echoed constantly.

"The Weeping Caverns," Medric said, glancing from one rock form to the next with a hint of panic in his voice. "They never let you out."

"Fear weakens you, lad," Acton said. "Breathe deep."

Medric didn't understand the words, but the smile that went with them heartened him and he put his shoulders back and nodded. Acton nodded approval at him, and he swelled with pride.

Men! Bramble thought. They just lined up to worship him. "This isn't the one we were in before," she said firmly. "We haven't been brought back to where we were."

"How can you know?" Baluch asked, curiously. "We could be in a different part of the same cavern."

Bramble shook her head stubbornly. "No. That cavern ran north and south. This one runs east and west." She repeated it in the old language, for Acton.

Medric didn't believe her, but the others did.

"Can you tell where we are?" Ash asked.

"South of where we were, I think." She concentrated. "The mine entrance is far behind us. The White River may be close. It comes out of these caves." She paused. "I am getting tired of being thrown around in time and space at the whim of the gods." She turned in to the cavern, her hand on one of the cold, slippery rock pillars, and shouted, "Tell us what you want!" Acton came to stand beside her. Even as a ghost, he was a reassuring presence.

Just as when she had asked for help from the Lake, something came.

Along the river bank, shapes stirred. Not every one—not the water sprite, but the boar, not the tree, but the woman. They moved, but they moved silently. The figures straightened and turned towards them in unison, blind rock eyes seeming to focus.

Bramble stood still, but Medric and Ash and Baluch all moved towards her until they were standing in a tight group. Acton walked forward to meet the shapes. The old woman, the boar, a weasel, sinuous even in rock, a fox, brush held high, an ox.

The boar stopped in front of Acton, but the others moved around him with the same unstoppable force as delvers had. The woman stood a little way from Bramble, mouth in a smirk. The weasel faced Ash, the fox, Baluch, the ox lumbered around to the back of the group to confront Medric.

Bramble moved forward a little, until she was face to face with the figure of the old woman. She held up her candle so that she could see the woman's face. It was no one she had ever seen, in her life or in Acton's. The kind of face a doll maker would carve for an evil-old-woman puppet—nothing but wrinkles and spite lines.

Acton's head flicked around, and he grinned at her, and then at Baluch. She smiled back, feeling the familiar rush of pleasure and excitement that danger brought.

The old woman raised a finger, as if reproving her. Her face writhed, and Bramble couldn't tell if the stone really shifted and warped, or whether it was simply the flicker from the candle.

Behind her, Ash cleared his throat, the first sound any of them had made since the shapes moved.

"Wild!" the old woman hissed immediately. "Ungrateful, undutiful, unwomanly! Not fit for anyone. The unloved daughter. The unwanted one."

Bramble flinched. Her voice was like the voice of the dead, rock grating on rock, but lighter, with changing tones like water falling. Behind her, she could hear the other figures speaking, and in front, the boar was roaring at Acton in his own language: "Murderer! Despoiler!"

The ox lowed accusations at Medric: "Coward, unwanted son! Sold for garbage. Unmanly, weak!"

She was glad that the weasel spoke quietly, and she couldn't hear what Ash was hearing. But her anger was building, because she knew that Medric, in particular, would be vulnerable to this kind of attack.

"Be quiet!" Ash's voice cut through with the resonance of power, and they were silent immediately.

"Oh, let them speak!" Acton said. "Words can't hurt us."

The others stared at him. Bramble saw that Medric had tears on his cheeks and Ash and Baluch both looked shaken. Acton had his solemn face on, the one that so often preceded some explosive physical action. Like smashing the rocks to splinters.

Then the old woman put out a hand and placed it heavily on Bramble's shoulder. She tried to move away, but her feet were stuck. She looked down: the bottoms of her boots were encased in rock, and the rock was spreading. She glanced at the others. The figures in front were touching each of them now, and the stone was slowly growing up their legs. They were being trapped.

The boar put a foot on Acton's, who promptly kicked it hard, unbalancing it and sending it crashing onto its side.

Acton came to Bramble's side, but waited to see what she would do. She glared at the woman. "What do you want?" she asked.

"Speak," Ash said reluctantly.

"These are the Weeping Caverns. None but the worthy leave here. And you, girl, are empty inside," the woman said. "You are the less loved, less wanted, carrying death with her like a plague! You betray the ones who trust you. You allow your loved ones to die like beasts!"

Bramble's earlier exhilaration drained away, but she was not the young girl who had left her family knowing she would not be missed. She thought of the hunter, and of Acton, and of Maryrose, who was waiting for her on the other side of death. And of the roan, dead because she had been afraid, just once, and let fear rule her. She wasn't going to do that again. Acton was right. These were just words.

"Yes," she said. "That's right. That's me."

Shocked, the woman moved back. As soon as she lifted her hand away from Bramble's shoulder, she froze back into rock. The stone around Bramble's boots melted into a watery slurry. She kicked it off and turned to face the others. "It's all true," she said. "Everything they say to us is true. You might as well accept it."

Baluch immediately spoke to the fox, which held his tunic in its jaws. "True," he said. "All true." The fox moved away and froze in position, its paw raised, its brush low.

Medric's shoulders were hunched and he was swaying his head from side to side, like a horse with the weaves. She went to him, ignoring the ox, whose heavy hoof was pinning Medric's foot down. Acton followed her and shoved the ox aside, despite its great weight. But the stone continued growing over Medric's feet.

"The worst of us is not the best of us," she said gently. "You can be everything they say, and still be worthy, because of what else you are." He stared at the ox as if he hadn't heard her. "Would Fursey have loved you if you weren't worthy?" she asked. "Would I have trusted you? Would you have bothered to help me? So your father didn't want you! What does that matter now?"

The ox spoke at the same time, "Coward! Weak! Always fearful!"

She stared at Medric, rubbing his shoulder, urging him to understand. Acton smiled at him and Medric blinked, turning his head to stare at Bramble for the first time.

He seemed to take something from her—not strength, something more like love.

Slowly, he turned towards the ox. "Yes," he said heavily. "I am."

The ox fell silent.

Ash understood, but Bramble could see that he found it hard to say the words. He managed, eventually, to concede whatever the weasel had said to him, but the weasel snapped, "Liar!" back at him and he flinched.

"Remember," Acton said to him, "we are all guilty of something." Ash stared at them.

Bramble felt her store of compassion, usually reserved for poddy calves and sick rabbits, rise like yeast. She smiled at him, like the big sister she felt she was to him. "I've been many people now, Ash, and I can tell you—we all fear the same things."

He stared at her, uncomprehending. The weasel was whispering, too quiet for her to hear, but Ash bit his lip.

"All of us," she said. "We fear being unwanted, alone, unloved. We fear the death of those we love. We fear that no one will miss us when we're gone."

She thought of all the eyes she had looked through: Ragni, old and facing her own death stoically, but distraught at the death of Asa; Piper of Turvite, fearing for her children, mourning Salmon; Baluch, hating himself for killing children but following Acton anywhere; Wili, letting Edwa kill herself because she understood the fear of being discovered as they were, used and degraded, worthless...Warmth overtook her and she hugged Ash, ignoring the weasel as though it were not there. "Come on, Ash. We need you."

"Worthless..." the weasel hissed.

The word was the same in both languages, as words sometimes were, so Acton understood. "This one? Worthless? Hah!" he said, evading the boar again as he spoke.

Ash blinked and turned to Baluch. "I can't hear her," he said.

"No," Baluch said, smiling with reassurance. "She lets you fight your own battles." He clapped Ash on the shoulder and perhaps that was what he needed, a physical shock, or perhaps it was the right reassurance.

Ash stared at the weasel. "I have been unloved," he said. "I have been useless. But not now."

"Truth at last," the weasel sneered, but it moved away and stiffened into rock.

The boar was shouting at Acton and trying to catch his tunic with a tusk.

"Oh, just talk to it!" Bramble said. "Or we'll never get out of here."

He gave her the sideways smile, but he obediently spoke to the boar: "Yes, yes, I am a killer, I am an invader. Those aren't secrets."

The boar stopped and froze in place. Bramble wished she felt better about it—Acton's tone had been so off-hand, so casual, as though the accusations hadn't bothered him at all.

But something else was disturbing her. All these things...had been alive once. She faced the old woman. "You're dead. Why haven't you gone on to rebirth?"

"Speak," Ash said. His voice was stronger, as if he were regaining confidence. The blind rock face stirred but only the mouth moved. "None are reborn from the Weeping Caverns," she said, and the eyes came alive, too, to stare despairingly at her. "None."

"I don't believe that," Bramble said. "It can't be true. The gods wouldn't allow it."

"The gods are young and this is not their realm, girl." She took a step towards Bramble. "Stone is ruler here."

"Not just stone," Baluch said from behind her. "Water, too."

"We can't leave them here," Bramble said.

"We'd never get them out," Baluch replied, assessing the size and weight of the rocks.

"None shall leave," the old woman said.

"The turns are turned!" the fox echoed.

"There is no way." The weasel rose up on his hind legs and giggled. Ash reached out and pushed it off balance so that it fell with a crash to the floor and lay there, panting and glaring.

"Then we will make a way," Acton said.

"Acton," Baluch said, "what are you thinking?"

"I am thinking stone can be broken." He came to Bramble. "How close are we to the surface?"

She extended that part of her mind that told her where she was, and figured it.

"Not far, I think." She pointed east. "That's the way we were going before the cave changed around us."

"If we can find a way out, perhaps our miner here can show us how to widen it enough to let these poor creatures out."

"That might work," Bramble said, "but not if the spell that holds them won't let them walk. They're too heavy to carry."

"But we have an enchanter," Acton said, looking at Ash. "Can you not find a way to bring them to the light?"

Ash looked at the old woman, his face full of pity. "Stone is no match for water."

He looked up. "Let them go, and the Caverns will be safe." His voice echoed in the dark around them, full of warning.

"Wait," said Acton, and he turned to the woman. "Who tasked you?"

"Dotta, daughter of fire," she said in his own language. "None shall leave but the worthy."

"Dotta," he repeated, the grating voice slow and considering.

"She was protecting you, Acton," Bramble said. "She knew I'd come back for your bones, and I think she was making sure no one too arrogant to accept their shortcomings would steal them first. But Dotta wouldn't have stopped spirits going on to rebirth."

The old woman spread her hands and shrugged with one shoulder, like a fishwife bargaining in the marketplace. "That is the Caverns. It has always been so. We have no power over it."

"Then it is time to end the Caverns," Ash said. Baluch came to stand beside him, to link arms. Acton watched him go with a curious look on his face, as though realising for the first time that Baluch had had a life — a long life — which had changed him in ways Acton didn't understand.

The old woman stared at Ash as though not understanding, and slowly the other figures stirred into life and ranked themselves behind her — not just the animals, but all the other figures, human and otherwise, which had lined the bank of the river.

They did not threaten. They did not speak. But Bramble saw a kind of hope in their blank eyes and slack muscles, as though they had been tasked for too long. Then Ash looked at Baluch and together they closed their eyes and sounded a single low note, their voices matching like one voice.

Bramble had no idea what was happening, but "water," Ash had said, so she moved away from the river, up to a promontory of rock that stood high. Medric and Acton followed her, but Ash and Baluch stayed still, standing in front of the stone figures, hands splayed, eyes closed, humming and singing without words.

The river began to sing in tune with them.

FLAX

THE WARLORD'S men came beating a gong that set every horse in Baluchston whinnying.

Flax ran out to calm the horses and went to the gate instead, to watch them going by on the main road—a party of messengers, just three of them.

Rowan and Swallow appeared at his shoulder.

"I'll start packing," Swallow said.

Rowan nodded. "Saddle up, boy," he said. A few moments was all it took and then they were ready, leaving the cottage tidy.

"When will my cousin be back?" Swallow asked.

"He was on foot," Rowan answered absently, head cocked, still listening to the now distant gong. "It will take him a few more days."

"Then we'll take all the bread," she said, darting back to collect it and stow it in her pack.

They led the horses by back paths, paths that Rowan knew well, it seemed; and they paused in a coppice of beech trees just outside town. There was no need to discuss why they were running. When warlords' men came beating gongs, Travellers made themselves scarce.

"Those were Thegan's men," Rowan said. "We should avoid Sendat."

Swallow nodded. "We could cut across the plains. It's a long way on foot..."

"Down river to Carlion and then to Turvite by boat?" Rowan mused.

In the end, they decided to cut across the Domain, avoiding towns, until they reached South Domain.

Swallow wasn't a rider and didn't intend to become one, so Flax tied their packs onto Mud and they all walked.

"It's a change, not carrying anything," Swallow said. "It makes me feel light. Now, Flax, tell me what you know about melody."

It was an inquisition. Swallow questioned him about every aspect of music, made him demonstrate breathing, projection, scales...He was woefully ignorant of the theory, but he could see that she liked his actual singing.

"Your breathing is shoddy," she said. "You could get much more power with proper control."

She waited to see his response, but he knew that look; his mam had used it on him often enough. He knew how to be humble when it counted.

"Will you teach me?" he asked, which was, after all, all he wanted to know.

She sniffed a little and settled back into walking. "We'll see," she said. But the look she exchanged with Rowan was amused and pleased, and he knew the answer was "yes."

This was plains country, a mixture of pasture and cropping, wheat, sheep and goats, some orchards. The dairies which leant against every barn were for ewes and nannies; cheesemaking was a major occupation. In this kind of country Travellers were regarded with great suspicion, and there were few officers' manors where musicians could find work.

"I've got silver," Swallow said. "We can buy what we need, if they'll sell it to us." They had stopped outside a small town to discuss food.

"Lucky at dice again?" Rowan said quizzically, and Swallow blushed a little.

"Aren't I always?"

"Better if I buy," Flax said. He got out a comb and slicked his hair back into a small ponytail. It was just long enough—Zel would have been at him this last week to get it cut, he thought. He groomed Cam until she shone and her tail was free of burrs and straw, then pulled out his good blue jacket and buffed his boots to a shine.

"That'll have to do," he said. "Do I look the part?"

He mounted and put on a haughty air, as an officer's son might, or the child of a wealthy merchant.

Swallow looked amused, but disapproving. "You could mimic an ape from the Wind Cities, I'm thinking," she said. He grinned and made ape noises at her, and she flapped her hands at him, then tossed him a purse. "Travelling food," she said. "But don't make it too obvious."

"I'll meet you on the other side of the village," he said.

The township was larger than a village. It had three shops: one for chandlery and farm goods, a butcher's and a store that sold everything else.

He tossed Cam's reins to a boy along with a copper. "Give her some water," he ordered, then walked in without looking to see if he'd been obeyed. Assume they'll obey and they will, he told himself, his heart thumping irregularly and his palms wet.

The shopkeeper hastened to serve him, and he bought all they needed without trouble. He even made a joke about young men with big appetites, and winked at the man's daughter, although she was squint-eyed and on the wrong side of thirty.

Cam was waiting at the horse trough, well-watered, and he tossed the boy another copper as he mounted and rode off south, feeling as though an arrow would hit him in the small of the back at any moment, or another axe would come singing out of thin air to take him down. But he made it away without incident and he went on down the hedge-lined track feeling very pleased with himself.

A half-mile went past before he began to get worried. There was no sign of Swallow or Rowan. There were hoof prints, and he recognised the worn shoe on Mud's off fore, where he pecked at the ground when he got bored; so they had come this way. But then he came to a widening of the road, a place where Mud's prints were scuffed over by other horses', several of them, it looked like, and riding horses, not the big half-moons that would have meant draught animals. There were droppings to the side as though the other horses had waited there for a while. But Cam wasn't reacting, which meant they were gone now, not hiding in the bushes and lying in wait, as his imagination feared.

Horses probably meant warlord's men.

Run, came Zel's voice in his head, but he couldn't do that. Ash wouldn't do that.

He sat down in the saddle carefully so that Cam stepped out gently, slowly, at a pace where Flax could listen for other horses up ahead. Then he thought that Cam would hear them long before he would, so he quickened her a little and watched her ears, ready for when they pricked forward, hoping he could stop her whinnying a greeting in the moment afterwards.

He puzzled out the tracks as he went. There were four horses, he thought, and perhaps a dozen people on foot. Some of the footprints looked like children's. They wouldn't be moving very fast, so he slowed down, then dismounted. They couldn't possibly be far ahead of him, not on foot. He hadn't been that long in the village.

As he neared a bend in the track, at a place where the road dipped into a hollow, he saw Cam's ears prick and her nostrils flare as she took in air to neigh. He lunged forward and pinched her nostrils closed, almost falling over her hooves.

"Shh, shh, sweetheart," he said, and although she rolled her eyes at him as though he'd gone mad, she snuffled out the air she'd taken in and let him lead her back the track a ways, until he could tether her between a hedge bright with unripe blackberries and a hayrick. She pulled content-edly at the loose strands of hay sticking out of the rick, as Flax ran back along the grass by the track, trying to be as silent as possible. He crept up to the bend and peered around, keeping low to the ground.

Warlord's men. Four, on horseback. Thegan's, again, like the ones in Baluchston. This was still Central Domain, and they held sway here. And with them—a group of Travellers, he thought, although one family had red-haired children and looked too prosperous, too fat, to be on the Road. They had stopped and were drinking from the stream which crossed the path in this hollow. He spotted Swallow and Rowan, who was still leading Mud. The warlord's men were lounging around, trading jokes with each other, and weren't threatening anyone. The sergeant was a big hairy man with red-gold stubble beginning to show on his face—the kind of man who had to shave twice a day to look smart. He was the only one who bothered to watch the Travellers, and even he did it lazily, as though he were sure they wouldn't run off.

Flax had no idea what was going on. He wished Zel were here—the burden of making decisions was heavier than he'd expected.

Rowan looked around at intervals, seeming casual, but Flax realised he was looking for him. He didn't want to make any movement so he stared directly at Rowan, concentrating on him. If you looked long enough, somehow people sensed you. Sure enough, after a moment Rowan looked in his direction, rubbing the back of his neck as though it prickled.

His gaze met Flax's and immediately he flicked a quick glance at the warlord's men. That told Flax what he wanted to know—this was not some nice picnic by the stream. They were prisoners, no matter what it looked like. Rowan tilted his head fractionally to signal, "Get away." Flax nodded, and wriggled backwards from his vantage point until he could stand up and run back to Cam.

Not that he was running away. His blood fizzed with excitement. Those warlord's men were sloppy, not expecting any trouble from mere Travellers. It wouldn't be hard to spirit Rowan and Swallow away from them. Mud would be harder. He considered that. He wondered how many of Thegan's horses his father had trained, and grinned. It only needed a few. Horses were herd animals. Where some of the herd went, the others would follow.

But he would have to wait until dark.

As the afternoon drew on, Flax became certain the warlord's men were taking Rowan and Swallow and the other Travellers to Sendat.

Why were they going with the warlord's men so willingly? Flax had grown up on stories of Travellers escaping from persecution by the skin of their teeth and their willingness to do anything to save their children: hide in cesspits, share caves with sleeping bears, even crouch in streams despite fear of water wraiths. But these people were just following along.

He had no idea why, and it disturbed him.

He trailed behind them just far enough so that Cam wouldn't try to join the other horses. He could follow their tracks, and when he came to a fork in the road it was easy to see which way they had gone. After that he relaxed a little.

By evening, they had turned on to the main road from Baluchston to Sendat. Flax blessed the lengthening shadows, and the fact that fear of the ghosts was keeping everyone close to home. There was no other traffic, which meant he was safe, as long as he kept well back from the warlord's party.

The sergeant called a halt at a broad meadow leading down to a small spring-fed mere. Flax tied Cam up on the other side of the coppice that edged the camp site, and made his way silently through the trees to spy. He watched the warlord's men organise the camp, giving a couple of the men shovels to dig privies in the coppice, getting the children to gather kindling for the fire, telling the women to get on with the shared task of cooking.

It was better not to make contact with anyone but Rowan or Swallow. That was his mother in him, he thought; she had never trusted anyone, and it had annoyed him. But this was the time for mistrust, and secrecy, and pretence, and all those other things she had practised in order to be accepted in Pless. Shame she never lived to see his father a town councillor. She'd wanted it so badly. Part of him knew it was that desire which had pushed her to attack him, but the thing was, he didn't remember it. She had drugged his cha, Zel said, and tried to smother him, but he was asleep and so it all seemed more like a story than reality. He believed Zel — believed she had no choice, or thought she had none. But he couldn't really imagine his mother killing him, and so he struggled to think of her with any anger or resentment. He wondered if that made him weak. What would Ash think?

The image of Ash in his mind smiled at him, and he was reassured. Aye, Ash'd choose pity over anger any day, he reckoned. So. It may be that Ash wouldn't choose to kill the warlord's men, either. He wished Ash were here.

When it was full dark, he pissed against a tree to make sure he wouldn't need to go later, then slowly made his way towards the camp. One of the guards was on watch, of course, but he was lying back, looking at the stars instead of the road. With any luck he was actually asleep. Then Flax realised that the man was lying on his front, not his back, and he was crying, trying to keep quiet by muffling the sobs in his sleeve. Flax's heart contracted. It was the young one, the one with the brown scarf at his throat. He wondered what a soldier had to cry about.

He knew where Rowan and Swallow were sleeping — near the edge of the trees, well-positioned for slipping away. No fools, them. But the horses were on the other side of the camp, the Sendat side. Was it better to go quietly off on foot, and lose Mud? Again he was racked with indecision. If they were on foot, the warlord's men would hunt them down easily. It was the memory of dogs baying on his trail, back in Golden Valley, that decided him. He never wanted to hear that sound again.

So instead of waking Rowan, he slipped across the road and made his way behind the bordering hedge to where the horses were tethered, then crossed back over and slid silently among them. His heart pounded the whole way and he was sweating. The horses didn't mind. They whuffled and sniffed at him. He was counting on the warlord's horses being accustomed to having many different people look after them, and he was right. They didn't treat him as a stranger. Mud shouldered others out of the way to get to him, nickering gently.

Flax froze, but there was no sound from the soldiers. Horses do make noises at night. 'Course they do.

"Shh, shh, there," he murmured, patting Mud on his side and gathering all the leading reins up, pulling the tethers off their pegs until he had all five animals on a rein. He collected a couple of saddles and slid them onto Mud's back, looping up the girths so they didn't trail. Mud shook his head but didn't try to dislodge them. They were the small, flat saddles the good riders used, so they weren't a burden to him.

Gently, quietly, he whistled the "follow me" signal his father had taught all his animals. Mud and two others pricked up their ears at the sound, and gladly fell in behind him. The others came along, as he had thought they would.

He led them further down the track and tied them to a gatepost. The "wait" whistle was long and soothing, and even the two horses who didn't know it seemed to settle when he tried it on them. Then, trying to move like Ash did in the dark, like a shadow himself, he crept back to where he had tethered Cam.

This was the big problem.

He could move silently, but Cam was much too big and heavy footed to pass the camp in silence.

He saddled her up and took her in a wide circle, thankful for the crescent moon as it showed itself above the hills as he threaded his way through the first field, trying not to damage too much—or leave a trail that could be easily followed.

Cam seemed to enjoy the ramble, walking quite confidently across the shadowy fields. He brought her back to the road well down from the other horses, then tethered her and began to run back the way he had come. Time was passing too fast. The moon had climbed from the horizon already, seeming to shrink as she swam higher, becoming colder and less welcome.

Flax threaded through the trees again as quietly as he could, to where Rowan and Swallow were lying.

He reached out and touched Rowan's shoulder. Immediately, they got up, slid their packs on and followed him behind the hedge and down the road to the horses; only then did they make a noise.

Rowan gasped as the big shapes loomed up in the darkness, but Swallow hissed. "Are you mad?" she demanded. "Horse stealing's a killing offence!"

"We're not stealing theirs!" Flax said, shocked. "I'm not stupid. We're just leaving them here so they can't come after us easily. Although, if we took just one, we'd each have a mount…"

Swallow considered it. "They're telling us they're here to protect us from massacres but it doesn't mean they won't stage one of their own when it suits them. No warlord ever cared about Travellers and none ever will." Her voice was bitter.

Rowan touched her arm. "Come, we must go."

Fumbling in the dark, Flax saddled Mud and a steady black cob he'd marked out during the day as the most sensible of the others. Then he helped Swallow and Rowan to mount, and they headed off towards Sendat.

"The one way they won't expect us to go," Rowan said. "We can turn off to the right before Garvay, I'm pretty sure."

"It's a long time since we walked those roads," Swallow said, and Flax couldn't tell if she were doubtful or nostalgic.

Rowan smiled at his wife reassuringly, "The road is long…"

Flax clicked his tongue to Mud and they moved off, the other horses trying to come with them at first and them settling, complaining, when their tethers held.

Under the cold moon, the Road looked very long.

"If we're lucky," Flax said to himself.

LEOF

THE SQUADS went out the next day, but Thegan kept Leof back at the fort, organising the Travellers into work groups.

"We might as well get some use out of them," he said over breakfast. "They'll be working for their own defence, after all."

When Leof went out to the big barn he was surprised at how much at home their guests had made themselves: cooking fires in a row outside, privies off behind the barn, each family's area marked off with rope. Alston had been very busy, it was clear.

The Travellers crowded towards Leof, and Alston motioned them back to give him room to speak. "As you know," he began, "we are fortifying against the enchanter's ghosts. You will be staying here until the menace is gone and there is no more reason for you to be afraid. That means that the fort's defences are your defences, and we would like your help in the work."

Some nodded, some looked sceptical; they probably thought Thegan had organised this to save himself the cost of a workforce. Well, let them. It would stop them from thinking darker thoughts.

Each of the masons and carpenters was assigned helpers from the mob in the barn.

"Keep them together with their own people, if you can," Leof told Alston. "The dry-stone waller, that big man from up north who is working on the rampart—give him a group of ten or so. Most of his time is being spent carrying the stones."

Alston nodded, but hesitated before he moved away. "My lord…I wanted to thank you. Faina and I, we wanted to thank you."

"For what?"

"The house…"

He had no idea what the man was talking about, and he didn't have time to find out now. A house in the town, married quarters? Probably something Sorn had organised. "I don't know anything about a house," he said. "Get to work."

As though the words had been a secret message, Alston grinned. "Of course, my lord. Of course!"

With an extra sixty people, the fort reminded Leof of home during a campaign against the Ice King's people. Cliffhold had been like this: always ringing with hammer blows from the smithy, horses whinnying to each other in the muster yards, the oath men drilling to their sergeants' shouts, children running, screaming, laughing. As he approached to inspect the fortification, he noticed there were lots of children today, most of them dark-haired, which was curiously disconcerting.

The waller—what was his name…? Oak, that was it—didn't look pleased when Alston spoke to him, but then he hadn't looked pleased for weeks. He looked exhausted, in fact. The work near the gate was almost finished but Leof felt he had been remiss in not giving the man help earlier.

On his way back he saw Sorn and her maid Faina gathering the children into the barn. Probably lesson time, he thought, and wondered how many of these children had any schooling. Well, he knew Sorn would sort it out. Some of these Travellers were perhaps even better off for staying at the fort for a time. Maybe.

It was a curious pleasure to watch her while she was unaware of him. She would be a lovely mother, he thought, seeing her cradle a toddler in her arms, smiling at him and tickling him under his arm. *If Thegan can't sire children, she'll never be a mother.* The thought slid treacherously under his guard, and he turned abruptly and headed for the smiths. They needed boar spears. Lots of them. Pin the bastard ghosts to the ground and see them fight then!

That evening Thegan and Leof spent an hour working out the details for the fortifications, provisioning, guard duties, night soil collection and the common meals. Sorn joined them for that part of the planning, and Leof marvelled again at her quiet competence. She seemed to have anticipated all of Thegan's questions, and found solutions to problems they had not imagined, like how to wash the babies' loincloths. She smiled a little at their blank faces.

"We're not accustomed to worrying about children on a battlefield," Leof said.

"Let us pray we never have to," Sorn replied, and it was a true prayer; he could hear it in her voice.

Thegan was oblivious to it, simply pleased with their combined efficiency. "Good. Good. Put all this in action."

A messenger knocked at the door and Thegan called him inside.

"Baluchston is refusing to give up its Travellers," he said. "Tomorrow go and get them. I've sent messengers warning them of your coming. If they will not surrender them, you will bring the town council back here to me."

That was all. Thegan turned immediately to Gard, who was waiting with a list of supplies commandeered from the various towns where they had collected Travellers. Thegan nodded dismissal to them both, and they rose together and walked back into the hall, which was silent and empty now that the meal was over and the cleaning done.

Leof could think of nothing to say that would be safe, so he bowed and left her without a word, casting a quick glance at her face. But he could read nothing there except her normal serenity, which he knew now was a sham. She was so beautiful.

That beauty tightened his chest into an insistent pain, so that he had to stop outside the hall doors to breathe and compose himself before attending to the next task.

Baluchston was not—yet—part of Central Domain. Except in Thegan's eyes, apparently. Leof wanted Alston for this, not Hodge. Someone he could count on to do the gods' will.

He tried not to think about what that might be.

Leof checked the saddlebags his groom, Bandy, had packed for him. Never trust anyone with the necessities of life, his father had taught him, and it was just as well, because Bandy had forgotten parchment and inkstone for sending messages.

He came with many apologies and rechecked everything himself, worried that Leof would leave him behind.

"Come on then," Leof said. "Mount up."

They set out very early, Leof riding a horse from the common herd, a bay gelding with two white socks. There was no way he'd risk Arrow or Thistle near the Lake, and besides, they had both worked hard this last week and needed the rest. This was one of the horses Bramble and Gorham had trained and, though it had an odd trick of tossing its head whenever another horse came near, it didn't bite or kick, so he counted his blessings. He led his men out, twenty of them, to escort the Travellers or Town Council of Baluchston back to Sendat, and thereby proclaim to the world at large that Baluchston was part of Central Domain now, like it or not.

Leof didn't think the people of Baluchston would like either option, which was why there were twenty horsemen instead of four, as there had been with the other collecting parties.

It was a relief to be out of the fort.

The rain was holding off, just, although the clouds were thickening and the wind rising slowly. Everyone who could be spared was out in the fields, gathering in the hay before the storm struck and the crop was ruined. His instinct was to go and help, knowing what a difference twenty workers would make; but Thegan's orders didn't allow for delays.

He sent a prayer to the local gods, to hold off the rain, and thought that the farmers' families in the fields were surely doing the same.

SAKER

THE FARM was heavily shuttered, like every building in Central Domain now. Even though the farm dogs were barking madly from the end of their chains, lunging at his scent, the farmer and his brood stayed cautiously, safely behind solid wood. Saker smiled grimly. It was a kind of victory, to make them cower behind their doors. But it made finding food harder.

He wished he had learnt to fish, or forage, or learnt any other way of feeding himself from the land; but that had not been part of Freite's skills. She knew only enchantment, so that was all he knew.

He could eat the dogs, he supposed. He knew how to kill dogs. Knew how to kill just about anything that was tied up, thanks to her. But he preferred something else.

The dairy was the best place. He made for it boldly, certain that the more noise he made the less likely the farmer was to come out and confront him. The dairy was shuttered, too, but it couldn't be bolted from inside, so he had no trouble forcing the door latch.

He set the door ajar so that the moonlight streamed in. Inside, there wasn't as much as he'd hoped, but there was enough: curds and whey, but no hard cheese that he could take away with him, milk in settling pans, the cream like clouds. There were stirring spoons on the drying rack, so he sat down on a churning stool and helped himself. Fatty cream, sharp curds, bland whey...He hated the smell of curds on the turn. He couldn't bring himself to take the rennet, which was soaking in a bucket. Goat's stomach *could* be eaten, he knew, but even roasting it to cinders wouldn't take away that smell.

He'd kill for a loaf of bread.

For a moment, he paused, realising that the idle thought was true. He would kill for a loaf of bread, or a handful of strawberries, or even a mouthful of hard cheese. Why not kill for that, when they had to die anyway?

111

He teetered for a moment between dismay and exhilaration at the thought but it was exhilaration that led him out to see what was growing in the kitchen garden. Strawberries *would* be nice. He kept his knife in his hand, just in case.

Action was what he needed now. He had sat, hour upon hour, racking his mind for memories, for theory, for any hint as to how he might amend the spell. Blood was the key to prevent the ghosts from fading, but how it was tied to the sun's rhythm he did not know.

He found, by touch, peas twining around cones of sticks, and snapped off the almost full pods to stuff in his scrip. The leaves were soft and pleasantly furry, but his fingers, questing, poked their way into a fat caterpillar, which squelched.

He jerked his hand back and left the peas alone to venture further along the rows.

Didn't carrots have these plumy tops? He knew that if he'd spent any time at all on a farm, he'd have a better idea. He pulled experimentally and when the noise came he thought it was the carrot screaming as it was wrenched from the ground. His guts clenched and he jumped back, dropping the carrot.

But it was just a carrot, and it lay there, seeming to mock his fear. The scream came again. A wind wraith, coiling and curling just above him. He felt a strong urge to void his bowels, but fought it back.

"Master!" it hissed in his ear. "What do you seek?"

He wasn't going to say he was foraging. Gods alone knew what food they'd offer him.

"I seek ingredients for a spell," he said. "A spell to allow the ghosts to stay in this world past the setting of the sun."

He could see the wraith now, almost invisible in the moonlight. The moon was only a sliver and it lit the creature from behind, so that it seemed he was looking at the crescent through a curtain of impossibly fine fabric. Finer than silk, and silver-grey. For a moment, he simply looked at it, without fear, and recognised its beauty. Freite had been beautiful too, in her own way. It seemed to him that evil often was.

"Ingredients?" the wraith said. "What more do you need, than blood?"

Freite had received many of her spells from the wraiths. There was no such thing as human spells, she'd told him once, on a day when he'd pleased her by giving her all the power from him she needed. He'd lain, exhausted, on a couch, while she strolled the room full of vitality, younger than the day before, lightly touching her collection of precious glass, piece by piece.

"All spells are stolen from or traded for with the spirits," she had said. "We have none of our own."

Hope stirred his guts into turmoil. "Blood alone is not enough," he said to the wraith.

"Blood and memory," it howled.

"Whose blood?" Saker demanded.

"The blood of thy heart, the blood of thy heart's enemy, what matter? Thy memory, thy army's memory, what matter? Feed us night and day, master. Day and night!" It shrieked with anticipated rapture and soared up in that fountain of movement he had seen so often and feared so greatly.

His heart thumped. Blood and memory. He ran through the spell in his mind. Yes. There were always memories that flooded over him at the start of the spell. He hadn't realised how important they were. He smiled.

Blood and memory. A way to renew the spell—to constantly renew it.

His ghosts were beings of memory. And they would find blood. Fountains of blood.

ASH

H E SAW with the River's eyes, which were not eyes at all. Every crack in the stone where water had once flowed was clear to Her; every opening, even a sliver, where she could reach was mapped. She knew the Caverns as his father knew his flute; it was instrument, where she sang, and home, and long familiarity.

"Smash it," Ash said to Her. "Crack it like an egg."

Was it asking too much, to demand that She destroy this long-held sanctuary? He and Baluch waited, breaths bated, hearts pounding, humming the notes that asked Her to help. The answer was not in words.

She laughed. It was wild, alive, unstoppable: the random, untameable force of flood let loose, delighting in destruction, wedded to change. She laughed, and the river rose.

It swirled around them as it came, sliding intimately between their clothes and their skin, tinglingly cold, pushing them but never so hard they were unbalanced. She curled past them, the current strengthening, the quiet flow of the river turning to rushing power, aimed like a spear at the crack where the river disappeared into the cavern wall. Like a spear, like a wedge for chopping hardwood, like the axe itself.

She did not let the river flow too widely as the rock resisted: it built up in a straight line, a long column of water banked only by air and Her will, far above the rocks. The water pounded in waves into the slit, against the far wall, over and over. Sound buffeted them, and Ash could faintly hear the stone figures screaming.

She laughed again as the rock resisted, and some power in the rock also, in the Cavern itself, whatever power kept the spirits from rebirth. He could sense it: this was the power of stone itself, as She was the power of water. The water sprites were hers and were like her, beautiful and dangerous. The delvers belonged to the earth, and were like it, unforgiving and irresistible. Except to water.

114

Ash could feel the battle building as tingling under his skin, across his hair, which stood on end.

"Give me your strength," She said, and although he thought She didn't really need it, not for this battle, it was his battle, and so it was right that She take strength from him. As he had helped Safred when she was healing Bramble, he sent support to her in a way he didn't understand. She relished it and grew stronger, wilder, the river rising higher and pounding more heavily until he felt, then heard, then saw the rocks at the end of the Cavern split apart like halves of a walnut and sunlight dive in, blinding them all, and rocks tumbled and danced and leapt and shattered, hurting his ears.

"Thank you," he said to Her.

The earth rumbled, a mixture of anger and defeat as the River sighed, "It's an old battle. I always win."

In the same moment, the stone figures cried out, throwing up hands and paws and tails in defence against the light.

As the sun hit the stone figures, they began to dissolve into the same slurry of water and rock that had come off Ash's boots when the weasel had let him go. Only bones were left as the stone melted away, some human, some animal. The weasel had really been a weasel, by the sinuous backbone, but one of normal size. The ox was a skeleton, but flesh still covered the old woman's bones. Bramble knelt beside her, supporting her head. It seemed that her body hadn't decayed before the Caverns had taken her.

Through the tears in his eyes from the harsh light, Ash could see she was younger than the stone had made her look, not much older than Bramble, with long blonde hair and fine clothes, the kind an officer's wife might wear. Around her waist, where simple women wore a belt, she had a sash embroidered with two names entwined: Brea and Calin. It was a marriage belt, sewn by an officer's daughter for her wedding.

"How did she end up here?" Ash marvelled.

"Unluckily," Bramble said. She bent and picked the body up easily and laid it out on a rock, smoothing the eyelids and crossing the hands over the chest. There was, surprisingly, no smell except that of chalk and water. She stepped back and bowed her head. "Brea, may you not linger on the roads, may you not linger in the fields. Time is, and time is gone."

"Time is, and time is gone," Ash and Medric said.

"May you find friends, may you find those you loved," Bramble said. "Time is, and time is gone."

"Time is, and time is gone," Baluch joined in.

"We have no rosemary, but remember us. We have no evergreen, but may our memories of you be evergreen. Time is, and time is gone."

"Time is, and time is gone," all of them said, except Acton. Perhaps, Ash thought, his people had had a different ceremony.

Ash began to gather rocks, to cover the girl over, but Bramble stopped him.

"No," she said. "Let her lie in sunlight."

So they left the body laid out on its rock, bathed in the white sunlight of early morning, and made their way out.

The river had sunk to its earlier level but it was still a hard, slippery climb over the rocks and out. They were huge, great slabs of limestone that shifted as they put weight on them, and settled into new positions with no more than a gentle push.

It took them until the sun was high above to reach the peak of the rock pile and all that time the River was silent in Ash's head. When he balanced on the topmost rock and looked out, he thought he understood why. She had carved out half a mountain to free them—the scar of the Cavern's collapse cut across acres of steep ground. The cavern river now cascaded down the mountain to join a larger river at the base. The White River? Bramble had said it was near.

The power involved...He shook a little. This had happened because he had asked for it.

"You'll pay for it, in time," Baluch said quietly, and it took Ash a moment to realise that he meant it literally, that he would pay with time, his own time, as Baluch had done. Ash shivered and wondered when he would have to start paying. He didn't want to leave everyone he knew just yet.

"No town here, thank the gods," Bramble said as she looked out beside him. She put her hand on his shoulder. "You have power, Ash."

"Not my power," he said.

BREA'S STORY

W E START out different, but we end at the same place.
So my mother would say to me after a funeral, after the stone
had been rolled back over the burial cave. But it seems to me we come
to the same place earlier than that, no matter what our life is like, no
matter if we are rich or poor or loved or unloved.

We come to the place where we first meet Lady Death face to face
and decide whether or not to take her as ally.

There were two of us; and on the surface we were alike, Linde my
cousin, and I. Born the same year, within days of each other. Grown up
the same—we could wear each other's clothes, and did, and from the
back no one could tell us apart, for we both had the same wheat-coloured
locks, and we dressed each other's hair in the knot of plaits they call
the Maiden's Prayer. From the front—well, Linde was always prettier
than I was, no doubt, but her figure wasn't as good, so I got the boys
who looked at a girl's body and she got the ones who looked at her face.
That did not trouble me. When a boy looked at my breasts and started
breathing fast, I felt strong and alive, heady with power. It was the only
power I could recognise in myself, then. One who has no right to make
choices has no real power, and I had no such right about anything more
serious than how to braid my hair.

Our fathers were twins, officers to the warlord, both of them, as their
father and father's father had been. Their lands adjoined. They had built
their houses on the edges of their lands so they could be close together,
and so Linde and I and our brothers and sisters grew up in two houses,
and both of them were home.

Officers' daughters don't choose their husbands. There's more to
marriage than four legs in a bed, my grandmother told me. Your task is
to make alliances for this family that will keep us safe and strong, that's
your life's work, she said.

And my mother nodded, warmly, because she'd been sent off halfway across the Domains to marry my father, to cement an alliance between our family and Cliff Domain. "Love doesn't count when you measure it against family and children and safety and loyalty and strength," she said. She touched my plaits, gently. "And you must trust your father to choose you a good husband, as mine did."

I smiled. It was a byword around the Domain, how my parents loved each other. I realise now that that was a bad thing for me. It brought me up to expect better than I was ever likely to get, being portioned off for strategic purposes as all girls must be.

At least I was not ugly, I thought, and *would* get married, unlike my aunt Silv, who was hare-lipped and squint-eyed and kept mostly to the kitchen and the linen closet. No one had even tried to find her a husband.

Linde went first. My uncle found her a young one, an auburn-haired officer from Western Mountains Domain, one of the warlord's officers who lived at the fort. Cenred, the warlord, was old and this officer was one of his son's best friends, so it was a good marriage. The bridegroom's name was Aden, and he came, blushing, to collect her.

"How you're going to miss her!" the aunts all said, because Linde and I spent all our time together, though we fought like water sprites when their backs were turned. We lived a layered life, she and I. On top, we were the good girls, the obedient, friendly, happy girls. Underneath, there was more going on and always had been.

We'd decided to do it that way one afternoon when we'd both been sent to Linde's room for pulling each other's hair. We can't have been more than seven or eight.

Linde climbed up to the wall slit and looked out into the golden autumn afternoon. "It's not worth it," she said. "Fighting with you isn't worth missing nut-gathering for."

I agreed with her.

"We shouldn't do it," she said. "We shouldn't fight in front of them."

"I don't like you," I said.

"I don't like you either," she snapped back. "But they don't have to know that."

It was a new idea to me, the idea of deceit, but Linde had been lying a long time. That was one of the reasons we fought—she put the blame on me for things she'd done. I saw a way to stop that. I remember feeling very clever and crafty at that moment, satisfied with myself, as young children are sometimes.

"I'll stop fighting in front of them if you stop getting me into trouble," I said.

She considered it, then slid down off the chest she was standing on and came over to me. She spat in her hand and held it out to me. I spat in mine and we sealed the bargain. And from then, we were known as best friends, the best in the world, though we snarled and scratched at each other in private.

It was excellent practice for marriage.

Because we were always together—therefore always chaperoned—they let us have more time alone than the other girls. And we became experts at stealing extra hours, at sneaking off and exploring the places we should not have known about. It even bought us time truly alone, because after a while they stopped verifying our stories, and we could go off by ourselves, ready with an alibi.

Linde found the enchanter's house, off the road to town, back from the road up a narrow drive lined with yew trees.

Freite, her name was, and she was dark haired but not a Traveller, because Travellers have pale skin and she was brownish, like someone from the Wind Cities. So we were unsure of the etiquette when she invited us in. A Traveller we would have scorned. But an exotic like Freite...

We drank cha with her in a lavish room full of carpets and cushions, with glass winking from shelves. There was more glass than I had ever seen in one place, more than the warlord had in his hall.

Linde was fascinated. Here was a woman who owned her own house, a woman who, she told us, made her own decisions. A woman of power. It was hard to know how old she was but I thought, *old*, though her face was unlined.

Linde wanted all the kinds of power there were, but Freite just smiled when she asked questions. It was like she was fishing for something, like she was using Linde to get something she wanted, but it wasn't Linde. She wasn't interested in Linde, though my cousin couldn't see that truth. She wanted me.

Half a dozen times she made a move as if to touch me—not as a man would touch, for pleasure, but just a gesture. A pat on the arm to get my attention, say, or reaching to brush a hair away from my collar. I pulled back, each time, sure somehow that no good would come of a touch from her. Her eyes grew angrier and darker as the time went on and I became nervous.

"We must get back," I said to Linde, but she was headstrong as ever and concentrated on getting this woman to reveal something—anything—about how she had come to this marvelous position, of being on her own, with wealth of her own, with no man to control her.

I stood up and said firmly, "We must go now."

Linde glared at me, but she came. That was the bargain—we would not disagree, even in front of a stranger. Freite invited us to come again, "Anytime," she said, "I am always here."

Linde smiled and said she would be back soon, sweet as honey, but two minutes out the door and she was berating me for being rude, for being stupid, for not seeing that we should be learning all we could from Freite.

"I don't want to learn what she could teach," I said, and shivered. It was true. Out of the house I felt clean, and that made me realise that inside it had felt dirty, filthy, though the floors had been spotless and the glass gleaming. It was Freite who had felt filthy, a grime on her soul spreading over everything. I said so.

No doubt the fight that followed would have lasted until we got home, but as we walked down between the towering yews a boy stepped out in front of us. Auburn hair, hazel eyes, younger than us, but not bad looking and well dressed. Linde took all that in with a blink and smiled and bowed, but he was looking at me, and I was looking at his pale cheeks and tired eyes.

"Don't go back," he said to me. "She wants your power."

"What power?" Linde asked sharply. "Brea hasn't got any power."

"*You* know," he said, still looking at me. "Stay away from her."

I nodded and he stepped back into the trees. Linde surged forward to see where he had gone, but there was no sign of him.

"What was all that about?" she demanded. "Do you know him?"

I shook my head.

"What power?"

And there it was, the underlayer that I had never shared with anyone, not even Linde. The shameful secret sleeping inside me. The power that only Travellers had, only the people with tainted blood, whose family line was not pure. I looked my blonde cousin in the eye and lied.

"I don't know what he was talking about," I said. "All I know is that she's a creepy old woman who kept trying to touch me. And you know what grandmother told us about women like her."

It was enough to distract her: a girl-fancier, or a girler looking for a blonde to ship to the Wind Cities' brothels, either option fuelled her speculation. Her vanity told her that Freite would want *her*, not me, and that she was in most danger. That gave her a pleasant thrill, but she was no fool, my cousin. The danger was real, and it kept her away from Freite. Fear of being used by her, of being *tainted* by her, kept me away too.

Then Linde got married, and I did miss her. Not she herself, but the time and space her companionship had bought me. I was drafted into the everyday work of the households, and trained intensively in the duties of a wife, the duties of an officer's woman.

But it was as though Freite's eyes and the young man's words had woken the power in me, from where I had buried it as deep as I could. I began to know things before they were told to me, to read people's eyes and see their thoughts showing as clear as speech. That was when I blessed Linde. Our life of dissimulation was a perfect preparation for this. For not showing what I truly was.

If I wanted a husband, I had to conceal myself. No one would want a wife with Traveller blood in her; it would shame the entire family, spoil the marriage chances of my brothers and sisters, possibly even get my father's lands taken away from him. Warlords don't trust Travellers.

Nor should they, because I found in myself layers and layers of deceit. Everything about me was a lie. My looks, my speech, my smiles, everything but my desire for my father to find me a husband so I could have my own place and my own family.

He found me one, all right, and the irony was he thought he was doing me a favour when he betrothed me to Linde's husband's cousin. He was an even better match than Aden, my father said, with a bigger estate and more silver. Moreover, he lived at the warlord's fort just as

Linde did, and had his land, up near the mountains, managed for him by a kinsman.

"You'll be glad to see her, no doubt," he said to me, beaming with satisfaction at having given me so great a boon. I thanked him properly, almost swooning with delight, it seemed, but my spirit darkened with fear. Linde knew me better than anyone. If she were to see the power which had awakened in me...

But then I reasoned with myself. She would not dare to speak out, because it would taint her family as well as mine. She would not dare take that risk. I was safer with her than with anyone. As I realised that, tears came to my eyes and my father hugged me, a thing he rarely did.

My husband Calin came to collect me soon after.

What is there to say? He is dead, after all. He was a boor and a bully but not an evil man. He was merely used to getting his own way, and Cenred's fort was a place of drunkenness and licence. Calin had lived like that for years, since he was a very young man, and it had shaped him to fit.

Cenred's wife was an invalid who wanted only solitude, and his son had not married, so there was no one to keep a check on the officers' young wives. For Linde and me it was a continuation of our old life, except that we avoided the hall, where the officers drank and whored and gambled.

Linde was besotted with her husband, Aden. A nice enough boy and with eyes only for her. I dealt with mine as best I could, and cursed my parents for filling my head with romantic ideas. But it was Calin who taught me my true power, a power I learnt in pain and dread, night after night in our bed. Night after night I wished him dead.

And day by day he died.

A wasting disease, the healer called it. He looked furtive when he said it, so I stopped him as he went out the door, pretending to want to thank him, and I asked, "What is wrong?"

He looked down at his hands, as though weighing his words. "Does your husband have any enemies, lady?"

I stiffened. "He is an officer. There are many who hate all officers." I paused, but I had to ask. "Why?"

"There is a feel about this... It's come on very fast for such a young man. It may be... wished upon him."

The blood rushed from my head to my feet and I swayed. No doubt he thought he'd frightened me, because he took my arm to steady me, and began to babble, "No, no, no reason to be frighted, lady, it was just a shadow on my mind, but it does happen so quickly sometimes, out of the deep sea and nowhere as they say..."

I forced my voice to be calm. "If this got out, there would be reprisals on innocent people."

He nodded, and never spoke of it again.

Calin was too frail now to come to our bed with any thought but sleep, but that night I caressed his head and wished him well because, although I dreaded his touch, I had never meant to harm him. Never meant to kill. I wished with all my heart, and I wished night and day, but it made no difference. I had no power to heal, only to curse.

He died only four months after our wedding day, and I thanked the gods that I was not carrying his child.

I went through the patterns of grief. I laid him out in proper form, cried at the funeral, Swith knows I looked pale enough. And on the third day I shut myself up in our room, the room where he had died, saying I wanted no one but myself at his quickening, if quickening there was.

I even hired musicians, saying that music often helps the spirit find rest. A flautist, a drummer and a singer, it was—typical Travellers, but the woman had a voice that would charm the soul out of your body. I set them to play outside the door, hoping that if I had to acknowledge my guilt the music would cover my words.

I was ready. Ready with the knife, ready to take the blame and offer reparation. Ready for Calin to accuse me silently.

He had died, as men often do, just before dawn. I sat up the night waiting, for it isn't always three days to the minute. I sat and listened to the flute and drum, listened to the woman sing songs about peace and love and the winds of dawn. I could hear nothing else, and even now I cannot close my eyes without hearing her voice again. I waited while the candle guttered, and the grey dawn slid in through the shutters, while the smooth bed seemed to grow bigger and brighter moment by moment, so that I strained my eyes time and again, thinking the white sheet was his ghost forming, thinking the pillow was his head, the bolster his body. The knife grew slick and I had to change hands and wipe the sweat on my dress. I felt sick with shame, feverish with guilt. As the first yellow rays cut through the gap at the window, I tensed. Surely now, surely this was when he would come, accusing and angry.

I waited until noon, until dusk, but he did not come. The healer had prepared him well for death, and even in the grave, it seemed, he did not realise I had killed him.

As I unbolted the door and came out into the corridor, the woman singer rose to greet me. They had played unstinting the whole time, taking turns towards the end so that it would be flute, or drum, or singer, to eke out their energy until it was over.

I gave the woman the purse I had ready.

"I hope all went well," she said, which was an impertinence from a Traveller, but she was pale and weary-looking and I felt grateful to them.

"He did not come," I said.

"That is good," she said gently. "He is at rest."

My eyes filled with tears, and they were real, because I hoped against hope that she was right, that my curse had not poisoned his afterlife as well.

Then her eyes narrowed a little and her head tilted to one side.

"If you try to deny who you are," she said, very quietly, "the power will overwhelm you."

I stared at her in shock, not believing that she could have said it, half-believing that I had imagined the words out of my own guilt and confusion. She turned away to help her colleagues pack their instruments, as though she had said nothing. What had she seen? How had I betrayed myself?

I took her by the arm and she turned to look at me, and saw my fear. "You are not the only one with power," she said reassuringly. "Others will see nothing."

But how could I be sure? Worse—how could I be sure that I would not curse someone again, unthinking?

So I came to my husband's lands, and to his house, which was mine now until I died, and I became, like Freite, a woman free of men, as widows mostly are. And I became, like her, a woman who lived alone, and saw no one unless they knocked at the door, and in the time honoured way I made sure that no one knocked, by being rude and parsimonious and meagre. They thought me a mad miser, down in the village.

So I protected others from a stray thought, a moment's anger, by becoming solitary. I protected myself from the guilt of their deaths, as well, and closed my eyes each night to the memory of the singer, of her songs about love and the winds of dawn, though I found no peace there. The only peace I found was walking in the mountains, and how could I know that my lonely explorations would lead so deep and to so much pain?

For one thing I was sure, and still am. Loneliness is better than murder.

FLAX

"WE NEED to be out of sight by dawn," Swallow said. She didn't like the idea of hiding, it was clear, but she accepted it. They had stopped at a stream to let the horses have a breather.

"This is mostly flat country," Rowan said, pulling at his ear in a way that Flax had seen Ash do when he was thinking. "Farm land. Not much shelter."

"There are coppices," Flax suggested and they nodded.

"The next one we see, then," Swallow said. She cast a worried look at the sky, which was now filling with clouds as a cool north wind picked up.

The moon would soon be covered, Flax thought, and they would be in pitch black—no riding then, they'd have to lead the horses. He touched his heels to Cam's flanks and they set off again with him in the lead. But there were no coppices on this stretch of road. It was all fields, mostly vegetables, from what they could see in the moonlight: cabbages, beanpoles, some hay fields and pasture. The hay hadn't been mown here; there weren't even any hayricks to hide behind and the hedgerows weren't high enough to offer shelter.

Not much further on, they came to a junction with a much wider track, a real road marked by wagons and horse traffic.

"Baluchston or Sendat?" Rowan asked the world in general.

To their left, the main route to Baluchston ran straight. To the right, the road led to Sendat.

"We've missed the turn, then," Swallow said.

Rowan nodded. "We could turn around and try to find it—I think maybe it was that little track about three miles back."

Somehow, that seemed like a bad idea. Flax felt a real urgency to keep moving, to get as far away from Baluchston as they could.

The sky was growing lighter.

"There are coppices on this road," Swallow said. "All the way down to Sendat. And there's another road about ten miles on that would take us east, to the Hidden River and North Domain. We could get a boat down to Mitchen and then one to Turvite from there."

She had the ordering of the family group usually, that was clear, just like his mam.

"We'd better get under cover then, before dawn," Rowan said.

The lightening sky was like a threat, like a deep dark chord sounded on that Wind Cities instrument with the big belly. He desperately wanted to sing, something cheerful to keep his spirits up, but it was too dangerous. The farmhouses were close to the road here, and villages too frequent.

They came to a village before they found a coppice, but they had no time to go around it. "Straight through," Swallow said, and they went on at a gentle canter, hoping the inhabitants wouldn't wake, or would think it were warlord's messengers coming back to the fort.

Flax, in the lead, came up on the first house, his heart beating fast, ears straining to hear anything, anyone, any sign that they were noticed. The village was revealed in flickers of moonlight as the clouds raced across the sky. All the houses were shuttered and barred. There was none of the usual clutter around: no handcarts or barrels outside the inn, no washing left out, no toys forgotten when it had been time to go inside. The tidiness gave the village an unnatural air, as though the townsfolk were already dead. That wasn't a comfortable thought. The dead were as dangerous as the living, now. It took only a minute to ride through the small collection of houses, but by the time they were on the other side he was drenched in sweat, and he wondered how Ash managed to live this kind of life all the time.

When there was no sound of pursuit, they relaxed a little, but Flax was still searching for any sign of cover—even a copse would do.

They left the plain behind as the road began to wind between small hills. Flax felt more comforted as the slopes rose up around them; they couldn't see ahead very far, but at least no one would be able to spot them a long way off.

The sun was winning over the clouds. It was a late dawn, but it was coming, slowly. The horses were tired, and Flax kept them to a walk, despite the urgency he felt.

Cam's ears pricked forward and she raised her head. He was too slow; he wasn't expecting it. She whinnied loudly and was answered from around the bend just ahead of them. Flax looked around wildly. Nowhere to hide. They would have to brazen it out, no matter who was around the bend.

He straightened in his saddle, reminding himself that he was a young merchant, travelling with his servants to — to where? Sendat? Carlion? Yes, going to Carlion to find out about their family's steward there, to get solid information about what had happened, rather than rumours and scare stories.

He took a breath and got ready to smile as they came around the turn.

Warlord's men. Thegan's men. Camped, but packing up in the early light, getting ready to move on. Flax's face froze, but he kept Cam moving, raising a hand to the soldiers as if in casual greeting. But one of them, a solid good-looking man in his thirties, moved across their path and raised a hand to stop them. He had the arm ring that identified him as a sergeant.

Flax reined in amiably, and nodded. "Morning."

"You're out early," the man said.

"Heading for Carlion. Long way, so we got off early."

"Where are you from?"

"Baluchston," Flax said, hoping it was the right choice. But it was the only free town on this road, and they needed to be from a free town if they were going to get away with this.

"Really?" the sergeant said, and he looked back at Swallow and Rowan. That was bad. Flax forced himself to not look. "Just stay here a moment, lad."

The sergeant walked back to speak to another man, a tall pale-haired officer wearing the signature ponytail, who was about to mount a big bay gelding.

He looked just like a warrior out of the old stories, the kind of man that Flax had secretly wanted to be as a very young boy, before he'd found his voice. He'd been ashamed of it, but all the same he'd dreamt about riding tall and fair on a chaser stallion — though he knew, as a horse trainer's child, that few stallions made really good chasers. For the first time, he thought that maybe he could go back, someday, when he tired of the Road, and help his father ...

If he didn't deal with this, there'd be no future, and no chance of ever seeing his father again. He swallowed down his fear, and prepared to lie until his face turned inside out, the way the old mothers said it would if you fibbed.

But he didn't have the chance.

The officer took one look at Rowan and Swallow, and a closer look at him, and simply said, "I'm sorry, but all Travellers from Baluchston must go to the fort at Sendat."

"I'm not a Traveller!" Flax tried to put as much indignation into his voice as he could.

"No?" The man seemed prepared to grant him exemption, but then one of the soldiers came and whispered to him. The officer firmed his mouth—gods, a gorgeous mouth!—as though he were disappointed, and turned to Flax. "Dern says he's seen you singing. A voice like a lark, he says. A Traveller."

That was bittersweet, to be skewered by his own talent. Flax shrugged and smiled as charmingly as he could. He didn't think it would make any difference with this one, but flirting worked with astonishing people sometimes.

"It was worth a try," he said.

The officer smiled, genuinely amused, but unfortunately not attracted at all. "You misunderstand. My lord Thegan is offering sanctuary to all Travellers—there have been killings right across the Domain and my lord is gathering Travellers for their own protection."

"So we've been told," Swallow said. "But we were in no danger in Baluchston."

"You were in great danger, whether you knew it or not," the officer said firmly. He turned to an archer. "Horst, take them to the fort." With a shock, Flax recognised the man who had pursued him and Ash in Golden Valley—the man Ash had saved from the wind wraiths.

The archer stared at him, and flushed as if remembering his fear of the wraiths, then turned away, pretending he didn't know Flax. Good. Flax was happy to go along with that. The officer looked at the ground for a moment, as though trying to decide what to say, then looked up and met their eyes, gazing at each of them separately, as though he wanted them to pay great attention. "My lord is generous, but he requires his orders to be followed. I would advise you to go with Horst."

It was clear he meant it. Just to add weight, Horst shifted his bow and fingered the arrows in his quiver. The officer hadn't ordered him to bring them down if they tried to escape, but it was clear that he would. They all knew it. Flax was suddenly, sharply glad that Zel was safe with Safred. No one would attack the Well of Secrets party.

"Our horses need rest," Flax said. "We've been riding all night."

"Take a break here, then, Horst, and have them back to the fort by tomorrow evening." Horst nodded. "Alston," the officer said to the sergeant, "let's be off."

The men mounted and rode on, the sergeant leading the squad.

The officer lingered a moment. "See my lady Sorn if you need anything," he said, then shook his reins and his horse began to trot after the others.

Flax looked warily at the archer.

"Down you come," Horst said. "Don't think I'm going to help you with your animals."

Well, that was clear enough. They dismounted and led the horses to the stream, where Flax, with some clumsy help from Swallow and Rowan, unsaddled, fed and watered the horses, then groomed them thoroughly before throwing himself on the grass and eating the food Swallow had ready for him. Flax was tired of resisting things. He was much, much better at just going with the current, like the little boats children made from leaves and twigs.

Of course, those boats always sank eventually, but once he'd made one that had floated right down a stream and launched itself off the cliff into the sea. It had flown, buoyed up by the air, for quite a way before it sailed down to the waves and was sucked from sight.

The archer kept them on the road all day and only found a camping place when the horses started to visibly labour. They were still some hours out of Sendat, but in such a settled, busy part of the Domain that Flax knew they had no chance of escape. As Horst had followed them along, they had been glared at, spat and shouted at, and threatened in every village, by every farmer, by every child with a handful of dung to throw, and only the soldier's presence had kept them from being dragged off their horses and kicked to death.

There would be no refuge in this country.

After they'd set up camp in a field with a stream that Horst simply commandeered from the farmer—"Warlord's business"—they ate their cold food in silence.

"What about a song, then?" Horst said finally, wiping the crumbs from his jacket.

Flax was astounded. Did this man really think they would entertain their gaoler? Then he looked more closely at the man. There was no scorn in his eyes, not even a demand. He'd asked as one person would ask another person for a favour, no more. Did he really believe all that nonsense about the warlord offering refuge? Did he think he was the hero in this story, saving Travellers from their deaths?

It worried Flax that the archer might be right. Maybe he was the hero.

Swallow cleared her throat, and looked meaningfully at him when he turned around. "Why not?" she said. "We have to practise anyway."

That was true, but it made Flax want to laugh. Practice, in the middle of all this!

Rowan found his flute in his pack and took out a small tambour as well. "Do you drum?" he asked Flax.

"Not as well as Ash," he said. They looked startled, as though they'd forgotten he and Ash had Travelled together, or as though they were surprised that Ash would drum for him.

"Try, anyway," Swallow said. He took the drum and sounded it—light but true. Good enough for a field and a warlord's man.

"Do you have a favourite song?" Rowan asked the archer.

The man seemed embarrassed. Probably liked some invasion song about killing Travellers, and wasn't sure whether he should ask for it.

"What about 'Homecoming'?"

Flax blinked, but he had his performing face on now, so he didn't show his surprise. "Homecoming" was a western mountains song, a miners' song, melancholic and somewhat sentimental. Not the sort of song a soldier often asked for.

Rowan set the beat by tapping on his thigh. Flax picked it up, holding a regular rhythm, then Rowan set the flute to his lips and played the simple melodic introduction.

Then Swallow began singing, and Flax's fingers faltered on the drum. He picked up the rhythm again, though, as she glared sideways at him, and he kept it up. Her voice was as pure as snowmelt—perfect, even after this long, long day, even without a chance to practise, to warm her throat and muscles.

The mountain is deep
And the mine is dark
And I have only one small light
Oh, pray keep me safe
In the pit-dark night
And bring me home
To the evening light

He came in on the chorus, softly, as he thought she would like, and saw her eyes flick sideways—in approval, this time.

Chains of gold, chains of gold
Bind me to you
Chains of gold, chains of gold
Bring me home

Afterwards, as the last notes of the flute died away, the warlord's man cleared his throat and said, "My mam was western mountains born." That was all, but it was enough. And they slept just as they would have if the archer had been another Traveller.

Sendat was a big town. They reached the outskirts in mid-morning and here, unlike every other place they'd passed, no one spat at them. The merchants in the market stared at them, and the townspeople too, but they nodded at Horst and a few shouted remarks—like, "More for my lord, eh? Fort's getting pretty full!"

Horst ignored their remarks with a shrug and an occasional glare, until one man yelled, "My lord must be crazy, feeding all those dark-haired bastards!" and then he was off his horse, his hand around the man's throat, his boot knife drawn and poised at the man's privates.

"Did you question my lord's orders?" he hissed.

The man shook and denied it and babbled about what a great lord Thegan was, and Horst dropped him, resheathed the knife and remounted without another word. The three travellers followed him up the hill to the fort, leaving complete silence behind them. Once they were out of earshot of the market, Horst cleared his throat and said, "No one questions my lord when I'm around."

"Loyalty is a valuable quality," Rowan said quietly, and Flax could tell that he meant it. The archer realised that, too, and his face cleared of its bad mood.

"Aye," he said. "The most valuable thing a man like me has to offer."

There were many people, men and women and even children, working on the fortifications around the top of the hill. Stakes, palisades, ditches — a whole ring of defences — showed the sharp edges and colours of new work. Thegan was serious about defending his fort from the ghosts. But would it be enough? For the first time, Flax wondered whether the Travellers were to be used as some other form of defence. He shivered slightly and turned to Horst. "What about our horses?"

"My lord's commandeered all horses. Travellers are sleeping in the barn, over there." Horst pointed to a group of dark-haired women and children cooking over fires. It smelt good. Rabbit stew, perhaps. Flax hoped there'd be dumplings.

But his appetite fell away as they walked through the heavily guarded gate and he noticed that half the warlord's men on the wall faced inwards, watching the Travellers.

LEOF

L EOF ORDERED his men to set up camp outside Baluchston. Their twenty men seemed a very small party when he remembered the army Thegan had assembled here only a few weeks ago. It was twilight by the time they had pitched tents, and he decided to give Vi and her council the night to talk the problem over.

He took Alston with him, but no other guards. Alston didn't comment. Thank the gods for a sergeant who didn't chatter! Leof could do things Thegan's way, or he could do his best to avoid conflict. This time, he wouldn't let his pride or his temper get the better of him.

Outside Vi's shop, they dismounted and found a youth to take the horses to a nearby inn. "Tell them my lord will want dinner," Alston said to the lad.

Leof usually ate with the men when he was on campaign, but Alston deserved a good meal, so he didn't contradict the order.

He ducked his head as he went through the doorway to avoid a swathe of white cloth across the lintel. That was a sign of mourning in these parts. He hoped that it wasn't Vi who was dead.

But there she was, lumbering forward to greet him, her shrewd eyes bright in the light from several lamps. Her mouth opened to greet him, then she noticed Alston following him, and changed what she had been about to say.

"Welcome back, Lord Leof," she said.

"Mistress Vi," he acknowledged. "This is my sergeant, Alston."

"Pleased to meet you," Vi said. "Come on through to the kitchen. The others are there."

The kitchen was even brighter than the shop, with a big fire in the hearth and lamps set around. Four men and women looked up from a table in the centre of the room as he came in, and his heart sank. Most of them had the closed-off look that meant they'd already made up their minds to deny him whatever he asked. Only truth would serve here, and he hoped Alston understood that.

There were two chairs vacant, at either end of the table. He took one and Vi took the other and there was a moment of silence. Alston came to stand behind him, in the second's position which, in an officer's court, meant that there was no trust in the host. Leof didn't know if Vi knew that custom, but she flicked her eyes over Alston and the corners of her mouth tucked back in a little.

"This is Reed, our leather worker," Vi said, indicating the older man to her left. "Minnow the chandler, Sar the weaver, Drago the ferryman, and Eel."

Leof nodded to them all in turn, and they nodded back, silently. The lack of any trade for Eel made Leof look closely at him. One of the Lake People, he thought, dark hair and dark eyes and skin that had spent a long time in the sun. And wise, humorous eyes. He nodded to Leof with a smile.

Vi ceremoniously poured them each a mug of water. "Lake water, for wisdom," she said as she passed one to Leof.

Eel dipped his finger in the water and drew a circle on the back of his hand, then drank. A sign that he belonged to the Lake? That he respected Her power? Leof pretended not to have seen, and drank at the same time as Vi and the others. The water tasted of nothing — or of everything: life and rock and moonlight. He shook his head to clear it of fancies. It was just water.

"What does Thegan want?" Vi asked.

"For now, he wants all the Travellers in the town," Leof replied. There was an intake of breath around the table. "Not the Lake People," he assured them. "Just any Travellers who are passing through." He had decided that it would be impossible to sort out the Settled Travellers from the Lake People, and this partial request might possibly be granted. "There have been massacres," he said seriously. "Many, many Travellers have been murdered. You must have heard."

They nodded, but kept silent, so he ploughed on. "My lord is offering sanctuary to all Travellers in his Domains. Messages have gone to Cliff Domain, as well, instructing his officers to protect Travellers, to gather them together in Cliffhold and keep them safe. He is doing the same in Central."

"But we are not part of Central Domain." It was the youngest of them, Minnow, a red-headed woman with startling blue eyes. She was someone Leof would have appreciated before he knew Sorn.

Leof chose his words carefully. "It's true you have not traditionally been part of Central Domain, but I think you must realise that you are now part of Lord Thegan's territory."

"So, Lord Leof, are you come to tell us our days as a free town are over?" Vi asked.

There was no way to soften the truth. "They were over some time ago, Voice. My lord has had no objections from other warlords to his intentions for Baluchston. Your independence is long gone."

They sat for a moment, taking that in.

"Others have tried to conquer the Lake in the past," Eel said softly.

Leof hesitated. He would not insult the Lake to these people. Not only would it make them antagonistic, Leof felt that it was profoundly dangerous to belittle the Lake so close to it. And whether Thegan would approve or not, he was going to honour that feeling.

"The Lake is the Lake," he said. "But my lord is able to bring armies on either side, this time. And he will have learnt from the last encounter. He won't try the same thing twice. And he will not give up." Leof spaced out the last words, because they had to understand Thegan; they had to believe he was implacable.

"Nor will She," Eel said.

Vi put her hand on his arm. "Eel, I think what my lord Leof thinks about the Lake and what his master thinks may be very different."

Leof forced himself not to look at Alston. Alston hadn't been part of the attack on the Lake, and he had no understanding of how powerful She could be.

"The Travellers are at risk as soon as they set foot on the road," he said. "We will take them to safety."

"They are safe already," the older man, Reed, said, "safer than they could ever be in a warlord's fort!"

"Are you sure?" Leof asked. "Are you sure the Lake can protect you against the dead?"

"It's not the dead we have to fear," Eel said softly. "It's what will follow them."

Leof decided that he had said enough. "Extend our invitation to the Travellers here. We will be in the town square tomorrow, two hours after dawn, to take them to safety." He stood up and bowed to them all, a gesture Thegan would not have approved of. And he could not tell them of the consequences of disobedience, or they would take to the Lake and be outside his reach. "I wish you a good night."

Leof left without looking back, but he could hear, and they said nothing until he was outside the shop. "Come on," he said to Alston. "Let's eat."

Alston paced silently by his side over to the inn. Just outside, he turned and said, "My lord, is the Lake so powerful?"

Leof paused, weighing his words. "I believe the Lake and the gods work together for our good. And that their power is Hers."

"Hers?"

Leof grinned. "Oh, yes, sergeant. She's definitely female. And that should be enough to tell us not to cross her!"

The town council was waiting in the square in the morning, the Lake behind them blindingly bright in the morning sun. Leof shaded his eyes and looked around the square, but of course there were no Travellers waiting compliantly to be herded off. Just the council, and behind them the people of Baluchston, standing in family groups, waiting. They didn't seem concerned. He noticed that some of them wore that smirk that meant they expected a good show. Leof's pride flicked at him. They seemed to think he was negligible, that Thegan could be flouted with impunity.

They would have to learn.

"Voice of Baluchston," he said formally, pitching his voice so it could be heard right across the square, "I am come to escort the Travellers of this place to safety."

"Sure enough," Vi said. "We're here and ready."

She swept a hand to indicate the people behind her. All of them.

He kept his face under tight control. "I informed you yesterday that we are inviting only those of Traveller blood to the fort."

137

Aye," Vi said. "So it is. All of us in Baluchston have the old blood, one way or another. There's been a lot of marrying with the Lake People over the years. If your lord wants to protect all of the old blood, he'll have to take us all. The whole town."

Leof fought down a smile. Swith, she was a cunning old fox! She knew Thegan couldn't possibly accommodate all of them. But they had, in a way, defied his lord, and he could not allow that, so it was time to fall back on the second part of Thegan's orders.

He had given his instructions back in camp, so when he raised his hand and dropped it the men went forward smartly, two to a councillor, riding them down and scooping them up without warning. It was a trick Thegan had used in battle before, to isolate the Ice King's officers from their men. They whooped as they split into pairs and targeted a councillor, bending down and grabbing one armpit each. Once the man was in the air, the right hand rider bent further to get an arm under the knees and flip him up over the opposite withers. It was a little harder with a woman, Leof noticed, and the men with Vi were having some problems, she was so stout. The red-headed woman fought tooth and nail and drew blood with both, but the men hardly noticed and dumped her face down with a slap on the rump for good measure.

Leof sat implacably, although something in him cheered when Eel wriggled out of the way like his namesake and ran for the Lake. The soldiers followed, but the townspeople were in the way; they shifted unwillingly aside, and boys ran under the horses' hooves, startling them into rearing.

Leof kicked his horse and chased him—he couldn't let Eel escape. His speed made even the boys jump out of the way, and he was gaining on Eel as they came to the end of the square, where the long piers stretched out into the water.

His gelding's hooves drummed onto the wooden boards of the pier and the horse spooked, planting his forefeet solidly, refusing to move, shaking all over. Leof almost fell. He jumped off instead and ran flat out after Eel, but there was a moment, just a moment, when his legs had to adjust to being on solid ground, and he was a pace or two behind when Eel, still running, flew straight off the end of the pier, and leapt high in the air, arms flailing. He hit the water and disappeared and only then did Leof realise that the people of Baluchston had been cheering Eel on, as now they fell silent, waiting for him to come back up.

Leof scanned the surface methodically. The water stayed an unbroken silver plain, except where the current stirred up choppy waves. Everything other than the ferry boats was swept away in that current, to the waterfall that fell hundreds of feet to the Hidden River. Leof wondered if even the Lake could save a man from that. He waited until there was no possibility that Eel was still holding his breath, still swimming under water, and then turned and walked slowly back, leading the gelding gently onto the solid earth and mounting. The stories of old battles said the Lake could move a man through time, into the future or the past — he wondered if she had done so to Eel, to keep him safe, or if he were drifting down the Hidden River, food for the fish.

"Regroup," he ordered his men, and they came, four of them with struggling councillors across their saddlebows. Three, rather. Vi just lay there like a sack of meal. He couldn't stop to check on her now. He pushed his gelding to a trot and the others followed, the people in the square running after them, some pleading, some cursing, some threatening.

"The Lake will save them!" one old woman screamed, eyes blazing, and Leof believed her, which was why they were not stopping anywhere within wave's reach. He managed to manoeuvre his horse to Vi's side and found that she was stoically staring upwards, mouth compressed.

She glared at him. "Didn't warn us about this, did you?" she accused him.

"Would you rather I had razed your town?" he asked. "I follow my lord's orders." He moved away before she could elicit more guilt from him.

Three miles out, when he was sure the Lake could not reach them, he halted so that the councillors could climb on double with their captors. He looked at Vi, perched precariously on the rump of a piebald mare, and his lips twitched. "Give the Voice her own mount," he told the soldier in front of her. "You double with Bandy."

"Aye, my lord," the soldier said, half resigned and half relieved.

Leof looked severely at Vi. "If you try to ride off, you'll be shot," he said, but he didn't really mean it and she knew it. The problem was, the five archers with them heard too, and put their bows at the ready. Leof looked at them and back at Vi. "Don't try," he said.

She nodded. "Thegan's orders, eh?" she said. "So you're following a man who doesn't even believe in the gods?"

Alston took a shocked breath. Leof paused. It would be stupid to reply directly. "Criticising the Lord Thegan is not permitted, Mistress Vi," he said firmly.

She sniffed, but stayed silent. She was a little pale; the ride couldn't have been easy for her. And it wouldn't get any better before Sendat. Leof sighed. When he had dreamt about being a warlord's officer, it had never been like this.

"Sendat," he said, and his men moved off immediately, in perfect formation, with perfect trust.

Too many people trusted him, Leof thought. He couldn't possibly satisfy them all.

It was slow riding, and instead of camping, they stayed at inns along the way. He had no orders to treat the council with anything but respect, and rumours would soon reach the other free towns. He didn't want to add fuel to an already dangerous fire. If Thegan wanted to keep both Baluchston and Carlion, he had to be seen to act as though he had no choice. And he could not treat the councillors of a free town like prisoners.

So he did not commandeer the rooms, he paid for them, as Thegan usually did, with a tax chit, and he allowed the councillors to sleep without guards; although some were posted at the outside doors. He didn't think they'd try to run.

Over dinner, he had asked Vi, "Did the Lake not give you instructions?" — not trying to be provocative, but wanting truly to know.

May be she sensed that, because she stared at him steadily for a moment, and then said, "Aye. She did. We're buying time, lad."

"Time for what?"

"Time for the enchanter to be defeated," Reed answered for her.

Leof had leant forward, as focused as he was during battle. "How?" he demanded.

Vi patted his hand, for all the world like she was his grammer. "Don't you worry, lad, the gods have it in hand."

"How many people will die before they settle it?" he said, remembering the bodies in the farmyard, his men at Bonhill, screaming as the wind wraiths feasted.

She paused, her face clouded. "Well, now, the gods don't worry much about deaths," she said. "Death and life, it's all the same thing to them. But coming back from death—that's a worry, and no mistake."

"There's things unseen in the world, lad," Reed broke in, his voice husky. "And things that aren't meant to be seen. The Lake says the enchanter could open the doors to the cold hell, and let the soul eaters in."

Leof could feel the blood leave his face. "They're *real!*" he said. He had always believed the soul eaters were a fireside story, a terror made up to scare children into being good: "If you don't do what you're told, when you die the soul eaters will get you and you'll never be reborn!" Horrible images filled his mind, ghouls that waited beyond death and ate the souls of the evil, the vain, the cowardly...There was no compact with the soul eaters as there was with the wraiths. If they entered the world of the living, it would not stay alive very long.

Vi gazed at him. "Aye, lad, they're real. And they're hungry. So it seems to me that your lord should concentrate on finding that enchanter."

"He's doing whatever can be done."

"So are we all," Vi replied.

"Pray it's enough," Reed said, and he shivered and looked up to the rafters of the inn, as though he expected to see something there, a demon, perhaps. He began to eat again, but his face was grave, as though he were preoccupied with more than the food.

No, Leof didn't think they would try to run. Whatever the Lake had in mind, she was buying time for the people of Baluchston, and the councillors were the price.

141

REED'S STORY

THERE'S NO saying what will happen next. That's what I learnt, that summer, that winter, watching her change. Losing her. They said at first that it was madness, wandering wits, but I knew better.

The gods talk to us but we don't see them. What if we could? What if *she* could, my Eaba? The first time, she looked up from the table where she was stringing beans for dinner, and her face lit up, as though she had seen a friend come in. I turned from punching a pattern into a belt length, but there was no one there. I raised my eyebrows at her, but she just smiled.

Well, Eaba and I have managed to share the same workspace for thirty years by keeping our noses out of each other's business. So I shrugged, although I puzzled over it later, in bed, her hand resting on my chest as it always did.

Then our children started noticing things. We've got eight, some grown and some half-grown and some still running about bare-legged. Two are married, though not the eldest boy, Wyst, and he was the one to say something.

"What are you looking at, Mam?" he asked one day, when she was smiling into the branches of the plum tree, though the blossom had long since disappeared and the fruit hadn't swelled yet.

"Why, that," Eaba answered, waving her hand to the sky as though it was obvious. But when we looked, we didn't see anything.

She picked her washing off the rosemary bushes and went inside, and Wyst and I stared at each other, then shrugged. Women! I think we both thought.

But it niggled at me and that night in bed I asked her, "What did you see in the plum tree, love?"

She laughed at me. "Don't try that on me, husband," she said, as though I were trying to trick her. "As if you didn't see it!"

"I didn't see anything except the tree," I said.

142

"No?" she replied, unconvinced, and settled down to sleep.

That shook me. What had she seen so clear that neither Wyst nor I could see? I wondered if it might be something to do with her being a woman, after all. *Could* they see things we couldn't? Nothing about women would surprise me, not after thirty years with Eaba.

The next time she got that look, she was combing the winter wool from her favourite nanny out in the goat shed, and I asked her straight out, "What are you looking at? And don't say 'that'! I can't see anything here except the shed and the goats."

Her face clouded over and she looked worried. She peered up again into the rafters—it was always up she looked, never down, when she had that expression.

"You don't see it?" she asked slowly.

I shook my head. Her eyes almost disappeared, she frowned so much. Then she looked up again.

"Why can't he see you?" she asked, and cocked her head as if listening to an answer. She wasn't pleased by it, whatever it was. Her lip stuck out in that stubborn way I knew so well, and she muttered, "That's no answer!"

She turned to me, still frowning, and asked, "I suppose you couldn't *hear* that, either?"

"No. I heard nothing."

She sighed. "It says that you don't have the right kind of eyes, but what sort of answer is that? It told me last week that I've only just got the right kind myself. Something to do with the veils."

Ah, I thought. Her eyes *had* been changing lately, growing the milky veils that had blinded her mother and her grandmother before her. She'd been resigned to it, starting to learn the house by touch as well as sight. Perhaps this—whatever it was—was just a missight, so to speak, because her eyes weren't working properly.

But she heard this thing as well.

"What's *it*?" I asked.

She opened her mouth as though to explain, and then shut it. She peered upwards, then shook her head.

"I don't know how to describe it," she said, tapping the wool comb on her knee in frustration. "The words aren't the right words..."

"Just give me an idea."

She paused, searching her mind, but shrugged helplessly.

"Is it alive?" I asked.

"Oh, yes!" she said.

"Is it human?"

"Oh, no!"

"A spirit?"

She shook her head. "Not like the water sprites, or the wind wraiths...I don't rightly know what it looks like."

"Well, what colour is it?"

She went very still, as though realising something for the first time.

"I don't know..." She looked up again, then slumped back on her stool. "Oh. It's gone. I don't think it likes being talked about."

"But—"

"It *is* beautiful," she said eagerly. "It's *very* beautiful. Like...like joy would be if it had a shape."

"But what shape?" I said, a bit loudly, frustrated myself. She looked hurt.

"I can't say. Can't, husband, not won't. I don't have the words."

After that, she didn't want to talk about it, but whatever the thing was, it came more and more often. The children all noticed, first, and then the villagers.

The little ones were convinced it was a wish sprite, like the ones in their stories. The older ones were worried, but no child likes to think their mother is going mad, so they didn't actually say it aloud.

We prayed, Wyst and I, at the black rock altar, but the gods have never spoken to anyone in our family, and they didn't now. When the villagers started muttering about wandering wits, I decided to go find a stonecaster.

Eaba was lighthearted. "It's like a holiday," she giggled, as she did when we were courting, and tucked her hand through my arm and snuggled close, and it was suddenly a good day, even if my worry for her was tugging at my mind.

She didn't look away from me the whole walk, and it was only then I saw that what I liked least about this *it* was how Eaba's face lit up when she saw it; the way she used to light up when she looked at me, or our babies. It was a kind of love she felt, not just delight, and I resented it hot and fierce once I realised it.

The stonecaster was a woman named Sylvie, a woman a few years younger than us, but not so young that I felt she wouldn't understand.

"You ask," Eaba said when we got there. "You're the one as wants to understand." And that was another annoyance. Eaba never seemed to care what the villagers were saying. Didn't even seem to be curious about this *it*—as though the presence of it answered all her questions, even when she couldn't tell anyone else what it was.

Well, I thought, I'm not going to beat around the bush. I spat in my palm and clasped hands with the stonecaster. "Is it real?" I asked.

She blinked in surprise and felt in her pouch for the stones. Brought them up, cast them.

They looked just like ordinary stones to me. Four landed face-up, with their marks showing. The other, a dark rock, face-down.

"New beginnings, Joy, Family, Spirit, face-up," she said, touching them lightly. Then she put her fingertip on the dark stone. "Chaos," she said quietly, and seemed to listen. Then she sat back and shook her hand as if her finger had been bitten. "Well," she said. "Whatever it is, it's real enough." She looked at the stones again, then sighed. "They're not saying much. There is some kind of spirit or sprite come to you, but what kind it is I cannot say. It brings joy."

"Yes!" Eaba said. "Only joy."

Sylvie looked her straight in her milky eyes. "For you. It brings joy for you. But for others it brings chaos, upheaval. A change in everything they have known or believed."

Eaba sat back on her haunches, brow puckered. "But why?" she asked. "What does it matter to them?"

"Because you love it more than you love us!" I burst out. "You'd rather stare up at it than do anything—*anything*—else."

She blinked and stared at me with more attention than she'd given me for a month. For a moment I could see through the veils in her eyes to the woman I loved. But her eyes filled with tears, and I lost her.

"I'm going blind, husband," she said softly. "I have loved you for thirty years, and I will love you until the day I die. But in all the world, it's the only thing that is bright to me. Would you take that light away from me?"

What could I say? I loved her. Love her.

I took her home and told the children and the neighbours what the stonecaster had said. I think some of the neighbours didn't believe me. I didn't care. I cared for her and I did her chores when she was too busy staring at the sky to notice what needed doing. She stared more and more, longer and longer, as though the sight was food and drink to her. I became father and mother, both, to our children and was relieved when they grew old enough to care for themselves and to help care for her.

I loved her. Love her. But when Vi told me the plan to stymie the warlord, and that like as not he'd take all of us councillors as hostage if we went to the square and defied him, I went anyway.

I'd like to think she noticed that I was gone.

BRAMBLE

HALFWAY DOWN the tumbled mountainside, they saw people gathering below, drawn by the thunder of the breaking rocks. Young men, the fastest runners, arrived first. Then children, then the adult villagers, more stolidly, but betraying in their bodies a mixture of fascination and fear. Not warlord's men, thank the gods. But dangerous for all that. There wasn't a dark head among them.

Acton waved cheerfully to them and Bramble suppressed a smile. Medric was excited and rather proud, Bramble thought, to be coming out of the mountain with Acton. She hoped he was right not to be afraid.

Ash looked worried, but with a touch of anticipation. "See if he can talk his way out of being a ghost," he muttered to Bramble.

"You talk for me, Baluch," Acton said, before they reached the waiting group.

"What do I say?" Baluch asked, a little out of breath. He was having more trouble climbing down than they were, Bramble thought, and she remembered the young Baluch, climbing a mountainside, springing from boat to shore, running.

"Tell the truth!" Acton said, his face surprised. "Tell them who I am and that I've come to defeat the enchanter."

The villagers were whispering to each other, pointing at Acton. Some carried scythes, sickles or hoes as weapons.

They halted a few feet above the crowd, and Baluch announced, in that clear, singer's voice: "People of the Domains, Acton has returned to you to lead you in victory against the enchanter!"

The suspicious faces cleared immediately, and they cheered. It astonished Bramble.

"It's the legend from the songs," Ash said. "The last thing he said as he rode away was, 'I'll be back before you need me.' In their hearts, they believed it, so they believe him, now."

Bramble laughed. "If they only knew!"

147

Acton sprang down from the rock and the villagers crowded around him. They wanted to touch him, despite the graveyard chill, and he let them, as if understanding the need to make sure he was real. He smiled, but it wasn't his mischievous smile, it was the smile of the commander, trustworthy and responsible and strong. She realised that it wasn't a false face. He just shifted as the need arose, because he could be whatever people needed. Maybe that's what he had always done—served other people's needs. The only thing he'd ever wanted, really wanted, for himself was to go to sea, and he'd never had the chance. That was what Tern, the enchanter of old Turvite, had done to him. She had cursed him: he would never have what he truly wanted.

The crowd grew more excited. "Acton! Acton!" they called.

Bramble was reminded of other scenes, battles, where Acton's warriors had done the same thing just before they killed. She hoped it wasn't a portent for the future. She drew Ash aside. "You gave him the perfect introduction. A mountain bursts apart, and Acton appears! The stuff of legend."

Ash scowled. "We're wasting time."

Acton put up a hand and the villagers drew back a little. He turned to Baluch and pointed to his own throat.

Baluch nodded. "Acton has returned from the grave for you, and he speaks with the voice of the dead. Be prepared. It is a harsh voice, but it is the voice of strength from the darkness beyond death."

The smith took a step forward. The village voice, may be.

Acton nodded gravely to him and said, "Where are your Travellers?"

It was the last thing Bramble had expected. Ash was as surprised as she was.

Baluch translated and the smith, a curly headed blond with hazel eyes, stared at them all, astonished. "Travellers?" he asked, looking around as if to find some. "Most escaped, my lord."

"Who from?" Acton said sharply. Again, Baluch translated.

"The warlord's men came," the smith replied. "And took a few of them. The others ran."

"Find them," Acton commanded. "They are your only defence."

Baluch translated again, but this time the smith and his people were

148

mutinous. "Travellers? What good are they?" He stared with narrowed eyes at Bramble and Ash, and she looked impassively back at him. She had no idea what Acton was planning. Medric moved slightly in front of her.

"The enchanter seeks to kill all of my blood," Acton declared. "Only Travellers, standing shoulder to shoulder with you, can defy him."

"He's mad," Ash whispered, and Bramble could see the same thought in the smith's eyes.

"No," she said slowly. "He's right. The enchanter may think he's doing what Travellers want. If they challenge him—"

Acton spoke again. "Find your Travellers. Reassure them. Plan your defences with them. And treat them well—because they are your shield and your sword."

"Stupid idea," a woman muttered. "Acton wouldn't say that. He just killed the bastards."

Acton turned slowly towards her and she backed away a little, reacting to the authority in his look. Bramble wasn't sure how he did it; his face was calm, not stern, but nonetheless he suddenly felt dangerous.

"For a thousand years this land has been divided, in part because I chose poorly at times. Division has led us to the dead taking revenge upon the living. Unity is our only defence. If we are not divided, if the people of the old blood stand with us, we cannot be defeated."

"Is that true, lord?" the smith asked. "We can't be defeated?"

Acton stared at him with compassion. "We will be defeated, my friend, if we are fighting each other. Work together, or die."

As soon as Baluch finished echoing him, he strode off, Northeast.

"Tell everyone what Acton wants," Baluch added. "Spread the word."

The smith nodded in obedience. It made Bramble's gut curl in a knot. Obedience, deference—Acton and Baluch expected them, just like any warlord's man.

But then she caught sight of the puzzlement and uncertainty of the other villagers, and almost laughed. It was so like him, to upset everything, to come back and take over, to do what everyone least expected.

"This wasn't quite what I imagined we'd be doing," she said. Ash was annoyed.

"He's heading the wrong way. We're supposed to go to Sanctuary." But when they caught up with Acton, he refused to turn around.

"Sanctuary's too close to T'vit," he said. "We have to stop this enchanter before he gets there."

"Since when is that *your* decision?" Ash demanded.

Medric moved in front of Ash and glowered. "That's Acton you're talking to!"

For a moment, Ash looked at him with hatred. Medric hunched himself, preparing for a fight. Bramble began to move forward, ready to intervene. She knew how Ash could fight. If he exploded, Medric would die. But Ash turned away from him, towards Acton.

Acton considered him. It had been a long time, Bramble thought, since anyone had challenged his leadership. Even Asgarn had pretended, until the end, to follow him gladly.

"Enchanter," he said with courtesy, "your business is spells and power. Mine is fighting. It's bad strategy to let your enemy get to your most valued stronghold. You must stop him early, before he reaches it. Or people die."

Bramble wondered which battle he was thinking of—one where he was a defender, or an attacker? Either way, he was right.

"We agreed to meet the Well of Secrets in Sanctuary," Ash said.

"She is a great prophet and healer," Baluch explained to Acton.

"We don't need her," Acton said. "From what you say, I must confront these ghosts. Do we need this Well of Secrets for that?" They hesitated, and he kept speaking. "Does it matter *where* I do it?"

"Not so far as we know," Baluch said. "But we may not know everything."

"Nobody knows everything," Acton said, his cheerful face at shocking odds with the terrible grating voice. "Baluch tells me that there is a stream in Central Domain which ran red with the blood of dead soldiers."

Information from the Lake, Bramble thought.

"Draw me a map," Acton said to Baluch, who crouched and sketched a rough outline of the Domains in the dirt. Acton beckoned over one of the young men from the village who had followed them.

"Show us where we are," Baluch said to him. The boy dragged his eyes away from Acton and pointed. They were much further east than she had thought. The Caverns had transported them a long way. Good, she thought, that would save them time.

"Thanks, lad," Baluch said, and Acton clapped the boy on the shoulder. The dead-cold sent him on his way shivering, but he was walking tall.

"Central Domain is where?" Acton asked. Baluch pointed to the map and Acton nodded. "Then the enchanter will make his way down to Turvite this way." His finger traced a route and stopped at the Fallen River.

"There's only two places to cross that river," Bramble said. "Up near the source, and here" she pointed—"at Wooding." Her voice had been steady, she thought, but Acton glanced up at her as though she'd betrayed her unease. Her parents and grandfather were in Wooding. If the enchanter crossed the River there... "That's where I'm from," she added. "I know that countryside."

Acton nodded and stood up, brushing the dirt from his hands. "We make for Wooding, then," he said.

Bramble reached in her mind for the local gods, as she had done so often. *Wooding?* she asked, but they didn't answer. All their attention was on Acton. Perhaps that meant they approved of his plan.

She had sworn not to become one of his followers. Giving in to her own desire to go to Wooding seemed like a betrayal of that, a betrayal of Maryrose. Then she remembered Ash's pouch. The gods could decide for them.

"Cast for us, Ash," she said.

Ash looked relieved to take some kind of action. He sat down on the grass and spread out the square of linen he kept tucked in the top of his pouch. Acton's face lit with interest, as it had in the cave when Dotta had cast the stones for him. He crouched next to Bramble as she sat opposite Ash, spat in her palm and clasped hands with him.

"Which way should we go?" she asked.

Ash cast five stones. They clinked as they fell. Four of the faces were up.

"Necessity, Danger, Travel, Uncertainty," Ash said, touching them one by one. As when he had sung Acton back, his voice was the voice of the dead, harsh and grating. As Baluch had said, it was a voice of power.

151

The final stone was plain black, blank faced. She waited for Ash to turn it over, but instead he touched it lightly as it lay. The blank stone, then, the one that meant anything could happen.

But Ash said, "Evenness," his tone full of dread.

"Evenness?" Bramble said. "Never heard of that one."

"It's new," Ash said, his face carefully blank.

Bramble stayed very still for a long moment. The other two, who came from a culture without stonecasters, looked puzzled.

"Change the stones, change the world," Bramble quoted, and Ash nodded. "But what does it mean?"

Ash took a long breath and let it out. "I'm not sure." He sounded light and young and a little afraid. "Justice? Equality?" His face seemed strained, as though this was not a responsibility he relished.

"So what do these stones mean for us?" Acton asked.

Ash looked down at the casting. "They mean that neither choice is perfect," he said. "We will be taking a chance either way, and the chances are evenly balanced, good and bad."

"Wooding, then," Acton said immediately, standing up.

"Because it's your choice?" Ash said, standing to face him.

"It's *Acton*," Medric protested again.

Acton waved Medric silent and turned to look at Ash seriously. "You brought me back because you have need of me," he said. "I think you need more of my skills than you know. We are enemies—I understand that. But I have stood shoulder to shoulder with my enemies before, because we were both confronted with a greater threat. And I think that is what you and I must now do against this enchanter."

"Under your command," Ash said bitterly.

"Are you a commander? If you are, I will follow you," Acton replied.

It was the simplicity of it that disarmed Ash. If Ash was a commander, Acton *would* follow. That truth was clear in his face.

Ash turned away and crouched down to pick up his stones and put them back in the pouch. Bramble expected his face to be red, but instead he was pale, as though Acton had said more than she had heard.

Acton nodded as if Ash had answered and began walking north-east, Baluch following after a backward look at Ash.

Bramble waited for Ash to pack up then slung her saddlebags back over her shoulder, in their accustomed place. She'd walked the length and breadth of this country, and it looked like she was going to walk halfway back. Her boots would be worn through, she thought with a grin, and she'd be forced to go barefoot, as she preferred.

"My family are in Wooding," she said, not looking at Ash. He walked ahead without meeting her eyes and she turned to Medric. "If you want to go home now, Medric, no one will think less of you."

He was surprised. "Go *now?* Oh, no. I'm following Acton." His eyes were alight with a vision of glory, of being part of legend.

"It will be risky."

"Fine with me," he said. That was bad, Bramble thought. That was very bad.

"We're not going on some kind of adventure," she continued, "where you can get yourself killed so you don't have to feel guilty any more, or so you can die in glory." Her voice was deliberately harsh, to startle him. "I need to be able to trust you, or you get out of this right now."

"You can trust me!" he protested.

"Trust you not to take the easy way out if an opportunity presents?" she demanded. "Not to dive into death to get away from your own thoughts?"

He flushed and looked away, and she knew she'd been right. He had been courting Lady Death in his mind as a way out of dealing with his need for Fursey, and Fursey's need for the gold buried deep in the mine Medric hated to enter. Lady Death would help him forget what the ox had said to him, back in the Caverns. And the promise of fighting with Acton had just made it easier to court her. Deliverance and glory, all in one.

But to Bramble's surprise he looked back at her, chin up. "Aye," he said. "I'll back you best I can till you don't need me."

She nodded. "Good then." Her voice softened. "Maybe by then Lady Death won't look so fair to you."

Medric grinned, a sudden sweep of humour across his face that brought an answering smile from her. "It's the first time a female's had any attraction, so might could be you're right!"

Acton and Baluch walked together and Bramble could hear that

Baluch was still giving language lessons—the names of things, the words he had used to the villagers, Domain and town names.

And they weren't travelling alone. Like Medric, some of the young men from the village chose to follow Acton at a respectful distance.

The first step, Bramble thought. He's raising an army.

LEOF

WHEN THEY arrived at the fort, Leof took Vi and the other councillors to the hall, moving through the muster yard slowly, to let them take a good look at the men training, the smiths hammering, the masons working on the defences. He had no hope that the huge, complicated apparatus of war being created here would impress Vi, but he wasn't sure of the others; it was worth a try.

He left them in the empty hall with Alston and went in search of Thegan, but found Sorn first, supervising the cleaning of Thegan's office. His heart jolted and then lifted as he laid eyes on her. She was instructing a young maid, a new girl by the looks of her, about leaving Thegan's map table strictly alone. Her voice was like rain after drought. He took a deep breath and let it out, glad she hadn't seen that first, unmistakable reaction.

Then she turned and saw him and he saw her eyes light, her mouth open to say his name and then close again, firmly, as she took control of herself. It broke his heart, an actual pain inside his chest, to see her in difficulty, but he could do nothing that wouldn't make it worse.

"Lady Sorn," he said formally, bowing. "I seek my lord."

"With the smiths, Lord Leof, I believe," she said.

"There are...guests, in the hall."

Her eyes lifted sharply to his, but they betrayed nothing.

"The town council of Baluchston," he said.

"They will be treated with honour and offered comfort," she said, the formal oath of a warlord's lady. It was a serious thing to say, and he was both solaced and worried by it. Sorn would honour that oath, and it might cost her dearly.

He bowed again and walked slowly back to the hall so his breathing would be as calm as her voice by the time he reached it.

The older man, Reed, spoke as he entered the room. "Where are the Travellers being kept?"

155

"In the barn." Distaste crossed their faces, and he was nettled. "I assure you, we have done what we could to make them comfortable, but as you have seen, our accommodations are stretched to breaking point. Stay here. My lord is with the smiths. I will come back after I have seen him."

Irritation at them went with him across to the smiths' forge and hardened his voice when he found Thegan with Affo, the head smith, and a group of other men he didn't know.

"I've brought those bloody Baluchstoners back," he said. "The whole town turned out and said they had Traveller blood and we should take all of them. I brought the council back. I've stuck them in the hall."

Thegan nodded. "Let them wait. I've been talking to the smiths and the weavers from town about making heavy weighted nets, like the ones the northern fishers make to catch the fish that are too strong for their lines."

Leof gladly dived into the discussion, gloom lifting from his spirits. Defence, weaponry, the organisation of their forces: these were what he had been trained for, and what he loved. Let Thegan deal with politics.

Sorn rose as Thegan entered, and bowed. "My lord," she said, and waited, hands by her sides.

Leof and Thegan had returned to the hall to find Sorn sitting with the town councillors at one of the lower tables, discussing, it had appeared, the music of the Lake People and how it differed from that of Acton's people. Leof hadn't realised she knew anything about music. There was so much he didn't know about her.

Vi lumbered to her feet and the others followed, a little reluctantly, and faced Thegan. Leof wondered what they saw: he himself was looking at Thegan a little differently nowadays, but he still saw a handsome, strong man in the full possession of his power. Vi's face gave nothing away, her heavy-lidded eyes blank.

"Our guests," Thegan said to Sorn, "have informed the Lord Leof that they have Traveller blood, so I think they are best housed in the barn with the others."

He ignored the council completely. Vi didn't react at all but Reed was furious, and the two younger ones showed a mixture of relief and indignation. Sorn nodded, and with her agreement Thegan simply turned and walked out.

Leof exchanged a quick glance with Sorn, and followed him, trying not to laugh. Punctured expectations were so often funny, even in people he quite liked.

Thegan turned and found him chuckling and smiled, the real smile. He couldn't help but return it. "They have no idea they have given us a weapon that we can use against this enchanter."

"My lord?"

"Not only Travellers as hostages, now, but Lake People." His tone was full of satisfaction. "After this is over, they will not be going home unless they tell me the secrets of the Lake."

There he was again, planning for the future. Leof found it both reassuring and irritating. He wanted to say, "How can you be so sure it will be over?" but knew it was possible that Thegan was *not* sure, and was just putting on a good face for his officers. Leof didn't want to find out that was true.

He left Thegan and went to check on the mason's gang strengthening the wall under Oak's direction. No time to rest just yet.

Sorn and her maid, Faina, crossed the yard, headed for the dairy. Oak's eyes followed them, and Leof stiffened. He would brook no indignity from a Traveller towards Sorn. But Sorn disappeared inside the dairy and left Faina outside, talking to Alston. Their bodies inclined towards one another. Oak's mouth tightened and he turned away suddenly, his trowel striking hard against the high stone block that was wrapped with ropes ready to be lifted, the note ringing out across the yard. Faina, not Sorn, then. Leof relaxed, filled with sympathy. No wonder the poor fellow looked unhappy.

"Keep up the good work, mason," he said. Oak looked surprised, as though Leof's words had contradicted something he had been thinking. Not feeling valued, maybe? Leof hadn't been an officer all his adult life without knowing how to deal with that. "Without you, mason, and your colleagues, we would be in a dangerous situation. Our lives are in your hands."

Leof looked around at the small gang preparing to use pulleys and rope to haul the heavy stones up into place, and clapped Oak on the shoulder. He expected the man to puff up a little with importance, or nod with understanding, but Oak stopped still, as though he had never thought of his role in this way. Finally, he nodded and turned away, trowel still in hand, to give an order to the lad he'd been assigned, a young man with light brown hair and soft hands, who'd clearly never done a hand's turn of work in his life. He looked familiar, and then Leof placed him—the one who had pretended not to be a Traveller, on the road to Baluchston.

"Flax!" Oak ordered. "We need to raise these blocks. Give us a work song to keep us in time."

The lad nodded. "Sea shanties are best for that," he said in a light voice, and waited until all hands had grasped the rope, then he gave out a note so strong and full that Leof almost jumped.

Lady Death will ring her bell
Heave away
Haul away
Call us all to the deep cold hell
Raise the mains'l maties

The men hauled on the ropes in time and the stone block slowly rose. Oak steadied it so it wouldn't swing.

There waves are taller than the sky
Heave away
Haul away
They'll crush your ribs and blind your eyes
Raise the mains'l maties

Oak called, "Hold it there," and then Leof heard the solid thunk of the stone settling into place.

Although he'd spent the day in the saddle, he felt the sudden need to get out of the fort, to prepare himself for dinner, the first meal he'd had in both Thegan and Sorn's company since he'd found himself loving her. He needed surcease. He checked that Thegan did not need him.

"Arrow will need exercising," he said. "If you'll excuse me, sir."

"You and your horses!" Thegan replied, waving Leof away.

Arrow did need exercising. She was spritely and affectionate and danced her way down the long road from the fort, shying at everything—wind blown leaves, a boy trundling a cart full of stone up to the walls, her own shadow. Leof found her innocent antics a great relief; and they kept his mind off everything else.

He rode down to the pool where he had seen the old man, half hoping to find him there again, but there was nothing except the cool, spreading water and moss-covered stones, which seemed to promise continuity, a sense of time far beyond a human lifespan. He dismounted and stayed there for a while, until Arrow grew bored and nudged him in the back. He reluctantly turned to go back, then paused and walked towards the water, Arrow's reins looped over his arm.

He stood with his toes just in the pool, feeling the cool wetness seep slowly into his boots. "Lady," he said, feeling absurd, "What should I do?" He didn't expect a reply. Part of him hoped fervently that there wouldn't be one.

But a voice sounded in his head, as though she were speaking from another room. "You are not one of mine," it said, which was curiously hurtful, because it was said in his mother's voice.

"I am in need of guidance," he said.

"No," the voice said. "You know what is right, which is all the guidance you need. If you will not go home to your mother, you must take the consequences." The voice was curiously soft and sorrowful, as his mother's voice had never been in his memory, and yet he knew that his mother could sound like this, as though she had crooned over him in this tone when he was too young to remember.

"But I will give you a gift," the voice said, "because you believe in me. Because you have tried your best to protect my people."

Something nudged his toe. He looked down and saw a little circle floating on the water. He picked it up. It was woven reeds, a simple ring as large as a woman's bracelet.

"For luck," the Lake said, her voice warm with laughter. "Just a token, to help you think of me. Keep it with you."

The water stilled, the ripples from where he had picked up the ring disappeared, smoothed away, and he knew she was gone.

He tucked the ring in his left pocket and felt a little flushed, as he had at sixteen when Dorsi's daughter, Gret, had chosen him for the Springtree dance: embarrassed and happy, with an undercurrent of fear.

FLAX

A S ALWAYS when Travellers came together, the barn that night was full of music, a complex lively music of drum and flute and oud, bells and rhythmic clapping, horn and gong. Rowan, Swallow and Flax were at the centre of it, of course, and Flax found it comforting.

"Give us a song, lad," Reed, one of the councillors from Baluchston, said to him, and he muttered to Rowan, "What will I sing?"

Rowan smiled at him and played the first notes of "The Distant Hills."

From the high hills of Hawksted, my lover calls to me
The breeze is her voice, the wind becomes her breath
From the high hills of Hawksted, above the settled plain
My lover sings so sweetly, sings the song of death

The last time Flax had sung this song was in the Deep, asking for acceptance from a group of demons. This audience was much easier.

By the time he finished, there were more than a few wet eyes. Even Oak looked teary, which he hadn't expected.

"Singing's all very well, my dearies," Vi said, "but that Lord Thegan's a cold-hearted boy and he'll sacrifice us all, sooner or later."

"Aye, that's so." It was Reed's voice, grave. "He'll not keep feeding us, not for long."

"We're not prisoners," Oak objected.

"I'd rather be here than back home," a woman said. "They slaughtered my cousins—and we've been Settled three generations!"

Disquiet circled the barn like a swarm of bees.

"It's bad out there," Vi agreed, "and we're better off here for the meanwhile. But let's not think he's doing it out of the goodness of his heart. We may not be prisoners, but we're hostages, sure as eggs is eggs."

"What would you know? You're not a Traveller." It was a man's voice, deep and authoritative. Flax looked around but didn't recognise the old man. There were people here from all over Central Domain.

"I've got the old blood in me, same as everyone in Baluchston," Vi replied. "I may not have been on the Road, but as far as Thegan is concerned, I'm tainted and he can do what he likes with me."

That silenced them.

Flax hesitated, but the memory of Ash confronting wind wraiths came back to him. Surely he could face a few questioning eyes? "We have to be ready," he said. "Sooner or later they'll turn on us, and we have to be ready. Have our escape routes planned, hide some weapons, figure out who stands with whom, and where."

Some in the crowd looked at each other, judging reactions, and Vi nodded.

"Aye," she said. "But quietly. Sing again now, in case they wonder why we've stopped."

Rowan's flute started and Swallow began to sing; it was beautiful and spare and delicate, in a language Flax didn't know. From the Wind Cities? No, something else. The melody sounded strange, too, with an unusual choice of notes. With a shock, Flax realised that she was singing in the old language, the tongue used by the people Acton had invaded. He'd had no idea that it survived. His parents had certainly never taught him any.

Then the words changed into his own tongue, as though Swallow were translating:

Water, fire, earth and air
Spirits live and spirits die
Flame upon the mountain
Wind across the sky
Water dark and dreamless
Earth in which we lie
Water, fire, earth and air
Blood is everlasting

"We're better off where we are," the old man said, when Swallow had sung the last note.

"But we have to be ready," Flax objected, "for when we're not better off."

"Young man's talk," the man said. Flax could see clearly now; he was a very old man, half bent over with rheumatism. "Young man's talk, young man's death."

A Traveller saying, and true enough. There were a few scattered chuckles.

"Old heads on young shoulders, sometimes," Reed said, and Flax laughed.

A child began to cry, and then another as the first cry woke the sleeping ones.

A woman groaned and got up to settle her child, and the assembly began to break into family groups. Some headed out to the privies.

Flax joined Oak and Vi and Reed in a corner of the room to plan.

OAK'S STORY

I CAN MAKE a wall will stand for a thousand years. I've seen 'em. Fences built in Acton's time, still there, snaking across the country like a stream. You can't build a straight wall that'll last, though. Have to follow the lay of the land, get the feel of the earth roundabout and put the wall where it lies lightest on the ground. Try to build a straight wall and it'll tumble over come spring, when the groundwater shifts with the snowmelt; it'll bulge when the tree roots feel their way through the cracks in the bedrock to get to the rivers beneath; it'll shake itself to death, slowly, with the heat and cold and heat of summer and winter and summer, over and over, making the rocks snap and crack apart, like as not—and then the wall has to bind those rocks together so that, even snapped apart, the wall still holds. Can't do that with a straight wall.

Build a straight wall, and you're having to repair it, year after year. That's most of my business, repairing straight walls. Guess I shouldn't complain about 'em then.

I know where I am with rock. Know my granite and my schist, sandstone and bluestone, basalt and limestone. Harder the better. Nothing beats a granite wall. Nothing.

But people...I have no idea about people. Never have had. Like my father, Mam said. Just like him. That's all right with me. My Da was a good worker. I've never seen a man make a wall with less wastage of stone. He could find the right chink even for a bit of rubbish—tufa, or even scoria, rocks that hardly deserve the name of stone. He taught me. Never said much. Didn't need to. Piece by piece is how you build a wall, and there's not much to say about it that you aren't better off showing.

He taught me masonry, too, working with mortar, even bricks. Some places just got no stone. I can build anything, near enough, thanks to Da.

So I never minded being no good with people. My da found himself

164

my mam, and I guessed one day I'd meet myself a girl who didn't want a chatterer, and it'd be sweet.

And maybe I would have, and maybe I could have, if I hadn't met Faina first.

Course I always thought I'd meet a Traveller girl. Who else? I'm no fool, ready to get beaten up or worse for looking above myself. And when did I meet other girls anyway? Walling, you deal with the man of the farm, or the house, not the woman. But my mam liked to visit the local gods wherever we went, and I came with her, though I don't feel them the way she did. So there we were a few years ago near Sendat, in a little village, and we went to the black stone altar early for the dawn greeting, just like a hundred times before, in a hundred little villages all over the Domains. And there she was. Fair-headed, blue eyed. Praying like she meant it.

My mam says my da made up his mind about her the first time he laid eyes on her. Takes some men like that. Guess I'm like my da that way, too.

Like I said, I'm not a fool. Didn't even think about it. Didn't even imagine...

But I knew there wouldn't be anyone else for me.

I did my job for a local farmer and we went on our way. Nothing else I could do.

My mam died the next year, and after that I Travelled alone. I had my round, meaning I called in to regular customers once every three years. Never short of business. South in the winter, north in the summer. Then this last year the call went out for wallers and masons to come to Sendat. My lord Thegan was building better fortifications.

I went because it was good money and it's better not to say no to a warlord.

So. She was there. At the fort. Acting as maid to the Lady Sorn. That first day, I was working on the new storage sheds and I saw her walk through the mustering yard after the Lady, so the next morning I was there at the altar stone before dawn, and sure enough she came. A little older; just the same. It was just the same for me, too. I don't think she even saw me. She was with a sergeant. He had a good face, that one, and tall, blond. I found out later his name was Alston and they were hand-plighted. I could tell, the way she looked at him.

There never had been any chance for me, so I wished her well. But I didn't go back to the altar at dawn. Made my visits during the day, when she was busy in the hall with the Lady.

She's a real lady, that Sorn. The weather was getting hot, and she made sure that there was small beer for all the workers, and good food at mealtimes, and decent lodgings, even for the Travellers. Alston organised things so that the Travellers and the blondies weren't working together, which made life better, too. He was all right.

But I heard that they couldn't get married yet. Alston didn't have a house to take Faina to, and her father wouldn't let her live in the barracks with the other soldiers' women. Don't blame him. No place for a gentle girl.

I heard Alston talking about it to my lord Leof. "I've got land," he said, "down by the stream, that my lord ceded to me after I got my sergeant's badge. But no house." He sounded rueful.

"And no chance of getting one until all this work is done," Leof said, looking at us, labouring to shore up the walls around the fort.

Alston shrugged. "We can wait," he said. But he sounded wistful, and I thought she was probably wistful too. "Even one sound room would be enough for the present."

I found out where the land was, and went to have a look. It was a good place. Alston must have pleased Lord Thegan, to get that land.

I used some of the things the demons had taught me in the Deep, and I scried the land underneath, to learn its strengths and faults. It's not a thing I do often. It takes too much from you.

The bedrock beneath it was solid, there was a spring as well as the stream, the earth flowed gently into a naturally level place, which is where, no doubt, they meant to build. But that place was where the spring started, and it travelled underground a ways before it came up. Put a house there and it would sink to one side in a year.

But down the other side was an outcrop of granite, which had calved enough stone to build with, and if that was cleared away there was enough room for a house. I scried that place, too, and felt the layers speak back to me, clear as quartz in the sun. Granite bedrock, solid as the earth itself. That was where they should put their house.

Well, I was a waller, and there were walls to build. What else could

I do for her? It was for living in, so I used mortar to give them straight walls (and maybe I thought I could come back and repair those walls in the future, and see her). I worked at night, after Lord Leof let us go from the fort.

I was tired, of course. Got tireder, working two jobs. Didn't matter. Walls went up, slow and then quicker once the foundations were done. I made her a good house. Strong. Facing south-east, with two windows, but none on the north side where the wind whistled.

Two rooms. Didn't let myself think about what might happen in that second room, between him and her. It didn't matter.

I made her a solid house, a house she could trust, with a chimney of river stones, all blue and grey, and a good white doorstep and a high-pitched roof to slide the snow off, because they told me it snowed mightily in Sendat. I traded some silver for slates in another village, told the man it was for my lord's work. Cut the trees for the rafters from their own land. I even put a floor in, flagstones, hard to cut. Didn't get much sleep that week. Alston got a bit short with me—told me to pick up the pace or get a whipping. Didn't hold it against him, much. He was right. I had been slacking.

Didn't matter. What mattered was, I couldn't figure a way to be there when she saw it.

I couldn't tell her. Alston was so much at the fort that he hadn't been to the land in weeks. I'd counted on that, but now the house was finished it was not so good.

I went to the altar at dawn and she was there, right enough, but—

I'm no good with people. Don't understand how they work. But I thought, if I tell someone else, and they told Alston, or her...

Couldn't think of who to tell.

So I went to the new stonecaster, Otter, down in the village. Didn't tell him what I wanted. You don't have to. He cast, but the stones were so mixed up, he said, that he couldn't make head nor tail of 'em. An empty house, he said, and a forlorn love. He looked curious, but trustworthy enough. So I told him. Not everything. Just that someone had built a house on Alston's land and I didn't know how to tell him. Didn't want to get involved, I said, but I think he could tell I was already involved, up to my armpits.

"I'll mention it to my lord Leof," he said gently. "Next time I go up to the fort."

He was there next day. I was working on the gate with Lord Leof inspecting the work when he arrived. I saw him talking to the Lord, and he was good to his word, because he didn't so much as look my way. He visited the Lady, too, while he was there.

So then I kept a watch and, sure enough, after dinner, Faina slipped out with Alston and they went down the hill together, taking the back way to the land.

I followed 'em. Heard 'em find the place. Alston had brought a lantern to light their way, though it wasn't full dark, and he took it inside. I saw them in the window, saying, "But *who?*" and concluding that it was my Lord Leof and the Lady Sorn, together, had organised it. She couldn't think of anyone else who would do something like this for her.

She was crying. That was all right. I'd seen my mam cry like that when my brother had his child. It meant I'd built her a good house, and she liked it. That was my satisfaction, right there. All I needed, I thought. Then he came up behind her and she turned her face to his shoulder and he put his arms around her.

I went away.

Nothing else I could do. For her. For me. Not while she loved him. Not even if she hadn't. Only time in my life, though, I've wondered what my life would have been if I'd had blond hair. If I could have gone up to her that first time, in her old village. Said, "Nice morning, isn't it?" as we walked away from the altar. Courted her. Won her. Built her a good house, a strong house that she could trust, for the both of us to live in.

Not in this life. Not nowhere in the Domains. Not now, and not never, probably. But I wondered. Wanted. Got angry for the first time, about how it wasn't fair and never had been. Thought, "It shouldn't be like this."

It shouldn't.

SAKER

SOLDIERS LINED the road ahead of him, checking everyone. Not that there were many people on the road to stop. Everyone who could be was hunkered down behind their shutters, shivering with fear.

Saker smiled, but his smile faded as he saw the merchant's party ahead of him sorted into two groups. One, blonds and red-heads, who were allowed to go on their way. The other, dark-hairs, kept in a group to one side, where the road widened into a water meadow.

His own hair was its customary reddish brown. He always carried some rosehips to make the dye, because they looked so innocuous if he was ever searched — "Oh, yes, sergeant, rose hip tea is very good for you, you know." Whereas anyone found with henna traded up from the Wind Cities was assumed to be a Traveller in disguise and treated badly. He had dyed his hair very carefully before venturing out of the mill. But would it fool the soldiers?

The pouch of stones he tucked inside his jacket. Stonecasters were not always Travellers, but most were. He remembered the red-headed woman from Carlion who had had Traveller blood — perhaps, like her, the stonecasters who were not Travellers had old blood in them after all.

His throat tightened as he walked towards the soldiers, conscious that if they found the bones in his pack he was dead on the spot. A sergeant was in charge of them, a large grey-haired man in his fifties. "Ho, sir!" he said with professional geniality. "Where are you off to?"

"Sendat," Saker replied, smiling. "I have family there, and they say it's the safest place in all the Domains right now."

"Family, eh?" The sergeant looked at him closely. "Who would that be, then?"

Saker blessed his years of roaming from town to town as a stonecaster. "Old Lefric, the chairmaker," he said confidently. "He's my great-uncle." And Lefric would confirm that, too, because he had decided, hearing Saker's made-up ancestry over a drink in the inn, that he was his niece

Sarnie's boy from Whitehaven. He'd invited Saker home with him that night and he'd stayed with the old man several times since, thinking there might come a time when being able to claim a family would come in handy. He was feeling rather satisfied with his forethought right now.

"Lefric?" the sergeant asked. "Bit of a drinker, that one."

It was a test.

"I think you may have him mixed up with someone else, sergeant," Saker said. "My uncle never drinks anything stronger than small ale."

The sergeant smiled. "All right, go along with you." He turned his attention to another party coming along the road, dismissing Saker without another glance.

Saker went on, deliberately ignoring the group of Travellers as he passed them.

He made it twenty paces down the road before his hands started to shake, his heart pound. Why would he be afraid now? It was over. He'd passed the test and he'd survived. It must be anger at the treatment the Travellers were receiving. But he had to tuck his hands well into his pockets and breathe deeply for more than a mile before he had himself under control.

Unlike the farms and villages he had passed on the way, Sendat was open for business. The market square was as full as always—perhaps fuller, although there was not as much produce on sale as there had been the last time he had visited two years ago. Saker thought that the farmers were not willing to risk the journey to town.

He noticed, too, that there were very few tools out in the open, and no axes at all. Had the warlord given orders to lock up the one type of weapon that would make these people vulnerable to his army?

He made straight for Lefric's house, in case the sergeant from the road, who had looked no fool, checked up on him. Lefric was in his yard, as usual, setting the legs into a stool.

He looked up as Saker came through the gate, and his face brightened. "Penda!" he called. He got up creakily and put the stool down on his workbench, then hobbled over to greet Saker. His knees and hands were even more swollen with arthritis than when Saker had last visited, but his eyes were still bright blue, unfaded. "It's good to see you, lad!"

He clasped his hands around Saker's arms and gave him a small shake of welcome.

Saker smiled. Although Lefric was one of Acton's people, he had always liked the old man. "Ho, uncle!" he said, smiling. "Thought I'd come and see how you were faring, these strange days."

"You're a good lad, Penda, a good lad, and it's good to see you. Come away in and have a bite. You look like you've been journeying a good while."

Saker glanced down at his clothes. They showed the wear and tear of sleeping rough and washing little. "Aye," he said, "I've come a fair step."

Over supper, he and Lefric exchanged news. He made up stories about his supposed mother, Sarnie, and his siblings; Lefric told him, in detail, all the goings-on of the warlord and the fort. Saker listened intently. Travellers being gathered together? Offered shelter and safety? He was shaken. Surely a warlord would never protect Travellers at the risk of his own people? Such an action would be beyond generous...He had always heard that this Lord Thegan was a hard man, although loved by his people. Could he be a just man, too? And if he were, what did that mean for Saker's plan?

The next day, he quartered the town, looking for the best place to cast his spell. With his army so large, now, Lefric's yard wasn't big enough. It wasn't easy to find a suitable place. He had to be sure of enough time to raise the ghosts, and the more he looked, it became clearer that there was nowhere within the town where he could ensure privacy.

He came back to the yard preoccupied, and was greeted by Lefric's request that he go to the coppice south of the town, to cut ash for chair backs. He had marked the tree with his colours, so Saker would have no trouble finding it.

"Save me the trip, lad," Lefric said, beaming as Saker nodded. "It's good to have family to help out." He paused. "Might could be it's time for you to settle down here, lad. Take on the business."

For a moment, Saker had a vision of what life might be like, living here, working at a solid, simple craft. Making friends. Marrying, even.

His vision faltered at that. His time with Freite had made him wary of touching any woman.

Just as well.

The guards on the road leading south refused to let him take an axe to the coppice. "Saws only," they said, and made him take the small hatchet that Lefric had given him back to the yard and lock it up.

"Aye, aye," Lefric grumbled. "I'd forgotten. Those are the new rules."

He couldn't set the ghosts to batter down door after door if the axes they needed were locked up in chests and cellars. They could get them, eventually, but the effort... Increasingly, he was looking to the fort for the weapons they needed.

It wasn't hard to find the tree Lefric wanted. The coppice was small enough, and useless for his needs during the day, being frequented by other crafters who shared Lefric's rights here: trug makers, wattlers, carvers. But at night... He looked around speculatively as he sawed at the ash tree.

Perhaps not right here, but behind the coppice looked promising. He put down his saw and wiped his brow as if tired, then walked towards the stream beyond the trees, in the little valley. At the stream's edge, he scooped water in his hand and drank, honestly relishing it. He poked at his hand, where a blister was already forming. No, he really wasn't suited to this kind of work.

By the stream was no good for his needs, either, at least not here. But a little way along there was a spreading pool under a large tree—a cedar? Its branches hung low, almost sweeping the ground in places. Under there he would be private, safe from interference. If he could get out here; if the guards were not too vigilant; if Lefric slept soundly enough.

He knew what his father would say to that— "Kill the old man. He's no kin of ours." But he was reluctant to repay Lefric's kindness with murder. "Weak!" He heard his father's voice again, and felt sweat break out on his brow. If he couldn't get out of the town, he'd need to stay at Lefric's until he could. He needed to keep him alive.

It was enough of a reason to still the accusing voice.

Tonight, Saker thought. I'll call them up tonight, and then tomorrow it won't matter what happens to Lefric.

The thought brought a mixture of excitement and terror.

ASH

THE STRAGGLE of youths behind them grew larger as they passed
each farm. They were starting to resemble a parade, like harvest
time in the northern towns, Ash thought sourly. And they were all so
young. He knew, objectively, that some of the gawking youths were his
own age, but somehow they seemed more like childer. They certainly
acted like childer, larking about and making jokes. They didn't seem
to realise the magnitude of the problem.

Acton, of course, just laughed at them.

"We need horses," Bramble said as they approached the next
village.

Ash groaned inwardly at the thought of riding, but he knew she was
right. It would take them weeks to get to Wooding at this pace.

"Will one carry me, d'you think, sweetheart?" Acton asked.

She shook her head. "Not a chance. But you're dead—there should
be no limit to how fast you can run."

It had taken courage to say that out loud, Ash thought, remembering
the searing longing that had flowed from Bramble when he and she had
raised Acton.

Acton grinned at her. "I never was very fast on my own legs. Might
be fun as long as I don't spook the horses."

In the village, Acton and Baluch went through their performance
again. Ash had to resist the urge to give them a low, regular drumbeat
as a background, because it *was* a performance. This time, there were
a few wary Travellers hailed out of their houses—or hauled out, Ash
suspected. They arrived in the town square with frightened or defiant
or deliberately blank faces, and gazed at Acton as though he were Lady
Death herself. Ash was glad to see that gave Acton pause.

"Without you," Acton said to them as gently as his death voice would
let him, "these people are all lost."

One dark-haired woman at the back of the crowd, her arm around a

173

young boy protectively, seemed to think that would be a good idea, and Ash wondered how badly she'd been treated in the past. He felt pushed to speak to her, so he slipped around the side of the crowd. She took in his dark hair and looked less suspicious.

"The ghosts slaughter," he said. "Children, women, old people, they don't care. They just kill."

She looked quickly at a group of very young children who, bored by the adult talk, had started a game of chasings around the village well. One of them had dark hair.

"That's what we're working for," Ash said quietly. "So they can play and work and live together without fear."

"A few hearts and minds'll have to change for that to happen," she said, and touched a scar on her arm. A warlord's brand, the punishment for insolence in these parts.

"Aye," Ash said. "They will."

She flicked her eyes at Acton. "That really him?"

"Yes."

"Shame he's dead already. I'd of killed him where he stood, otherwise."

"We need to stand together against this enchanter."

She sniffed. "And after that? When they don't need us any more?"

Ash touched the pouch at his side.

"There's a new stone in the bag—evenness. Who knows what that means?"

"A new stone?" she asked, her eyes alight. "Then the world *is* changing."

"Aye," he said. "And how it changes will depend on us."

Ash realised that this was his task—as Acton raised the countryside, he would spread the news about Evenness. Everyone knew the adage: change the stones, change the world. If hearts and minds had to shift, thinking about the new stone might be the first step. He felt better, having a task, instead of just trailing behind Acton.

The Voice found them horses. Not good ones, by Bramble's expression, but saddle horses nonetheless. Bramble claimed the best of them, a lumpy bay, Medric was given a piebald, which looked half-carthorse but could carry him and the feed bags, and Ash and Baluch got shaggy dappled geldings, clearly brothers. Baluch simply paid for them, and for food.

"Where did you get that much silver?" Bramble asked him.

He smiled, looking older than ever. "Singing," he said, and for some reason that made Bramble laugh.

The horses didn't like Acton at first, but Bramble took them, one by one, and whispered to them and made them smell him until they stopped skittering away with wild eyes at his approach.

"But don't touch them," she warned him, "and don't talk to them."

He made a face, but obeyed in silence. Baluch, standing next to Ash, chuckled, and Ash wondered if Acton had ever obeyed anyone before.

The horses let them leave their escort of youths behind, which was a great relief. The boys were planning to mass at the borders of their Domain, Travellers and blonds alike. Acton wished them well and waved goodbye.

"Run!" Bramble called, turning the head of her ungainly mare to the north-east. "Run, little rabbit!"

Acton laughed and they surged off together, Bramble pushing the mare to a canter, Acton seeming to will himself to go faster, and faster, until he was keeping pace easily. His feet weren't quite touching the ground, Ash noticed.

Ash and Baluch enticed their horses to keep pace, but their slow start meant that Bramble and Acton remained some way ahead of them. Medric lumbered along behind, but the carthorse was faster than it looked.

"She loves him," Baluch said, glancing across at Ash.

"He's dead," Ash replied.

"Aye, but—" Baluch watched the two flying figures jump a low wall, Bramble's hair escaping from its tie and streaming out on the wind. "He may have met his match in her."

"And what's *she* met in him?" Ash asked, and wished he hadn't because no matter what the answer was, it couldn't be good for Bramble.

MARTINE

THEY WERE rounding the cape between Mitchen and Carlion, and the captain was looking worried.

"Bad water around here," one of Zel's aunties said. Martine could never tell them apart they were so alike—sun-browned, wiry, greying. "Things happen," she explained grimly.

Zel cast her a cynical look as she filled Trine's hay net. Trine butted her on the shoulder, but not unkindly. They had come to a closer understanding in the last few days. "Sailors' stories, Rawnie," Zel said.

Rawnie shrugged. "Believe what you like. But we'll be saying our prayers till we're past Carlion, Rumer and me."

"And keep a lookout for sea serpents?" Martine asked. She was sitting on the side of Trine's enclosure. She wanted to swing her legs like a child, she was so happy whenever she thought about Arvid. He was doing his accounts nearby, sorting out how much each Last Domain farmer and crafter had to be paid from the cargo they had sold in Mitchen. He glanced up briefly and gave her a look that recalled the night before, when he had stared into her eyes and said her name as he made love to her.

Her mood over the past days had veered from happiness so great she had felt drunk, to pessimism and gloom. The weather matched her: the clouds flitted across the sun, sending them from glare to shadow moment by moment.

She turned back to Rawnie and Zel, who were staring at her knowingly. She flushed.

"Well, sea serpents?" she prodded, embarrassed.

"No," Rawnie said seriously. "They swim further south, past the Wind Cities. Stranger than them."

The captain whistled. Rawnie jumped out of the hold to run to the mast. She seemed to skip up it, moving from rope to cross-mast to belaying pin.

Zel watched her thoughtfully. "Useful on ship, being a tumbler," she said, as if she'd never realised her physical skills might have any other application than performing.

"Your aunties seem happy," Martine said. It would be good for both Zel and Flax, she thought, if Zel took some time on board a ship.

"But what would Flax do?" Zel muttered as she shovelled Trine's dung into a bucket. She washed down the deck before spreading a fresh layer of straw.

Martine enjoyed the sun on her back as she watched Zel complete her chores. But slowly, subtly, she became aware that something was wrong. The sun was on her back, all right, but she wasn't growing any warmer. It wasn't the breeze—she was in a protected corner here. The sun's rays were growing weaker instead of stronger, although it was approaching noon.

"Something's wrong," she said. "Call Safred."

They didn't have to. As they came out of the hold Safred emerged from below deck, followed by Cael. The captain was at the steering arm, conferring with the steersman, and they both looked unhappy. Arvid came from the stern to join them as Martine and the others approached.

"What's happening?" Arvid asked.

The captain pointed off the starboard bow. Between them and the coast was a long, low bank of fog, rolling silently over the water towards them. It was a pure, cold white, and it should have reflected the sun brilliantly, but instead it seemed to drink the light in.

Martine found it terrifying. "Can we outrun it?" she asked.

The captain shook her head. "Normal fog, maybe. Not it. That's peril fog, that is. No escaping. All we can do is batten down until it gets what it came for."

"What is it coming for?" Cael asked.

"Memories," the captain said, in the same way she might have said "murder." The fog was coming faster. "Keep hold!" she called, bracing herself against the steering board, the steersman on the other side equally braced.

Martine moved back to the mast and grabbed a stay. She saw Arvid vaulting over a crate to get to her and then the fog reached them.

It blanked out not only sight but also every other sense. Martine couldn't hear, or speak, or feel her hands or feet. As though she had been imprisoned in fleece, but she couldn't even struggle against it. She tried stamping her feet on the deck, but it made no noise.

Then she heard, finally, and wished she hadn't. Someone was weeping. The steersman, she thought. The voice was a man's, close by, but he was crying like a child. Martine moved, without thought, to go to him, but without any sense of her body she had no idea how or which way she was moving, and she froze in fear. She could walk straight off the side of the ship unwittingly.

Then another voice — Safred's — cried out, "No!"

Martine sensed power in that rejection: the fog seemed to thin in that direction. Having a direction at all was so great a relief that Martine wanted to sink down and collapse, but she moved towards Safred as fast as she could.

Safred was muttering, "I will not..." over and over, and Martine used the words as a home line, like the ones they strung between houses in the Last Domain in winter, so that someone caught out in a blizzard could grab on and follow it to safety. She followed the words and found the white nothingness dissipating, so much that she could finally see Safred, in a column of clear air.

Others were coming, too: Arvid was next to her, Cael sprawled on the deck at Safred's feet — had he been weeping? A small whirlwind of fog lingered above Safred's head, seeming to be drilling down. Martine's Sight struck her and she almost fainted. She could feel the hunger in the fog, a hunger that could not be satisfied. The hunger of the dark for the light, the hunger of the dead for life, the hunger of emptiness.

"I will not. I will not..." Safred's face was set but she kept repeating the words.

The captain stumbled into the clear air. "Let them have it!" she pleaded. "It'll go if you let it have the memory. It only ever takes from one or two."

"No!" Safred cried out. "They want all of them. They're not mine to give!"

Martine understood. Safred had not only her own memories, but the memories of all the people she had helped over the years. All those secrets, the deepest part of herself, were not hers to give. She had a hunger for secrets equal to the fog's, which meant that to it she was a feast. The fog would not let her go.

"We'll be stuck here forever!" the captain said. "I beg you, Well of Secrets."

Cael dragged himself up and put his hand on her shoulder. "Niece, I think you must."

"They trusted me," she said, eyes fixed on nothing.

He pressed her shoulder. "They are only secrets. You are more than the secrets you hold."

The fog crept back slowly over them, so that Martine gradually lost feeling in her toes, her feet, her legs.

"*Now*, child," Cael said, in the voice of a father.

Safred closed her eyes, and the fog enveloped her. She screamed; it sounded like a toddler's tantrum, but then it changed and Martine could hear real pain in it, searing distress.

Tears ran down Cael's face. The fog around her head darkened, became more like smoke, formed curls and wisps. Complex patterns emerged, like watermarks in silk, and Martine realised that it was, in its own way, beautiful. And her Sight told her that it was satisfied after all.

The screaming softened to a whimper, and Safred slumped to the deck. Cael gathered her into his arms, wincing as his own wound pained him. They were now only vaguely shrouded by the swirling patterns of light and dark.

Then they were not—the fog was gone, speeding across the water towards the open sea. It looked darker, but still pale, still formless.

Martine crouched beside Safred and took her hand.

"All gone," Safred moaned, laying her head on Cael's shoulder. "All of them, gone."

The steersman stumbled forward, and it was clear from his face that he had indeed been the one weeping.

The captain embraced him. "What did it take?" she asked.

"My childhood, I think," he said. "I can't remember anything before I was twelve, when I came on board ship the first time."

The captain breathed out a sigh of thankfulness. "That's all right," she said, smiling and hugging him. "You had a bastard of a childhood anyway!"

179

She waved at the crew and they cheered.

"Saf? What can you remember, sweetheart?" Martine asked coaxingly.

"They took the secrets," Safred said, without opening her eyes. "Only that. So much." She was exhausted.

"Your own memories?" Cael asked.

"I don't think so. Some small ones, perhaps." She sat up. "I can't remember the first time I healed someone," she said.

"Your childhood?" Cael prompted.

"I remember you, and Sage, and Nim and March," she said slowly. "So I think they left me that."

"They?" Arvid said. "The captain said *it*."

Safred shook her head. "They," she said definitely. "Like a swarm, like a hive of wasps feeding off a beehive. Parasites."

She shivered then leant over and vomited. They helped her up and Martine and Zel supported her towards the companionway, passing the steersman. They stared at one another with pity and comradeship.

"It was a bastard of a childhood," he said. "But now all I have is—emptiness."

She nodded, shivering still. "A great emptiness," she said. "It will never be filled."

SAKER

ALL DAY Saker wondered when he should raise his army. What if his new spell didn't work? What if they attacked the fort and then the ghosts faded, leaving him helpless?

He decided to cast the spell just before dawn, and wait until sun-up. If they faded, no harm done. If they didn't—on to the fort.

After they had retrieved the axes they needed from the fort, they would turn back and go through the town. He smiled to himself. It was a good plan.

He ate dinner with Lefric and enjoyed it, the first meal he had really enjoyed for weeks. The old man made dumplings and treacle for dessert, something he'd had only rarely—inns hardly ever cooked them, and Freite had never cooked, unless it was for a spell.

He licked the sweetness from his fingers and smiled at Lefric. When they went through the town, he would make sure this one was saved. The decision made him feel powerful and magnanimous; life and death were in his hands, but he would use it wisely.

The sky was still black. He had mapped out his route that afternoon, but finding it again, now, just before dawn was proving difficult. He hadn't brought a lantern; it was too dangerous to show a light. So he fumbled his way along the street, grateful for the chinks of light that came from an inn door, from an upstairs chamber where someone was getting ready to go to work, or making love, or sitting up at a sickbed.

As he stumbled past the locked houses, each one with its own occupants, each its own world, Saker felt completely alone. He was always alone, but having to go past each house and know he had no place there, no family, no role to play, tonight it seemed more difficult. He felt like a ghost himself, forever excluded from human company, human love. He touched wall after wall to keep himself walking straight, and each

181

touch was another place he didn't belong, each house another rejection. His breath came loud in his ears, ragged and sobbing.

He was almost running by the time he reached the last house, along a laneway that he had earlier calculated wouldn't be guarded. Just as well he'd been right—he hadn't thought to go slowly, carefully. He simply needed to get away from those houses, from all the things he would never have.

But after Acton's people were gone, surely then he could think about a place of his own, even a family...His steps slowed and his breathing returned to normal.

It was no lighter, but the clouds were lifting and soon there would be starlight to see by. The wind seemed to blow the loneliness away—being alone out here was different from being alone in a town. He walked briskly along the lane, which curled in a wide loop before it came back to the coppice.

When he reached the pool, with its overhanging branches, something made him hesitate. It wasn't a strong feeling, like Sight, but...He turned and walked towards the coppice instead.

There was a small clearing where the charcoal burners worked, but in early summer they were long gone, leaving only the smell of charred wood behind. Here he made his preparations, laying out the bones on a linen cloth, bringing his father's and Owl's skulls out last and placing them in the front row. His father would be impressed by their army, Saker was sure. He looked up. The sky was beginning to lighten to that clear grey that meant it would be a sunny day.

Saker waited for as long as he dared. He couldn't risk the ghosts being seen if they were going to fade at sun-up. But the remaining clouds were turning pink. It was time.

"I am Saker, son of Alder and Linnet of the village of Cliffhaven. I seek justice..."

The strength of the spell lay in memories, and finally he understood that, could draw on them and on the memories that had been buried with these bones: phrases of music, a particular scent, a scream. It was harder than he had expected, to draw on the memories in the bones as well as his own. It meant he had to experience their despair. And their anger. Yes. Their anger would feed his own righteous rage, giving him enough strength to call them again.

"Arise Alder and Owl and all your comrades, know my blood as your own, seek only the blood of strangers..."

He heard something, and paused—something high and disquieting, like bat calls, a sound so high he almost felt it rather than heard it. It ran along his veins like ice water. He looked around quickly, but there was nothing to be seen except the trees and the lightening sky. Perhaps it was the souls of his army, keening to be brought back from death. He raised his knife and brought it down, despite his unease.

When the blood spattered on the pale bones, his father and Owl rose up first, by a heartbeat, before the blood had stopped spouting from his palm, and were followed by the others. The sound at the edge of his hearing grew as they appeared until he could barely hear anything else.

Then he said the final words in the old tongue, the new part of the spell: "Blood and memory raised you. Blood and memory feed you. Blood and memory keep you."

The sound in Saker's ears vanished. At least his father would understand him easily. No need for the few words of the old tongue he had to use with Owl and the others.

"We are outside Sendat, a large town with a warlord's fort at the top of the hill. Inside the fort are weapons—axes, halberds, tools we can use to get *inside* the houses."

Alder nodded enthusiastically.

"This is our second big raid—we took Carlion." Saker was both proud and a bit worried that Alder would be angry he had been excluded. "I wanted to make sure we were ready for this," he added as Alder frowned. "This is the important one, the one that will allow us to take Turvite back."

Alder looked like he wanted to argue it, but Owl clapped him on the back and urged him out of the coppice.

"No!" Saker ordered. "Wait!" He held up a hand to them all to mime "Stop." "Wait until the sun is up." He pointed to where the sun was beginning to show above the hills.

"Blood and memory!" he said in the old tongue. "Remember your losses."

Each person there, man and woman, turned solemnly to face the sun, grief and anger on their faces. The light crept across the landscape and finally came to them, there in the hollow, last of all.

They did not fade.

Saker felt himself shaking inside. He had not really believed it would work... "Now!" he said to his father, buoyed by relief and triumph. "Let us take the fort!"

The ghosts understood. They raised a silent chant of triumph and shook their weapons in the air. When they stamped their feet, the ground shook.

His father stepped forward and embraced him, his face glowing with pride. Saker leant into him and laid his head on his father's icy shoulder. Just a moment, that was all, to fortify him for the task ahead. He stepped back and took a breath.

A shepherd out early saw their approach and raced ahead to raise the alarm. Saker let him go. Let the townsfolk shut themselves up in their houses. It cleared the way for the real fight.

By the time they reached the first houses, in full sunlight, there was nothing but silence and children crying behind closed doors. Signs of work just begun and hastily abandoned were everywhere—a spindle unravelling its new thread, a butter churn spilling cream onto a doorstep, a last with a shoe half-stitched overturned outside the cobbler's shop. Every door was barred, every window shuttered.

He and his men passed them without a glance. The road to the fort led clear and easy, right up to the first gate and palisade.

Over the main gate was an observation post, a roofed platform raised above the line of the wall. Saker could see officers gathered there, watching. The warlord's men lined the walls, weapons ready. The new sun glinted on their armour, their weapons.

The might of the warlords, ranged against them. Every other time, Acton's people had won. Every other time, this concentration of weaponry and trained men had smashed his people's defences, and each defeat had ended in a massacre. There would surely be a defeat, today, but it would not be his people slaughtered. Not this time.

Saker stood outside the gate, out of bow range, and motioned Owl forward. He was expecting arrows, shouts, spears from the waiting men, but there was nothing. Then a handsome blond man standing at the observation post cupped his hands and shouted, "Enchanter! Do you hear?"

Saker exchanged glances with his father and Owl. What would he do if this warlord simply surrendered? His father's eyes were hard. Saker knew what he would say—exactly what Acton had said: *Kill them all.*

"I hear," he shouted back.

"Behind these walls I have one hundred and thirty-six Travellers," the warlord said. "Leave Sendat now, and they live. Attack, and they die."

Rage overwhelmed him. Treacherous, murderous bastards! Come and live in my fort, I will give you protection, he'd told them. And they'd come, because the rest of their people were being slaughtered in their beds. He knew his people would have come with trust, and faith, and hope. And now they were to be turned into cattle for the slaughter. Goods to be bargained with.

The warlord motioned behind him and a young woman was brought forward—black-haired. He put a knife to her throat, and seemed to spit words in response to another man, an officer, standing behind him. That man was dragged away by soldiers.

Saker looked around—his ghosts were staring at him. They hadn't understood the first exchange, but the girl was clearly one of them, and the threat was one they understood.

She was crying, sobbing, pleading for her life. Saker swallowed hard. He couldn't condemn her. Not one of his own people. His head lowered until he stared at the stones of the road.

Alder pushed him hard, to make him look up. Saker stared into his father's face, a face from childhood, the one that made even the strongest men of the two villages back down.

Owl, behind him, raised his scythe, and the ghosts around him followed his lead.

Saker looked at them, not understanding how they could demand to go on. Then he realised. This was the moment. If they backed down now, every warlord, every town, would hold their people hostage. Prisoners, forever. Instead of bringing people of the old blood freedom, he would have brought them slavery.

One hundred and thirty-six sacrifices to buy freedom forever.

He closed his ears to the girl's sobbing, and stared up at the warlord. "Each of their names will be remembered. They will be honoured for the freedom their deaths have bought." Saker saw approval in his father's eyes.

"Did you think I would not do it?" the warlord shouted, and dragged his knife across the girl's throat, blood spurting out and falling in a shining red cascade over the wall.

Owl howled silent anguish, then leapt forward onto the gate. Alder boosted him up and over, where the warlord's men slashed and hacked at him in vain, then ran.

Saker stood, watching, as his men and women climbed and scrambled, hit and killed. He heard the screams of Acton's people as the old blood took their revenge.

But the girl on the hill was silent.

DAISY'S STORY

I WERE UGLY, ugly as an unkind word, my gran used to say. I'd had
pox when I were just walking, and the scars'd stretched into ridges
and holes. Bad to look on. She were kind, but she spoke as she saw,
my gran, and so when my mam said, "Oh, don't listen to her, you're
beautiful," I didn't believe it. Travellers don't have mirrors, much. Too
expensive, too breakable. But I looked in still pools and I saw that my
gran were right. My body were all right, but my face were ugly as an
unkind word.

Even when I were little it itched at me. My sister were pretty, with
hair so light brown she could've pretended to be one of Acton's folk, if
we'd had the right clothes and boots. But we was Travellers, and poor,
like most Travellers. My mam was a painter — she did those patterns,
friezes, around the inside walls of houses. Clever as clever, my mam. She
taught me: ships for Turvite, dolphins for Mitchen, wheat sheaves for
the northern towns, flowers for Pless and leaves for Sendat, the standing
wave for Whitehaven, fish for Baluchston, pots and scales for Carlion,
the moon in all its phases for Cliffhold.

I don't think Mam were a woman of power, cause otherwise she'd'oa'
warned me not to mix 'em.

I found out first in Baluchston, after she died of the wasting fever
and my ser married a tinker and I took the Road alone. I were painting a
main room for a ferryman. His wife were new to the place, from Sendat,
and she wanted something as reminded her of home, but he were Lake
through and through, and he wanted fish. So I mixed 'em up for them,
autumn leaves and fish, and it felt funny as I painted, but I put that down
to the lack of air in the room. The fish seemed to thrash around a bit in
the corner of my eye, and the leaves floated gently down — but when I
turned around to check, there they were, safe on the wall.

I were almost finished when the Voice come rushing in, all wheeze and
pant, for she's a big woman, Baluchston's Voice, and older'n stone.

"Stop!" she said. I were just about to paint the last fish, and I were cross and a bit flummoxed. What was it to her what I painted? It weren't her house.

"Stop," she said again, but gentler, like. "Lass, you have danger in your hand."

I looked down at my brush and its load of grey paint. I'd never seen anything less dangerous in my life. "Mad," I said.

She laughed. "Aye, may be so. But mixing those two...They'll be pulling up nets of leaves and the fish will be jumping up in the trees by day's end if you keep going."

"Nah," I said, laughing too.

"Aye," she said, and she weren't joking.

The Lake had sent her, and that shook me up properly, 'cause my mam had told me oft and oft about that Lake, and how never to go against Her or Hers.

So I painted over each leaf and put fish instead—a different kind, trout instead of pike, so the design would stay balanced. Afterwards, Vi, the Voice, took me for a meal at the inn and talked it over with me serious, like.

"Painting's a kind of enchantment," she said. "You call what you paint, if you paint with love. And each frieze must be a circle."

"Aye, they must be unbroken." I nodded. "That's why they have to run over the top of doors and windows."

"Haven't you ever wondered why?"

I thought it through, then shrugged. "I always reckoned it was just...design."

She shook her head so hard the flesh on her arms wobbled. "Nay, lass, each circle's a spell to bring prosperity."

"Autumn leaves aren't prosperous."

"Harvest time," she said. "Don't mix them up, lass. Every place has its wellspring of prosperity, and it's bad luck to mix them."

Well, I kept to her advice, because I were no fool, and I still remembered the way the leaves had seemed to fall out of the corner of my eye. But I brooded over it, and brooded more when the lad I wanted, a tall, strapping cobbler I met in Gardea, wanted nothing to do with me. He mooned after a pretty little tumbler who tumbled him and then left him behind without a backward glance, I heard. But I was long gone by then, because I couldn't bear to watch him watching her perform outside the inn, her and her brer, a skinny boy who sang like a nightingale.

I thought about power a lot that summer, and calling, and how painting might be a path to power, and I wondered, wondered, wondered, until the wondering turned into planning and the planning, finally, became decision.

To work, I needed somewhere I could paint a frieze that would be unbroken and stay undisturbed forever — or at least until I were in the burial caves. And that thought gave me an idea. Most caves are taken for the dead, but in the Western Mountains there are still some, high up, where no one goes but bear and wolf. Seemed to me that were a good place to set a spell down in paint.

I Travelled that way so as I got there in the summer, when the bears were out of their caves, and I went up past Spritford to Hidden Valley, which I'd not been to but I'd heard it had caves in the valley walls.

So it did, right enough. Oh, that's a pretty place, Hidden Valley. I thought I'd like to go back there, someday. Maybe even Settle.

I found me a cave was just right, with a low entrance that hollowed out into a space about the size of a room. There was old bear scat there, but none recent, so it didn't trouble me. The bear wouldn't hurt the paintings — all its scratching points, which were rubbed smooth, were below where I'd paint.

I took my gear as well as my paints up there, 'cause I knew it would take me more than a day, and I set to work as the dawn light first channelled into the cave, grey and pale. I painted, and I painted, until the light was red with sunset, and I left the brush still wet so that the painting would know it was not done yet, and I started before dawn the next morning, as soon as I could see my hand in front of my face, and by dusk it was finished.

This frieze was me, and I painted it with love. Painted the way I *ought* to be, the way I *should* have looked: better than my sister, even, with two sides of my face the same, and big eyes and soft lips and the smooth, smooth curve of skin like that tumbler had, but *me*, and I painted it around the cave until the design met above the door. But the faces weren't all the same, and that was where the power lay.

No, they were different, each one: side face and full face, laughing and smiling, serious and mocking, all the expressions I could think of, except crying. Each one I finished, I could feel the power build, feel something shift inside me. And when I put the last stroke in, the final brush mark that tied the last image to the first, the power burst out.

Ah, gods, it hurt! I fell to the ground, screaming. My face were being ripped off, it felt like, ripped and torn and seared with vitriol. I would have scrubbed out the brushstrokes, but I couldn't stand up. I were curled around myself in pain, spasms rippling through me so I arched and jerked like someone with the falling sickness.

Pain like that seems eternal when you're in it, so I don't know how long it took. I fell asleep, or maybe unconscious, after, and next I knew it was day. I got up, carefully, not touching my face in case a touch made the pain come back. I ached in every bone. When I looked up at the frieze, I didn't know whether to laugh, or cry, or purge myself. Each of those images was ugly. Ugly as an unkind word.

I touched my face then. No pock scars—not one. And I felt different even down to the bone. Beautiful. Aye. I knew it in that moment, and I were full of triumph and...I don't know the words for that feeling, but it were good.

I walked out into the early morning and though it were a grey, wet day, it felt like sun and blue skies to me. I were weak as a kitten, and it took me long, long months to get strong enough to Travel. I had to work in the inn there, and the nightmares of pain came every night, but I didn't care, because the inn had a little mirror in the stairway and I could see myself as I went past with the chamber pots or the wood basket. I were beautiful.

When I got strong I went looking for my cobbler, thinking, hoping...and I found that Travelling on your own as a beautiful young woman has problems of its own. But I had what I wanted, and I knew I would find him again, and he would look at me the way he looked at that tumbler, and we would be happy. We would Settle in Hidden Valley, and I would paint our house with happiness.

I heard he was in Sendat, so there I went. My cobbler, he were there all right, gathered up with the rest of us Travellers, there with his new wife and his new baby and though I hated him, hate him, I hope he's all right, hope that baby's still alive, hope for them better than I got.

The lord picked me because of my face. That lord, that bastard, he looked at all the girls—just the girls—and he picked the most beautiful, to make a better show for the enchanter.

So I got my throat cut because I were good-looking, and that were such a joke, don't you think? A joke on me.

His new wife weren't even pretty.

LEOF

LEOF, ON duty at the gate, saw the messenger come up from the town just after dawn, sweating and gasping, "They're coming!" A mixed band of townsfolk followed him, the ones who had no homes, or who didn't trust the stoutness of their doors.

"In quick as you can!" Leof told them. They needed no urging, moving as though Lady Death herself was after them—and maybe she was.

He despatched a runner to ring the alarm bell and he made sure the gate was secured behind them.

As the bell tolled out, all of Thegan's people, men and women alike, well-drilled over the last week, went into action. The muster yard boiled briefly as soldiers, sergeants and civilians ran desperately to get to their posts. Sorn crossed the yard at a quick walk, even in this emergency a centre of calm. Leof smiled involuntarily at the sight of her.

Only the Travellers stood still, until they were chivvied into the barn by a picked handful of soldiers, led by Horst. Leof, watching to make sure they weren't treated roughly, saw him talk briefly to a couple standing next to the boy who had flirted with him on the road. Flax, Oak had called him. The couple nodded at Horst and moved to the back of the barn, but the youngling shook his head and stayed put.

Leof continued watching as Horst corralled the Travellers behind the line of the open doors, and set his men on guard outside, back and front. The Travellers, impassive, watched the activity in the yard; and Vi, Reed and the other councillors from Baluchston took positions at the front, near the boy.

The yard was now clear again, and Leof knew that Sorn and her women would be in the big hall, ready with bandages and strong drink and, gods help them, saws and hot pitch in case they needed to cauterise a stump. He prayed for her safety, and touched the amulet in his pocket, then turned his attention back to the road.

They approached, rounding the bend below. Thegan had had all trees

192

and bushes cut back from the roadside, so they had a clear view. The enchanter was leading his army, flanked on one side by the same ghost who had almost killed Leof at Bonhill, a short man with beaded plaits, and another stronger looking man.

And there was no sign of wind wraiths.

Leof prayed that they would stay away, but he didn't hold out much hope. A shudder went through him at the thought, but he kept his face calm, as an officer must.

"My lord!" Leof called, as Thegan appeared at his shoulder. Wil and Gard and some of the sergeants followed, Hodge and Alston among them. They crowded into the observation platform above the gate and stared down the road.

Thegan's mouth tightened as he saw the ghosts. "Get her," he said over his shoulder to Hodge.

Hodge started towards the barn and Leof didn't want to know who Thegan meant by "her," but he could guess. If he were a warlord showing a hostage to an invader, he'd pick the prettiest little thing he could find. It wasn't sensible — an older man's life was just as valuable as a young girl's — but it wasn't sense they were dealing with.

Leof forced himself to watch. Hodge disappeared into the barn and came out dragging exactly what Leof had pictured: young, pretty, frightened. Flax tried to block Hodge's way, but Horst and two men forced him aside and back into the barn.

Vi's face was unreadable, but the set of her shoulders told him what she was thinking. She spat something at Hodge, and his face flamed bright red, but he held the girl's arm firm.

Leof was sweating, the cold sweat of fear. He could smell it on himself. He couldn't let Thegan just murder this girl to make a point. He couldn't, even if it was his warlord's direct order. Could he?

He'd never prayed harder in his life than he prayed that the enchanter would respect the hostages' lives and retreat. It was their only hope.

Hodge brought the girl over to Thegan. Eighteen, maybe, and a bit like Bramble would have looked at that age. She was frightened, sobbing. Even if she didn't know what was happening, being dragged off by a warlord's man to a group of soldiers was a terrifying situation for any girl. Unlike Bramble, she wasn't even trying to be brave.

On the faces around him, Leof recognised that mixture of pity and irritation that a weak victim so often evoked in the strong. But Thegan's face was completely expressionless, as he waited for the enchanter to come within earshot. He didn't even glance at the girl. The rising sun glinted off his hair and made a nimbus around it, so that he looked like a vision sent by the gods.

"Enchanter! Do you hear?" Thegan shouted.

Behind him, in the yard, on the walls, in the barn, there was complete silence.

"I hear," the enchanter shouted back.

"Behind these walls I have one hundred and thirty-six Travellers," the warlord said. "Leave Sendat now, and they live. Attack, and they die."

The Travellers began to shout and protest from the barn, Flax the loudest.

Let it work, Leof prayed. Gods of field and stream, gods of sky and wind, gods of earth and stone, make it work.

Thegan motioned to Hodge and the sergeant brought the girl forward.

Yes, Leof thought. Show him the girl. Make the enchanter see her face. Move his heart.

Then Thegan brought out his knife and placed its tip at the girl's throat.

The world went very still for Leof. He was aware of a stir among the men there, but none moved. None protested. Was it fear of the ghosts, or loyalty, that kept them silent? Or did they just not care because she wasn't one of theirs?

The moment, the heartbeat, seemed to stretch forever, as though he were poised at the crest of a wave that would never break. Loyalty was the officer's creed, central to the warlord system, the heart of their beliefs, the core of their lives. Loyalty and obedience. He owed Thegan his life. Thegan had saved him at Bonhill at the risk of his own life. He had commanded him in so many battles, and Leof had followed blindly, sure that whatever his lord said would be right, and it had *proved* right, time and again. What if he was right now? From the corner of his eye, he spotted Sorn, hurrying towards the gate, followed by Faina, and that meant he had no more time to think, because Sorn would do anything, would throw herself under the knife, to save this innocent, and he couldn't let her.

"My lord!" he said, moving forward, putting his hand on Thegan's arm. "No, my lord!"

"Take him and chain him," Thegan said calmly to Hodge, as though Leof were merely another law-breaker brought before the warlord's justice. The blue eyes were as cold as hell. As though Leof's years of loyalty and comradeship meant nothing to Thegan—had never meant anything. He had been a tool, like all the others.

"He is no officer of mine," Thegan said. "Cut his hair off."

Leof grabbed at the knife at the girl's throat, trying to twist it from Thegan's grasp, but Wil and Gard and Hodge were on him and dragging him away, hands grabbing his arms, his legs, picking him up bodily, one limb each, in that lift that is the hardest to break free from. He had nothing to push against. He kicked, tried to wrench his way loose, but three to one was too much.

As they dragged him back he heard the girl pleading, and saw Alston, white-faced, take a step towards Thegan.

"Did you think I would not do it?" Thegan shouted at the enchanter. The girl screamed and the scream was cut off in the gurgle of a cut windpipe, a sound they all knew too well from the battlefield, and it was too late.

Leof stopped struggling. They lowered his legs to the ground and he stood, shaking, hung between Wil and Gard, who were shaking too. Wil, apology mixed with determination on his face, drew his belt knife and sawed off Leof's ponytail, and threw the bright hair on the ground, where the wind lifted a few strands of it into the air, whirling it around. Leof watched it, feeling oddly calm. There was his old life, he thought. Maybe some birds would use it to line their nests.

Sorn no longer hurried. She stood in the middle of the yard, Faina clutching her arm, tears on her cheeks and staining the front of her plain grey gown. She stared at Leof and took a deep breath, wiping emotion from her face.

"We have to chain you," Wil said. Leof nodded and they trudged towards the whipping post beside the barn, past the Travellers standing in the doorway, looking between Horst and his men, who stood with bows strung and arrows nocked.

Flax glared at them, fury flushing his cheeks, and Oak, the mason, stood at his side with shoulders hunched and heavy. The red-headed councillor wept silently, and Reed's face was turned away, covered by his hand. Vi simply stared at him.

"Don't blame him," Wil said, nodding at Leof. "He tried to stop it."

Leof wondered why he said it. It was an acknowledgement, of a kind, that what had happened to the girl was wrong, but it was worthless, because Wil had done nothing.

"What will happen to you?" Vi asked him.

Leof shrugged. "The noose or the pressing box." He didn't much care. He'd spent his life under Thegan's command, keeping their Domain safe from attack, and now it seemed that all he had done was help evil rule.

"Hope you make it that far," Vi replied. "That enchanter, he won't respect hostages. We'll all be dead, come sunset."

She was probably right.

They chained his hands and looped the chains through the high hook above the whipping post, dragging his arms up painfully. He could hear in the distance the unmistakable sounds of battle starting.

Sorn stared at him, her face expressionless but her hands clenched at her sides. He turned his head deliberately away from her towards the Travellers in the barn, and then back again. He had tried to save the girl, and failed. But there were still one hundred and thirty-five more souls to be saved.

Sorn nodded. Her hand on Faina's arm, she walked around the side of the barn. There was a back door, a back gate. If she could get the guard away... *Run*, he thought. *Save yourself as well as them.*

A scuffle at the barn door brought his attention back. Flax and Oak were trying to push out, shoving against the soldiers, who pushed them back.

Flax turned to the Travellers clustered close to the door, but hanging back. "Are you going to wait here to be slaughtered by the warlord?" he demanded. "If we wait, it will be too late."

The boy was right. "Do it!" Leof called.

Horst whipped around, his face contorted with anger. "That's treason!" he yelled, and he brought his bow up to aim at Leof. His arm drew back, and Leof braced. Better Horst's arrow than the pressing box.

The soldiers at the door had turned at Horst's shout. Flax slid past them, jumped Horst from behind, dragging him down. Oak acted at the same moment, thumping the next archer on the side of the head, and the barn erupted as Travellers came flooding out, barrelling towards the soldiers.

Reed snatched the knife from Horst's boot and went for one of the archers, but he was too slow—an arrow took him in the chest and he fell soundlessly, still clutching the knife.

Horst twisted beneath Flax, bringing his arms up to break free, but the boy was stronger than he looked and held on grimly, bashing Horst's head against the ground. Young Scarf lunged at Flax from behind and plunged a knife into the boy's side. Flax arched backwards, astonishment on his face. Horst sprang to his feet and drew his sword, slicing towards the nearest Traveller.

Leof lost sight of them as the Travellers spilled out into the yard, the alarm bell ringing.

Thegan strode back from the gate, directing archers on the walls with hand signals.

"Kill them all!" he shouted and turned back to the wall defence.

Arrows rained down. Leof was protected by the whipping post at his back and the barn wall next to him, but the Travellers were too slow to take cover. They fell, one by one: the red-headed councillor went first, shouting defiance. She fell on top of Flax's body. His head faced Leof, his eyes wide and blank. There was a trickle of blood drying at one nostril.

Vi and Oak had been pushed back towards the barn by the fighting. They both ducked in behind the door, marshalling the few who had escaped the arrows towards the back where, surely, Sorn was waiting.

Run, Leof thought towards her. *Run.*

But of course she came back for him. Striding through the barn, she carried the pole that could unhook his chains from the whipping post.

"Don't let them see you help me!" he yelled, but she ignored him, moving even faster towards him.

Then the wind wraiths came, shrieking hunger and delight, and the

197

walls began to spill ghosts from three sides. Her steps faltered, then steadied, and she came on.

"Run! *Please*, Sorn!"

Ghosts streamed over the walls, but she didn't seem to care. She was braver than anyone. Braver than he was, for sure and certain. Brave to the core.

Then Thegan came from the gate, running hard, followed by Wil and Alston and Hodge, and swept her up in one arm, sword in the other. He dragged her to the back door of the barn, but she managed to throw the pole to Leof, for what good it would do, before she was gone.

Thegan didn't even look at him.

The archers were scrambling from the walls, soldiers with boar spears massing to form a line to cover their retreat. The ghosts simply walked up the spear, ignoring the shaft through their bodies, as a boar will run up it, until they reached the end. Thegan's men had thought of this, and had set the crossbar much further back than normal, allowing for their reach with a sword, so the line was holding.

Then, from behind, Oak came lumbering, swinging a halberd, chopping at the spearsmen and shouting.

Once the line was broken it was outright massacre. Affo was there, wielding an axe as tall as himself, buying time by hacking at the ghosts' arms and legs. It took a moment or two for each one to reform, the delay too short for them to gain any real advantage.

Oak was not the only Traveller fighting alongside the dead army. Living flesh was grabbing swords and bows and axes from the withdrawing soldiers and wielding them inexpertly.

"Retreat!" Leof shouted at the soldiers. "Get yourselves away!"

It brought the wind wraiths' attention.

They descended, screaming, from the wall heights, talons reaching out. Leof braced himself and stood tall, taking hold of the chains with both hands.

As the first wraith came at him, he took all his weight on the chains and swung his legs up high in the strongest kick he could manage. It took the wraith in the chest and it fell backwards with a squawk, although Leof could feel a sharp sting from where a talon had cut his leg.

They regrouped and began circling him, just above head-height.

"Master, master!" they called. "Come and feed us the pretty one!"

The enchanter appeared in the yard, flushed and triumphant. He carried no weapon, but the ghost with beaded hair followed him, hefting an axe. Leof recognised the weapon and turned away. Affo's. The wind wraiths made another darting sortie towards him, and he swung from side to side, kicking them off.

The enchanter nodded to the ghost. "Kill him, Owl. *Disgara.*"

Owl raised the axe.

"No!" It was Oak, running heavily out of the fray. "He tried to stop Thegan."

They stared at him for a moment, Owl slightly lowering the axe but clearly not understanding anything but Oak's tone. He didn't look like he enjoyed being stopped. He looked enquiringly at Saker, hefting the axe again.

"He's one of them," the enchanter said. "An officer." He nodded to Owl to strike, and Owl raised the axe high with satisfaction.

At that moment the wraiths plunged towards Leof again, shrieking. He had to lift his legs above his waist to kick them off, the Lake's amulet falling from his pocket to the ground.

Owl let the axe drop. He knelt, cautiously, by the amulet, and looked closely at it. Then he stood up and looked at Leof, suspiciously. He mimed dipping his fingers into water and drawing a circle on the back of his hand, then with his eyes, put the question to Leof.

Leof remembered seeing Eel make the same sign with his cup of Lake water. A sign of respect for the Lake, he had thought at the time. Leof nodded to Owl. Oh yes, he respected the Lake.

Owl stood for a moment.

The enchanter laid a firm hand on Owl's arm. "*Disgara!*"

Owl shook his head, but Leof wasn't sure if it was in disagreement or in puzzlement. He stepped forward and tried to use the axe to unhook Leof's chains from the top of the whipping post, but he was too short. He looked at Oak and gestured for him to help, and Oak reached up with the halberd and let them loose.

The relief on Leof's shoulders was immense, though he hadn't been aware of any pain up until then. He shrugged movement back into his shoulders and bent down slowly to pick up the woven circle of reeds. The wind wraiths had moved on to easier prey; he could hear the screams. He looked up and shock kicked him in the gut—the wraiths carried Faina. She was bleeding from a hundred wounds and as he watched she stopped screaming and her head dropped back, eyes closed. Then, from below, an arrow took her in the chest; Leof knew from the fletching it was Horst's arrow. He had saved Faina's spirit, at least.

Leof looked around wildly—did they have Sorn? Faina never left Sorn. He would drag this enchanter's heart from his body if Sorn had been taken by those monsters.

But there was only Faina.

"Your lord has run away, with his lady and his men," the enchanter taunted him. Leof relaxed. Smiled. Sorn safe.

The enchanter stared at him and Leof stared back. Not a strong face, he thought, a nothing face, an ordinary face on an ordinary body. He wished he had killed this man when he'd had the chance, at Bonhill.

"Owl refuses to kill you," the enchanter said. "Why?"

Was it more dangerous to tell him or not to tell him? Leof's inclinations ran to the truth. "Because the amulet was given to me by the Lake," he explained. "To keep me safe."

The enchanter frowned. "The Lake? What does she have to do with this?"

So, Leof thought. Thegan was wrong. The wave that defeated them outside Baluchston was conjured by the Lake, not this murderer. He kept his face blank.

"Let him go, then, Owl. *Vara, vara.*" The enchanter pointed to the gate and Owl nodded.

Owl kept a tight hold of his arm until they breasted the gate, then he reached out and gently touched the amulet in Leof's hand. It was a gentle gesture.

Leof looked at him, surprised, and saw tears in his eyes. Then the dead man looked towards the town and his eyes grew fierce. He hefted the axe and gestured for Leof to go.

Leof ran down the hill, shouting, "Ware! Ware! Run! They have axes! They're coming!" expecting any moment to feel an arrow or a spear in his back.

BRAMBLE

THEY VISITED three villages on their way, stirring the young men into dreams of glory and ensuring that Travellers were included in any defence. They learnt to leave Medric on the outskirts with the horses, because the animals—all animals—went crazy at the sound of Acton's voice booming out across the village green.

Ash spread his own news more quietly, Bramble at his side. The Travellers of each village, reassured by the promise that the world was changing, cooperated with their neighbours and began to forge a new kind of alliance.

It was late afternoon when Bramble called a halt on behalf of the horses. They had reached a stopping place near a stream, which was clearly used by Travellers. There was a pile of kindling next to the fire circle, and the ground had been flattened by boots and bed rolls.

"We need to keep moving," Acton said. "There is sunlight left."

"You can't just ride horses like you ride a boat," Bramble replied, looking him right in the eye. "They need rest. And *we're* still alive, remember. We need rest too."

Acton nodded reluctantly but Bramble was irritated. She knew he had ridden horses—well, the sturdy ponies that passed for horses in his day. He should have more sense. But he'd been buoyed up by the reception he'd received in each village, by the excitement of a great enterprise, and he was impatient to continue.

When they dismounted, Bramble was piercingly reminded of her first riding days, learning on the roan, and how sore she had been. In months of walking through the Forest with the hunter she had lost her riding muscles. Ash was in a better state, but Baluch and Medric could barely walk.

They tethered the horses and Bramble recruited Medric to help groom and feed them while Ash and Baluch built the fire and prepared the meal: cold beef and cheese, fresh bread, onions, raisins. Baluch used the opportunity to give Acton another language lesson.

By the time they ate, it was growing dark and the fire was welcome.

"How about some music?" Bramble asked Baluch. He smiled at her and pulled a small pipe from his belt pouch.

"Play that one you made up for your father's wedding," Acton said.

Bramble sat up straight. "Eric got married again? Who to?"

"Ragni's daughter, Sei," Baluch replied. "She was a widow. Her husband was killed by the River Bluff People."

Her face must have changed.

"What?" Ash asked.

"These two and their men killed every last man, woman, child and baby in that village," she said bitterly.

"They chose to fight!" Baluch protested, but he looked pale, and he put down the pipe like an old, old man.

"I thought..." Acton said slowly, considering, "I thought they would go on to Swith's Hall, to feast forever. I believed that."

Ash stared at him with contempt. "You were wrong," he spat. "You just murdered them."

"They killed one of my men," Acton said.

"And that justified killing a whole village?" Ash said, his voice like a whip.

Acton flinched back from it. "No," he said. "No. But it seemed to, at the time."

Ash rounded on Baluch. "Why is there no song about River Bluff?"

Baluch looked at him, fighting for calm. "Because I was ashamed of it." He paused. "Perhaps we should make one now."

Acton looked down at his hands. "The beer was good. Put that in." Ash made a wordless exclamation of disgust, but Acton put up a hand in defence. "No, no, I meant that honestly. They were clever people. They built good houses, they made good beer, they fought like wolverines, even the women and children." His voice, even through its stone-on-stone harshness, was admiring. "They were fine enemies."

Ash stared at him with a kind of bewilderment, as you might stare at a slug that had perched on the top of your shoe in the night. It was a stare that asked, *What are you?* Medric, too, was troubled, staring at Acton as though he wanted the legend to explain everything away, to make it all right again.

"Times were different then," Baluch said, and Medric's face cleared a little. That was an excuse he could accept.

Bramble wasn't minded to let Baluch off so easily, remembering the mixture of exhilaration and horror he had felt in that battle. He had known they were doing wrong, even if Acton hadn't.

"People were the same," she said. "They grieved just as much when someone they loved was killed."

Baluch looked at her, a thousand years of memory in his eyes. "That's true," he said. "Love doesn't change."

In the morning, Bramble was as stiff as any old grandam and every sinew protested each movement. She swore quietly to herself and went off to piss away from the camp.

They breakfasted on the leftover bread and cheese and then caught and saddled the horses, which took longer than it should have because the dappled geldings had chewed through their tethers and were two fields away, happily gorging on a haystack.

"We should avoid villages if we can," Ash said, readying to mount. "We don't have time to stop everywhere."

To her surprise, Acton nodded. "Agreed. We stop only where we must," he said, the sound of his voice sending the horses into a panic. Bramble swore at him and he raised his hands placatingly at her, smiling.

Gods help her, that smile was enough to melt her clean through. He didn't have to know that, though.

They bypassed five villages, but now, mid-afternoon, they faced a broad stream that seemed to have only one crossing — the ford at a small town.

"We need food," Bramble said to Ash. "Acton might as well give his speech while I buy it."

Acton smiled at her and Ash nodded.

"I doubt they'll let us through without questions, anyway," he said.

"Medric," Bramble said, "take the horses across the ford and wait for us on the other side."

Medric looked long-suffering. He loved to stand next to Acton, proud as a boy with his first bow. Taking the horses across the ford wasn't his idea of glory. But they had taught him to obey orders at that mine of his, because he never complained.

This was clearly a village that had heard of the slaughter at Carlion. The windows were heavily shuttered, even though it was the middle of the day, and there were no tools in sight.

A party of strangers riding in to any town was usually all it took to bring villagers out from their midday meal.

But Acton's presence sent a couple of men running off, and women pulled their children behind closed doors and watched fearfully through gaps in the shutters, leaving brooms and spindles littering the street. Only two men grabbed axes and stood their ground.

They dismounted and Medric took the horses and began to lead them away. Acton raised his hands peacefully and nodded to Baluch to start.

"Good people," Baluch said sonorously. "Do not be afraid. This is no ghost come back from the dead to seek revenge. This is," he paused for effect, "Acton, returned to defeat the enchanter!"

There were exclamations from the villagers. Bramble could hear women talking to each other behind the shutters. She realised that this was the first village which was too far from the Weeping Caverns to have heard the mountain burst asunder; she wondered if they would find it as easy to convince the villagers that Acton was back. The legend of his return in times of danger had always been strong in the west, where he had died, but not so much in the central and eastern parts of the Domains.

Then the men who had run off walked back into the village, followed by five of the warlord's men, pushing Medric in front of them. Three of them had strung bows and quivers on their backs. One of them, a blond sergeant, seemed young to have gained that rank. A villager led their horses.

Dung and pissmire, Bramble thought. Trouble.

Baluch moved to address the sergeant. "Good day—"

"Enchanters! Shoot them!" the sergeant yelled, staring at Acton. He nocked an arrow as he spoke, and aimed straight at Ash.

Medric turned at the shout and saw him take aim. "Don't!" he cried and cannoned into the man, sending him sprawling. The other two archers hesitated, but aimed and fired at Acton.

The arrows stuck in him and stayed there, quivering. He looked down at them and Bramble saw that irrepressible sense of humour rise up and take over. He put one finger on the end of an arrow and flicked it, making it twang, and grinned. She couldn't help but grin, too. The archers turned pale, nocked and aimed again.

"Not the ghost, you fools!" the sergeant said, scrambling up. "The enchanter!" He pointed at Ash, the only dark-haired man in the group.

Ash grabbed a broom and held it like a singlestave, but Acton had already moved forward and had seized the man's arm as he reached for his bow. "Would the enchanter come with a single ghost?" he asked.

The dead-cold touch and terrible voice froze the sergeant in place and Acton took advantage of the moment to snatch the bows from the other two archers. One of them ran, the other stayed stock-still, brittle with fear. The two men with swords weren't sure who to attack, so they faced down the only one with a weapon. Ash.

"I am Acton, come back from beyond death to defeat the enchanter." Acton said the words in their own language and released the man's arm; he stood back, waiting.

"Oh, that's likely, that is," the sergeant said.

Bramble noticed his strong South Domain accent and knew they had to be near home. The warlord's men of South Domain were both badly trained and brutal. The sergeant stood firm, full of bravado and furious about being disarmed in front of his men. She had seen this kind of thing too many times before, whenever someone in Wooding had dared to question anything a warlord's man did.

She stepped forward and laid a warning hand on Acton's arm.

The sergeant drew his own sword and turned to Ash, ostentatiously ignoring Acton. "Enchanter!" he said. "Surrender to my lord's justice."

"I am *not* the enchanter," Ash said. "We are not a threat to you. Call off your men."

The sergeant swivelled and aimed a great blow at Acton's shoulder. With no sword, no shield, he shifted back with a fighter's instinct and the sword sliced down on his upper arm.

Bramble felt the shock as it hit him. The arm fell cleanly off, the bows in his hand clattering to the ground. Acton just stood, looking puzzled. Her heart stopped, and thudded, leapt and steadied as she realised that he was not really hurt.

The men with swords began to close in on Ash and the sergeant raised his sword again, this time to strike Bramble. She braced herself so she could kick him in the groin and then hestitated, remembering the last time she had kicked a warlord's man, and killed him.

"No!" Medric yelled, and he flung himself at the sergeant, who jumped back and swung his sword around. Acton spun and shouldered him aside, but although the blow went awry, it still landed, hitting Medric in the neck. Acton smashed his left hand down on the sergeant's arm and the sword went spinning. Bramble kicked him in the groin, then turned to Medric.

There was blood all over her. All over Acton, the sergeant, Medric himself. It spurted out as though glad to be free of his body. She knelt next to him as he fell and he gasped for breath, reaching for her. She took his hand and held on tight, knowing it would be only a matter of seconds. Acton would deal with the sergeant.

"Thank you," she said to Medric, though her throat was so tight she could barely make the words.

His eyes were already unfocused. "The only warm thing," Medric breathed, and then he stopped breathing.

She closed his eyes, laid his hand carefully down, and stood up with murder in her eyes, rage scorching her. All the times that warlord's men had ridden roughshod over the people of Wooding boiled up in her, all the times she'd bitten her tongue or held back her blow because it would cause danger to her family, all the times she had watched and fumed and hated. She would kill him, now, and die for it if she had to.

A lot had happened in those seconds.

Ash was standing over one swordsman, pressing the broom handle hard against his neck. Baluch had the other sword, but the soldier who had held it was running away. Acton, his arm whole again, yanked the arrows out of his chest and drove them up under the sergeant's chin until the points drew blood. The two soldiers stood very still, watching.

Bramble hoped he'd simply push them through, and make the sergeant's lifeblood spurt out as Medric's had. Baluch tossed a sword to Acton, who caught it one handed. He let the arrows fall to the ground and held the sword to the sergeant's throat.

"You killed one of my men," Acton said, low and furious. He looked up at the villagers, who were still watching, not sure which side they should support. Then Acton said accusingly to the villagers, "And you let him."

Neither the sergeant nor the villagers understood him, but the words were like ice down Bramble's spine, an unwelcome echo of the past. She took a step forward, the red rage draining out of her and leaving cold behind. "This is not River Bluff," she said, forcing the words out.

At the same moment, Ash said to Baluch, "This is not Hawksted."

Both men flinched. Baluch lowered his sword. Acton paused for a moment, long enough for Bramble to wonder what she would do—what she could do—if he chose to strike. Was she prepared to die to save the sergeant? To throw herself on Acton's blade? She didn't think she was, but she wished she were. She wished, for the first time, that she didn't hate warlord's men so much. Because then she could save Acton from another murder.

The sergeant was brave, she had to give him that. He stared ahead, unflinching, and his bladder hadn't loosened with fear.

"He was doing his duty for his lord," she said quietly. "Would you have believed it, if you were him? A ghost from a thousand years ago, come back to save everyone?" She smiled at him wryly.

Acton's sense of humour reared up, as she'd hoped, and his hand loosened on his hilt. He took a step back and let the sergeant move away. "Aye, it's hard to believe, right enough," he said. He flicked a glance at Baluch, who came obediently to stand next to him. "Tell this man that I am who I say I am, and he owes fealty to me before his fealty to any other lord, because I am the Lord of War."

Bramble watched it happen as Baluch spoke. The sergeant, who had been so hostile, so disbelieving, suddenly believed. Because Acton had spared his life? Or because he had had more time to observe the ghost, and he saw now that he truly looked and behaved like a Lord of War?

Men simply followed him. They felt greater in themselves when they did. Even poor Medric. She knelt by his body and wished she had known him better, wished she had asked him about how he and Fursey had met, about his family, his work. She'd had the chance, on the walk and the ride from the mountain, but she'd been too preoccupied with Acton.

Because when people followed him, they stopped seeing anything else.

Not her, she swore to Medric. Not her any longer.

Thornhill, the fort above Wooding, was visible in the late afternoon light even from across the river. It was on the only high ground, and its palisades picked up the late sunlight in a grey gleam. Far below it, they could just make out the roofs of the town, the herringbone pattern of reeds visible on each thatch. That was Udall the thatcher's pattern. Unmistakable. The only other thatcher who used it was that girl who'd been his apprentice, Merris, who married the butcher over in Connay.

Her whole life rushed back into her head: Widow Forli, the brewer Sigi and her children, old Swith with his arthritic hands. Her parents, and grandfather. Maryrose.

They were a few leagues above the narrow bridge which spanned the deep chasm that she and the roan had jumped, once, escaping from Beck and the other warlord's men. She had died, here. Right here. She dismounted and looked down. Below, the Fallen River resounded, its spray climbing in swirling clouds of mist. Swifts rode the air currents, constantly in motion.

Looking at the astonishing jump the roan had made, pride and love and grief for him rushed into her heart. No other horse could have done it. She dragged her eyes from the chasm and looked back at the town she had grown up in. She could just make out the roof of her own house.

In old songs and stories, when someone came back home they either felt right at home, and sentimental with it, or they felt like a complete stranger. Neither was true of her. Perhaps it was because she had never felt at home here to begin with.

Ash and Acton were arguing. Again.

"Who is in command there?" Acton said, gesturing at the town. "If we go to him, he can help us get information, better horses—"

"Go to the *warlord?*" Ash and Bramble exclaimed together.

Acton blinked at their vehemence. "Even Asgarn would have understood this situation," he said. But Bramble shook her head decidedly.

Baluch put up his hand in peacemaking.

"I don't think you understand about warlords and Travellers, yet," he said. "Just take my word for it, Acton, no warlord is going to believe two dark-haired people who show up with what they claim is your ghost."

Acton opened his mouth to argue, but Ash lost patience. "Silence," he said, and Acton could no longer speak.

Bramble had had enough of this sniping. "I'm going home," she said, and she strode off, then thought to look back and say, "You'll have to lead the horses; they won't cross the bridge otherwise. They panic."

The men were staring after her. Acton had that look—a mixture of admiration and laughter, and she thought of Medric saying "the only warm thing." She was pretty sure he'd been talking about Fursey. Men did think of the person they loved most, just before they died. She'd heard enough men in the pressing box calling for their mothers to know that. But although his look warmed her, it was the same admiration he'd shown to Wili, or the girl on the mountain. To any woman. She was just another in a long line whom he'd looked at like that.

Suddenly, she wanted fiercely to go home, to see the familiar look of exasperation and puzzlement in her mother's eyes, to see her father's slow smile, to feel her grandfather's hug. To feel *normal* again, as if she had not died twice, as if she had never loved a ghost or seen the battles and love affairs of a thousand years ago.

As she stepped off the bridge, leading her lumpy bay, the men following behind, she could feel familiarity rise up through her boot soles, and her spirits lifted. In her mind, she sent a greeting to the local gods, as she had done every day in her childhood.

They did not reply.

"We have to go to the altar," she said, and mounted.

She led their party the woods way to the altar, along narrow trails used mostly by deer. The black rock altar looked as it always did. Bramble slid to the ground and led the horses to a large chestnut and tethered them, then approached the altar.

Greetings, she thought to the gods. She laid her hand on the cold rock and felt relief wash through her. They were there, they were there after all. But their attention was elsewhere, far away.

Greetings, she thought again, and this time a small spark of their notice flickered towards her. When they recognised her, suddenly all their attention turned to her.

Child, they greeted her. *Why are you here? Go to Turvite.*

And that was all. Their attention immediately turned away from her. She had the sensation that they had returned to a battle, a fight of their own, and a sliver of the same coldness, the same dread, that she had felt as they raised Acton went through her.

She backed out of the clearing and rejoined the others. "We have to go to Turvite," she said. "Now."

Ash simply nodded, and Bramble thought that perhaps he had heard them too. But Acton set his mouth and frowned. Bramble turned to Ash.

"Let him speak," she said.

"Speak, then," Ash said.

"Why Turvite?" Acton asked immediately.

"Because the gods say so," Bramble said.

He considered that, shaking his head. "But—"

"It's the *gods*, you idiot," she said, furious. No one could stir her to greater annoyance than Acton. No one.

"They're not *my* gods," he said simply, the statement sounding doubly blasphemous in the dark grating voice. "Who knows how much they know? They could be wrong."

She could see them getting dragged down into an argument which would go on for too long. They didn't have time for this.

"*I* am going to Turvite," she said. "Ash is coming with me."

Acton glanced at Ash and saw his assenting nod.

"And without *Ash*, oh Lord of War," she continued, "*you* cannot speak."

"The gods are not the only powers in this land," Baluch said, as if unsure of his own words. "We all agreed to follow Acton's leadership—"

"No," Bramble interrupted. She faced Acton and stared right into his eyes. "I am not your follower. I never will be."

He smiled at her, the sideways smile that had melted hearts over and over again, but her heart kept a steady beat. The nuthatches that nested in this glade were calling to one another, an alarm call because of the noisy humans. She had seen them nest and raise their young every year. This was the place where she had always been strongest, the most at peace. Where she knew who she was, and who she was not.

Acton stared into her eyes and gradually she saw his face change. The warm expression shifted into a frown, then into something else. She was reminded of old Swith's face as she rubbed the swelling from his arthritic hands—a combination of pleasure and pain. But this was deeper than anything Swith had ever felt. It seemed to her that Acton's pale eyes flickered with the vivid blue she remembered, as though the living man had looked out, for a moment, from the ghost's eyes.

His face showed a mixture of exaltation and loss, the expressions flowing so fast that she wasn't sure she'd even seen them. Her heart beat faster, and she flushed.

He turned away from her for a long moment, as if regaining his composure, then faced her, and smiled. It was not the cozening smile. She had never seen him smile like this before—in his life or his death. It was a smile of regret at something lost. Something precious. Did he regret that she wouldn't follow him? Was the loss he felt the loss of his life? His vitality? She couldn't tell, but it seemed to her that he had grown older in those few minutes, and it sent a spear through her heart, robbing her of breath. His eyes were pale again. He was dead, and she had to remember that.

Acton turned to Ash and gestured to his mouth.

"Speak," Ash said, in almost a whisper, as if he, too, had seen something that moved him.

"We must raise the defences of this place first," Acton said firmly.

She nodded, unable to speak. Yes, that was right, she thought. Even the gods would want that. She felt a flash of relief that her parents would be protected, at least as well as they could manage before they left.

"We'll start with my family," she said. "They're used to Traveller and blondies working together."

"Let's go, then," Ash said.

211

* * *

Although the houses were shuttered fast, the shops around the market square had their counters down as usual for evening business. Wooding had a big market square, being the warlord's town. They stopped on the edge of the open space, not sure if they should attract notice or not. In every other village Acton had just walked straight out into the open, but here...A warlord's town was different, and even Acton seemed aware of it. Bramble thought that after Medric's death, he didn't want to risk her or the others by being overconfident.

"Hey!" a voice called. They started, and Acton drew his sword. He had kept the sergeant's and had seemed happier with a weapon in his scabbard.

One of the warlord's men had taken a loaf of bread from a stall, it looked like, and the owner, a very young man, was objecting. "The warlord's son said you had to pay for what you took!" the man, a red-head, insisted.

Beck. The warlord's man was Beck, the man who had trained the roan with whips and spurs. The man who had chased her and the roan until she had jumped that chasm out of desperation, and died. Beck, the man the gods had intended to be the Kill Reborn. The roan had decided otherwise, and changed her life.

Beck was a veteran of too many encounters like this one. He simply walked over to the stall and spat on the biggest basket of loaves set out on the counter, then turned and hit the man across the ear with his fist. The man fell to the ground groaning, and Beck's companions helped themselves to the clean loaves from the other baskets.

They walked away without saying a word, leaving the man still moaning and clutching his head on the ground.

Acton started to surge forward, his face thunderous, but Bramble called him back. "What do you think you're going to do?" she said bitterly. "Even if you beat the piss out of all four of them—" he opened his mouth and she cut him off— "yes, I know you could beat all four, but what then? Those are warlord's men and there's a barracks full of them up at the fort. Are you going to fight them all?"

Acton stood still, angry and unhappy.

Ash was obviously enjoying Acton's discomfort. "Speak," he said.

"Something should be done," Acton said. "Warriors should protect their people, not exploit and beat them!"

"Yes," Bramble said seriously, "they should. But they don't. And they haven't, for a thousand years."

For a moment, there was such anguish in Acton's eyes that Ash looked away.

"We'll go around the back street," Bramble said. "And find my family. They'll know what's happening." She added, with a flicker of humour, "Or we could ask the Widow Forli. She always knows all the gossip."

Her parents' house was shuttered tight, but so was every other house. She led the others around the back and left Ash to tether the horses while she tried the door. It had been nailed shut with a board across it. No one around here could afford proper locks, so this was the way a house was left secure when the owners were away.

They weren't here.

A mixture of relief and regret swept over her. She wouldn't have to face her parents' grief for Maryrose — but there would be no homecoming.

"What are you doing, there, you?" A sharp voice, as familiar as the roses growing over the walls came from behind them. Widow Forli. Bramble turned to face her, smiling despite herself.

Widow Forli was plumper than she had been. She looked like she'd been eating properly at last. Then Bramble remembered. Maryrose had told her that her parents had come back to Wooding for the Widow Forli's wedding to . . . to whom? She couldn't remember.

"Bramble!" Forli exclaimed, and her hands went to her mouth in a genuine display of surprise.

Bramble glanced around. Acton was nowhere to be seen, nor Baluch. There was just Ash, with the horses.

Forli cast one look at him and jumped to the obvious conclusion, with avid interest. "Brought your young man to meet them, have you? They're not here. They're up to Carlion—" She faltered to a stop, face crumpling a little as she realised she'd have to tell Bramble why her parents had gone.

Bramble took pity on her. "To bury Maryrose?"

Forli nodded, solemn, pity in her eyes. She seemed kinder than she had been, Bramble thought, or maybe it was she who had changed.

"You know then? Aye, they went as soon as they heard the news, though I told them it was too dangerous."

"Nowhere is safe, these days," Bramble said.

Forli made the sign against the evil eye. "So I hear." Her old pleasure at knowing all the gossip took over, and she added, "The warlord's gone to Turvite, they say, for a warlords' council about this enchanter and his ghosts. And Eolbert, the warlord's son, too. That Beck is acting overlord!" She looked sideways at Ash. "They're taking everyone's horses. I'd be careful if I were you."

Bramble nodded. "Thank you, Forli," she said, and the woman looked surprised. Bramble remembered just how rude she'd been to her in the past. "We'll stay tonight, and be off in the morning. But if they're taking horses, I'd appreciate you didn't tell anyone that we're here."

Disappointment shone in Forli's eyes, but she nodded. "Aye, that's best. Sure and secret."

To reward her, Bramble said, "I hear you have some news? You're married again?"

"To the smith," she said proudly.

"Congratulations. He's a good man."

Astonishingly, Forli blushed. A love match? Amazing. Anything was possible, if Forli was in love.

Ash gave Forli some coppers and she went off to the market to buy them bread and milk and cheese. "And some pasties!" Bramble called after her. "Some of Sigi's ale would be good, too."

As soon as she'd left, Acton and Baluch came out from behind the shed and with his sword Acton prised off the board nailing the door shut.

Bramble stood for a moment in the doorway before going in. This house was full of memories of Maryrose, and hatred of Saker surged back, stronger than ever. He would pay for his murders. She set her mouth and walked in, dropping her saddlebags in the corner; she took the bucket and fetched water from their well.

She sat down, finally, on her stool. Her own stool, at their own table. Although her parents had gone to Carlion to live with Maryrose and

Merrick, it was clear the house was well kept. Her grandfather must have stayed here, or come back for frequent visits. That made sense. He'd never liked towns anymore than she did. She blinked back tears. Time to get on with the job.

"How do you say 'new beginning' in their language?" Acton asked Baluch, catching her thought.

She left them repeating words like "peace" and "justice," and went into the room she and Maryrose had shared. Her mother had kept it as it was, except that there was a new cover on Maryrose's old bed. Her mother had woven it—she recognised the pattern as one her mother had been working on in the year Bramble left home.

That made her want to cry, suddenly, but she forced the tears back and fed her anger instead. Saker would suffer. She would turn the knife in the wound, herself, and make sure.

MARTINE

WITH A good following wind, they came to Turvite faster than Martine had dared to hope for, and found other ships heading the same way. Safred was still keeping to her bed; she shook every time she tried to stand up, and Cael spent most of his time sitting on a stool next to her, keeping watch. He seemed a little stronger after days on the water, and Martine hoped against hope that his wound would heal after all.

"That's Eni's colours," Arvid said, shielding his eyes from the afternoon sun so he could sight the two-master a league or two ahead of them. It was just about to make the tack into the narrow entrance to Turvite harbour. He turned to look astern, where a three-masted galley rowed. "And those are Coeuf's."

"You haven't displayed your colours," Martine said.

Arvid grinned. "I didn't bring them with me. Didn't think of it, to tell truth. I was just going on a trading trip to Mitchen, remember?" He ran a hand through his brown hair and frowned. "Someone must have sent out the muster for the warlords' council. It's always held in Turvite."

There was a note in his voice she hadn't heard before, a mixture of wariness and distaste. "You don't like the council?"

It was a daring thing for a commoner to ask a warlord, but he didn't seem to notice that. He seemed to view her as his equal. She found herself testing him like this all the time, trying to find out, once for all, if he really believed in Valuing or was just mouthing the words. He hadn't failed, even a little bit, not once. She should stop doing it.

He sidestepped the question. "I wasn't brought up to politics. It's different in the Last Domain. We're so isolated that we're all in it together. There are very few officers' families, and most of them have intermarried with merchants and farmers and even crafters. We don't stand on ceremony much."

Martine imagined what it was like, going from that to a warlords' council, with its rigid and exacting etiquette, its precise gradings of status and worth...And he was so young, much younger than the other warlords she knew of.

She slipped a hand through his arm and hugged it to her, the most spontaneous show of affection she'd given him in public. "You'd better not be seen with me," she said. "I'd destroy your standing completely."

He went still, avoiding her eyes, and she realised that this was something he'd thought about, had already made a decision on. Her mouth went dry. This was the moment when he would say, "I'm sorry, but you're right..." Because the truth was that warlord and Traveller just couldn't be together, and this time on the ship was stolen time, honeyed time, like childhood summer days that seemed to stretch on forever but had to end in darkness.

He picked up a short length of rope from a barrel in front of them, and started twisting it in his hands, as though he wanted a reason not to look at her.

That was when she realised that she *did* love him, because instead of being angry about it, she wanted to make it easier for him, even if her heart felt that it was splitting in two.

"It's all right," she said, letting go of his arm. "I understand. You have a job to do. The council is more important—"

He turned to face her, grabbing at her hand, his mouth set stubbornly.

"I will not deny you," he said furiously. "If what we are building in the north means anything, then I *must* not deny you. Let them say whatever they want—I am the warlord, I will do as I choose!"

She stared at him for a moment, astonished, and then laughed, helplessly laughed until she sank down on the deck, gasping. He stared at her in bewilderment.

"Meet arrogance with more arrogance?" she managed to say. "Protect equality by demanding respect for your rank?"

A smile tugged at the corners of his mouth and he raised his head in a parody of a proud officer. "Ex-actly," he said, exaggerating each sound. "Pre-cisely."

"Let's hope it works," she said.

He stared at her, as if suddenly uncertain, running the length of rope through his hands. "So...you will stand with me?"

It wasn't ex-actly, pre-cisely a marriage proposal, which was good because she wasn't ready for one yet. But it was a big thing, a large question. It would change her life forever. She should think it over sensibly before she gave him her answer.

"Of course I will," she said.

LEOF

LEOF RAISED the alarm well enough for some of the people of Sendat to run. But not all. Not even most.

The ghosts didn't chase the ones who ran. Perhaps they thought they'd have time later to track and slaughter them. Perhaps they were right. If no one could stand against them, nowhere was safe.

Leof stopped running, and stood in the middle of an open field of hay, hay that should be harvested, and let the sweat cool on his back and neck.

He had nothing. Was nothing.

He sank to the ground and sat cross legged, his head hanging. No longer an officer. Forsworn. A traitor. Without allegiance, or family, because his family was cut off from him now, for their own safety. Without home, or goods, or even a horse. He had a sword he was no longer permitted to use, a small pouch of silver, and a woven ring of reeds.

Should he go to the Lake? The Lake, alone, could keep her people safe from the ghosts, he was sure. He thought he would be welcomed there, but what would he do? Learn to fish?

With everything else taken away, there was only one place he wanted to be—within sight of Sorn.

Sorn was on her way to Turvite.

A free town, where traitors were protected.

He might catch a glimpse of her there, make sure she was safe. Make sure she was still alive.

He picked up a handful of dirt and let it run through his fingers. It was good soil, in Central Domain. Full of life. He didn't want to see it become a wasteland peopled only by ghosts. He could offer his services to the Turvite Council, to other warlords even. He could still fight.

Leof dusted off his hands and stood up, his head swimming a little. He hadn't eaten for a while, or drunk...There was a stream nearby. He went to it and drank, then took the reed ring from around his neck and held it in his hand. "Lady?" he said, not expecting a reply.

He remembered her last answer: *If you will not go home to your mother, you must take the consequences.* Going home to his mother was no longer possible, not if he wanted to keep her safe.

"I can't go home to my mother now, Lady," he said. "I am a traitor. Should I go to Turvite?" But this time there was no answer. Perhaps he had exhausted her patience, or maybe the answer was so obvious she didn't need to give it.

It was a long way to Turvite, so he stole a horse, one of Thegan's breeding stock from a farm across the valley. It was a good mare, by Acton out of Dancing Shoes. Not as good as Arrow, but fresh. He took a spare mount, a chestnut gelding, so he would lose as little time as possible. He wished he could have taken Arrow, but he knew she would have been taken by Thegan's party.

He stole saddle and tack as well, from the empty stable block. The farm workers were holed up in the strongest part of the farmhouse, behind shutters and bars. He saddled the horse and rode up to the door. He could at least give them a warning.

"Take the horses and go to Turvite," he yelled. "My lord Thegan will meet you there."

An eye peered out from a crack in the shutters. "My lord Leof?"

"The ghosts have taken the fort," he said. "Make your escape while you can. Take the horses to Turvite and my lord will be pleased."

The eye stared at him, and he was suddenly conscious of his short hair, blowing across his face.

"The fort's gone?" The man's tone was incredulous, as though he couldn't imagine it.

"Aye," Leof said. "And the ghosts have tools, now, axes." The eye disappeared and he heard a flurry of activity start inside. "Be safe!" he yelled, and he kicked the mare into a canter, down the wide grassy ride to the back road which led south. The main road would be choked with those who were fleeing Sendat. He hoped enough people had got out for that to be true. Or else there was no good that had come from his betrayal of his lord.

SAKER

HIS NAME was Oak. He was a man about Saker's age, dark haired and thick-shouldered, with grey eyes that burned.

"I want to join you," he said. "It shouldn't be like this."

Saker nodded. Oak was talking about the bodies around them — bodies with dark hair like his, who had been slaughtered by Thegan's men, cut down by arrows, most of them. They were being collected and reverently prepared for burying by some of the ghosts. The rosemary bushes in the kitchen garden were almost stripped bare; and they'd had to send a party to the coppice to collect enough pine sprigs.

"We all want to fight. Take back what was ours."

A group stood behind Oak — about thirty people. All that they could save of the Travellers in the barn, although Oak had told him that some had escaped before the ghosts stormed the walls.

Saker was filled with elation. This was what he had hoped for, dreamt of: his people, joining him in the fight. Living comrades, fighting for justice.

Tears came to his eyes. "You are welcome," he said. He clasped arms with Oak and then turned to the others, a mixed group of men and women, all ages from fifteen to sixty. "We've taken over the warlord's hall. Go find yourselves food and drink. Tomorrow we bury our dead and then we march."

They stood together in the muster yard in the red, dying light of dusk and used one of the warlord's men, a young officer named Wil, to get the blood they needed. Oak had found him hiding in the barn loft.

"Blood and memory," Saker said as he wielded the knife, trying not to remember Freite with her knife, trying to convince himself that this was no different to killing in battle. It was the first time he had killed a

221

human with his own hands. The man was his own age and some quirk had also given him hazel eyes. He was on his knees, not pleading, his head up. But his eyes showed white as Saker raised the knife.

"Gods of field and stream," he began, "gods of sky and wind, gods of earth and stone—"

His father, impatient, seized the knife from Saker's hand and slashed it across the boy's arm. The blood welled up, not pulsing, but streaming steadily. It would last long enough for each ghost to taste, or touch, or whatever they pleased.

Saker heard again, at the edge of his hearing, the thin, high keening he had heard as he had called up the ghosts in the coppice. No one else, not even his father, seemed to hear it. There were others, he thought, whose bones he'd not found, who watched them and wanted to join their fight. It was their grief he heard when the spell was loosed.

Alder dipped a finger in the man's blood and drew a line across his forehead. It stood out startlingly dark against his pale skin. Owl followed suit.

Saker swallowed. His father should have left the knife stroke to him. But he said nothing and turned to the ghosts, who were queuing for their share of blood.

"Blood *and* memory," he said to them as they walked past. Most chose to mark their faces, like Alder, but some bent and licked at the blood. The officer shuddered at each touch.

There were hundreds, and by the end, when the sun was almost gone, the last of them were hustling to claim their share, so that the man was pulled this way and that, his blood smeared uselessly on the ground. He fainted, moaning, his face as pale as theirs.

And then the sun disappeared.

For a moment, only a moment, Saker found part of himself hoping that it hadn't worked, that they wouldn't have to go on, day after day, finding blood, sacrificing.

Saker waited a heartbeat, two, three. The ghosts stopped moving, turned their faces to the west. But they did not fade.

His father slapped Saker on the back, smiling, and Owl nodded at both of them, his face intense with satisfaction.

Alder indicated the land below them, spreading his arm wide, and Saker grinned.

"Yes," he said, "we take back all of it. Starting with Turvite."

How wonderful it was to finally talk to someone freely—to be honest, truly himself. Saker tried to remember the last time he had been able to tell the truth. He thought it was when he'd warned that officer's daughter against Freite. A long, long time ago.

He discussed it with Oak, over a dinner of fine roast kid and carrots, strawberries from the garden, clotted cream and honey. It gave him great satisfaction to sit in the warlord's chair and drink mead out of an actual glass goblet.

And to discuss conquest with a friend of the old blood was a joy he had anticipated for a very long time.

"Turvite's the key," he said, leaning to fill Oak's glass again. "It always has been, which is why Acton wanted it."

Oak nodded, reflecting. "Lot of people in Turvite."

"It's the only way. Otherwise they will regroup and take it back from us. If we wipe them out, our people can live in peace and plenty."

"There's some good folk, though," Oak replied, "with Acton's blood."

Saker scoffed. "So tell me how to sort them out from the other kind, and I'll save them. I've thought this through, Oak. There's no other way."

Oak looked thoughtful and downed the last of his drink.

"Get some sleep," Saker said. "Early rise tomorrow."

He slept in the warlord's bed, which smelt still of the Lady—gardenias and roses. Saker dreamt of gardens torn apart by wind wraiths, and woke in the hour before dawn, that high, ominous shrilling in his ears, ready to provide more blood for his army. But by the time he got out to the muster yard in the grey light, Owl and his father had already bled two victims dry, a blonde dairymaid and a saddler.

Saker watched the ceremony with a sinking feeling in his gut. They hadn't bothered with a prayer to the gods, and no one was reminding the ghosts of blood and memory. It was far more businesslike than the day before, with two orderly lines that meant no one had to hustle for their share. All arranged without him.

As the saddler slumped back on the ground, dead, Saker saw something move out of the corner of his eye — a tall, sinuous shape. He spun, mouth open to call an alarm, but there was nothing there except an aspen, shivering in the dawn wind. He shivered too. An illusion. Nothing more.

His army was getting ready to march.

He wondered, for the first time, whether he had the power to break the spell and send the ghosts back to the grave.

ASH

THE WARLORD'S men slammed both doors open just after dawn. They came in two groups, yelling, "Out, the lot of you!", waking Ash from the deepest sleep he'd had since Oakmere. He roused instantly, rolled out of bed and jumped through the window; but they were outside, too, and grabbed him roughly, dragging him around to the front door where the officer stood.

He had just enough sense not to fight back. They threw him on the ground and he rolled to his knees, hands ready, just in case. But there were at least ten men, and he had no chance; they held boar spears and bows, as well as swords. He didn't even have his belt knife. He'd taken his belt off the night before, wanting for once to sleep comfortably, and feeling safe in Bramble's house. That had been stupid, although it had probably saved his life — he'd have used the knife, if he'd had it, and he'd be dead by now.

They threw Bramble down after him. She grimaced at him and wiped a smear of blood away from her mouth. She'd fought, then.

The River reached to him, sensing his fear. *"Beloved?"* She said.

"I am here," Ash replied, calmed by Her touch.

"Stay alive," She ordered, with a flicker of humour.

"Good idea," he answered in kind, and She laughed and retreated, as though She trusted him to deal with this current danger. It gave him confidence.

The officer was a man in his forties, maybe, with a small beard, and a hard voice. "Travellers," he said, "you are fortunate. The warlord has decided to give you shelter at the fort."

"Shelter from what?" Ash asked.

"From those who would take revenge against all dark-haired folk because of your enchanter's evil." He said it like he didn't believe it. Like he didn't care if it were true or not.

Bramble drew a breath and one of the warlord's men looked at her with some interest. That look was unmistakable. Where in the cold hell was Acton?

"Beck!" a voice called from inside. "There's another one!"

Bramble flashed a look at Ash and he wondered what she meant, then remembered. *Beck.* He'd heard that name. The Well of Secrets had named Beck as the man whom the gods had intended to be the Kill Reborn. A man of mixed blood, as Bramble was.

Baluch walked out the door, hands spread wide to show that he was weaponless, followed by a couple of men who were clearly not sure whether Baluch was a Traveller. He looked strange enough, it was true, in his leggings and tunic, his plaits hanging around his face. But he had blue eyes, the particular blue that you only got with no trace of the old blood, and that might save him.

"Beck, is it?" Baluch asked, his beautiful voice taking on a tone of authority, as an officer's would in these circumstances.

"Second in command at Thornhill fort, in temporary command in my lord's absence," Beck answered immediately, responding to the tone.

Baluch nodded. "I hope you have good reason for rousting us from our beds."

"My lord's orders. All Travellers come to the fort." There was no room for negotiation in that voice. "Everyone with Traveller blood in them, Settled or not," Beck added, to make it clear that Bramble living in a cottage didn't make her safe.

Ash could see the pattern, suddenly. There was a song from four centuries ago, "The Red-headed Lord," told the story of a warlord who took his enemy's children as hostages to prevent a massacre.

"Hostages," he said, the refrain of the song running through his head. "You want us as hostages."

"What my lord wants with you is no one's business but his," Beck said, and gestured to his men to haul Ash and Bramble to their feet.

"Your lord is wrong." Acton's voice had come from the corner of the house. Dark and grating and terrible, it was as though Ash heard the voice of the dead for the first time, inspiring the terror of death. Acton had spoken in the modern language—a fast learner, Ash thought, or Baluch had taught him the words he would most likely need.

The warlord's men whirled, then stopped, faltering, as they saw Acton.

"Stand fast!" Beck snapped. The men settled into formation, clutching their weapons.

Acton held his sword, the one he had taken from the sergeant who had killed Medric, and it looked menacing against his white hands and white chest.

"Your lord is wrong," Acton repeated. He took a step forward and the men started to back away slowly; he kept one eye on Beck, who had drawn his own sword.

"Where are the rest of you?" Beck asked, circling for a better approach.

"You don't recognise me," Acton said gently. "I have been gone a thousand years, but I'm back now."

Beck stared at the ghost before him. "Impossible," he said, finally.

Acton needed no translation—the tone was clear. He smiled.

"You're not Acton," Beck said loudly, for the benefit of his men. "You're an imposter trying to sow discord." He smiled back at them. "You—" he spaced the words for effect—"are a creature of the enchanter's."

The men firmed in their ranks, gripping their spears and swords more tightly.

"No matter who I am," Acton said, "I resist the enchanter, and I advise you to do the same."

"We are—"

"Hostages won't work," Bramble cut in. She stood up and took a step forward, facing Beck down. "The enchanter kills Travellers who get in his way."

Acton came forward, sword point on the ground, Baluch next to him, ready to translate.

"The enchanter will sacrifice these people if he has to, for all Travellers. Instead of holding them hostage, you should be begging these people to save you." Baluch translated so fast that it was as though he were Acton's echo.

Beck looked disbelieving, but a murmur came from the men. "And how can they save us?" he asked.

"Stand together with them in defence. Let them convince the enchanter

227

that they doen't need his help. That they are strong and respected and safe in this town."

"Hah!" Bramble scoffed, and Beck flicked her a glance of dislike.

"You must make them your shield and sword," Acton insisted, speaking the modern words himself.

"I will make them our shield," Beck said. "As my lord ordered." He gestured to Ash and Bramble. "Take them to the fort."

Acton smiled and stood next to Bramble. There was something in his face that made Ash shiver. Something primitive. For the first time, Ash felt in his gut that Acton was a thousand years dead, because the light in his eyes, his willingness to slaughter with a smile on his face, came from another time. And it was clear, from the way he stood, that he would protect Bramble at the cost of a hundred lives.

Ash was filled with a vast impatience. Beck's men didn't deserve to die because their officer was too hard-headed to submit to fate.

"Do you want to die?" Ash exclaimed. He pointed at Acton. "Don't you understand? That's *Acton*. Alive he could have crushed each one of you. But he's dead. He has a sword and he *cannot be killed*. Lay one hand on her and he'll slaughter the lot of you."

The men backed away but Beck grabbed Ash, pointing a knife at his gut. "Which is why we need hostages," he said.

For a long moment no one moved. Then Beck turned to Acton. Ash kicked Beck in the groin and as the man bent over in pain he brought up joined hands fast under his chin, snapping Beck's head back. The warlord's man fell, retching.

Ash stepped back, panting a little, Beck's knife in his hand. He knelt by Beck's side and held the knife in the same place Beck had used on him, under the ribs ready to strike up at the heart. His hand shook with the desire to push it in. But this wasn't a decision he could make on his own. He looked up at Bramble. Her eyes were hard with hatred, too, but she shook her head, flicking her eyes at the other men, poised now to attack. The River touched his mind again as if sensing his turmoil. *Stay alive.*

"I could kill him," Ash said slowly, for the benefit of the men. "But we are not here to kill." He stood up and tucked the knife into his belt. Beck vomited again and rolled up onto his knees, then climbed to his feet, wiping his face.

He looked at Ash, a long measuring look that marked Ash down for later retribution.

"I could kill all of you," Acton said. "But we're not here to kill."

It gave Ash a jolt of satisfaction to hear Acton follow his lead. Acton had been telling the truth, earlier—he was prepared to follow if someone else led. But they had reached an impasse, and Ash didn't know how to break it.

Bramble walked over to Beck and spoke quietly to him. "You have the old blood in you, just like me," she said.

Beck's face went blank and he shook his head. No, not true: Ash could see the thoughts hitting him, making him shake a little. "You're lying," he said.

Bramble said, "The Well of Secrets told us."

He dragged a breath in and held it, then let it out slowly, fighting for calm, to not let his men see his reaction. It was as though Bramble had told him something he had always feared. Then his face hardened. "Acton or not, I take these Travellers to the fort."

"We'll go," Bramble said, and then to Acton and Ash, "there may be someone with more sense up there."

Beck waved his men back to let them walk freely. The men were visibly relieved.

As they walked up to the fort, through the busy market square, the centre of all eyes, Acton grinned at Ash. "So," he said, "you're a warrior as well as an enchanter."

"No," Ash said quietly. "I've been a killer. And sometimes I'm a safeguarder. But I'm not a warrior, and I never will be."

The townsfolk followed them, drawn by the sight of Acton, not knowing if he were a messenger from the enchanter, or an advance scout for an army.

At the gate of the fort, with guards outside and inside, Ash felt his stomach churn. To be escorted into a fort by warlord's men was a verse from a song which ended on the gibbet. The soldiers unbarred the gate at Beck's order and it swung open slowly.

As Ash readied to walk forward, one of the soldiers looked up over Ash's shoulder to the sky, and horror twisted his face.

"Run!" he screamed and ran inside the fort, throwing his spear to the ground.

They all spun around.

Wind wraiths. Gods preserve them. Wind wraiths were arrowing their way across the sky, turning and dipping and dancing with joy. Ash was flooded with shame. Were these the wraiths he had sent south unintentionally, from the cliffs above Golden Valley? Had he saved himself then at the cost of other lives? He had saved Flax and Horst, too, he reminded himself, but the shame stayed, mixed with fear as the wraiths came closer to the fort.

They circled high above, shrieking down to them. "Our master has conquered the central fort and we have feasted! Soon, soon, we feast here, humans!"

They cackled and played in the air before disappearing north, towards Central Domain. The silence they left behind was broken by one of the men sobbing.

"He has broken the compact," Baluch said, his voice shaking.

"He commands spirits as well as ghosts in his army," Acton said, not seeming to understand what the compact meant. But the thought that a human being had deliberately invited wind wraiths to feast on other humans made Ash want to retch.

"Sendat has fallen," Bramble said slowly. She looked up at Beck, who was white around the eyes but who stood firmly, not showing fear to his men. "Did Thegan have hostages?"

Beck nodded.

"Much good it did him," said Bramble. "I hope the wind wraiths ate his heart out."

Ash shivered. There was a terrible intensity to Bramble's eyes. She hated Thegan—it was his men who had tried to kill her in Golden Valley, when she and Ash first met.

Acton came forward and stood in front of Beck.

"Hostages are useless, it seems. Work with your Travellers and you may survive."

"Why would they stand with us?" he asked. "If I were them—" He stopped, unable to frame the words.

Ash felt the weight of the pouch at his belt grow suddenly heavier, as if the stones wanted to remind him of their presence. "I can convince them," he said. "Let me talk to them."

* * *

The warlord's house had fine stone steps and Ash stood on them, Beck by his side, while the soliders chivvied a small crowd of Travellers from one of the outbuildings to stand in front of them. Behind, the townsfolk clustered at the gate.

Acton and Baluch stood behind Ash, but Bramble slid away from them as they climbed the steps and joined the crowd.

Ash had never made a speech before, but he'd performed often enough, and seen his parents control a crowd.

He took the pouch from his belt and held it up. "I am a stonecaster," he said, realising that it was the first time he had said those words. "And in this pouch is a new stone."

A shock ran through the crowd like a drum roll. He could feel the River listening, and he knew that the gods were leading him.

"Change the stones, change the world," he said as the murmurs quietened. He let his voice build, as his mother would at the climax of a song. "The stones have spoken. It is time for us to change the world."

LEOF

IN THE shadows of the enchanter's progress, Leof made mental notes about the ghost army's numbers, groups, skills. He was an officer, trained in scouting and assessing an enemy, and knew they would want that information in Turvite. So Leof curbed his desire to just ride until he reached the city where he was sure Thegan had taken Sorn.

But they were a rabble, not an army. Their only show of organisation was at dusk and dawn, when a ceremony took place in which they queued for something. Leof couldn't get close enough to see exactly what.

More worrying was the number of Travellers who had already joined their ranks. Two hundred, maybe, men and women and children. Leof suspected that many didn't want to fight, but felt safer with the ghosts than they did with Acton's people; and who could blame them?

He rode across country to avoid the hordes of people fleeing along the roads, streaming in every direction, but mostly towards Turvite. Carlion was closer, but clearly no one trusted that it was safe. Turvite would need warning, he decided, that it was about to receive a domain's worth of visitors, hungry and probably without any silver to pay their way. And for how long?

Cross country on a decent horse was faster, anyway. They were in Three Rivers Domain now, and the warlord here did not spend money on roads the way Thegan did. They would be in South Domain soon, and the roads there were even worse. Should he stop at the fort at Wooding and let them know what was coming?

Over his evening campfire—the ghosts didn't travel at night, although he didn't understand why not—Leof considered his own position. His short hair meant he no longer looked like an officer. His sword—if he had any sense, he'd throw his sword away and figure out how else he could earn his living. It was the pressing box for anyone but a warlord's man to carry a sword. But he couldn't throw it away. He'd trained with the sword from the time he was old enough to walk—toy swords, wooden practice-swords, blunt half-size blades, and finally the real thing. He couldn't just discard it.

Besides, he might need it.

The decision settled him, made him feel less like a dandelion clock floating willy-nilly on the breeze. If they all made it through, there would be time enough to worry about the rest of his life.

The people running ahead of the ghosts had left a lot behind them. He'd had no trouble finding a ham and some cheese in the last farmhouse. He'd hesitated about whether to leave silver for them, but figured that if he did, the farmer would probably never get it. So he had ignored the guilt of theft and packed his spare horse with a light load of food that would last—plus a good supply of oats. If worse came to worst, the horses could make do with grass, and he could live on porridge. He'd done it once before, when he'd been snowed in to a cave for two weeks on a scouting trip.

That time Thegan had come to find him. When the blizzard had stopped, Thegan had led a rescue party and dug him out. So many qualities: loyalty, courage, intelligence, foresight. Tears pricked Leof's eyes; it felt like his commander, the commander he'd fought behind for so long, believed in for so long, was dead. But he had never existed.

Leof watched the ghost army as it approached the bridge over the chasm of the Fallen River. He was near Wooding, on a small rise, obscured from view. A scout from the town, an older man with grey hair, was cut down by one of the ghosts as he tried to make it back to the small force holding the bridge. Men with axes stood ready to hack through the bridge supports and send the bridge crashing into the chasm. The ghosts would then have to go the long way, down to the ford near Three Rivers Domain. If they didn't break the bridge Leof knew the people wouldn't live long.

Then someone moved forward, towards the ghosts, and stopped, the people behind pushing, trying to see what was happening.

Leof expected the ghosts to surge forward, killing as they went, but nothing happened. The enchanter came to the front, flanked by the two ghosts who had seemed to control the fighting in Sendat. They talked—talked!—to the man on the bridge and then, astonishingly, the entire ghost army turned and began to walk down the river towards the ford. It seemed impossible.

Leof found himself shaking. What had happened here? Had the South Domain warlord found a way of defeating the ghosts? He rode a little closer for a better look at the men still ranged across the bridge. They weren't warlord's men, most of them, although their leader seemed to be an officer. Were they... Travellers?

By the time the ghosts and their human allies had walked down river, the men on the bridge were relaxing, sitting down and pulling out flasks and bread, celebrating. Leof rode up and dismounted, tying the horses to a nearby tree.

The officer stood up, ready to be welcoming, and then hesitated as he saw Leof's short hair.

Brazen it out, Leof thought. "Greetings," he said with an officer's authority. "I'm Lord Leof, from Sendat. Congratulations. You're the first group to have been successful against the ghosts. How did you do it?"

The man smiled with thin pride. "Beck, second-in-command to Coeuf, Warlord of South. We heard about Sendat, so we knew the hostage plan wouldn't work." He hesitated. "Do you know about Acton, Lord Leof?"

That was a strange question, Leof thought. Beck read his expression and went on quickly. "He's back. His ghost, that is. And he can talk. He told us to make the Travellers our shield and our sword."

Leof stared at him. The man seemed to believe what he was saying. And why not? If all the other ghosts had risen, why not Acton? He felt a flicker of hope. If Acton were fighting with them... perhaps they had a chance at last.

"So our Travellers told the ghosts, 'This is our home. Go elsewhere'," Beck continued. "The old ghost, the big one, didn't like it, but the enchanter said we had the right to make the decision for ourselves. He said, 'They have weapons. They don't need us to fight for them.' I think he was pleased about that."

Leof raised his voice so they could all hear.

"You've done very well indeed. You are the only people to save their homes so far. We need to send messengers to other districts to let them know of your success." He spoke more quietly, to Beck, "Your warlord can organise it."

Beck shook his head. "Coeuf's gone to Turvite for the warlords' council. His son, too. I'll do it."

"I'll take the news to Turvite," Leof said. "They will be glad of it there."

Beck grinned. "If they can get their Travellers to do it. Without the stonecaster journeying with Acton I'd've had trouble convincing them."

MARTINE

THEY ENTERED Turvite Harbour on an evening tide, riding the swell through the narrow channel with the captain shouting instructions as fast as she could speak and the sailors up and down the rigging like wrens in a berry bush.

Their party met on deck, Safred and Cael both looking pale, but Safred more cheerful at the thought of land ahead.

"I must go to the Moot Hall," Arvid said, turning to Martine. "You will come with me?"

"Not immediately," Martine answered. "I have business here. I have to see Ranny of Highmark."

"She'll be at the Moot Hall. She's in the council. With so many warlords arriving, the council will be there."

Martine felt her back crawl, as it had when she had last walked through Turvite, expecting a knife between her shoulder blades from Ranny. She had no idea if the woman still wanted to kill her, but it seemed likely.

"All right, then, I'll go with you. But the others must go straight to Sanctuary."

Arvid looked at them with surprise. "It's too late for that," he said. "Too late for secrecy. If the warlords are out in force, whatever must be done should be done before them, with their support. We will send to Ash and Bramble, bring them to Turvite."

Cael looked at him kindly. "Lad, do you really think they'll believe us?"

"The Well of Secrets? Of course they'll believe her!"

Zel refused to go, and none of them pressed her. She wanted to take Trine off to the inn Arvid always used, The Red Dawn.

Trine had recovered all her old snappiness, seeming to object to everything about Turvite—the noise, the smell of fish, the lumbering handcarts, the hawkers.

236

"She'll look after me," Zel said, smiling, and they smiled back, but as she walked off down the road in front of them, leading Trine because the horse's legs were a little unsteady after the long voyage, she looked very small.

"Perhaps you should go to the inn too, and rest," Safred said to Cael. He looked pallid and shaky, but he shook his head.

"I'll see it through. If they've all come, you know—"

"Yes. My uncle will be there," Safred said. "Perhaps my father."

She was staring off at the sea, but her hands were clasped tight. Martine couldn't tell if she was frightened, or hopeful, or simply confused. Perhaps all three. It was the most she had spoken since the fog had been fed. That should be encouraged.

"Your uncle?" Martine asked briskly. "Which one's that?"

"Thegan," Safred said. "My father was Masry, his older brother, the heir to Cliff Domain, but after... When I ran away from him, he followed me into the caves and we met delvers. They say it warped his mind. Changed him. He became very religious, went into seclusion. So Thegan took over the Domain when my grandfather died. Then, of course, he married that poor little Sorn and now he has from cliff to cove, except for the Lake."

"Poor little Sorn?"

"Married off to cement alliances, like all the warlords' daughters. That's what my mother saved me from. What a prize I would have been!" Her voice was bitter. She had paid a high price for her freedom, and she hadn't been the only one who had made sacrifices.

Martine glanced at Cael, but he was concentrating on his balance. Holly, Arvid's guard, stepped forward and gave him her arm. The fact that he took it told Martine that he was very bad. But how he used the last of his energy was his choice.

"Do the gods tell you what we must do next?" Arvid asked her.

Safred shook her head. "I am hollowed out," she said. "I think they will not speak to me again."

There was nothing they could say to that without sounding falsely hearty.

They walked down the dock guarded by Arvid's soldiers, Holly still supporting Cael, and made their way through the streets to the Moot Hall past some locals, staring and speculating at the new arrivals. Martine could hear them:

"That's the young warlord from up north!"

"No, no, it's Coeuf's son from South. Has to be—look at that nose. Just like Coeuf's. You could hide a horse up there!"

Martine felt happiness sliding over her, as it did so unexpectedly these days. She managed not to giggle, but she couldn't resist peeking at Arvid's nose. It was a definite nose, admittedly, but surely not so prominent as all that?

Immune to public attention in a way she would never become, Arvid ignored it all and chatted with Safred and his guard. Finally, as they approached the hall, he turned to Martine. "Do you have yourself under control now?" he asked, his own mouth twitching just a little.

It almost undid her. What was it about this man that brought out the giggling youngling in her? Then the fear at the heart of love overtook her and her eyes stung with tears. "Be careful," she said. "In there, all the rules are already overturned."

She could hear it as she said it, the Sight coming through without her intention. His gaze sharpened on her as he heard it too, and he nodded, once, the warlord's nod acknowledging information from an officer.

One of his guards called out to the safeguarders on the doors, two big men Martine recognised as working for Doronit: "My Lord Arvid of the Last Domain requires entrance."

The men swung back the big doors and they entered in strict precedence: Arvid, then Safred, Cael, then Martine, the soldiers flanking them all.

At the door to the great hall the Turvite councillors, Ranny among them, stood to greet the arrivals. Arvid went through the formalities, but when he looked around in preparation for introducing his party, Martine shook her head very slightly.

Ranny had seen Martine already, and didn't look pleased. There was no need to antagonise her by making her formally acknowledge someone she thought of as an enemy. Martine wished that she had never withheld the full casting she had done for Ranny. But then—perhaps she would never have left Turvite, never seen Elva or been sent to the Well of Secrets. Never met Arvid. Too many connections, tumbling like stones in a landslide.

"My adviser, the Well of Secrets," Arvid said.

A stir went through the people assembled, and Martine saw someone slip out the door to the hall to spread the news.

Ranny smiled, a genuine smile of relief. "We are glad indeed to see you here, my lady," she said.

"Lady?" Safred said, her freckles standing out against her pale face. "I think not."

Martine winced. The whole of the Domains knew that Safred, Well of Secrets, had refused her heritage as a warlord's daughter; refused to be part of the ruling elite.

Ranny realised she had misspoken, but she carried on with the aplomb of the seasoned diplomat. "Please, enter."

The others walked on, but Martine lingered, moving closer to Ranny. "Two weeks after mid-summer, twenty-three years from now, here in Turvite," Martine said softly, ensuring no one else could hear.

Ranny stared at her, instantly suspicious. "What?"

"I swear to you, that is what the stones told me," Martine said.

Safred had returned and overheard. "That was an old fate," she said gently, "cast before the enchanter arose with his army. All fates have been broken by that—it was outside the gods' control. No fate cast is certain, now."

Shocked, they both stared at her. Then Ranny smiled. "So you do *not* know. No one knows when I will die." Tension went out of her shoulders and her head lifted. "Good. That's as it should be."

"Are you ready?" Arvid asked reprovingly. He had come back to collect them.

Inside the hall the servants had taken the tables up and set one large, long table in the middle. The Turvite councillors were at one end, the titular head of the Council, Garham the wine merchant, in the centre. Garham had been a customer of Martine's—a blustering but not stupid man, he rarely listened to anyone other than Ranny, who stood beside him.

Warlords and their men stood around, eyeing each other and the table, working out precedence and who would sit where.

Martine recognised a few of them: old Coeuf was there with his son, Eolbert. She smiled to herself when she saw that he had inherited his father's nose. Merroc from Far South was easily picked out, too, as he was famous for his bright red hair. He was in his fifties but still robust. He'd outlived three wives; two dead in childbirth and the other from a fever. They said he was cursed: even as a warlord, he'd had trouble finding a fourth wife.

Some others: Eni from Three Rivers, so stout he could hardly walk; Berden from Western Mountains, it must be, he was supposed to be very tall and despite the stoop of age he towered over them all still. Then a young man, younger even than Arvid, with reddish-blond hair. Would that be Gabra, who held Cliff Domain for his father, Thegan? But not all the eleven were represented. Some would still be travelling, she figured, and Henist from Northern Mountains might not come at all; he ran his domain as though it were separate from all the rest.

Garham called out, "My lords! Councillors! Please take a seat."

She moved towards the wall with Cael, certain she didn't belong at that table. "Let's find you somewhere to sit down," she said to him, taking his arm.

He nodded with effort and they walked slowly towards the door.

After some initial jostling, the warlords sat at the table, their officers standing behind. The councillors were grouped at the head of the table, Ranny on Garham's left hand. Safred sat at his right, her spine straight and her head high. But Martine could tell she was unhappy about being there.

Garham cleared his throat. "This council was called by the Lord Thegan—"

"And it was a warlords' council!" Merroc snarled. "What do you think *you're* doing here, merchants?"

Garham paused, trying to control his temper.

Martine and Cael had almost reached the door when it slammed back and a man strode into the room, followed by several officers and a woman. The leader was tall and blond and ridiculously good looking, and he moved like he owned the world. He wore Central Domain's colours, as did the officers. The woman was auburn haired and graceful, but looked tired and drawn. Thegan and Sorn? Martine wondered. It seemed likely.

Thegan walked to the foot of the table and suddenly, like a picture

turned upside down, it became the head, simply because he stood there.
Everyone there turned subtly to look at him.

He stared down the table challengingly—not at the warlords or the
councillors, but at Safred. "Are you satisfied?" he asked her. "If you had
done your duty by our family we would have had warning of this before
it happened!" He slammed his fist down on the table. Safred winced,
but recovered.

Cael was already halfway to the table. Martine followed helplessly,
sure this was going to end badly.

"Well?"

"Don't blame her for your own incompetence," Cael said.

Thegan whirled on him, hand going to his sword. He was unshaven
and tired, Martine saw, and deeply, vigorously angry.

He checked when he saw it wasn't an officer insulting him, and
looked to his officers as though expecting them to drag Cael away.
Then he realised that they were in Turvite, a free town, and Cael had
the right to say anything he wanted. That no warlord had power within
the city bounds. Martine could see it happen, because his face went very
calm, and behind her the woman drew in a sharp breath, as though
frightened.

"You look a bit like your brother," Cael went on casually. "I suppose
we're some kind of relation, since my sister married your brother."

It took the wind out of Thegan's sails as nothing else could. Martine
smiled.

"Your brother couldn't capture her, and you have no right to even
try," Cael said, the amiable tone at odds with his sharp gaze.

Safred stood up. She still looked pale to Martine's eye, but she
spoke firmly enough. "Thank you, uncle," she said formally. "But I am
sure this council has more pressing things to discuss than our family
disagreements."

"She's right!" Merroc snarled. "What can you tell us, Well of Secrets?
Can we stand against this enchanter and his dead?"

Thegan and Cael still glared at each other, but Thegan turned away
after a moment, preserving dignity by pretending to discount Cael.
Martine saw him flick a glance at one of his officers, and saw the man
nod in return. Cael's life wouldn't last long if that man got near him.

Martine forced herself to approach Cael. "Come," she said. "Leave her to explain."

Safred nodded, and Cael turned to go, all his energy deserting him so that he had to lean heavily on Martine's arm to make it out of the hall.

Behind them, as the door closed, they heard Safred's warning, "The gods have provided a way of defeating the ghost army, but it will not be easy, and we must not kill the enchanter before it is done. That would be the worst folly..."

The woman who had accompanied Thegan followed them out and sat on a bench in the corner, collapsing the last few inches onto the seat as though exhausted. Martine helped Cael onto the bench beside her.

"I am Sorn," the woman said, gathering herself.

"My lady," Martine acknowledged, and Cael echoed her.

"No lady now, I think," she said bitterly. "Sendat is taken by the enchanter."

"Then he'll come here soon," Martine said.

"They will have axes," Sorn said. "Many of them."

Martine considered the possibilities. "The stonecasters of Turvite bespell their doors against ghosts," she said slowly. "Is it possible, do you think, to bespell a whole city?"

SAKER

SAKER ADDRESSED each new group of allies the same way. "There's no need to steal. No need to loot. Everything will belong to us, by the time we have finished. Just take what you need now and decide which house you want later, after we have conquered. There will be enough for everyone."

They cheered him, each time, and joined him, more every day. Whenever they were sighted, Acton's people ran for their lives and the Travellers came out to meet them. The warlords further south hadn't been as efficient as Thegan at gathering up the Travellers. Or massacring them. But there were no more towns like Wooding; no Travellers asked them to just pass by.

"No safety being Settled, not any more," one old man said to him in a small, prosperous town. "Is there? We might as well fight."

Saker clapped him on the shoulder and smiled as his people gathered whatever they needed from the market square. They didn't linger and didn't loot, but finding enough food for their growing army always took some time.

His father and Owl were impatient with the needs of the living.

"These people are our future," Saker reminded them. "Once the invaders are destroyed, these are the ones who will build our new land."

Alder and Owl shared a glance that Saker could not read. Then, almost reluctantly, Alder nodded.

They took over that village for the night. All of Acton's people had vanished, except for the innkeeper, who pretended to be glad to see them. "Welcome, welcome, come in!" he babbled, clutching at his apron.

He had the same brownish hair as Saker himself, but Owl shook his head when Saker asked if the man had Traveller blood, and used him as one of the evening sacrifices. Oddly enough, his family had old blood in plenty, and the wife served them with tears running down her cheeks, two young childer hiding in her skirts.

"You're safe now," Saker told her, but he could see that only fear stopped her spitting in his face. Fear for her children. "Your children will grow up able to look anyone in the eye," he said earnestly. It was important that she understand why they fought. "No more warlords. No more Generation Laws. No more injustice."

"My husband was a good man. Where's the justice in his death?" she demanded, her voice breaking into sobs.

"We all have to make some sacrifices to bring the future into being," he said, but his words sounded hollow even to himself, and he wondered if they should have spared the man, for the sake of his children.

Each night and morning, Alder and Owl conducted the blood ceremony. Saker had nothing to do with it, but by this time he was glad. The shrilling sound grew stronger in his ears each time, until he could hardly bear it. On the third day, as he watched his father slit the arm of a young woman, a blonde-haired woman much the same age as the girl Thegan had killed at Sendat, he realised something. The sound was not the yearning of spirits beyond the grave who wished to join them. It was the keening of those they had killed and sent to the darkness beyond death, calling out for revenge. No one else seemed to hear it, and Saker accepted the sound, and the shapes he saw, writhing in the corner of his vision, as part of the price he had to pay to secure their victory. He was haunted by the dead—that was fitting. He would bear that alone, so that none of his people, alive or dead, would feel the burden. After each ceremony, exhausted by pretending to be unaffected by the deafening shrill, by controlling his reactions to the horrible, distorted shapes which clambered at the corner of his eyes, he sat down and found some consolation in that thought. He was protecting his people, as he should, from evil.

BRAMBLE

BRAMBLE RODE through the day half-expecting Swith himself to descend from the clouds. Anything might happen, she felt. Beck, hated for as long as she could remember, was an ally. Acton, despoiler and invader, was her—well, call it friend. Wind wraiths were abroad in settled land. Ash, whom she had thought of as a younger brother to be looked after, had stood on the warlord's steps and made a speech that had stirred an entire town to cooperation and action.

And here she was, riding to Turvite to confront an enchanter who was capable of the darkest betrayal in all human history. To confront him, and make him powerless, and then kill him. The peace she had felt in the forest with the hunter was so far away she could barely remember it.

Acton ran at her side like a young deer, tireless and oddly comforting. Occasionally he would grin up at her, and although she grinned back she felt there was something false about it, as though he were forcing himself.

Close to twilight, deep in South Domain, they entered a long stretch of woodland, to Bramble's relief. The summer green of the trees, the rustle of life, bird calls, everything was a blessing.

After an hour's riding, they found a clearing with a stream that crossed the road, and decided to camp there.

Bramble was grooming the bay when the hair on the back of her neck stood up. The bird calls were all wrong. She could hear woodpeckers' *ki-ki-ki-ki* alarm calls from some way ahead.

"Ware," she said. "Someone's coming."

They drew off behind an enormous holly bush and waited. A few moments later a band of Travellers came into view, but Travellers like she had never seen before. A big group—far larger than the Generation Laws allowed. Twenty, maybe, mostly men and a few young women, although there was one family with a small child and a babe in arms. They walked warily, carrying hatchets and knives like weapons.

Bramble stepped out and raised a hand in greeting. They stopped and scanned the trees for anyone else, then relaxed a little as they noticed her colouring.

"Fire and water," she greeted them, remembering her grandfather's lessons in Traveller ways.

"Fire and water and a roof in the rain," the man in front replied. "Are you alone?"

She shook her head and the others came out of hiding. The Travellers gripped their weapons more tightly at the sight of Baluch, smiled as they saw Ash, and seemed excited when Acton finally appeared.

"Are you with the enchanter?" a young man asked eagerly.

"No," Bramble said. "Why?"

"We're going to join him," the leader said. "We've had enough."

"Enough of what?" Baluch asked.

The leader glared at him. "Enough of being murdered in our beds! Do you know what's been happening?"

Bramble answered quickly, before the others could say anything. "Some of it. But joining the enchanter isn't the way to—"

"It might keep us alive!" the mother with the baby exclaimed. "They killed my sister and her two sons. For nothing! Nothing..." She began to weep. Her husband put an arm around her shoulders and glowered at them, as though her tears were their fault.

"The enchanter can't be stopped, they say. His ghosts will protect us." He looked at Acton, assessing his bulk and the sword at his side with some satisfaction.

Acton was listening thoughtfully, assessing each member of the group, but he stayed behind Baluch and said nothing.

"The enchanter wants to kill everyone in the Domain without Traveller blood," Ash said.

The Travellers looked at each other. It was news to them, and a shock. Some faces were troubled, some implacable, but others wore a touch of satisfaction.

"Might be the only way," the leader said finally. He looked up at the canopy of leaves. It was growing darker. "Camp here," he ordered.

These were people who lived on the Road. Bramble admired their competence as they set up camp, built fires, dug a privy. They kept their bags packed, so they could leave at any moment. She and the others helped and by the time they were all sitting down to eat, the Travellers made a place for them in the fire circle.

They shared what they had, and it was the best meal Bramble had eaten since the morning she'd woken up in Oakmere, unexpectedly alive and ravenous. Carrot soup, roasted rabbit and greens, griddle scones and a dark fruitcake that the woman with the baby said kept well on the Road.

After they'd cleaned up and repacked their gear, Ash took out his pouch and glanced at Bramble. She nodded. It was worth a try.

"There is a new stone in the bag," he began, more gently than he had at Wooding.

They listened, but unlike the Travellers at Wooding they had seen recent murder, and not by ghosts. They would not be convinced. Acton tapped Ash on the knee.

"Speak," Ash said readily.

"Greetings—" he began.

The dark, grating voice brought the Travellers to their feet. Parents lifted children into their arms and two of the littlest began to cry.

"There's no need to be afraid—" Ash said.

"I am Acton, come from the darkness beyond death—"

They stared at him white-faced. One man picked up his pack. The woman with the baby took a step backwards, covering her child's face to shield it.

"He won't hurt you," Bramble said.

"Ghosts don't speak," the youngest man said. "Ghosts don't speak!"

He began to back away, his eyes fixed on Acton. The others moved too, slowly backwards, gathering their packs as they went until they were at the edge of the clearing.

"We mean you no harm," Baluch said in his most soothing voice, but they weren't listening, Bramble saw. Their whole attention was given to Acton. Acton the invader.

"Are you really Acton?" the leader asked, his voice rough.

Acton spread his hands in a gesture of good faith and took a step forward.

"I am Acton," he confirmed. I am here to—"

The young man broke and ran and the others followed, disappearing into the trees.

"Come back!" Ash cried.

He might as well have been mute. In a few moments, they were alone in the leaping light of the fire.

Acton looked down at his hands. They were shaking. "Afraid. So afraid of me," he whispered.

Bramble wanted to reassure him, tell him that they feared a nightmare story, a figure out of legend, not him. But it was him they were afraid of—and if it had been a thousand years ago, they would have been right to run.

Ash said so. Bramble thought for a second that Acton would hit him, but he clenched his fists and walked a little way into the trees.

He came back some time later.

"Speak," Ash said.

"They will join the enchanter," he said.

"They're right," said Baluch, the first time he had spoken since the Travellers had gone. "They're safer with him."

Acton said nothing, but something had changed in his face; a new awareness, Bramble thought, of the consequences of his actions. He would not be so fast to declare himself the next time they met Travellers.

The next day they passed through fields and woodland and more fields.

They were ahead of the enchanter's march, which fretted Acton. When they stopped for the night where a stream formed a clear pool he paced around the fire circle.

"We should make our stand here," he said, indicating the broad sweep of pastureland they had ridden through that afternoon. "Before he gets to Turvite."

Bramble hesitated. What if he were right? She drew Ash aside.

"Why not cast?" she said.

Ash looked over at Acton. "See what the gods say? You're right, now is a good time."

Since the wind wraiths had appeared he had barely spoken, except to spread the word about Evenness and a new world waiting on the other side of this crisis. Bramble had believed him, too. The world was shifting. But somehow she couldn't see the new one. It seemed too far away, as though she only had the time she was living in, moment by moment. As the hunter had lived, moment by moment.

They stepped through the ritual and Ash examined the stones. "They say we must go faster."

"Well, we can't!" Bramble said, exasperated. "The horses won't stand it."

"There's another way." He hesitated, as though he were about to say something she shouldn't hear. Baluch, sitting beside him, put a hand on his arm.

"Bramble has met her," he said reassuringly.

Ash looked startled. "You've met the River?"

Bramble shook her head. "Not me. I met the Lake."

Baluch waved his hand dismissively. "The same being in a different mood."

"The River is the Lake's little sister," Ash said, as though he parroted something he'd heard many times.

"All rivers, all streams, all lakes in the Eleven Domains are part of her," Baluch said gently. "It's why we can hear her everywhere." He looked at Bramble. "She will take us the River's way to Sanctuary, if you wish."

The River's way, she thought. Faster than horses? The way Ash came into the Weeping Caverns? Acton moved closer, listening with interest, and Ash sat back, saying nothing more.

"Will She take Acton, too?" she asked.

Ash and Baluch both considered for a moment, as though listening to someone speak, then shook their heads. Acton moved away, his face expressionless for once.

"Sorry, Bramble," Ash said, as if he were not sorry at all. "We'll have to raise him again when we get there."

Bramble felt her gorge rise at the thought. She had been able to do it once, when she hadn't known what it would take, but to deliberately banish Acton back to the darkness beyond death and then go through that, that flaying alive. "No," she said.

"Bramble—" Ash said, exasperated.

"With you two gone, we can make a better pace," she said briskly. "I can ride each of the horses in turn, and go cross country. We'll be there much sooner. It's better this way." She forced herself to grin at him. "Neither of you are really riders, after all."

At least there was no argument about her not being safe on her own. She could have no better protection than Acton. His own people worshipped him and he terrified the Travellers.

"You won't be able to talk to him," Ash warned.

She shrugged. That might be a relief.

Ash looked at her with some compassion in his eyes. "If you have anything to say, say it now."

She did have something to say, and knew that she had better say it convincingly. She walked around the fire to where Acton was saying goodbye to Baluch.

"I want to make something clear," she said. "We are not going to confront the enchanter here. We are going to Turvite as quickly as possible. I will not wait for you. I will not turn aside. Whatever dreams you have of raising an army and marching on Turvite, forget them. That's not going to happen twice."

"I want to protect it, this time," he said, and paused. "A way of paying part of my debt."

"You're not here to fight," she said. "You're here to help others, not to lead."

He smiled at her. It had a hint of the cozening smile in it, but it was far warmer, and full of laughter. "Yes, Mother," he said.

"You've been spoilt from the day you were born," she said in mock reproof. "You've always had everything you wanted."

"Not now," he said, suddenly serious, looking younger, eyes open with that impossible flicker of blue. "I can't have what I truly want."

He meant her. It was clear. He wanted her. But was it real, or just that, for the first time, he couldn't reach out and take what he fancied?

She stared at him, but she didn't know what to say. She was not going to pour her heart out in front of Baluch and Ash.

"You will be together in your next lives," Baluch said.

She blushed, hard, feeling the red climb up from her heart to her face.

Acton looked startled and then laughed. "I promise," he said, serious again. "In our next life."

She couldn't speak. Not in front of the others. But she nodded, feeling exultation climbing through her, filling her with something wilder than joy. They both smiled. Whatever linked them was as tight as a bowstring.

"I think we can go now," Baluch said to Ash, and his voice was a mixture of amusement and a kind of regret. He looked older than before, as though their exchange had exhausted him.

"Aye," Ash said.

He hugged Bramble goodbye and the warm pressure of his arms was both comforting and a reminder of what Acton would never feel like to her. She let out a breath as Ash and Baluch walked to the pool and stood beside it.

They looked back and raised their hands, then took a step forward into the water, and were gone.

She walked down to look at where their footprints ended, then turned back to Acton.

He was gone too.

MARTINE

MARTINE DID not want to go back into the council chambers, but Sorn insisted. "Come with me," she said.

They left Cael sitting on the hall bench and opened the door.

The warlords were still arguing.

"Apologies won't stop them!" Thegan said forcefully. "He's prepared to sacrifice any number of his own people to take his revenge — do you think apologising would make any difference to him?"

Sorn coughed politely and he whirled, impatience clear on his face.

"My lords, councillors," Sorn said. "This is Martine, a stonecaster who lived formerly in this city. She has a suggestion."

"Well?" Thegan said, pre-empting Ranny or Garham's right to speak first.

Garham's face closed in with anger, and somehow that bolstered Martine's courage. "In Turvite," she said calmly, "we bespell the doors of stonecasters' houses, to prevent ghosts from entering."

"Can you bespell the whole city?" Ranny asked.

"I don't know," Martine said. "I've never tried to do more than my own door. But I am not the only stonecaster who can use that spell. If we worked together..."

"Good!" Garham said. "At last, a sensible suggestion. Boc, send for the stonecasters of the city. I want them here now!"

Boc hurried out with a spring in his step, and faces lightened around the table.

"If it works for Turvite..." Merroc said.

"We can protect all our towns and villages," Arvid said, finishing Merroc's thought. He shot Martine a look of admiration and mischief. "If our stonecasters agree."

"I am sure they will," Martine replied. What was the man thinking, to even suggest otherwise? Did he *want* to see stonecasters imprisoned and forced to work?

"And we have the Well of Secrets," Merroc said, inclining his head politely to Safred.

Safred raised a hand in denial. "My lords, I am not a stonecaster, nor a caster of spells. I can relay messages from the gods, and I can heal, but that is all. If I can help, I will, but do not rely on me for spell casting."

Thegan scowled at her as though she had personally betrayed him. The others got to their feet and stretched.

"No sense waiting here while these casters are gathered," Coeuf said, leaning heavily on his son's arm. "I'll be at my inn."

He was followed out by the rest of the warlords and councillors, Ranny last. Thegan nodded to his men to take a break and they left too. Only Thegan, Sorn, Safred and Thegan's son, Gabra, remained.

Martine was struck by the resemblance between Safred and her cousin. They might have been mother and son, if she'd had him young. Safred was looking at him, too, and then at Thegan.

Martine's Sight stirred, and she moved forward to Safred's side. "Don't," she whispered. "Whatever it is, don't say it."

"I have to," Safred said. "It's part of this pattern, I can feel it." She turned to Gabra and nodded. "It's good to meet you, brother," she said slowly.

He frowned. Thegan stood very still, his face blank.

"Cousin," Gabra said.

Safred ignored him, looking at Thegan. "Did you really think I wouldn't know my father's son?" she asked.

Sorn was even stiller than Thegan. Then she took a deep breath in, her face pale, her green eyes cold, and faced him. "Time we had a child, you said. Were you going to pimp me, too?"

Impatience swept over him. "I didn't *pimp* her! She always wanted Masry, but he was obsessed with the green-eyed Valuer bitch. She only took me as second best, and when I gave her the chance to lie down with him, she jumped at it!"

Gabra stood with his mouth tightly closed, looking more like Thegan than he had done before.

"And me?" Sorn demanded. "Who did you have in mind for me?"

He looked at Gabra.

Sorn laughed, her voice hard. "Your *nephew*? Oh, perfect!"

"It's the bloodline that counts," Thegan snarled. "Masry was the true heir anyway—his son inherits, his son's son inherits. The way it should be."

"As if you cared!" Sorn shot back. "If you'd been a *man* and sired your own sons, you would never have allowed Masry's get to have any part of your lands."

He struck her across the face, a full back-handed blow that sent her sprawling on the floor. Gabra and Martine both moved between them as he took a step towards her.

Sorn did not cry out. She fell in silence, as though she'd done it many times before, and climbed back to her feet in silence, and faced him down. "I am my father's daughter, and the true heir to his Domain," she said softly. "I renounce you as husband."

Thegan smiled. "I own you, wife."

"I have had time to study my position, these last years," Sorn continued, "since I have not had children to occupy me." He flinched, and her voice gained strength. "There are ancient laws, little used but still valid. Since the Domain passes through my bloodline, if you are not able to give me heirs, I can renounce you for the sake of the Domain, and take another husband."

"I'll kill you first," he said. "You know I will."

"This is not Sendat. You are not ruler here. If you kill me without heirs, my cousin Coeuf's son inherits."

"He'd have to take it by blood."

"It's already been taken," Martine said, annoyed. "Have you forgotten?"

Thegan nodded, still looking at Sorn. "She's right. Truce, until the enchanter is defeated?" His voice was as soft as honey, as reasonable as rain after drought.

Sorn stared heavily at him, red from his blow spreading across her cheek, and then nodded. "But I will not sleep where you sleep," she said.

"Stay with us," Safred said immediately.

Thegan flicked a hand as if to say "Do what you like," then walked out of the room. Gabra hesitated, but followed him.

Martine and Sorn and Safred looked at each other.

"Don't trust him to keep this truce," Safred said.

Sorn gave a half-smile. "I know him too well to trust him with anything," she said. She sat, exhausted, on one of the chairs and raised a hand to her face.

"That wasn't the first time he'd done that," Martine said.

"No, no, he's never struck me before," Sorn said.

"It wasn't the first time you've been struck, though."

Sorn bit her lip and shrugged. Safred laid a hand over the red cheek and sang softly under her breath. When she took the hand away the skin was back to its normal pale glow.

Sorn looked up with awe. "A true prophet," she said. "The gods are good, to have sent you to us."

A flush swept up over Safred's freckled face. "The gods love *you*," she said. "They yearn for you."

But Sorn only laughed, as though that were impossible. She dug inside her belt pouch and brought out a small scroll of paper. "I don't know who to give this to," she said. "I made a list of the Travellers at Sendat. I've marked the ones who escaped before the ghosts came. Most of the others were killed, although some may have survived. I thought someone, somewhere, would want to know who they were..."

Safred took the list gravely, and looked over it. It was long. Halfway down, her expression lightened.

"Rowan and Swallow escaped," she said to Martine. Martine knew that they were Ash's parents. Ash had been going to find his father...

"What about Ash?" she asked, in sudden fear.

"There is no Ash on the list," Sorn replied.

Martine realised only then that her heart had stopped beating, when it resumed with a sudden thud. But there were tears on Safred's cheek.

"Who?" Martine asked. "Who is it?"

"Flax," Safred said numbly.

Martine drew in a sharp breath. No, she prayed. No.

"A young man," Sorn said. "A beautiful singer. I know he died, trying to lead the others to escape. I am sorry...you knew him?"

Martine turned away. Zel. Gods of field and stream, what would Zel do?

"I should have known this had happened," Safred said numbly. "*Why didn't they tell me?*"

"Because," Martine said bitterly, "human death doesn't matter to them, remember?"

"I have to tell Zel," Safred said.

Martine and Sorn went with her. Martine passed other stonecasters coming to the Moot Hall, but didn't stop. Let them sort out a strategy, she thought, and she would help. They knew as much about spell casting as she did. She had to be with Zel.

As soon as they came around the stable door, Zel realised something was wrong. "Are the ghosts here?" she asked, springing up from a straw bale, bridle and cleaning cloth in her hands.

Safred just stood there. Martine didn't know what to say, either.

"What's wrong?" Zel asked.

Sorn moved forward, her face full of compasssion. "I am sorry, but we have bad news. You have a brother named Flax? A singer?"

Zel nodded slowly.

"He is dead."

Her head moved from side to side in denial. Sorn took her hands, pressing them in sympathy.

"He was very brave," she said. "He was trying to free his people when he was cut down."

"Free them?" Zel whispered. "From the ghosts?"

"No." Sorn's voice was even gentler. "The warlord at Sendat held Travellers for hostage against the ghosts. But the enchanter attacked anyway, and the hostages... Some managed to escape, but your brother..."

"The warlord killed him," Zel said flatly. "What about Ash? Is he dead, too?"

Sorn looked at Martine for help.

"We don't know what's happened to Ash," Martine said. "Oh, Zel, I'm sorry."

"He promised he'd keep Flax safe," Zel explained to Sorn, as if it were very important that she understood. "He *promised*. He's a safeguarder, see, and he said he'd look after Flax like he were his little brer." Her voice cracked on the word and she drew in a long, sobbing breath.

"So he's still alive? Right? He's alive and my brer dead?" She turned to Safred. "That right?"

Safred nodded. "I think so. But we don't know why—"

"Don't matter *why*!" Zel said. "Don't matter. He's alive and my boy's dead and he promised." She threw the bridle and cloth on the floor. "Where's the enchanter now?"

"On his way to Turvite," Safred said. "Zel—"

"Warlords gatherin' to fight, eh? Kill more people? Seems to me this enchanter are the only one stayed honest." She walked out the door.

Sorn went to follow her, but Safred stopped her. "Let her go."

"Is this part of the pattern, too?" Martine asked with bitterness.

"I pray so," Safred said.

SAKER

SAKER LOOKED across the plain to the rising hills in the distance. Turvite, and beyond that, the sea.

It had been fifteen years since he had been here, the year that Freite had come to barter with the trader from the Wind Cities for some special herbs for a particular spell against plague.

The trader had refused to sell them to her, and she had been furious. Saker found himself thankful for that, now that he thought about it. Had she been planning to loose a plague on her enemies, and refrained only because she could not guarantee her own safety? It seemed likely, looking back.

He had been only a boy, then, cowed and obedient. He had gawked at the high hill with its golden houses, flinched at the noises that clamoured in every street, slept lightly on a pallet at the end of Freite's bed, and slept heavily on the nights after she drew strength from him. She'd had customers: a woman with eyes the colour of sapphire, a man with a raddled nose, an old man in rich clothes who ordered her about like a lackey. She hadn't liked that, but after he was gone she turned to Saker and said with satisfaction, "He's got a canker and he'll be dead in a year, no matter how high his mark is!"

There had been some significance to that, which he hadn't understood, some complex bit of politics or social interaction that she had never bothered to teach him. Now, he realised with a jolt of surprise, none of that mattered. The old ways were about to end: old families would die, old wealth would be shared among his people. Social standing would vanish; equality would stand. Evenness. All the things he had never quite understood would be unimportant.

They would work their way through Turvite street by street, and no one, this time, would escape.

ASH

A SH STEPPED onto the riverbank.
The smooth curve of bank was dotted with small jetties, and here and there clumps of willows and alders grew down to the water. He and Baluch used the branches of one to swing up the steep bank, the sky bright above them, mackerel clouds a coverlet of rose and gold. Ash's safeguarder instincts made him assess their position immediately. There was no one in sight.

A light wind seemed to blow them dry in the instant that they stepped ashore. That moment, leaving Her, was full of sorrow and loss.

He saw his pain reflected in Baluch's face.

"It's always so," Baluch said gently. "To leave Her is to break your heart. Every time."

Ash nodded. It was the same as human love, then, like the songs said. A mixture of joy and pain, desire and longing, delight and misery.

He accepted it with some relief. If his bond with the River had been unalloyed happiness, it would have felt false to him, like the happiness poppy juice bought. Temporary.

"The heart of love is the dagger, the soul of love is the lance," he quoted. It was a song from the north, a couple of hundred years old. His mother liked it.

Baluch smiled with quiet satisfaction. "That was one of my good ones," he said.

Ash stared for a moment, then burst out laughing in a kind of shock. Had Baluch written every song he liked from the last thousand years? He sobered, thinking about that song, "The Warrior's Love." A life of fighting and music, that was Baluch, and that song brought both of them together. He wondered if Acton were as complex, if that were the reason Bramble loved him.

There were voices, beyond the curtain of trees. Many voices, talking

259

in a low contented buzz. They paused to listen. Occasionally a voice was raised in a shout or a laugh.

"Sounds like an inn," Baluch said.

Ash nodded, and now he brought his attention to it, he could smell beer, and piss, and sausages cooking. "I think it's the Dancing Bear, at Sanctuary," he said. "I've been here before." Several times, he remembered, on jobs for Doronit. The innkeeper was one of her customers. His stomach growled. It had been a long time since the last of the cheese. "I could do with some food."

"An inn is the best place to get news," Baluch said.

They moved to the edge of the green willow curtain and paused, listening still. It felt dangerous to Ash, to push aside that curtain and walk back out into the world. He had a deep conviction—almost Sight—that the world had changed since he entered the River. That he would walk into the inn in another time, another place, another country, even.

He put his hand out and pulled the trailing willow withies aside, and walked into the inn yard.

There were tables set out on the river bank, full of people drinking, and the inn behind them was busy. It *was* the Dancing Bear, the largest inn on the river outside Turvite, so large that he couldn't see beyond it to the town. As he stood there, assessing, someone inside lit candles and the night suddenly seemed darker.

He and Baluch took a couple of steps towards the drinkers, and the people at the nearest table turned around to look.

Dung and pissmire! Ash thought. It was Aylmer, Doronit's right-hand man. Aylmer, and Hildie, and tall blond Elfrida, and two of the Dung Brothers. The third Dung Brother walked out of the inn, carefully carrying three tankards. He stopped dead when he saw Ash.

There was a moment when everyone froze. Then the others looked at Aylmer—even Hildie.

"You've got a hide thick as an ox, coming back," Aylmer said. "She'll take you apart, and she'll do it slow."

For a moment Ash's memory played for him a recent song: the speech he had made about the world changing, there on the steps of the warlord's house, in the stronghold of the enemy. He had taken the crowd with him, lifted them up with the image of a better world, a greater world where justice was the same for everyone, officer or commoner, Traveller or Acton's folk. It had been a great and wonderful feeling, while it lasted, while they listened, and then afterwards as they worked together for the first time. He had felt like a different person, as though nothing was beyond him.

But the eyes that looked at him now saw just Ash, the Traveller boy whom Doronit had employed, trained, been betrayed by. A nothing. A cipher. Ash felt his confidence drain away with the memory of Wooding. This was Sanctuary, Turvite, the real world, and here he was just a safeguarder.

Baluch was still behind him. Ash motioned with his hands behind his back: go, stay hidden. Baluch melted back into the willow fronds.

This situation, he realised, wasn't about his task, it was simply about his own survival. Perhaps this meeting was why the stones had sent him here. He only had one chance to get Doronit's people on his side. What would do it? All he had was the truth.

"She wanted me to murder Martine, on Ranny's orders. I don't do murder for hire."

The two Dung Brothers scratched the backs of their necks as if in puzzlement. The third moved to do the same and spilt some beer, then put the tankards down on the table and stared at him. They weren't hostile, but they weren't important. It was Aylmer and Hildie who would decide. Ash kept his eyes on them. Hildie looked scornful and somehow satisfied, as if she'd always known he was weak and was glad to have it confirmed. Aylmer pressed his lips together, but he seemed—wistful? As though he wished he'd made the same choice.

"She'll take *us* apart if we doesn't turn him over to her," Hildie said.

"Aye," Aylmer said slowly. "That she will." He sounded regretful, but there was no hesitation in the way he got up and came to Ash's side.

Ash knew better than to fight them. Or to run. Hildie was faster, the Dung Brothers stronger, and Aylmer more cunning. Even Elfrida had put him through a window, one time. All of them together could have stopped Acton himself. He shivered at the thought, and remembered Baluch, hiding and listening.

"What are you doing in Sanctuary? Who needed so many safe-guarders?" Ash asked.

"Big shipment of jewels and velvet, coming down the river from Whitehaven," Aylmer said. "Merchant's landing it here so his rivals won't get wind of it. Not till early tomorrow, though. We thought we'd make a night of it."

"And we're going to," one of the Dung Brothers said, settling more comfortably in his chair. "Don't need all of us to take him to Doronit."

Aylmer looked at him steadily. "Well, if you don't want to share the reward, that's fine by me. Come on, Hildie. I reckon you and I can keep him in line."

Hildie laughed. "Sure and certain," she said. "Off we go, cully." She came behind Ash and he felt the nudge of a knife in his back. They had been colleagues, he and Hildie, but he knew she wouldn't hesitate to use that knife. "It'd be more work to deliver you to her with your hamstrings cut, but we c'd do it," she said.

He laughed. "Aye, that's for sure." He felt almost free; he could make no decisions here except to go with them or die fighting, and that was no decision at all.

They walked him from the inn yard, Aylmer on one side and Hildie just behind. "So, cully, you've come full circle," she said.

"Not yet," Ash said.

Sanctuary was almost connected to Turvite. Houses and market gardens lined the road between the two, and at halfway there was another inn called the Last Chance. Last chance to get good beer before leaving the city, or last chance to buy beer at country prices? Both, maybe. His good mood continued, and he could just make out, at the edges of his hearing, Baluch whistling "The Warrior's Love." Following, then, but not trying to break him free. Just as well.

He pretended to have caught a stone in his shoe, and as he bent over to dislodge it, he saw Baluch watching from behind a house a hundred yards or so back. He shook his head and flicked his fingers discreetly to say, no, don't try. Baluch looked puzzled, but nodded and disappeared behind the corner of the house. Ash knew Baluch wouldn't do anything stupid. He had been a fighter once, but he was no match for Aylmer or Hildie now.

Walking back into Turvite proper, they strode up the long hill that he and Martine had struggled down in that storm, close to a year ago. Ash felt like a different person to the boy who had left, but he wasn't sure why. It wasn't just the passage of time. It wasn't even the sense of being involved in a task of huge importance. It was mainly the memories of young Ash and of the River. He had a home, now, and a stake in the future; a year ago he had been without any ties, without anywhere he would be welcome, without the sense he had a future. It was why he'd followed Martine so doggedly—she was all he'd had.

Turvite itself hadn't changed. It was still loud and busy and smelly, and full of people going about their many businesses, even though it was coming on to full dark. The ghosts lingered, too, pale and insubstantial compared to the warriors Saker the enchanter had summoned, but still clear in the fading light. They looked at Ash with concern, recognising him from the Mid-Winter's Eve when he had commanded them, on Doronit's orders, to reveal their secrets. It was her source of power in this city, all those secrets stolen from the dead. It was a bad memory, but it was important to remember what he had done, what he was capable of.

A year ago, being a Traveller in Turvite had attracted no comment. This evening, he and Hildie were given black looks and mutterings. Men spat on the ground as they passed, women made the sign against evil.

"What's that about?" Ash asked Hildie, after a woman had cursed her for a black-haired slut. Hildie just shrugged.

"Don't say you haven't heard about this Traveller enchanter?" Aylmer cut in.

"I've heard," Ash said. "But I didn't know people were sure he was a Traveller."

"Lord Thegan announced it," Aylmer said. "Figured it out somehow from what had been done in Carlion."

Ash felt cold sweep over him. If people in Turvite, famed for tolerating anyone from anywhere, were spitting at Travellers in the street, what was happening in the rest of the Domains? Stories of massacres abounded in the old songs, and some not so old. The Generation Laws had been enacted originally to stop large Traveller groups being attacked on the Road—the warlords decided that their various services were too useful to lose. With a touch of panic, Ash wondered about his father and Flax.

He sent a prayer to the local gods, and heard them reply, saying his name over and over, as they had when he lived here. Then, it had filled him with panic and a kind of shame. Now, he welcomed the sensation. He reached out to the River in his mind and found her, very faint, far below the city. *Belonging*, he felt her say, and was comforted.

As they climbed the hill, coming into the richer quarters, lanterns were hung at gates, candles lit inside houses, curtains drawn, and the streets began to empty. By the time they reached the very top and walked past the huge, sprawling mass of Highmark, they were the only ones around.

Then there he was, back at Doronit's house, back to where he'd sweated and yearned and maybe even loved a little. He'd always heard that places seemed smaller when you went back to them, but Doronit's house loomed larger: she'd built another storey on, half-timbering, painted sand-colour to mimic the sandstone houses further up the hill.

He was glad it looked different.

The office was the same, though, and Doronit herself, when she finally walked in, looked just as she had the day he'd killed the girl in the alley: wide navy trousers tucked into yellow boots, skirt and blouse of a lighter blue, a shawl pinned by a sapphire brooch. And her face, he thought, meeting her eyes at last, looked as smooth, as beautiful, as...cold.

The thought reminded him of what he carried with him, and he reached out gently to the River, sensing Her to the north, and deep below. A phrase from "The Distant Hills" played in his mind; his love was far away.

Ash stared into Doronit's sapphire eyes and wondered how she was going to kill him.

BRAMBLE

H E WAS gone.
   She looked around wildly, but there was nothing except the
silent pool, and the fire burning low.

Acton was gone, as a ghost fades after quickening and never comes
back.

She felt as if she were disintegrating, shredding apart on the wind,
her heart flaking away, uncoiling like a ball of thread. She couldn't
breathe.

Ash. It was because Ash had left. Ash had sung him up, and without
Ash he had faded. He had not gone on to rebirth, as a ghost that fades
after quickening. He could not have, because he had promised he would
help her, and he never broke his word.

That thought steadied her. He had promised, and what he had
promised he would do. That was a certainty, and she clung to it. They
could bring him back. She would take his bones to Turvite and find Ash
and they would sing him up again. It would be all right.

Bramble deliberately put her feet down in the cold water, trying to
shock some sense into herself. She had lived without Acton until now.
She would survive without him, as she had survived without the roan,
without Maryrose. But as she walked over and picked up the pack full of
his bones, part of her didn't believe it. They felt even lighter than before,
as though some essence of him had gone, too.

It was a long, lonely night with only the horses for company.

In the very early morning, Bramble saddled the mare and took the
other two on a leading rein. They weren't as fast, but at least she could
spell the mare. As they cantered along the grass by the side of the road,
she found anxiety growing in her chest. Not her anxiety—at Obsidian
Lake she had become adept at sorting her own emotions from those of
others. This was coming from somewhere else.

Then she saw the black rock altar among the trees and realised that the gods were calling her. Thankfully, she headed the mare towards the clearing and slipped off her back, tethering her to a sapling.

As she placed her hand on the altar, the anxiety rose to an almost panic.

Why are you here, child? they asked. *You should be in Turvite. Now! You should be in Turvite now!*

She cursed Acton. If she hadn't listened to him, they would have gone straight down the river and been in Turvite by now.

I will hurry, she said to them.

Too late, too late, they said with sorrow, and turned away from her towards whatever battle they were fighting.

She backed away and stood by the horses, fighting her own anxiety. She could ride — of course she could ride, but on these horses it would take too long. If only she had the roan.

She remounted and urged the horses to their best pace, but she knew they couldn't keep it up for long. They weren't chasers; they weren't even in top condition.

Rounding a bend screened by willow trees, she saw the barred fences, white-striped, that marked a horse farm. A stud, because in the fields beyond were chasers. Long legged, short backed, beautiful. Valuable.

Horses that could get her to Turvite much faster than the slugs she had.

Horse stealing was a killing offence, but that wasn't what made Bramble hesitate. She didn't want to take a horse who might be loved as she had loved the roan. But she had no choice. She'd bring them back, if she had the chance.

She wondered if any of these horses had come from Gorham's farm. There was an easy way to find out. Perched on the fence, she whistled them up: the come-to-me call all Gorham's horses learnt.

Across the field, three of them threw their heads up, whinnying, and whirled to canter over to her. Her heart lifted as they came — she was sure she remembered at least one of them. By Acton out of Silver Shoes — a great lineage, but the colt had been so wild that the owner had gelded him. He'd be fast. With him were two mares, a bay and a liver chestnut who lagged behind the others.

She took the tack off her other horses and turned them loose with reassuring pats. They were happy to graze and went off to meet the others in the field, who were now crowding towards them with that insatiable equine curiosity.

She saddled the gelding and put the bay on a leading rein, and then left, wondering why no one on the stud had come out when the horses had whinnied. Too afraid they'd meet ghosts?

The gelding's canter was smooth as they rode down the flat even road. Not bad, and the mare could keep pace. But could they jump? If they could ride cross country it would be much, much faster.

There were wooden fences all along this stretch of road—perfect. She set the gelding at one and he sailed over, the mare following willingly on a very long rein.

Chasing had always been her great passion, the one thing that could set her alight: the speed, the freedom, the thundering, shaking ground flicking past like a dream. On the roan, chasing, she had lost any sense of a separate self; they were one being, acting as one, and her exhilaration was his, and his was hers.

It wasn't like that with these horses, but it was still wonderful. In the broad light of morning, over field and stream, over wall and ditch, over hedge and fence, the three of them raced together, and Bramble laughed each time they jumped. They sped like an arrow towards Turvite, her sense of direction taking them in a straight line, no matter what the obstacle. There were no big rivers between here and there, and nothing smaller that they couldn't jump.

They galloped and jumped and trotted and walked, Bramble switching from horse to horse every couple of hours, until the sun set, and they had to rest.

With these horses, she would be in Turvite by the next night.

MARTINE

MARTINE WENT back to the gathering of stonecasters, because there was nothing else to do. She had left Sorn and Safred together eating an evening meal, but she wasn't hungry. Flax and Zel. She'd only known the boy a very short time, but he'd been as sweet as new butter. She wondered, again, where Ash was and why he'd let Flax go anywhere alone.

Zel had a right to her anger, but surely Ash had had good reason. Safred thought he wasn't dead, but she didn't know for sure. The gods were being coy, apparently. Martine felt a quick surge of anger. She should be grateful they were intervening at all, she supposed, but their lack of care for individual humans set her teeth on edge. At least the fire saw *you*—the individual woman, the actual person. He knew each of them by name, by more than name...but He was no help now.

The stonecasters were in the big hall, with Ranny trying to organise them from the mayor's podium. It was like herding snakes, as the saying went. They were talking to each other, sitting on the floor, some of them, casting stones; some argued over the right spell to use. There were only twenty or so, but the noise was immense. When Martine came in, they quietened and turned to face her, their backs to Ranny. Another thing for Ranny to get upset about, she thought. She found their deference surprising. She was a good stonecaster, yes, but she'd never claimed to be better at it than anyone else. Still, she did know most of them...She realised that they'd all come to her for readings at one time or another, which showed they trusted her skill, if nothing else.

"The ghost army is almost certainly on its way here," she said, pitching her voice as loud as she could. "We thought we could try to bespell the city the way we bespell our houses, to keep ghosts out."

"But that only works because they're *our* houses," a portly auburn-haired man objected. She'd forgotten his name, perhaps because she'd never liked him.

"And this is *our* city, isn't it?" Martine asked. "Do you want to find a new home in a countryside ruled by ghosts? I doubt they need castings very often!" She tried for a laugh, and got a few chuckles.

Wila, who cast mostly for the whores down by the harbour, cleared her throat. "My spell is for walls and door," she said. "I don't think it would work for streets. Or squares. Not empty space, see?"

Martine looked over their heads to Ranny. "Can we get barricades built across the outer streets? If we can make a ring of bespelled houses and barricades..."

Ranny nodded, shortly, and jumped down. "I'll get it organised. You assign them districts. Don't forget the harbour."

Fortunately, most stonecasters lived in the poorer parts of town — near the harbour and on the outskirts. The middle of the city, on its hill, was the preserve of the respectable. Martine found a clerk to fetch a map of Turvite and allocated an area for each stonecaster to cover, the area nearest to their own home whenever possible.

One of them was a stranger to her, after all — he had come with Thegan from Sendat, an odd-looking bald man without any eyebrows. Otter, his name was. He studied the map with intensity and spoke of the enchanter with real hatred.

"The others are afraid of the enchanter," Martine said to him. "But you hate him."

Otter's mouth thinned. "I'm from Carlion." He stared unseeing at the map of the city. "For twenty years I've been working towards equality for Travellers. Me and others, some Traveller, some not. We were getting close to having the laws repealed in Carlion. We had the ear of the town clerk, a few other councillors. We were so *close*! Twenty years...and that blood-hungry bastard destroyed it all in a night. We'll never recover from this."

He turned abruptly and walked out with the others, as though he were sorry he had said so much. He was strong, Martine thought, feeling regret for the future he had been working for, and slightly ashamed that it had never occurred to her to do so. She hoped he could cast a good spell — and the others. But she knew it would only buy them time.

Where was Ash? And Bramble, where was she?

* * *

Since Martine had no home in Turvite now, she took a part of the city that no stonecaster had a stake in—around the road to Sanctuary. It was the route into the city the ghosts were most likely to take; and she might see Ash. She stood at a barricade made of carts and barrels and boards, stretched across the road.

"Why don't stonecasters do more spells, if you can?" Sorn had asked her, back at the inn.

"There aren't many to cast," she had told her. "Only a handful, and most of those backfire on you—cast a love spell, someone ends up hating you; give the evil eye, your eye sees only ugliness afterwards."

"Balance," Sorn mused.

"Something like that. The spell to keep ghosts away is different, somehow. Maybe because it doesn't try to change anyone, just preserve what is—your privacy."

So here she was, trying to preserve a whole city's privacy.

The stonecasters had agreed that the spell might be stronger if they all cast it at the same time—at sunset. It wasn't a difficult spell, but to do it on this scale required all their strength, and sunset or sunrise were the easiest times to cast a spell. Martine didn't know why, but dusk and dawn seemed to enhance Sight and other gifts.

She waited, conscious of the Turviters who had built the barricade, and others who lived nearby, watching her critically, hopefully, nervously.

It had been three years since she'd cast this spell. It was usually done alone, inside your own home. She had never performed any public enchantments before. She took a deep breath, feeling like the butterflies in her stomach were as big as sparrows. She looked around to embed the area in her mind and saw Arvid, standing beside one of the houses, a few steps away. He smiled at her. She was flooded with warmth; she hadn't expected him to be there. The nerves retreated as though they had never existed, and she spread out her hands on top of the barricade, feeling the timber warm from the afternoon sun, slightly rough under her fingertips.

She had loved living in Turvite. This *was* her city; these were her people. She knew them inside and out—their fears, their hopes, their loves and hates, their greed and generosity. They had brought all of themselves to her and she had cast the future for them, for good or ill.

Take that feeling, she thought, and weave it into the spell.

"I am Martine, of Turvite," she said aloud, "and this is my home. Spirit without living body, come not within my home; spirit without living body, be barred from my home; spirit without living body, enter not my door."

The usual spell—"Spirit without body, enter not my door unless I set it ajar for you"—left two big holes for the ghost army. They would have needed only one sympathiser within the city to undo the protection; and who knew if the ghosts had an actual body rather than merely having bodily strength?

The rest of the spell wasn't in words, but in feeling—the desire to protect, the desire to make whole, the desire to be safe. Martine's Sight could sense the other spells reverberating on either side of her.

She could feel her energy flowing out with the spell, and she gave all she had; the others were doing the same. She had to push the spell from the barricades to the walls of the houses on either side, and then further. She thanked the gods that Turviters didn't like trees or shady yards; their houses abutted each other. But each house needed a spell in itself, and pushing the protection from one house to the next took more energy than she had expected. She pushed sideways and out to the limit of the barricades and houses, to the space that was neither city nor countryside. The edge of Turvite.

Her head was light and empty now, her legs shaking; but they weren't finished yet, they hadn't joined. She wished Ash were here, to give her strength in the way he had given it to Safred once, but she was alone. She swayed, fighting dizziness, and felt Arvid's hands come under her elbows, to support her. He wasn't Ash; he didn't have the ability to channel strength to her. But his presence, his warm body behind her, his concern, steadied her.

She reached out as best she could, ensuring that her protection reached the casters' on either side, closing the gaps. Her Sight took her around the spell, which now stretched all the way around the city. It was like a protective girdle shaped like a crescent, because it took a curve in at the harbour. But there, at the point where the crescent curved inwards, there was a weak spot. A lack of feeling, a lack of desire. She knew who it was. Otter, from Carlion. He didn't feel strongly enough about the city to protect it properly.

She sent her own love, her own strength, to that part of the spell, and felt it firm up, like a rope pulled taut. It was a maternal kind of love, she realised, as though the city and its people were her child. She could sense other weak spots being shored up by the stronger stonecasters.

The words of spells were taught when a stonecaster took an apprentice. But only the words — you couldn't teach the feeling. How could you teach the searching out, the recognising, that Sight allowed?

The protection grew, and grew, and then stopped. The rope was taut, all around the city. It *felt* all right. But whether it would keep out solid ghosts, she had no idea.

She had just enough strength left to end the spell, tying it off as one tied embroidery thread when a design was done, and as it ended her legs gave way and she fell.

Arvid caught her.

"I'm all right," she whispered. She was not all right. She could barely feel her legs and hands. Every bone in her spine hurt. But she was breathing, and the spell was tight and full.

LEOF

IN EVERY town he passed through, Leof told of the success of the Wooding Travellers. To the Travellers left alive, to the village voices, to any warlord's man he found. Most Travellers were too scared, or too angry, to do anything; but a few began to band together to protect those of Acton's people who had been good to them.

There were at least some of these: people who had given Travellers shelter when scared mobs came for them, or those who had hidden Travellers in barns or haylofts or in their own bedchambers, and denied all knowledge of them. Sometimes there were family bonds to explain their actions — but sometimes, as far as Leof could tell, they had acted out of sympathy, and abhorrence of murder.

But there were fewer of those stories than of Travellers massacred, or imprisoned, or sent to the warlord.

When he told one voice about the Wooding group, the woman said, "Why would they protect us?" Leof couldn't fault her logic: why, indeed?

As he neared the outskirts of Turvite, his two horses tired but still sound, Leof remembered his last visit to the city, two years ago, to ride in a Spring Chase. It had been after he had met Bramble, but before he had recognised his love for Sorn. Before Thegan had actively planned war. Before the enchanter, before the Lake, before he had been anything but an enthusiastic officer who liked chasing and idolised his warlord.

He had been a child.

Coming up the hill to Turvite he saw the entrances to the city were barricaded. Flimsy constructions of boards and carts that wouldn't keep an army of children out, let alone the ghosts. Surely the Turviters weren't relying on these inadequate defences?

When he reached the barricade he found some of the Moot staff, with what looked like hastily recruited deputies, allowing people in and out of a small gate.

One of the staff, an older man, was instructing a young deputy. "You *must* close the gate after each person," he said. "The stonecasters say the spell will only work if we keep a wall around the whole city, like the walls of a house, see? So people can go in and out of a house, but to keep the house safe you have to close the door."

The younger man, a tanner by the smell of his clothes, nodded earnestly. "Aye," he said. He looked up at Leof, clearly preparing to put his training into practice. "Are you blooded?" he demanded.

"What?"

"Show us your blood," the older man said.

Leof frowned. "How?"

"You may," said the young man, parroting, "pull down your eyelid and let us see the red; cut your hand and bleed; or punch yourself on the arm and show us the reddening."

"Isn't it obvious that I'm alive?" Leof demanded, both amused and affronted.

"It will be when you show us," the older man said stolidly.

Chuckling, Leof dismounted and pulled down an eyelid. The young man inspected him solemnly and then opened the gate, closing it again carefully once Leof had led the horses through.

"The stonecasters?" Leof queried.

"They're casting a spell to keep these ghosts out," the older man said happily. "We'll be safe in Turvite!"

"There are a lot of people hoping you're right, and they're all on the way here," Leof warned him.

He rode to the Moot Hall first. He had considered his options all the way to the city, and had decided that Turvite's council needed warning of the countryfolk fleeing to their city, and to learn of the success at Wooding, although he doubted *any* argument would convince the enchanter to turn away from Turvite. He would have to risk meeting Thegan.

At the door of the Moot Hall he was inspected again for blood, and then passed from clerk to clerk until he was in a small room with a thin, blonde woman.

He hesitated on the threshold, but she waved him to a seat. "I'm Ranny of Highmark," she said.

He'd heard of the Highmark family. They had a breeding farm which produced wonderful piebald chasers. "Leof, originally of Cliff Domain," he said. He'd thought quite a bit about how to present himself. "Former officer to Lord Thegan."

She raised an eyebrow at that, but let it go. "You have news?"

"Thegan is in the city?" he countered.

She paused, weighing whether it was valuable information, but he could have found out from anyone at the hall. "Aye," she said. "He came straight here."

"So he would not know, I suspect, that the whole countryside is following his example. Half of Central Domain is on its way here, hoping for shelter."

"We can't take them all in," she snapped.

"Best be prepared, then, to send them elsewhere. There may be alternatives." He explained the situation in Wooding, where the Travellers had protected their village. "I've been encouraging other towns to do the same," he said. "I'm hopeful at least some areas will remain untouched."

"Interesting," she mused. "We have quite a few Travellers here. Settled for generations, some of them. We might call a muster..." She stood up and bowed. "Thank you for your assistance, Lord Leof. Perhaps, since you are no longer on Thegan's staff, we can call on you for advice about our defences?"

"I'll give you some advice right now—the enchanter has acquired human allies. Travellers who were attacked by our people and who see him as their saviour. Your barricades may stand against the ghosts, but the humans will demolish them in a single charge."

"What do you suggest?"

"Archers at high points and behind the barricades, pikemen in front, and a good solid group of soldiers set in ambush behind them. The humans will be at the back, I think, when they attack, and if you surprise them you could cut them down easily enough with a trained force, particularly if you have enough archers. They are not trained fighters, you understand."

Part of him sorrowed as he said it—there were women in that group, and children, too. Perhaps they would not fight, and might be saved.

"We would prefer not to call in assistance from warlords."

275

"Set the ambush on Merroc's soil—then you won't need to let his men into the city." Merroc was the warlord of Far South Domain, which surrounded Turvite.

Ranny nodded. "Will you command the city forces?"

"Not if you want to keep Thegan as a friend," he said. "In fact, I would count it as a favour if you did not mention me to him."

Ranny assessed that information. She nodded. "Agreed, for now, if you keep me informed of your whereabouts."

"As to that, can you recommend an inn? Something modest, I'm afraid." He smiled at her, the smile that so often helped him make a friend.

It worked on her, too. Her lips twitched, even if she didn't smile back. "The Red Dawn is not a bad place," she said. "And I think Lord Thegan is unlikely to go there."

The Red Dawn was stripped of staff. The innkeeper had to come out and take the horses himself, apologising and promising that he'd be with his lord as soon as he'd put them in the stables and found the stable boy to groom them. He suggested that Leof wait in the inn chamber, he was sorry, but there would be no one there to serve his lord. Everyone was out working on the city defences; he hoped his lord understood. Of course he understood.

The first person he saw when he walked into the inn chamber was Sorn.

She was sitting alone in a window seat, gazing up at the sky. He had never seen her in repose before, and for a moment he simply didn't believe it *was* her. Why would she be here, instead of at the Moot Hall, or a more expensive inn? Then he saw the curve of her cheek, the light coming through the window onto the warm glow of her hair, the long hands clasped around her knees, and knew without doubt that it was her. It was as though someone had punched the breath out of him; the moment of shock was followed by a surge of feeling so great he couldn't identify it. It brought tears to his eyes, set his hands shaking.

She was alive. She was here. He didn't care whether Thegan punished him—he had to speak to her.

She hadn't noticed him. He set his bags on the floor and walked slowly between the inn tables towards her.

He stumbled a little, pushing a chair across the floor with a sharp noise, and she looked over at him. He stood still, thinking of nothing. Just looking at her.

Sorn looked back for a moment, eyes wide, and he had just enough time to wonder what to say before she sprang from the seat and flung herself across the room to him. "You're alive, you're safe! You're alive!" she babbled — quiet, controlled Sorn! He caught her, held her close. Her hands were at his face then, cradling it, then at his chest, grasping his tunic, shaking him a little. "You're *here*!" she said breathlessly.

He was already a traitor. What did one more betrayal matter? But he couldn't do it — couldn't hold her and kiss her the way he ached to. It was the only shard of honour he had left.

She saw it in his face. "I've renounced him," she said, and pulled Leof down so she could kiss him. "I'm free."

He didn't understand how she could do that, but he had no resistance left. They kissed as though parched for each other, kissed and held — the urge to pull her tight to him, to make sure she was really there, was as strong as the urge to make love to her. He twined his hands in her long hair and held her head firmly as he kissed her. Desire overwhelmed his relief at seeing her alive, and she felt it.

"Come," she said, pulling him by the hand upstairs.

They didn't make it to the bed, falling to the floor instead. He had never felt this need before, not even with Bramble. It wasn't a need for pleasure, or release, but to be with, to be *one*. Joined together, joined forever... He fought against climax because it would be the beginning of separation; he slowed but she wouldn't let him, moaning his name. Her voice, his name; it started an avalanche in him, of pleasure and tears and joy and sharp, sharp pain at the centre. He clutched at her and said her name in return, and felt her tears start, her body clutch his.

They lay in a welter of clothes, still half-dressed, feeling cold air and warm skin and sweat cooling. Shaking, both of them, still, and not from pleasure.

He'd always thought that shagging was shagging, no matter who the partner: always good, always fine. He tightened his arms around Sorn and she made a curious little snort of satisfaction, and he laughed.

She looked up at him, laughing too, and then fell silent. "Too much need for too long," she said.

He stroked hair back from her eyes. "I love you," he said.

She closed her eyes as if in pain, and he winced, wondering if he'd completely misunderstood. Then she turned her brow into the curve of his shoulder, and he realised she was weeping. He wiped the tears away for some time before she raised her head.

"No one, in all my life, has ever said those words to me," she said.

"Your parents, surely!"

"My mother died in childbirth. My father...was not a loving man."

"Your wetnurse?" he ventured. "Your maid?"

"They changed, depending on who owed tax bondage."

He was appalled at the vision of the lonely little girl, growing up without comfort or affection in all the isolation of the fort.

"Then how did you become so wonderful?" he exclaimed.

She laughed with more freedom than he had ever seen in her. Then she sobered. "Thank the gods," she said. "They were my refuge."

The words brought them back to the present, and to the dangers of the present.

"There's a good deal you don't know," she said.

As they dressed she shared all the information she had, including the plan to raise Acton's ghost.

"The Well of Secrets says that Bramble has gone after his bones." Sorn was pretending to fold a scarf, but looking sideways at him.

He caught her at it. "Wondering about her and me?" he asked. "One night, a long time ago, and never again."

She relaxed and continued her story, finishing with Thegan's intention to have Gabra sire a child on her. He stood rigid at that point, every instinct telling him to find Thegan and kill him.

She came and clasped her hands over his. "I have renounced him," she said. "Before witnesses, including the Well of Secrets. After—after this is over—I will choose me a new husband." She smiled coquettishly at him, a look he had never seen from her before. "I wonder who I might choose?"

He laughed, but sobered quickly. "We must not be seen together, or

Thegan will claim you are only renouncing him to have me, and I am a traitor, condemned to death. I'll find another inn."

"No," she said, blinking slowly. "You will take a separate room, but you will stay here."

It was the warlord's daughter speaking, and his impulse was to obey, but he had to make her see that it was dangerous for her. "Sorn—"

"I am willing to take your oath of allegiance, Lord Leof."

Even with her hair tumbled around her shoulders and her lips red from his mouth, she looked older suddenly, and far stronger.

"You need to put your case to the other warlords before Thegan gets to them," he warned, then he picked up his sword from where his belt had fallen, and drew it, presenting it hilt first to her in the ancient ceremony, but she shook her head.

"I am not a commander," she said. "I value the oath more than the sword."

"Thou art my lady," he said, "and I shall be loyal unto thee until death." They were not the same words he had used to Thegan. To Thegan he had pledged his sword and his honour. Thegan had used his sword and trampled on his honour. So for Sorn, whose honour was brighter by far than his own, he could offer only loyalty. But it seemed to be what she wanted.

Formally, she placed her hands over his. "I am thy lady," she said. "In return for thy loyalty, I shall care for thee until death."

It was the promise warlords made to officers who did not serve directly in their command—the officers who husbanded their lands and paid tribute. They were both aware of the double meaning of the words; it sounded like a wedding pledge. He smiled at her and she turned her head away slightly, trying not to smile back, then punched him lightly in the arm as if to rebuke him for levity.

She plaited her hair swiftly and pinned it up until she was once again the poised warlord's daughter.

"So, now you're mine and I can do what I like with you," she teased him as they walked out of the room.

His breath caught in his throat at that thought, but he brought his attention back to the needs of the moment. "We need to find Bramble. Where's the stonecaster?"

The sun had lowered while they had been in the chamber, and the innkeeper had lit the lanterns below.

"I have reported to my lady," Leof said. "What room have you put me in?"

The innkeeper looked slyly at him. "I wasn't sure you'd be needing a separate room."

Leof crossed the room in two paces and pushed the man back against the counter. "You cannot possibly have meant to insult my lady."

The innkeeper didn't cower, but he lost the knowing expression. "Nay," he said. "No insult. I'll put you in the room at the end of the corridor."

Leof nodded and let him go. Another woman was coming down the stairs: stocky, sandy-haired, around forty.

"Safred!" Sorn said thankfully, going to meet her. "Leof, this is the Well of Secrets."

It was strange to meet a legend in the flesh. Leof bowed very low and straightened feeling curiously exposed. It was said that the Well of Secrets knew the past and the future and everything in between. The way she flicked a glance between him and Sorn, and then lifted her eyebrows just a fraction made him believe it.

She walked over to him, closer than was polite. He didn't know whether to move back. Then she put out her hand and touched the circle of woven reeds that hung around his neck. "Are you a man of power, Lord Leof?" she asked.

He shook his head. "It was given to me. As a great boon. It saved my life."

"You are blessed," Safred said. "Keep it close. If we survive this, you will have a son. Give it to him, when he is born."

A shiver went through him. Prophecy. True prophecy. It felt different from stonecasting, where the stones somehow seemed to have the power. The Well of Secrets was linked tight to the gods...A son. *If we survive this*, she had said.

"Will we win against this enchanter?" he asked.

She sighed. "You want a prophecy? Fine, here it is." Her eyes looked into space, and she spoke as if from a long way away. "The dead will be reborn, the quick and the quickened will both taste blood, the killers will be brought together to confront the killed. The voices of the dead will echo through the world, and the evil dead shall triumph over the evil living. If we're lucky."

Her gaze sharpened on him again and he was sure she could see the trembling in his body.

"Happy?" she asked.

"Don't take it out on him, Safred," Sorn said sharply.

Safred turned to look at her closely. "So, you've found your strength, have you? Don't let Thegan intimidate you again."

"I won't."

The three of them stood there as if waiting for something. Outside, the sun set.

A shiver went through Safred and she clutched at a chair back to steady herself. "They have set the spell," she said. "The city is protected from ghosts."

"As long as the barricades are intact," Leof said. "It will be a fight to remember, keeping them so."

ASH

"TELL ME everything you know," Doronit said. It was the part of her that he'd never fully understood, the merchant in information. But more than that, there was a need to know what was happening, as though knowing could protect her. He thought for a moment of Safred, to whom secrets were meat and drink, but this was different: more rational, more ruthless.

"And then you kill me?" he asked.

"That depends on what you tell me," she said, sitting down behind her desk. She didn't offer one of the chairs she kept for clients, but he took one anyway, staring at her, not sure how he felt.

Thanks to the River, his desire for Doronit had been washed clean away. But the other emotions—especially gratitude for her taking him in when no one else wanted him, not even his parents—stayed with him and made his mind whirl. He knew she'd had her own reasons for taking him, but she'd given him the first home he'd ever known and she had truly valued him, the first person to ever do so. The skills she had taught him had saved his life, and Bramble's.

So he told her the truth. Exactly, leaving nothing out but the River.

At the end, she looked at him closely. "What are you not telling?"

He brushed the question away. "Nothing important to you."

She assessed that, a look on her face he could not read, and for the first time he could take breath and simply look at her. Just a Traveller woman. Richer, cleverer, but important only because of the secrets she held. He would never share her desire for power, but having walked through the streets of this city and seen the contempt and hatred for Travellers that lay just under the surface, he understood what had driven her to compel the ghosts of Turvite to give up their secrets. Compassion for her twisted in his gut.

"This enchanter wants to take back the Domains for our people?" she asked, looking away at last, twisting the fringe of her shawl between her fingers, something he'd never seen her do before.

"Yes. By killing everyone."

She nodded slowly and raised her head to gaze at him. Her eyes were alight. "That would work," she said.

He pushed out of the chair, sending it spinning to the floor behind him. "Thousands of people!"

"*Their* people," she breathed.

He should have seen this coming—he'd known how much she hated Acton's people. He had to appeal to the merchant in her. "There'd be no trade," he said. "Life would just collapse! No customers, no merchants, no *farmers*. You'd starve in a month."

"You think our people couldn't learn to be farmers, if they had the best land available to them, tools, animals, barns and all just handed to them? Some of them already know how! I grew up on a farm, Ash. I could run one. With a little help."

He was as startled by the idea of Doronit on a farm as by the plea in her voice. "You would let thousands of people—children—be slaughtered, just for revenge?"

She smiled, hard as the sapphires in her brooch. "Not for revenge. For justice! This is *our* land, and always has been. Do the old powers come for the blondies? No! Does the River acknowledge them? You know she doesn't."

Shock hit him, a moment ahead of understanding. She had all the secrets that the ghosts could tell. Of course some Traveller man had told her about the River. She didn't know, couldn't know, about him and Her.

Outside, the sun set. A shiver went through both of them at the same moment, and Ash's head reeled. Something was happening, outside, at the edge of the city—at all the edges of the city. A spell... One that felt familiar.

Doronit was quicker than he was, as always. "The spell to keep out ghosts! They've set it all around the city."

They stood for a moment silently. Doronit smiled.

"They'll be resting secure now, in their feather beds. Thinking they're safe. But all we have to do is break the barricade, and they're all dead."

She saw the revulsion on his face and came closer.

"We could help him, Ash, you and I. There's no sign that he can make them talk. Think how much more effective he'd be if he could

283

talk to them, discuss plans of attack, strategy. We would be his most valuable officers."

He knew that voice. It was the voice she'd used to try to convince him to kill Martine. Then he had been torn, but not this time. He moved closer to her, as though drawn despite himself. For a moment, he'd lost his compassion for her, but now it came back. She was like a child, not caring how she got what she wanted, just wanting it now. In that thought, at last, he found affection for her as well as compassion and gratitude; she could have been so much more. In another world, a different time, before the landtaken, she could have been anything she chose.

Her eyes warmed as she came closer, seeing the warmth in his. "We could tip the balance," she said softly. "You and I together. The way it was meant to be."

"Yes," he said. "We could tip the balance. *You* could tip the balance."

He could see it, too clearly. Turvite overrun. She would simply send out her people and tell them to break the barricades where it wouldn't be detected. The ghosts would storm through into an unprepared city. The enchanter, so far, had shown no great sense of strategy or cunning. His strikes had been clean, simple, brutal. With Doronit to advise him, with her capacity to communicate freely with the ghosts, with her huge network of spies and safeguarders — and worse, with her viciousness — Acton and Bramble had no chance of even reaching the ghost army. Doronit's agents would find and stop them before they came anywhere near. She would destroy any hope they had, and condemn thousands to death, right across the Domains. And one of those thousands would be young Ash, probably, and Mabry his father, certainly. Their precious home in Hidden Valley would be smashed apart with swords and screams and death, and the child he had sworn to protect would be the most vulnerable thing there.

He didn't reach to the River for guidance. She had no say in this. Just this once, he was not following. This time, he had to decide for himself.

Ash reached up, gently, delicately, and took Doronit's face between his hands. He felt very calm, as though time had slowed. She smiled, triumphant, blue eyes finally alight for him.

He broke her neck.

MARTINE

SORN WANTED to go back to the Moot Hall immediately. If she were to claim Central Domain, she needed to be part of any discussion, to set herself in the council as if it were natural. Turvite was the perfect opportunity—she had as much right to be there as the warlords did.

Martine would have preferred to rest, but she followed Sorn. Curiosity drove her as much as duty, she acknowledged to herself. And the desire to see Arvid.

When they walked into the hall, Ranny and Garham were poring over a map of Turvite spread out on a huge table. They were allocating areas. Each warlord was to defend a section of the city, using his own men to direct and train Turviters.

Martine kept back, but Sorn joined the group around the table, ignoring Thegan's glare and the questioning stares of the others. Ranny glanced at her and nodded; Garham scarcely seemed to notice her. Arvid looked up and saw Martine at the back of the hall and smiled involuntarily, as though his whole spirit had lightened because she was there. Her thoughts wandered: to his arm, supporting her during the spell; his gentleness as he had returned her to the Red Dawn, the way he had stroked her hair back and handed her over to Sorn and Safred reluctantly. She forced her attention back to the present, to the discussion around the table.

Ranny had given the harbour to Coeuf, Martine suspected on the grounds that his senility would be least dangerous there, and put Eolbert, his son, in actual control. Thegan was given the southern sector.

"I should take the north-west," he demanded. "I'm the only one who has experience against them!"

"Much good it did you," Sorn said mildly.

Each warlord snapped his head around to stare at her. Thegan couldn't hide his astonishment, which gave Martine some satisfaction.

He'd never so much as spoken a word to her directly, but her dislike was already deep and burning.

Merroc smiled at Sorn in appreciation. "I will take the north-west," he said. "It leads to my domain."

Thegan stared at Merroc; then, with a slight nod, accepted this as reasonable. Or appeared to.

The others took their assignments more graciously, and were introduced to the Turvite Moot staff who would be their offsiders.

Before Merroc left, he bowed to the council and said, "Far South Domain is at the service of Turvite!" It was a display for the benefit of the assembled officers and councillors.

"South Domain is at the service of Turvite," Eolbert followed quickly, simultaneously, with Arvid: "The Last Domain is at the service of Turvite." The two men smiled at each other, a little embarrassed. The other warlords waited for each other to speak.

Sorn noticed Thegan open his mouth. "Central Domain is at the service of Turvite," she said.

There was a pause, as people registered who had spoken. The women councillors smiled slightly.

"Cliff Domain is at the service of Turvite," Thegan said smoothly, smiling at Sorn as though at an errant child. "And the men of Central and Cliff Domains will fight together, as always."

It was a good recovery, Martine thought. But Sorn had sown a seed, at least, in people's minds. Eolbert's, for example. He was her age, after all, and not married, although rumour said he had a mistress who lived at the fort and had borne him several children. That was no barrier to a formal alliance between warlord families. Sorn would have to encourage Eolbert to hope that, if she renounced Thegan, he would be in the running to marry her.

She clearly knew that, because she smiled at him gently, and walked out the door with him, and let Thegan hear her say, "You have several children, do you not, my lord, at Wooding?" It was a dangerous game, and Sorn was braver than Martine had thought to play it, but Thegan was too fully occupied with the enchanter to focus on her just yet. It would come. An attempt to kill her, probably, before she could announce her intention, so he could inherit from her. And then he could forget about siring a son on her.

"I would so love to have children myself," Sorn said.

Eolbert's eyes widened and the dissipated folds around his mouth deepened. So, he had understood, and was rapidly calculating her intentions. "A big family is every warlord's dream," he said. "One I certainly share." He glanced at Thegan. "But not in this current situation. We must deal with this enchanter before any of us can think of the future."

Say something, Martine urged Sorn silently. Reassure Thegan of your promise, or he will draw sword and slice you down right here.

As though she had caught the thought, Sorn nodded. "Indeed, my lord," she said gravely. "Nothing can be thought of until after this crisis."

Arvid came up behind Martine and, careless of who was watching, put his hands on her waist and drew her back to rest against him. She allowed herself to relax. Sorn was safe for now.

It made sense for the council to use the most experienced commanders, but the people of Turvite didn't like it, and showed they didn't like it by obeying orders slowly or sloppily or by simply ignoring them. Martine and Sorn and Safred watched as Merroc tried to organise the defence of the western road. He had made an inn his headquarters, despatching orders from there, but it wasn't going well.

Martine almost laughed. It was one of the things she'd always liked about Turviters, their independence. But it might get them killed. She yawned behind her hand. Every bone still ached slightly, as though the spell had hollowed them out. But how could she rest? She'd never sleep, not tonight.

"I can't be everywhere at once, man!" Merroc snapped when an aide asked him to talk to the tanners who were forming the guard at the gate.

"Perhaps an extra officer would be useful, my lord Merroc?" Sorn queried.

He frowned. "An *experienced* officer would be invaluable, my lady, but—"

"I have one in my train," she said smoothly. "He has...parted ways with my lord Thegan, but he is an excellent officer."

"Who is it?"

"Lord Leof."

"The chaser? Gods, yes, get him here as soon as you can."

"Thegan won't like it," Safred warned.

Merroc smiled. "Let me worry about Thegan. Time he learnt he's not the warlord of the whole eleven!"

They sent a messenger to fetch Leof from the Red Dawn. When he walked in, Sorn bit back a smile, and he flicked a quick, searching glance at her before bowing formally. Ah, Martine thought. Sits the wind in that quarter? That explained a great deal. He was certainly good looking enough to make a young woman's heart beat faster. Sorn was playing a much more dangerous game than she had realised. Thinking of Arvid, Martine was sympathetic. You couldn't choose who you loved, could you? Especially a warlord's daughter, married off when she was still half a child to a ruthless man twice her age. Poor Sorn, she thought. Yet when she looked at Sorn, who was following Merroc's plans intently, a small frown on her face, her body upright in her chair, *poor Sorn* seemed inappropriate. Sorn was no longer a child—and she had a strength that men might not easily see, hidden inside the calm poise of the warlord's wife.

Leof had no time to even speak to them. Merroc sent him out immediately to place the archers in the houses nearest the road.

More people were going to die, Martine thought. More and more.

ASH

HE WALKED out into the training yard, putting every ounce of energy he had into seeming confident.

Aylmer was waiting, sitting on a bench honing a knife in the light from a lantern. Hildie was lying full length on another bench. They both tensed as he walked out the door, and Hildie swung her legs to the ground, eyes on his.

"She's letting you live?" Aylmer asked, voice neutral.

"Better than that," Ash forced himself to grin. "I'm the heir again!"

Hildie swore, but Aylmer raised both brows and half-grinned back, caught between admiration and disbelief. He stood up and made for Doronit's office.

"Wouldn't go *just* yet if I was you," Ash said slowly, before Aylmer had reached the door. "She might need a few minutes to, er..."

Aylmer's grin was genuine this time. "Shagged your way back in, did you, lad?"

Hildie laughed and lay back down on the bench. "Old fool," she said, and it wasn't clear if she were talking about Doronit or Aylmer.

Neither thought for a moment that he might have been a threat to Doronit. A year ago they would have been right.

His hands felt heavy with the memory of her weight sagging down on them as he'd lowered her to the floor.

"I need a drink!" he said with feeling, and raised a hand casually to them as he simply walked out of the yard, and kept walking slowly until he reached the inn on the corner. Hildie watched him go. He didn't turn to confirm it, but he knew she would be watching. She was less trusting than Aylmer, and immune to men's charms.

So he walked into the inn and past the outside benches into the quiet of the parlour, ordered a mead and, after he'd had a few sips of its dizzying sweetness, headed out to the privy in the back lane.

He couldn't see anyone watching the lane, so again he kept walking. He had to find Baluch. Meet Bramble. Be ready for the enchanter's next strike.

But he didn't make it to the end of the laneway before the Dung Brothers caught up with him.

They stripped him of weapons, purse and pouch and hauled him in front of the council, where Doronit's limp body lay on a sheet on the floor as evidence. She looked like a stranger, some brown-haired woman he'd never met. Small, much smaller than she'd seemed to him alive. Ash drew a deep breath and looked away from her.

Turvite's Town Council was five members, including Ranny. They stared at him with identically suspicious blue eyes, and he had never been so aware of his black hair.

The Council were furious, especially Garham, who shouted and banged the table in front of him.

When he drew breath, Ash said, "Clear the room."

"What?" Garham yelled. "Don't you give me orders, you black-haired bastard!"

Ash looked at Ranny, who had sat composed through Garham's tirade. The last time he had seen her had been in her own office at Highmark, with Martine. He could tell she remembered him. He spoke directly to her. "Clear the room."

The other councillors began to object, but Ranny cut through them.

"Why?"

"Because you don't want anyone else to hear why I killed her."

That silenced all of them.

"Clear the room," Ranny said.

Reluctantly, Hildie, Aylmer, the Dung Brothers, Boc and the other Moot staff trailed out and shut the double doors behind them.

"Well?" Garham demanded.

He told them almost everything. Acton's brooch, the gods in Hidden Valley sending him and Martine to the Well of Secrets, meeting Bramble, meeting Safred and Cael, the tasks the gods had given them. They listened impassively, although their eyes widened when he described raising Acton's ghost.

"You left him behind?" Garham said. "With some chit of a girl?"

"The gods sent me ahead—perhaps to get you ready for when he arrives, so we can meet this enchanter next time he comes, to lay the ghosts to rest and bring peace."

"His story matches that of the Well of Secrets," Garham said reluctantly, at the end.

"She's here?" Ash asked eagerly. "Let me see her."

"Later," Ranny said. "Perhaps."

"You say someone has to give Acton his voice, let him acknowledge his wrongdoing, like at a quickening." That was the thin one, a spice merchant Ash had once worked for, guarding a saffron shipment. Ash nodded.

"What if he won't acknowledge it?"

"Why should he?" a thickset, red-faced man broke in. Wine merchant, that was it. Garham, his name was and he was as influential as the Highmarks, Doronit had told him. "He didn't do anything wrong! He's a hero!"

The others were silent.

"No matter what we think of him in the present day," Ash said carefully, 'to the ghosts he is the man who invaded their homeland and organised their deaths. And he has promised that he will go through the ceremony."

"Why not just kill the enchanter?" Garham said, looking crafty.

"Someone else will raise the ghosts. And the ghosts will come, and it will all start over again. It is the ghosts who must be—dealt with."

"What do you want us to do about it, eh?" Garham asked.

"Let me go. The Well of Secrets and I will go to bring Acton here." They stared at him.

"You need me to finish the task the gods have given me."

"Wait. There is still the matter of Doronit's death," Ranny said.

"Doronit was going to support the enchanter," Ash replied. "To break the barricade and, once the city was overrun, hand over her entire organisation to support him. You know how much information she had..." they looked, shiftily, at each other, as though assessing how much each knew "...but you don't know how she got it."

"How?" Ranny demanded.

"She was like me. She could make ghosts speak. She made the ghosts of Turvite tell their secrets. And she was going to join the enchanter, so he could talk to his army whenever he liked, discuss strategy, plan attacks..."

They shivered in unison.

"So I killed her." Ash kept his voice flat. "It was the only chance we had."

"Why would Doronit...?" the thin spice merchant asked.

"Because she wanted to be sitting where you are sitting, and she knew she never would."

"She was ambitious, yes, but surely she never imagined that a *Traveller*..." Garham spluttered.

"No," Ash said. "She knew better than that."

That was all he trusted himself to say. He ached all over. Head and legs and back and stomach, where the Dung Brothers had kicked him and Hildie had punched him. He'd fought, but to stop them he'd have had to kill them, and he'd had enough of killing.

Ash waited all night in a small room off the hall. They didn't bother to bring him a candle. He sat away from the window, staring at the green wall with its frieze of little ships, to represent the mercantile wealth of Turvite. The longer he stared, the more they seemed to dip and lift with the stylised waves they rode upon.

Safred had called him a killer, in her kitchen back in Oakmere. He'd known it was true, even then, but he'd hoped that he could leave that behind him. Become someone else. When the River had chosen him he had felt washed-clean, new, ready for a different life. To be a different person.

But here he was with blood on his hands, again. Doronit. He sat with his hands hanging between his knees, remembering her. He hoped, with all his heart, that he had killed her for the reason he had told the council. To save them all. Not because he had hated her. Not because he had loved her. Not because she was beautiful and untrustworthy and unrepentant.

He didn't think he had killed her for those reasons. Before the River, maybe he would have. Since She had accepted him, he had felt no desire for anyone else. So, surely, he had closed his hands around Doronit's neck for good reason. Surely.

Killer.

He did not reach for the River, and She did not try to contact him. He refused to wonder if she would ever touch his mind again. If not, he deserved it.

He didn't know what would happen, but he clung to two things: Acton walked; and Safred was here, nearby, and would no doubt find him eventually. But he might still hang for Doronit's murder, if the ghosts were defeated.

BRAMBLE

SHE RODE for a day and a night, stopping only for water and privy breaks. When the horses tired, she stole new ones from abandoned farms. By the end, she was lightheaded from lack of food and sleep, in a high exalted mood.

The Turvite headland hadn't changed much in a thousand years. She had seen it then through Piper's eyes, coming up from the harbour. Now she stood on its northern edge, where it started to rise from the surrounding fields, and saw that it formed a quarter circle, bounded by the cliffs on the sea and harbour sides, and by the stream to the north. It rose and became a plateau at its height, dotted by boulders and rocks, turfed by hardy grass and small shrubs in the lee of the boulders. There was a clear path up from the town which, protected a little from the rising wind, seemed as good a place as any to wait.

She drank from the stream and then leapt over it, her body feeling heavy after the fast ride. She had no food, but that didn't seem to matter. Perhaps she should sleep, though, before she went looking for Ash. It was very early, the sky only just beginning to lighten. A couple of hours, and then she would go searching. She trudged up the hill towards the ring of high rocks. As she approached, she realised that someone, a man, was waiting for her.

Baluch. Without Ash.

"Where is he?" Bramble called, unable to disguise her urgency.

"If Ash can get away, he will come here." Baluch said. "The River will tell him where I am. He is imprisoned in Turvite, but not harmed."

"We need to get him out," Bramble said. "We need him to sing Acton back."

"He is not with you?" Baluch said tentatively, then realised what must have happened. "Could you not sing him yourself?"

She shook her head. "Ash has the brooch. I don't think...I don't think I could do it alone." She didn't know why she was so sure, but she

294

was. The thought of trying to sing Acton back by herself was nauseating. "Can you do it?"

"I can try," Baluch said, but he was troubled by the thought, too, she could tell.

They spread the scarf out and laid Acton's bones on it. "Best to wait for sunrise," Baluch said, and she nodded understanding—sunrise or sunset were the best times.

So they waited, and they talked over other things—memories in common, Ragni and Sebbi, Harald and Swef...Friede.

"I loved her," he said. "I've never said that to anyone else, because no one else knew her."

"So you wrote songs for her."

He dropped his head for a moment, then brought it up again. "Yes...a poor monument."

" 'The Distant Hills' will keep her alive forever," Bramble said, but he shook his head.

"I should have put her name into it. *Then* she would have lived forever." He paused. "Strange. I put all those memories aside, but talking with you has brought back all the pain."

"It's the same pain the ghosts are feeling. Just as fresh." He looked at her with surprise, but she was angry again, at the way people talked themselves out of guilt. "You're a good man, Baluch, but you killed a lot of people in your day. Acton has taken responsibility for that. Time you did, too."

She pushed herself to her feet and walked out of the circle of boulders, feeling the salt spray on her face and hands. The wind was building again, clouds scudding across the sky, waves smashing into the cliff. She walked to the edge and peered down. The rollers were crashing against the sheer rock, sending spray shooting up and over the cliff face. Bramble grinned, tilting her head back to the sky and letting the spray coat her face and neck, letting the wind whip her hair out of its tie. Her spirits rose. Too much talk. She wished she were back in the forest again with her hunter, but this rampant display would do. Wind, water, stone. The things that lasted. The same as they were a thousand years ago.

She took comfort from that; the land, at least, would remain no matter what the enchanter did.

After a while she turned and went back to Baluch, whom she found watching her, standing, leaning on one of the boulders as if he'd been there a long time.

She was wet from sea spray, but she didn't care.

"I can see why he looks at you the way he does," Baluch said. Her heart skipped a beat with sudden longing to see Acton again, even as a ghost. To see how he looked at her. To see that berserker grin he gave just before he did something outrageous. The hollow under her ribs was enormous. She felt like a shell around thin air, as light and empty as an egg whose hatchling has flown away.

As the sun showed its first edge, Baluch began to sing. His voice was much better than Ash's—more trained, more controlled—and the song rose like a bird song, like water flowing. Bramble hung her head and yearned for Acton, feeding all her longing into the music. It was harder than with Ash, which surprised her, because she wasn't revealing anything this time that Baluch didn't already know. But she and Ash had been attuned, and she and Baluch were not, exactly. Perhaps it was the missing brooch. Perhaps it was the place, so far from where he met his death.

She remembered being Baluch, being inside his head, inside his music, and felt the connection between them grow stronger.

Come back, she sent to Acton. *We need you. I need you.*

But she could tell, even before Baluch's voice faltered to a stop, before she lifted her head, that he had not come.

SAKER

SAKER WOKE and looked out the window to the east. A day's march to Turvite. Perhaps two. The road curved and looped between low hills, following the path of the river. There were well-built villages along the way, smaller streams with bridges over them, large inns next to docks on the river, all the marks of prosperity.

He ran his fingers over the rim of the wash basin. He had to make sure that, when the spoils of war were distributed, it was done fairly. His people had had everything taken from them: they should receive everything equally.

But that might be difficult, sometimes. There were not so many ceramic basins of this quality... Who should get this level of goods?

Better to smash the luxuries and start even than have disputes about mere things, Saker resolved. Or else inequality would be built into the foundation of their new world, and he would not let that happen.

The yard below was seething with ghosts. They had finished their morning blood ceremony. Saker had decided to let Owl and his father just do it. He tried not to admit to himself that he was relieved not to have to use the knife on another person — it was not because of that, not at all. It was because he was finding it increasingly harder to avoid reacting to the terrible whining of the spirits of those they had killed. With each sacrifice, the sound grew louder, though no one else could hear it. Each dawn and dusk, the distorted shapes crowded his vision more and more, writhing towards him against an invisible barrier. He had nightmares about what would happen if that barrier ever broke, and he shuddered.

In a corner of the yard, the wind wraiths devoured the remains of the sacrifice. Saker turned away from the sight. Better to avoid the whole ceremony, lest he break down in front of his army.

They had organised themselves into groups for the march: ghosts first, human allies behind them. It was time he went down.

As he came out of the house into the bright glare of the dawn sun, the lead wraith flew to him like a scrap of cloud and hovered.

"Master," it said. "Today you go to the city of the woman."

"The woman?"

The wraith shivered. "The enchanter who made the compact, long ago. The compact is strong, there. Too strong for us to follow you, unless you break the walls and invite us in. Can you?"

Saker felt his spirits rise. At last, a battle without the horrific shrieking of the wraiths. "I will try," he said graciously.

"Call us and we will come." The wraith shot up in the air and was joined by his companions, until they were no more than specks in the sky, and then were gone.

Saker looked down, his eyes blinded by the morning light, and he noticed a woman walk through the gate into the yard. She stood for a moment, staring at the ghosts, and then she shrugged and came in. A black-haired woman, young, with the grace of an acrobat. Saker realised he was staring, and flushed.

It had been longer than he could remember since he had looked at any woman that way.

She asked a question of one of the living, and made her way over to him. He could see that she had cried a lot, recently. His heart contracted a little with pity.

"My name's Zel," she said. "My brer was killed by Thegan at Sendat."

She has come to reproach me, Saker thought immediately. And she is right — I am responsible for those deaths.

"So. Can I join you?"

It was like a reprieve; she did not blame him. He nodded. "Welcome, Zel," he said. She bobbed her head, as though she didn't know what to say but felt she should say something. He reached out and put his hand on her shoulder. "Walk with me today," he said, "and I will explain our plans."

She half-smiled at him; it was the best she could do, he surmised. Her grief ran deep, very deep. Freite had taught him how to draw on the power of such emotions, but he didn't need to. The ghosts were all the power he needed. That realisation made him feel light, free of the past. He walked with Zel to the head of the army and took the front wagon.

They found Owl, Oak and his father waiting for him to lead.

"This is Zel," he told them. "She has suffered greatly from the warlords, as we all have." They nodded to her with respect, and Oak smiled at her, stirring a flick of jealousy in Saker. He put a hand on her back, to guide her into place, and saw that Oak registered the touch.

"Come," he said, raising his voice so they could all hear. "Let us make Turvite our own."

They drove off to the sound of human cheering and the deathly percussion of the ghosts banging their weapons together. Even without the wind wraiths, they were invincible.

Saker and Zel talked, and he learnt that her brother had been a singer, and she a tumbler, as he had thought. She was so slight that she made him feel stalwart, and he was determined that she should go to the back when the fighting began.

"Why should I?" she demanded. "I want to fight the blond bastards."

"I understand. But it's better if the ghosts can swing their weapons without worrying about hitting a living ally." He dropped his voice and leant closer confidentially, her scent suddenly warm in his nostrils, making him dizzy. "They're not trained soldiers, you know, and half the time they hit each other!" She turned surprised eyes to him and he chuckled a little. "It doesn't matter, of course, with them. But with you..." He shook his head magisterially. "It would hinder our fight, and that cannot be allowed."

She stared at her feet resentfully. Her boots were scuffed and worn, from long Travel. He would find her a cobbler to make a new pair. All his people would have new boots, he amended hastily. Not just her.

On the outskirts of Turvite, they passed through a deserted village. "This Sanctuary?" Zel asked, looking around intently.

"Aye," Saker said. "They've all hidden in the city, but it won't help them."

Zel frowned, and kept frowning on the long slope up the hill towards the city. He tried to engage her again in conversation, but she replied absently and he let it drop. She looked at him often, and he took comfort from that, although she never smiled, just looked around at the ghosts and the city ahead. It was natural that she should be afraid. He said so.

"Not fear, cully," she said.

"What, then?"

There were tears in her eyes as she looked up at him. "Just the past coming back to bite me," she said. "I'm going to die. I knew it when I found out about Flax. And I thought, if I'm going to die, I'd rather die fighting with my own kind."

"You're not going to die!" he protested. "I'll look after you."

"You'll have enough trouble looking after yourself. D'you think they'll just let you stroll in?"

"They can't stop me! Us!" he said. "We're invincible!"

She smiled at him then, but it was the smile of a mother to a young child who had said something foolish.

"No such thing in the world as invincible," she said. "Not in this world or the next. Sorry."

That was all she would say.

As they came through the houses and market gardens that surrounded the city, Saker could see that the road had been blocked off. But this was no proper fortification, as there had been at Sendat. This was just a motley collection of carts and barrels and boards. No one stood guard, although he noticed faces at windows nearby, watching. It was unnerving. Then, as they came closer, he felt the hum of enchantment running through the barricade.

It seemed familiar to him, somehow, but he couldn't place it. He called a halt a few hundred yards from the barricade and got down from the cart. Owl, his father and Oak came to him with questions in their eyes.

"There's a spell on the barricades," he said. "I don't know what it is, but I don't want our living allies anywhere near it. We'll have to storm it and see."

Owl nodded and hefted his battleaxe. He was hung with other weapons: knives, a short cudgel.

Oak stepped forward. "Are you sure you should send the ghosts against a spell?" he asked, and Alder nodded strongly, as though he shared Oak's doubts.

"It's not that type of a spell," Saker said. He was sure of that. "Believe me. It feels quite different from a destruction spell." He looked at his father, who was still frowning. That annoyed him and put a sharper note into his voice. "Spells are my business. This is *not* a destruction spell."

Reluctantly, Alder nodded and moved back with Owl to the head of their forces. They exchanged glances and grinned at each other. Saker, as he had before, felt suddenly excluded. Owl, he thought, was the kind of son Father really wanted. Warlike. Fearless. He set his shoulders straighter. Well, it wasn't Owl who had brought them to this moment of triumph. It was him.

"Attack!" he shouted.

The ghosts moved forward, men and women and youths armed with axes or swords, moving more quickly as they neared the flimsy barricade.

A few yards away from it, Owl recoiled, pushing back against the men behind him. Alder flung up a hand and skidded to a stop, putting out a hand for balance and pushing over the woman next to him. The line came to a standstill. Saker watched, puzzled. What had happened?

Owl tried again, walking forward as if through deep water, thrusting his leg ahead at each step with visible effort. Then, head down, pushing as hard as he could, he could go no further. Saker felt the spell's power surge against him. It was very strong.

Owl turned and walked back, and the power in the spell waned.

"I know what it is," Saker said, turning to Zel. "It's the spell stonecasters use in Turvite to keep ghosts out of their houses." He thought for a moment. "It will only work if the barriers go all the way around the city."

Oak planted the handle of his axe in the dirt and smiled a little.

"Time for us to do some work, I reckon," he said.

LEOF

O AK? SURELY that was Oak, the stonemason from Sendat. Leof felt sick to his stomach. He was angry with Oak as though the man had betrayed him personally, but he remembered that the last time he had seen Oak, Thegan's men had been trying to kill him. It wasn't surprising that he had joined the enchanter's army. Where else could he go? Who should he side with—the man who was trying to take his country back for him, or the ones who had tried to murder him?

Merroc had given orders that the barricade should appear deserted. They had waited, sweating—in attics and bed chambers, a rabble of safeguarders and huntsmen for archers—while the enemy sorted themselves into the dead and the living, and the dead had advanced upon them. Behind them, in the city, Leof had heard the news of the ghost army's approach spread. Shouts, screams, weeping, running feet loud against the cobbles. He had hoped that Eolbert, down by the harbour, would realise that he'd have to hold the barricade against the Turviters trying to get out, more than against the enemy. *Just let them through*, he thought, *let them run if they want, as long as the spell stays strong.*

And it stayed strong, but now the enchanter's human allies were massing together—too close for proper fighting—and walking up the road, led by Oak, axe in hand. There were women, too, but Leof was relieved to see the men kept them at the back out of harm's way. Except, of course, that would put them closer to his spearmen who were waiting for just this moment, when the living enemy was between them and the archers.

Merroc was in the house across the road, with a sightline to Leof. He nocked his bow and looked at Merroc, who had his hand raised, waiting for the Travellers to advance enough to be sure targets, but not so close that any could break through the barricade. The others in the room found places at the windows, bows ready but not pulled.

Leof watched. They were within bowshot now.

He took aim, but not at Oak. He couldn't bring himself to cut the man down. Two along from him were a pair of twins, tall men with shiny black hair like raven's wings.

Leof pulled back and aimed at the one on the left. He felt the familiar heart-stopping anticipation that built just before battle—a mixture of dread and excitement, nausea and exhilaration.

Merroc's hand dropped, and the archers let fly. The whir of arrows was loud, shouts and screams erupted from the enemy. Leof's man dropped. Oak reeled back with a shaft in the shoulder. He dropped his axe, picked it up again with his other hand and tried to rush forward.

Leof took another arrow. This was where practice paid off.

He was twice as fast as the others so it fell to him to stop Oak from reaching the barricade. There was no choice: a living city depended on it. He pulled back and let fly, then nocked another arrow and shot again as Oak's throat blossomed with blood. The third arrow hit him in the side as he spun away; he fell.

Around him, his companions were panicking. They had been prepared for hand-to-hand fighting, Leof thought, not for death falling from the sky. Just as his men at Bonhill had not been prepared for the wind wraiths. He hardened his heart and shot, and shot again.

The line broke and ran back towards the ghosts, who had started advancing. But the spearmen emerged from hiding and spears sliced through the air towards them. A few realised what was happening. Leof saw one young woman jump over a fence like an acrobat and run between houses, away from both the spearmen and the ghosts. He followed her flight to avoid looking at the slaughter; she ran, but she ran in a wide circle, coming up behind the ghosts and rejoining the enchanter, who stared, stricken, calling his people back.

The ghosts turned on the spearmen, but Merroc waved and a horn sounded in warning. The spearmen turned and ran back into the houses on either side; bespelled against ghosts, they were temporary havens.

The spearmen slammed the doors closed and the shutters were already nailed up. Outside, the ghosts couldn't even reach the walls; one strained to touch the door, but couldn't make contact. He snarled frustration—even at such a distance, the expression was clear.

In the street below him, people began to cheer. He should be happy, too, Leof thought, but he could see Oak's body, and the others he had killed, sprawled on the road. He could not quite feel the elation he had always felt before when a battle went well.

They were retreating, all of them: the few remnants of the living, the dead, the enchanter. Leof thanked the gods that the wind wraiths had not come; that had saved the spearmen.

He realised then, with a little shock, that they had not lost a single man; and at last a sense of achievement came to him.

BRAMBLE

SHE WOULD not let herself panic. She would not. "We need Ash," Bramble said. Briskly, she began packing Acton's bones back into the bag. She refused to dwell on the feel of bone beneath her fingertips, the curve of his skull. "We'll have to go into Turvite and find him."

She had to raise her voice. Baluch had walked away after their attempt to raise Acton had failed, and was looking down at the city from the landward side of the boulders.

"That might be harder than it sounds," he answered over his shoulder.

Bramble moved to stand beside him, gazing down at Turvite, which was spread out before them like a bowl, the tiers of houses leading down to a harbour full of white caps from the night's wind.

A thousand years ago a woman named Piper had looked down at what had been a simple fishing village. Bramble felt as though she saw both places at the same time, as one sees frost on the windowpane and the scene outside, overlaid on one another. She shook her head. *This* Turvite she could smell, a combination of old fish and spices, woodsmoke and cooking bacon. She was starving.

Then she saw, around the town, a continuous barrier blocking all the inward streets, with men behind it, guarding. "They're trying to keep the ghosts out," she said.

"Doesn't mean they'll let us in," Baluch said. "People from the countryside will be flooding in soon, when the ghosts advance. Their only hope of survival is to keep everyone out except their own people."

Bramble remembered when Baluch's folk had made the same choice—to accept the people running from the Ice King or fight them off. They had chosen to fight. It was the constant attacks from those pushed from their land that had led to Acton planning the settlement over the mountains.

Instead of going down the slope to the harbour, they walked along the ridge that connected with the hill at the back of the town. They found a well-worn track, and halfway along they understood why; they had to stand aside to let the milked cows return to their pasture. They passed in stately file, their udders swinging loose, and their solid warmth was reassuring to Bramble, their twice-daily trek seemed the only unchanging thing.

"I want to see what's happening on the other side," Baluch said. He was assessing the city with a warrior's eye, as he had once assessed River Bluff.

The barrier extended all the way around the city, but as they came closer it was clear that it was so flimsy it wouldn't keep anyone out.

"A spell," Bramble said with surety. "They're using enchantment to strengthen it."

"Let's hope they know what they're doing."

The headland grazing area ended on a high knoll. Beyond it on one side were market gardens stretching down to the river. Lilac, rosemary, lavender and dung from the gardens mixed in Bramble's nose. Down the hill, the road west cut through a mixture of houses and vegetable patches.

It was strange to see her enemy, finally, coming down the road towards Turvite. It had been months for her since that day in Oakmere when Safred had told her that a man named Saker had killed Maryrose, and offered her the chance to stop him.

They needed Acton, right now. "We have to try again," she said.

But Baluch shook his head. "It won't work. I could feel it—something is missing in the spell. I'm not sure if it's the brooch or Ash, but we can't do it as things stand."

"Then we have to find Ash."

"Battle is about to be joined," he said, flexing his right hand as though a sword might appear there. "And Ash is in the middle of the city, somewhere. I don't know where."

"But he's alive?"

Baluch nodded, and she felt a surge of relief. It wasn't hopeless, then. Risky, but not impossible.

She grinned and hoisted her bag of bones onto her shoulder. "If they're coming in the front way, let's you and I go in the back, round the harbour."

306

They retraced their steps to where the path began to lead down towards the water, but Baluch put out a hand and stopped her. "Look," he said.

There was a fight at the barricade leading to the harbour. People were panicking, trying to reach the few ships in port. The guards at the barricade were letting people through one by one, closing the gate after each one, but it wasn't fast enough to satisfy the crowd. Some leapt over the barriers, others climbed up inside the houses that formed part of the city's defence, and jumped from their windows. The ones who made it through rushed to the ships, all of which had pulled up their boarding planks and were making ready to sail.

It didn't stop the crowd. They pulled on the mooring ropes until the ships were crammed up against the dock, then swarmed up the sides. The sailors fought them off with belaying pins and knives. Bodies dropped back onto the dock — some sailors, but most Turviters.

"Don't go down," Baluch said. "Please, Bramble. I can't protect you down there."

She spared a flick of a smile for the idea that he had to protect her — that came from his old life, for sure — but the scene below was sobering enough. Going down into that mob was too foolhardy even for her. She had Acton's bones, and they could not be risked.

The desperate Turviters had almost overwhelmed the ships when a horn blasted out from the top of the hill.

"The ghost attack!" Baluch said.

They ran back to the knoll in time to see the ghosts retreat, confused, leaving a welter of dark-haired bodies in front of the barrier.

"More deaths," Bramble said.

"More will come, unless we do our job," Baluch said.

SAKER

H E CALLED his people back in horror, and they died as they came, bodies falling, pierced by spears or arrows; some screamed as they lay in the dust of the road, their blood coating themselves and their colleagues.

Blood.

He could smell blood, and the stench of guts cut open.

Blood and memory.

"Arise!" he cried, putting all his grief and terror into the call. "Arise, comrades-in-arms! Oak and Ber and Eldwin and Fox, arise! We seek justice for you, my friends. Arise!" He called, and kept on calling, as long as their blood flowed.

It was easier, this spell, than any other had been, fuelled by his pain, strengthened by his sorrow.

They rose as they died, one by one, the ghosts forming quickly, their weapons still in their hands. There was no confusion—they knew what had happened, they had died hearing him call. Their ghosts moved with purpose as soon as they formed, gathering with the others; they were the newest part of his army, the most valuable.

Zel had arrived, panting, at his elbow as he began the spell, and she supported him as it ended, when his legs gave way and his head spun. She was stalwart; he gave thanks to the gods that she was still alive.

Saker turned to his ghosts again, and whispered, "Try the barrier again."

Owl and his father looked sceptical, but they went, all the same. The bigger group overwhelmed the road and spilt off into the yards on either side. Saker could feel the spell again as they approached the barricade: just like last time, its strength rose as his army came nearer. But this time, this time, it was almost not enough. He closed his eyes so he could sense it better. The spell only just held, now that there were more ghosts trying to break it.

Saker opened his eyes. His father looked furious, storming back to him, brandishing his sword. Owl followed, just as angry, and the others came behind, disappointed, frustrated.

"We almost had it," Saker said to them. "With the new ghosts, we were almost enough to break it. I need to think. I need somewhere quiet to think."

"Up on the headland," Zel said, pointing. "It's quiet up there."

She was right. The headland was deserted.

The wagons were no good up there. He left them with the few living allies in the yard of an inn halfway down the slope. Zel organised guards, shifts, rosters — he had needed someone like her. Then they walked up to the headland together, near the river, the ghosts trailing behind. His father brushed past them, impatiently, and Owl followed him. They climbed to the highest point and stood, looking down at the city.

When Saker turned away and sat by the stream, Zel followed. He didn't think that his father saw Turvite as he did, as a jewel to present to their people, a symbol of everything they had lost. His father, he suspected, just wanted to destroy it and everyone in it.

They needed more ghosts. That was the key. Those just arisen had almost been enough. But to get more . . . Travellers had to die. Or else he had to find more bones.

He outlined the problem to Zel, relieved to have someone to talk to, someone to share with. "If only I didn't need the bones!" he said despairingly.

She patted his hand as it lay on the grass, and he flushed. He turned his hand over quickly, so that her hand came down on his palm, and he curled his fingers around hers. It was the first time he could remember welcoming a human touch. It was so different from all the times he had taken a hand wet with spit and stiff with excitement. Zel's hand was gentle, although rough with calluses from her tumbling.

He smiled at her, and she smiled back.

A hand came down on her shoulder and pulled her roughly away, sending her sprawling almost into the water. His father.

Alder grabbed him by the shirt and shook him like a terrier shakes a rat, pointing in rage at Zel, frothing that he couldn't shout, couldn't berate him. Saker knew why his father was angry — because he had taken a moment, just a moment, to be simply Saker, a Traveller man, sitting with a Traveller woman in peace, instead of being committed, heart and soul, every moment, to their cause.

Unforgivable.

His father threw him down and hit him across the face, the shoulders, the back, as he curled into a ball to protect himself.

There had been many beatings in his childhood. Alder was known for having a hard hand. One family had even cut off all contact with his because Alder had beaten their daughter for lying.

Saker was vaguely aware that Zel had scrambled up and pulled Alder away, shouting insults at him. Alder shrugged her off, but he stopped and moved back a pace.

Saker forced himself to hands and knees, panting with pain. So much pain, all his life, from his father, from Freite...

Anger bloomed in him. Wild anger, so huge it seemed about to split him in two. He seemed to swell larger than any human, as vast as the sea, as vast as the sky. His sight was red, as though his very eyes were bleeding pain. He could kill his father easily, just by removing the spell from him. He'd *never* have to see him again, never see the look of disdain on his face, never...No! No, that wasn't right. Couldn't be right. His anger was for the invaders. If his father had lived, seen him grow to be a man, surely they would have found mutual respect, understanding...

It was the invaders' fault, all of it. Acton's fault. All over the Domains, people lay in shallow graves and burial caves because of him. The invaders had to be crushed. His father was right. But the anger...the anger was still there, still building. He felt as though his eyes were going to break open; his heart was beating too fast, it would burst itself and there was no one to bring him back, no one to call *his* spirit back from the darkness beyond death...He felt like a wind was rushing through him, lifting him to his feet.

His father backed up a step as he rose, and Saker was glad to see it. Glad to see alarm on his face.

Blood and memory.

He remembered them all. All the songs that Rowan had taught him, all the names he had conned over the months of collecting bones, all the faces, the places, the pain, the death...He remembered them all.

Blood and memory and anger would bring them all back.

310

He took out his knife and slashed his palm wildly, and the anger swelled as he cut and cut, the blood swirling out as he began to spin, so that all the Domains would be touched by it, south and north and west and east—all corners blessed by his blood.

He called them: "Arise, brothers and sisters! Arise, all of you. All who have died who would not have died without Acton; all who have died untimely and unjustly; all who have been murdered, had the life ripped from them because of Acton's invasion; come to me, all of you, all my brothers and sisters, all the dead who rage; all whose lives were shorter because the invaders came through Death Pass. Arise and come! Come! Come now! Come and be given all my strength!"

And as the spell grew, as the power grew, the terrible singing in his head returned, louder than ever, but he ignored it. Let them rage, those he had killed! Let them shriek against the barrier of death for revenge. No one would call them back. He didn't care if the ululation split his head wide open, he would not stop. He would call them all, all his kin.

The anger and the pain and the loneliness spun out of him and spread out across the Eleven Domains. He could feel it go, feel it spread, feel it fly across the landscape like clouds before a gale. It spread like night, like shadow, like sunlight. As fast as dawn.

He felt it hit the nearest burial caves, felt the spirits stir within. Felt it go further, further, travelling as a dove flies, straight and quick. It was huge, growing no weaker as it spread, pushing all other enchantments before it. Something about that troubled him, but he did not know what it was.

The high whining in his head began to pulse and move, as though whoever made it was looking for a weak spot in him, a chink they could use to climb through, to come back like his kin was coming. But he was too strong, too fearless. He resisted, thrust it away from him.

Then he felt the first of the new ghosts moving up the hill, faster than anyone could walk, faster than a chaser; and the whining died away. They were invisible: flying, swimming through time and air to be with him. They only firmed to visible shapes when they came near enough, and they kept moving until they stood before Saker, dazed and wondering.

A young girl was in front, holding a knife with comfortable familiarity. She looked around and blinked, then tilted her head to the side as though assessing the situation. She looked Saker up and down, then Alder. Owl. Then she saw Zel, and relaxed a little, as though the presence of a young woman reassured her. The others were a mixture: old and young, men and women, clothes of different fashions and quality.

Saker saw that his father, at last, was looking at him with some respect. But somehow it mattered less, now. He could not turn aside for Alder. He had to stay here, until the spell was complete.

They were coming with the speed of dawn light. And when they were assembled, nothing would stand against them.

BRAMBLE

BRAMBLE COULD hear shouting from the other side of the headland, a rhythmic shouting. The bones in the bag on her shoulder seemed to move in time to it. A half-familiar noise rang in her head — the same noise she'd heard when they raised Acton's ghost. It was the sound of the dead being brought back. She dropped the bag and watched, in a mixture of relief and consternation, as Acton's ghost rapidly formed.

He seemed to be fighting against something that was pulling him towards the top of the headland. He was being dragged up towards the shouting. She reached out to help him, but her hand went through. He was a real ghost, then. She moved closer to him, desperate to help but helpless, barely able to think through the ear-splitting noise in her head. And then the shouting above stopped.

His hand clasped hers with the chill of the burial caves.

She almost let him slip from her grasp, but grabbed hold with her other hand as the whining howl subsided. The enchanter had called up more ghosts, she realised, and Acton had been in the ambit of his spell.

"Hold on to him!" she called breathlessly to Baluch. The pull up the hill was very strong. "We have to keep him here!" She dug in her heels and despite Acton fighting it, too, with all his massive strength, they were dragged up a yard or so before Baluch added his weight, coming around and leaning against Acton from higher up the slope.

From the harbour below, ghosts appeared and rushed past them: sailors, city people, all the recent dead.

Acton shook his head as if to clear it, set his jaw in that look she knew so well, and simply stopped. Immovable, like a mountain.

Bramble exchanged glances with Baluch, and they both smiled, very slightly. If this were a battle of wills, they had no doubt who would win it.

Acton seemed to send down roots into the ground, so that his feet

313

were planted as solidly as an oak tree. Still, it was not only will, but power, being used against him, and even an oak tree may be pushed over by a strong enough wind.

It brought out the best and the worst in him. When strength of will faltered, stubbornness took over. She saw it happen, saw the mulish set to his mouth, the same expression he had worn when he set himself to explore the Ice King's realm.

Her hands, on his cold, cold arms, were going numb. She would reach a point where she couldn't grasp, and then what? "Gods of field and stream," she hissed, holding on. "Gods of sky and wind, gods of earth and stone, help us!"

Her shoulders and legs were alight, burning with effort. She looked at him and laughed to herself—this was not how she had imagined touching him, that moment back on the hillside when he and she had been alive. He grinned at her as if catching the thought, and mimed a kiss. They both laughed silently, Bramble gasping for air, hearing only her own heartbeat and Baluch's panting breath.

Bramble was suddenly aware of noise above them. It wasn't talking, but a *shush*, like the sound of people moving silently over grass.

And Acton seemed to be planted solidly now, as though the spell were running thin.

She released Acton's arms and waited a moment to make sure he was firmly set, then put a finger to her lips and climbed the hill half-crouched, hands steadying her against the high slope. She lay down before she reached the top, and slithered up to peer over the edge.

Ghosts. Hundreds.

They were many, many more than had attacked the city that morning. Thousands, maybe.

Silent. Roaming the headland in small bands. More arriving, dragged to the spot by the spell, just as Acton was being pulled. They flew, it seemed, or came through the ground itself, and formed on the hillside in front of a man, the enchanter. Saker.

It was her first close sight of him, and she was disappointed. He was just a man. Not old, not handsome, not ugly, not tall or short or anything unusual. Just a man that she might have passed in the street.

How could this... *nothing* be responsible for so much grief?

314

He looked exhausted, and when the arrival of ghosts slowed and then stopped, he slumped to the ground. Good. Acton should be free. But she didn't go back immediately, because something was happening.

The few humans and some of the ghosts which were already there were organising the new ghosts into lines, as if they were assembling for inspection. Then Bramble saw that at the head of each line was a person, hogtied. Scared. Next to each prisoner was a ghost with a knife. Two ghosts, a big man and a small one with the beaded hair of Hawk's people, seemed to measure how far the sun had to go in the sky, then nodded to the ghosts at the heads of the lines. They bent as one and cut the arm of the person kneeling in front of them, and tasted the blood that welled up.

Bramble scanned the scene and her stomach clenched as she registered the ceremony unfolding before her. Blood was part of the spell. Blood to keep the ghosts there, blood to give them strength. Some of the new ghosts were hanging back, reluctant to taste the blood of a living sacrifice.

The enchanter came to address them, supported by one of the Travellers. A girl. Zel.

Bramble stared, uncomprehending. How could Zel? Why would she? Some plot of the Well of Secrets? It had to be. Zel was probably feeding information back to the city. That could be useful. And it meant that Safred and Martine were here, which had to be good.

"Take some blood before sunset," the enchanter called to the ghosts. "It will keep you from fading. But it is not only blood you need, but memory. Blood and memory will keep you here, to take your revenge." Some seemed confused, and his voice sharpened. "You will fade without it, back to the darkness beyond death."

Bramble didn't wait to see if they were convinced. Acton needed blood, right now.

She scrambled down the hill, fumbling for her belt knife. Acton was free, standing, moving his shoulders as if to get the kinks out of them.

Cutting her arm just above the wrist, she offered it to him. He stared at her, puzzled.

"Blood and memory will keep you from fading at sunset," she said. "The enchanter is feeding all his ghosts blood, and you have to drink, too, like in a quickening ceremony."

315

His people hadn't had quickenings. They happened only in the Domains, like stonecasting. He didn't understand, and shook his head.

Baluch put a hand on his arm. "Take the blood, Acton. We need you."

It was a hard thing for him to do, she could see, and she was filled with a familiar impatience with him. Why couldn't he *see* what was happening? "Just drink the blood, idiot!" she snapped.

His eyes lit with laughter at that, and he bent obediently, his tongue flicking out to her skin. She shivered violently as the death-cold hit her, but at the same time was pierced with sudden desire; heat and cold striking through her with equal force, leaving her trembling. His eyes were no longer laughing; he swallowed her blood down and stared at her with matching need. Baluch turned away.

Acton put his hand out to stroke her cheek, but instead of touching her, he curved his palm so that his fingers followed the line of her jaw without contact. Slowly, sadly, he shook his head.

Her chest was tight with desire, but he was right. There would be no surcease for them, not in this life. Not in any, may be. She turned away, fighting tears.

"Acton can face the ghosts and acknowledge his guilt," Baluch said thoughtfully, looking at the cut on her wrist. "But the quickening ceremony needs blood, as well."

He and Acton exchanged glances. Bramble didn't trust that look; she knew it too well. "What?" she demanded.

"I think," Baluch said slowly, "I think if we are offering acknowledgment of the landtaken, I should be the one to offer blood."

Bramble badly wanted to argue against him. Let the warlords do it! They're the real criminals. But she had to accept that he was right. He had been there. He had killed, and more than once. He owed blood.

"There are a lot of ghosts," she said. "That much blood might kill you."

Baluch grinned at her, a familiar gleam in his eyes. The music in his head would be horns and drums, she thought.

"I have to die *some*time," he said.

MARTINE

SORN WALKED into the hall without considering etiquette, Safred, Martine and Cael behind her. She was gaining in authority with every passing hour, Martine thought, as though the free air of Turvite was feeding some part of her that had been starved all her life.

The council was consulting with the warlords, Merroc included. Thegan looked up and anger flashed across his face so quickly that probably only they had seen it. Then he smiled. "My lady! Come to join our celebrations?"

"Celebration is premature," Sorn said, standing stiffly in front of the council table. "The enchanter has let loose another spell. The Well of Secrets tells me that he has begun calling for reinforcements; that there will be more ghosts arriving, from all over the Domains."

A buzz arose as the warlords turned back to their map, reassessing the defences.

Martine spoke reluctantly. "With this number of ghosts against it, I don't think the protective spell will survive."

"It's time to negotiate," Ranny said.

"I'm not negotiating with that piece of filth!" Merroc snarled.

"I will negotiate with him, if none of you will," Arvid cut in.

Martine wanted to smile at him, to give him support, but she forced herself to look at Sorn instead. It would do him no good in the warlords' eyes to get encouragement from her.

Ranny dismissed one of her people to find a set of antlers, the sign of parley across the Domains. In Turvite, so far from the nearest forest, they weren't common.

"I will take your spell workers with me, my dear," Thegan said to Sorn. "We might have need of them."

"I will take them with me," Sorn said, staring him straight in the eyes as she had never done before. She saw fury flare up in him, and she nodded calmly before walking away to join Martine and Safred.

"It's a fine line you're walking," Martine murmured to her.

"It's necessary. There has to be someone in that parley who respects the gods."

"One thing more," Safred said to Ranny. "I believe you have a young man arrested. Ash. A safeguarder."

Martine's gut clenched. Safred hadn't mentioned this—how long had she known? And who had told her? Were the gods talking to her again?

"A murderer!" Garham said. Martine flinched. What had Ash done?

"Even so," Safred said. "We need him."

"If the Well of Secrets needs him, Garham, I think we have more to worry about than a single death," Ranny intervened smoothly. Seeing Garham's slow nodding agreement, Ranny turned to one of the Moot staff. "Get him."

As the parley group gathered and bickered over precedence, until it was established that Ranny was the least threatening person to hold the antlers, they brought Ash in.

His shoulders were hunched, hands in pockets. He looked profoundly unhappy. But his expression lightened as he saw Safred, and even more when he saw Martine.

She smiled as easily as she could. "In trouble again, are you?"

He tried to grin, but couldn't. "I killed Doronit," he said baldly, as if he wanted to get the worst over with immediately.

Martine paused, her breath stilled. Without willing it, her gaze flicked to Arvid, for support, but she looked back at Ash immediately. This was no business of Arvid's. Ash was watching her as if waiting for a sentence of death. Martine remembered the night he had refused to kill her on Doronit's orders—he had given up everything so that he would not have to murder. Only extreme need would have pushed him to killing Doronit.

"No doubt you had good reason," Martine said gently. Ash's shoulders relaxed.

Safred turned to him. "It's time to meet the enchanter."

SAKER

THE WIND wraiths were circling, over the sea, as though they were
waiting for something. Saker watched them with unease. They
had said they could not come close to Turvite. Why had they appeared
now? He remembered, with a twist in his stomach, the feeling that
some other spell had weakened when he called in the spirits.

But the wraiths were offshore, a league or so away, so he didn't have
to think about it now. It was time to address the new ghosts. There
were so many of them. And such a variety. He now knew that Traveller
blood existed in the most unlikely people, but even so, some of these new
arrivals seemed strange to him. A beautiful woman in modern dress, her
shawl held by a brooch, looking around with calculating eyes. A scraggy
old woman dressed in fur skins. She had laughed and refused the blood,
but Owl had taken some and smeared it across her face. Saker wondered
if they had known each other.

Owl had then soaked a rag in blood and unceremoniously dabbed
blood on the cheek of each new ghost. It was much more efficient; the
sacrifice hadn't even died.

So many. There was even one who seemed not quite human, who
was hard to see, except out of the corner of Saker's eye. It moved like a
cat instead of a person, with hawk's feathers in its hair.

He could feel that the spell was still subtly working—the last of the
ghosts had not yet arrived.

He moved to higher ground and clapped his hands to draw their
attention. What language should he use? The old or the new? He decided
to start with the old and then repeat himself.

The ghosts gathered around. His heart was breaking, there were so many
untimely dead. He found the words he needed in the old tongue and pieced
them together in his mind before he spoke. He could wait no longer.

"Welcome!" he shouted. "I called you so we can take back the land
that was stolen from us."

319

Some of the ghosts nodded and clapped their hands together, but others looked blank. The old woman in skins shook her head in dismay. He didn't understand, but he kept on.

"The invaders are in fear of us, because we can overcome them. We will attack the city—" he swept his arm towards Turvite— "take back what was ours."

When he repeated the words in his own language, and saw with astonishment that some ghosts shook their fists at him, or turned their backs. His father and Owl seemed as puzzled by the dissent as he was.

Zel came up behind him. "Not all of them are Travellers, Saker," she said. "Her, for example." She pointed to a young woman dressed in current fashion, not like an officer's daughter, but better than most. The woman had an arrow in her breast and was kneeling, praying. "She's one of Acton's people, sure and certain."

He recognised the woman. It was the maid, the warlord's wife's maid, from Sendat. He had never expected this. Brothers and sisters, he had called for, the ones cut down before their time by the invasion.

"Your spell were broad," Zel went on. "I reckon it called *everyone* who died because of the invasion. Including the ones you've killed."

Saker searched the crowd more carefully and recognised the tall red-headed woman from Carlion who had thrown herself in the way of Owl's blow. She had been of the old blood, but she was standing next to the husband she had tried to protect, and he had been one of Acton's people. He saw some others from Sendat. Not many, because the wind wraiths had feasted there. Those spirits were truly dead. But there were some soldiers, and there—the first sacrifice, the young officer they had bled to keep the ghosts alive. He was standing, arms folded, staring at Saker as though calculating the best way to kill him.

And there was a young man coming towards them, looking excited. Zel stared as though she couldn't believe it.

"Flax?" she whispered, and then ran to him, throwing herself into his arms. She pulled back, shaking him. "I told you to stay out of trouble! I told you to be careful!" Saker felt his heart skip a beat, but it wasn't a lover's voice she used as she scolded him. "You went and got yourself *killed*!" Her brother, maybe? She began to weep, hands covering her face, and the boy patted her on the back, a curious expression on his face, a mixture of pity and consternation at the tears.

Saker noticed an older woman, dark hair showing clearly despite her paleness, staring intently at Zel and Flax, but standing away from them as though she didn't have the right to come closer. She seemed to hesitate, then turned and walked to the back, losing herself in the crowd.

Saker forced himself to look away from Zel. The important thing was that they had more than enough ghosts to break Turvite's defences. Perhaps not all of them would join in, but that didn't matter. They were invincible.

Alder began organising the ghosts who had come to Turvite into groups, to march down the hill to the city. Owl gathered the new ones who had welcomed Saker's words, and directed them to Alder's groups, which were swelling rapidly.

They would take the groups down and the force of numbers would overwhelm the protective spell. The other ghosts could wait here.

Flax looked across and realised what was happening. His face, so soft before, firmed and he looked older. He moved away from Zel, searching for others in the crowd. He found an older man, a couple of young ones. His face lit up when he saw Oak, and he went towards him enthusiastically. Then he saw that Oak was one of a group preparing to fight—checking weapons, settling knives in belts. He shook Oak's arm, but Oak stared at him stonily and drew his belt knife. Flax backed away.

He moved into the crowd. Saker watched him closely; he didn't know why, but his Sight was telling him that Flax was important. Zel was watching, too, and her face was unreadable. Flax approached the young officer they had bled to death. They faced each other. Flax pointed at the city, and shook his head. The officer spread his hands—they were empty, of course, because he had not died fighting, with a weapon in his hand.

Flax made a motion dismissing that as an excuse, then turned and marched towards the path down to the city. He stood on it, feet planted, and stared challengingly at the officer, and at the other ghosts who were not joining the groups. Saker couldn't believe it. This boy had been killed by the warlord's men only days ago! He should have been hungry for revenge. Why was he siding with the Turviters?

Other ghosts were joining him. A tall beautiful blonde woman in ancient dress, who stood next to Flax and regarded everyone with a calm eye. The scraggy old woman, the tall red-head and her husband, the maid, a girl leaning on a crutch, and others, following them, seeming to realise that they had a choice of who to support. They stared at Saker with varying expressions, a mixture of disdain, hatred, and fear.

He wished, agonisingly, that he could talk to them properly, and have them talk back. That he could explain everything, so that they would understand, and respect him, and join him.

Owl and Alder, occupied with readying their troops, realised what was happening too late. The path was blocked by a solid phalanx of ghosts, of all sorts and sizes, Traveller and Acton's people alike, standing ready. More joined them, including the young officer. Although their numbers were not large, there were too many for the path, so they spread out along the ridge, forming a half-circle of resistance.

Flax looked at Zel, and motioned her to join him, but Saker reached out and took her hand tightly. She made a movement towards Flax, but stopped. Her hand tightened around Saker's, and he was filled with a warmth he'd never known before.

Alder snarled at Saker as he pushed past him to confront the newcomers. For once, Saker was glad the ghosts could not talk.

The sun was lowering. Saker was overcome with impatience. They had to act now! Or it would be too late. He didn't know why he was so sure—it wasn't Sight, not as it normally felt. It was something else, some animal sense that told him they had very little time left.

"Push them aside," he said to Owl. "Don't hurt them."

Owl laughed at him. Then he took a step forward and swung his battleaxe straight at Flax. Zel cried out and leapt forward, pushing Owl to the ground before the blow could connect.

Flax dragged her upright and pushed her back to Saker, making shooing motions with his hands as he might have shooed chickens back to roost. He was right, Saker thought. Zel was one of the few who could be hurt. One of the few still left alive.

Owl stood up, his face contorted with rage, and raised the axe again.

"Stop!" Saker said. This time he put power into it, and Owl, thank the gods, stilled with his axe high, then slowly put it down, resting the blade on the earth.

"Fighting each other will not help," Saker continued. But Alder turned to him and took him by the shoulders, shaking him. Shaking his teeth loose in his head, making his neck feel it was about to crack.

"Someone's coming from the city!" Zel shouted. Saker followed her to a vantage point. The ring of new ghosts parted to let them look down.

There was a party coming up the path: the leader, a small blonde woman, carried antlers, a symbol that warlords had used for centuries in the borderlands between domains, to show that they were a hunting party, not a party of war.

"Someone's coming up this way, too!" a man shouted from the back of Alder's group. "A man and a Traveller woman—they've got a ghost with them!"

Saker relaxed. More recruits. He looked down the hill again. There were warlords in that band—he recognised Thegan, from Sendat. How dare he show his face! And others—Merroc, from Far South; old Coeuf, from South. There were women, too, and a handful of officers.

They would want to negotiate. To save their city. But they had chosen badly, if they thought he would negotiate with Thegan—with any of them! Sendat had shown there could be no peace, no justice, no surrender.

He could feel that the ghost coming up the other side of the hill was the last one, that the spell was finally ending. He glanced over and saw the ghost, a big man, flanked by a Traveller couple, step onto the plateau.

The spell faded away. Then the world shook beneath him.

BRAMBLE

As THEY climbed the hill, Bramble was aware of a great hissing murmur. The ghost army couldn't talk, but the noise of their movement was like the noise of the sea on a calm day.

Acton looked out over the plateau. It was filled with ghosts, and they had spilt into the market gardens below as well. Thousands upon thousands.

"They are opposing him," Baluch said thoughtfully, pointing to a group blocking the path to the city. "They are refusing him access to the town."

Acton wasn't listening. He was still looking down, his face stricken. He gestured widely, to include all the ghosts, then tapped his own chest and looked at Bramble questioningly, pleading.

"All your fault?" Bramble asked. She paused. What should she say? What did she truly believe? It was hard to find the right words. She had tussled with this herself: how could she love a killer? Unless she accepted that she, too, would have fought and killed and invaded, if she had been him. But although she loved him, could finally allow herself to accept him as he was, that didn't mean he had been blameless.

"Some are not your fault. The ones Hawk killed. The ones that someone now has killed. But there are others. River Bluff. T'vit. More. You invaded, and you killed, and you took. I accept that Hawk had to die, if only to rescue Wili. But after that—after that you just took what you wanted, because you wanted it. Because you wanted a harbour. Because you wanted to go to sea. Because you thought a death in battle was a good death, but it's not. It's just death."

Tears were riding down his cheeks, and he bowed his head as though accepting her judgment. Bramble looked away from him, and once she had she couldn't look anywhere else but at Maryrose, who was staring down the enchanter's forces with disdain. Bramble's heart was flooded with warmth and she felt her hands loosen from fists.

"He's called them all," Bramble said, finding her voice, fighting tears. "He's said the wrong words, and called everyone who died because of the invasion."

Acton pointed and she looked and saw another group of ghosts forming—warlord's men, and by the way they were behaving, they knew each other. Men Saker's army had killed, perhaps. They'd died with weapons in their hands, so they had swords and pikes now. They began to make their way across the headland towards Saker, swords drawn, a wedge of order in the throng. They were going to attack.

Acton ran onto the plateau, straight for Saker, grabbing a sword from another ghost as he passed. Baluch ran after him.

Bramble took a few steps after them when something under her feet shifted, putting her off balance. Then the gods cried out to her: *Help us!* And she fell to the ground as it seemed to shake beneath her. The force of the cry was so great that she began to crawl back down the slope, to get to them. They needed her.

She scrambled back to her feet and looked down to the harbour below, the quickest way to the altar from here. The ships were bursting into flame, the harbour boiling with water spirits. The mob that had clamoured to get onto the ships now scrambled to get off, pushing and shoving back along the docks to the city. The entrances were now held by warlord's men, and they were ruthless; they chopped down anyone who tried to break the barricade.

The only other way into the city was to cross the plateau through the army of ghosts.

She turned back to the headland. Below her, Acton was fighting off a group of warlord's men, standing in front of Saker like Lady Death herself. She ran down, pushing the cold bodies of the ghosts aside as she went, so that it felt like she was running into winter, her veins freezing moment by moment. It was hard to run away from the city—the call of the gods was still drawing her, pulling her hard.

As she ran, she shouted. "Don't kill him! We need him! Don't kill him!"

She heard Baluch's voice added to hers. "The Well of Secrets says not to kill him!"

Those were words of power. When she reached the enchanter, the two sides had stopped fighting and were facing off. Baluch stepped between them and Bramble wished hard that Ash were there, to let Acton speak for himself.

"The Well of Secrets," Baluch said slowly, looking at the ghosts of the warlord's men, "has told us to keep him alive until she gets here."

The leader was a young officer, very young, with only a small wound, a cut on his arm. He gazed at the enchanter and at the ghosts around him with absolute hatred. The officer sheathed his sword and motioned to his men to do the same. But he stood his ground, as though merely waiting for permission to attack.

The enchanter turned to Acton. "I thank you, sir," he said formally.

Bramble was impatient. She had to get back to the altar in the city. But the pressure to return to Turvite suddenly lifted, as though the gods no longer needed help. Or had found it elsewhere.

Ash, Bramble thought, taking a deep breath. Martine. Maybe Safred. She relaxed a little, but it didn't feel as though the crisis was over; the gods were not shouting in her ears but they were still distressed.

Maryrose smiled down at her. Touching Acton had been horrible, but she couldn't help it: she threw her arms around Maryrose, ignoring the burial cave scent and the cold, cold skin. Maryrose hugged her. Stroked her hair. And for a moment, just a moment, everything stopped. They were at the centre of the world, the centre of life itself. But her body rebelled against the chilly embrace, and she shivered, the movement bringing her to the here and now.

Bramble pulled back and blinked tears away. "We'll solve this," she told Maryrose. "And then you can just wait for me, so we can go on to rebirth together."

Maryrose nodded seriously, her eyes approving. Bramble felt a familiar warmth grow under her ribs; only Maryrose had ever really approved of her. Maryrose and Acton, maybe.

When she moved up the ridge to get a better view of the city, her gaze was drawn by an odd movement in the sky. She gasped. Wind wraiths were streaming towards the city from out at sea, a long arrowhead of wraiths heading straight for them. They had a long way to come, but they were so *fast*. Bramble had never seen them before, but she knew immediately.

Wind wraiths, fire spirits—Tern's compact was crumbling. That was why the gods had cried out.

Bramble grabbed the enchanter by the shoulder and spun him around. "Look what you've done!" she cried, pointing to the sky. "The compact is broken apart!"

He paled and took a step back, as if to run from the wraiths, then stood his ground. "I did nothing to the compact," he said.

"Your shagging spell broke it!" she hissed. "Fix it or we're all dead."

He stared at her and she realised he was no older than she was, certainly no more than thirty.

"I don't know how," he said. He frowned, his eyes unfocusing as she had seen Martine's do, and Safred's, when they used the Sight. She thought to the gods, urgently, *What should he do?* but they didn't reply.

ASH

A SH AND Martine kept in the back of the parley group as they
walked out of the Moot Hall and up the hill, Ranny in the front
with the antlers. Martine pushed Arvid forward, her hand in the small
of his back so unconsciously intimate that Ash stared, and she flushed.
What was it with women and warlords? First Bramble, now *Martine?*
He felt like all certainty was crumbling. *Martine?*

"He's a good man," she said defensively. "A Valuer."

Of course he was a Valuer. A warlord Valuer. That made perfect
sense. Ash snorted his disbelief.

They walked up the hill in silence, towards the waiting death, danger,
stone and water.

Safred came back to join them. She gave a brief outline of the attack
on the city and how the ghosts and their human allies had been repulsed.
"There was panic, though, and people stormed the ships in port," she
said. "I healed the ones I could, but many of the sailors died. Zel's aunty,
for one."

Zel's aunty? He'd never even heard of Zel's aunty. He didn't know
what to say.

"Ash...are you all right?"

He shrugged. What could he say? Yes? No? Both were lies.

"You killed Doronit?"

"Broke her neck," he said harshly, glad in a way to make her wince.
It may be he *was* dangerous. "She would have broken the barricade and
joined the enchanter, else."

Safred nodded sadly. It infuriated him, as though this was all her
fault.

"Well, you wanted a killer, didn't you? You needed someone who
could do whatever needed to be done. *Didn't you?*"

"Yes," she said. Her green eyes were bright with tears, but she
didn't cry.

The fury drained out of him. At the same moment the gods cried out. He and Safred and Martine all jerked to a stop. *Help us!* the many-layered voices cried into their minds.

They all forgot the parley and turned to run downhill, towards the old part of the city where the black rock altar stood under its canopy of oak leaves. Martine called back: "Sorn, the gods need us!" Sorn ran after them.

As they came towards the open space where the great oak tree grew, Ash could hear the local gods shouting, *No! NO!*

A shudder went through them all and the ground shifted under their feet. Ash was thrown to the ground. He didn't know what was happening. Part of him felt a strong urge to run, run to the headland. Another part wanted to run as far from there as he could.

"His spell of calling is ending," Safred said, her voice shaking. "He has called all the ghosts. All the angry dispossessed of the Eleven Domains. All of them are here, now."

The pressure of the spell increased before it tapered off, but underneath it Ash could feel something else—something being pushed, stretched, bent past breaking point. Another spell, old, old, deep in the ground... it was cracking under Saker's power, as a weir will crack in a flood. The water doesn't care. Doesn't even notice the weir. But the cracks widen...

"The compact!" Safred gasped. She was white with terror. "The spell is breaking apart the compact. Breaking into pieces!"

Ash dragged himself up and they ran on. In quick flashes, Ash remembered: water spirits lying in wait in the Sharp River; wind wraiths above the cliffs of Turvite, long claws reaching for his throat; wraiths in the uplands of Golden Valley, slashing at Horst, harrying him for sport. Only the compact stopped that happening, all over the Domains.

They could hear screams coming from the harbour. He looked involuntarily down a side street, and saw the topmost masts above the nearby houses. As he watched, balls of yellow light descended on them and they burst into flame. He had never seen a fire wraith before, and his whole body went cold. The protective spell might keep them from the city, but for how long?

At last, they reached the open space where the altar was. The ground around the altar was churning, in a wide circle that matched the oak tree's shade.

"Delvers!" Safred gasped.

In the circle of broken earth there were boulders moving, seeming to wade through the ground, pushing cobblestones aside in waves. They advanced slowly, but inexorably, towards the altar. Their circle grew smaller.

Ash hesitated. Delvers: no one knew their weaknesses; they did not vanish in air, they could not be hurt by sword or spear or fire or water or any human strength. He gathered his courage and ran towards the altar, leaping over the circle of delvers and turning to face the nearest ones, his back to the altar.

Safred and Martine gathered their skirts up around their knees and leapt, too, crowding as close to the altar as they could. Safred spoke out in the voice of the dead, the healing language transmuted into a challenge. Ash had the impression that they had turned their backs as if uninterested, although the shapes didn't actually turn. They moved towards the altar with purpose, and all Ash and the others could do was stand and watch.

"We have to strengthen the compact!" he said to Safred.

"I don't know how!" she wailed.

"It's hurt." He shook her shoulders. "Heal it!"

"I'm empty! Ever since the ship...I am empty!"

He didn't know what she was talking about, but they had to act, or it would be too late. He put his hand on her shoulder and willed his strength to her, as he had done when Bramble was dying.

"I'm full," he said. "Use me. You've done it before."

She put her hands flat on the altar and closed her eyes, Ash's hands on her shoulders from behind. Ash closed his own eyes, and straight away he could sense the cracks in the old spell. Beyond them was chaos. Safred began to sing, her harsh voice cutting through the air.

Ash reached for the River, to see if She could lend her strength, but She was distant. He could feel a strange ambivalence from Her, and realised, with a shock, that the water sprites were Her creatures, after all, born of Her, living only within Her. He would think about that later. Now he turned his attention to Safred and poured whatever strength he could find to her. There was a curious emptiness about her, a hollowness in the centre of her presence, but it was surrounded by power and strength, and he guided her to that, drew on it himself and fed it back to her.

He might be a killer, but he could also help heal.

Safred's song wound itself down into the altar, into the spell itself, but it was as though it was as insubstantial as the air she used to make it. It did nothing, merely seeped between the cracks and dissipated.

She stopped singing and looked at Ash in despair. The delvers had slowed, but they were still advancing, and they were closer than before, inside the circle of oak tree shadow.

Martine joined hands with Safred. "Let's try again."

They closed their eyes and Safred started to sing again. This time, as the song went down, Martine's strength was there. She was speaking.

"It's like the other spell, to keep the ghosts out," she whispered. The words were like a shout in Ash's ear. "Safred, it goes like this: 'Spirits, come not within my home; spirits, be barred from my home; spirits, enter not my door.' "

Astonished, Ash realised that she was singing the same five notes that Doronit had taught him, to send away the wind wraiths.

Safred sang the same tune, but the cracks kept growing. Safred worked harder, her voice hoarse with effort. There were layers to the compact spell, Ash realised. It was like a cloth with four layers, and the bottom layer was unravelling. That was why the delvers could come right inside the city while the fire and wind spirits were still kept outside. But to get to that layer, to repair it, Safred had to go through the top layers, and it was only where the cracks were deepest that she could do it without causing more damage.

"The spell's not right!" Ash said. "There are four layers. There has to be four—something."

They paused for a moment; Safred's song stopped. They could feel the old spell breaking further apart every moment, and the noise of the delvers grinding through the earth was louder each moment.

What would happen when they reached the altar? Ash wondered. Would they simply grind it into pieces, the compact destroyed, the gods made homeless?

"Wind, water, stone..." Martine hesitated. "Fire, too, I suppose. Try this, Safred: 'Spirits of wind, come not within my home, spirits of water, come not within my home, spirits of fire, come not within my home, spirits of air, come not within my home.'"

"No," Safred said. "Didn't you see what was happening? Ash's strength went to the third layer, yours went to the second, and mine to the top. We can repair one layer each, I think, but I don't know why."

Ash knew. Of course, now he thought about it.

"The third layer is water," he said.

Martine looked down at her hands, as if admitting something embarrassing. "The second is fire," she said. "I think the top one must be air."

"We sing to our strengths?" Safred said doubtfully, but they had no time to debate it. "We have no one for earth, then."

"Use me," Cael said. He had limped into the square after them without Ash noticing and was being supported by Lady Sorn.

"Cael is earth," Martine said. "Anyone can see that."

Cael looked at Safred, and smiled slightly.

"No choice, niece," he said.

Safred bit her lip and held out her hand.

He gauged the height of the delvers—barely past his knees, but he shook his head. Sorn lent him her arm for balance and he simply walked over the top of one, putting his boot down on it firmly and thrusting off. The delver made a crashing noise that almost split Ash's head in two but Cael was unaffected, although the effort of stepping down opened his wound again—Ash could see lines of blood and pus seeping through his shirt.

Cael leant thankfully on the altar. They joined hands again and all began to sing the words Martine had suggested, each taking one element.

"Spirit of water, come not within my home," Ash sang, in the voice of the dead, feeling like a traitor to the River, knowing there would be a reckoning with Her, one day, for this, but also feeling that it was one way to make up for sending the wind wraiths south.

"Spirit of fire, come not within my home," Martine sang, and the words felt sad, as if she were relinquishing something valuable.

"Spirit of air, come not within my home," Safred sang, in the voice of the dead.

"Spirit of earth, come not within my home," Cael sang, his voice gravelly and low.

This time the cracks started joining, supporting, reforming.

Cael had no power of Sight or healing, yet his voice resonated somehow with the lowest layer and at first they were hopeful, as they saw the cracks slow in their progress. Ash marvelled at the size and complexity of the compact spell. Whoever had done it had been a great enchanter, with a mind as complicated as—Ash didn't know what to compare it to.

But the lowest one was the hardest to reach, and the one that had cracked most, and it resisted every effort he made. After the three top layers were mostly healed, they tried to help him, all singing "Spirits of stone, come not...", until they were all exhausted, propped up on the altar stone like drunks against an inn table, but it did no good. Cael was not strong enough. His song was barely reaching the top part of the lowest layer. Caught in the middle of the spell, Ash could sense how weak he was. How near death.

They paused, just for a moment. The three top layers stayed firm and steady, but the lower one began to fragment further immediately.

"Don't try to heal me, niece," Cael said, and took a deep breath.

"No, don't!" Safred cried, but it was too late. Cael let out the breath in a last, long, passionate song.

"Spirits of stone, come not within my home," he sang, and poured out all the strength he had down into the lowest layer of the spell. All his love. All his devotion to Safred. All his decent, kind, cheerful life. The life of someone without gifts, without power, without anything except circumstance to make him special. The life of someone who had wanted to be an ordinary husband and father, until those things were ripped away from him. Ash felt it go; honoured him; envied him. It wouldn't have been enough. Ash could See that it wouldn't have been enough; but as his life poured out, something else went, too—the remnant power of the Forest, which had been keeping his wound fresh, which had been killing him slowly. That power went down deep, deeper even than the River, and as Cael died that power left him, spearing into the earth, returning home by a route deeper even than the fourth layer. That spear of power took Cael's strength with it, down deep enough, strongly enough, to reach the cracks.

Then Cael was dead, and his body fell against Ash's shoulder. But the cracks in the lowest layer had stopped growing.

And the delvers had disappeared. Ash sighed with relief. He took a deep breath and stepped back, well away from the altar. Martine rolled her shoulders and shook her head like a dog coming out of water.

Safred rubbed at her eyes, her face white. "It's not fully healed," she said with difficulty. Trying to stay intent on their task. Ash wanted to pat her on the shoulder, but guessed that would take away the last of her self-control. "That lower layer is beginning to fray again."

The ground burst open beneath their feet.

Ash staggered, tripping and falling on his back, rolling as he had been taught and coming to his feet with his knife in his hand—but of course there was no human enemy to face. Safred had fallen on her side. He hauled her up and away from the altar. Martine backed away on the other side of the altar.

"They're coming!" Safred cried.

The ground was roiling around the black rock, heaving and splitting, cobblestones spinning away, mounds rising and falling. Then some of the mounds shook themselves and became the dark shapes of delvers, hard to see in the bright sunlight. They had moved slowly before, but now they were much faster, as though they were running out of time.

The gods were silent. The delvers crowded around the altar and it began to sink into the ground, as a foundering ship sinks into the sea.

"No!" the lady Sorn cried out, as though her heart was being ripped away.

It was so quick, Ash didn't have time to move. The altar, Cael's body still on it, was sucked into the dirt and disappeared in a few heartbeats, and the delvers followed it, leaving the ground beneath the oak tree looking like it had been dug over for planting.

The tree itself seemed unharmed. Everything was exactly the same; but the altar was gone.

Sorn sank to her knees and wept.

Ash, Safred and Martine went to the spot where it had been, and stared helplessly at the ground. Where had they taken him? Then Martine knelt and brushed away some dirt. The toe of Cael's boot. Safred's face sagged with relief, and she looked a decade older than she was.

"They have buried him," Martine said. "As a mark of respect, I think. But the altar..."

"This is what the gods feared," Safred whispered to herself. "The enchanter has broken the compact—the lower layer kept the delvers out." She turned and looked at Ash, green eyes wide in a white face. "We must defeat him and rebuild the compact. Or the world crumbles for everyone, including Travellers."

BRAMBLE

DO SOMETHING!" she screamed at the enchanter.

He shook his head, his mouth open, watching the wind wraiths with clear terror. Useless. The wind wraiths were closing in, and someone by the stream yelled out, "Water sprites! There's water sprites in the creek!"

On the edge of the plateau, the ground shifted slightly, as though something moved underneath. Bramble knew what it was. Delvers. She was glad there was nothing to burn on the headland to tempt fire wraiths. They would head for the city. Then she was ashamed of the thought.

Suddenly the wind wraiths paused in their arrow flight. She could hear their harsh shrieking even from here. They were protesting something.

The gods had found help, Bramble thought. Safred? Ash? Where in the cold hells were they?

The fine trembling beneath her feet died out of the ground, and the world felt solid again. Almost. Something was still not right. But the wind wraiths cawed frustration and wheeled again out to sea, and the water spirits let the cascade of the stream take them over the cliff into the wild sea. Bramble took a breath, and looked at the enchanter. He smiled at her in relief and she wanted to hit him more than she had ever wanted anything. But she couldn't kill him yet. The compact had to be fixed, first, and the ghosts laid to rest. *Then.*

Acton moved behind the enchanter, and Saker turned his head and nodded, as though Acton was one of his men. Of course he would believe that of someone who had just saved his life, but Bramble wondered why Acton was letting him believe it.

"Where is Ash?" she asked Baluch.

He swallowed as though he found it difficult to talk. "He was helping the gods," he said. "She isn't happy about that."

Too bad for Her, Bramble thought. She turned and noticed a parley group being led up the hill by a woman carrying antlers as a sign of

336

peaceful intent. Warlords, most likely. Yes, there was Thegan. It was a measure of how perilous their world had become that Thegan seemed barely a threat to her now. She recognised Coeuf from Wooding, puffing and wheezing after the climb, and Leof. It was odd to see him again, as if she'd met him in another life. He looked older, tired.

Flax motioned his ghostly allies back, to let the parley group through, and Bramble looked around for Acton. She found him staring at the crowd with intent eyes. Assessing, as a commander sums up the situation before attacking. A female ghost moved to his side and touched his arm. Asa! His mother. She hadn't gone on to rebirth, had waited all this time . . . and Friede was with her, greeting Baluch with mock astonishment at his advanced age. Baluch's eyes were bright with tears and she touched his cheek comfortingly.

Other people were greeting their dead—Thegan's sergeant, even Thegan. He went to the band of warlord's men and greeted them; they stood straighter, and whatever he said made them feel proud. Then he motioned them back. That isn't over, Bramble thought. He's the only warlord here with armed men at his back, now. He'll use them, sooner or later. She looked at Acton to warn him, but he was already watching Thegan, eyes narrowed.

Saker stepped forward, looked around at each member of the parley group, and said, "My name is Saker, son of Alder." He indicated the scowling ghost standing behind him.

"What do you want?" Thegan asked in a reasonable tone, as if he were in command of the parley. But Saker had Thegan's measure, she could see.

"Justice," Saker said. "Justice for murder and dispossession that has lasted a thousand years."

"There's no justice this side of the grave," Thegan said.

"Then we shall send you to the other side to seek it," Saker said through gritted teeth. "My ghosts—"

Flax shook his head and raised his hand outwards against Saker, and so did the others with him. Saker stopped speaking, as though waiting for them to move back.

The ghosts who had stood with Flax moved closer together to show their support. The parley now stood in a circle of ghosts. As more ghosts came from lower down the slope to see what was happening, the circle widened to let them see, until it took up almost all of the plateau.

Bramble watched Acton. He seemed to just stand there, but the ghosts on either side of him had moved back, without realising it, she suspected, to leave him a little ahead. Baluch stood, as always, at his shoulder. The ghosts who had noticed Acton looked at him as often as they looked at the enchanter and the parley group. None seemed to recognise him.

The parley leader laid the antlers at Saker's feet, as though the warlord hadn't spoken. "I am Ranny of Highmark, of the council of Turvite," she said. "I come to parley with the enchanter Saker, son of Alder."

"I greet you, Ranny of Highmark," Saker said.

"Saker, enchanter, we in Turvite seek to do no harm to you or yours. We ask for truce, so that a peaceful settlement can be reached which is satisfactory to us both."

"Our land was taken from us. We want it back. That would satisfy us."

"All of it?" she said disbelievingly.

"All." Saker looked disdainfully at her. He glanced behind him to his father, who was nodding approval.

"You would have to kill thousands of people," Ranny said.

"Yes," Saker said.

Bramble grew hot with rage, and then cold. She would gut this madman from stem to stern, and be doing the world a favour. He spoke as though lives were nothing, as though he were Lady Death herself, with the right to pick and choose who would die.

The ghosts moved on the grass, some in excitement, but some in unease. Not all of Saker's army wanted to kill. But that solved nothing. At the worst—or the best—it meant an unending battle between Saker's ghosts and the others, with neither side vulnerable, neither side bearing any losses.

Saker sensed his army's unease and turned to them, his face reassuring. "The world will become safe again, for us and our blood," he said. The Turviters who had been summoned during the last spell shouted silently at him, shaking their fists. They shouldered their way through the crowd and came to stand behind Flax, their arms linked to block the path. Bramble realised that Cael was one of them, and felt her stomach clench. He winked at her and she smiled a little back.

"Not all your army is of your blood," Ranny said. "Not all obey you."

Saker whirled. "Do you think I cannot winnow them out? Do you think I cannot send them back to the darkness beyond death?"

"Wouldn't surprise me if you couldn't," Bramble spoke up. "As long as they feed themselves blood before sunset. Blood and memory."

He turned to her, his face white, and she fought down the urge to take out her boot knife and gut him. It wouldn't solve anything. She drew breath and let it out again.

Zel came up to Saker and laid a hand on his arm.

"Don't matter," she said. "Don't worry about that. What matters is this: we've got the upper hand first time in a thousand years, and we gotta use it right."

The enchanter's father nodded urgently, staring at Zel approvingly. Saker shook himself and stood upright, opening his mouth to make some kind of proclamation.

There was a disturbance on the path leading down to the city. The solid ghosts of Turvite were moving aside, shoving each other out of the way, as four people clambered up hastily.

Thanks the gods! Ash, Martine, Safred. And Sorn.

Sorn walked straight to Saker, still panting from the climb. She was more beautiful than when Bramble had last seen her, and seemed stronger, somehow.

Sorn caught her breath. "Saker, son of Alder, do you respect the gods?" she asked in a gentle voice.

He drew himself up as though she had insulted him. "Of course I do!"

"But your actions have harmed them. Your spell—your last spell—damaged the compact."

The enchanter paled and cast a look over his shoulder at the wind wraiths. They had pulled back, but they were still there. He cleared his throat. "The compact was repaired. I felt it."

Sorn shook her head. "Not fully. It will fragment again, soon." She turned and motioned Safred forward. "Saker, enchanter, greet Safred, the Well of Secrets."

Safred paused, weighing her words. "If you continue, there will be nothing for anyone—for the Travellers you want to help, the other inhabitants of this land, even the gods themselves. Is that what you want?"

Alder gestured vigorously, mouthing angry words. It was time to act, because apparently Acton wasn't going to do anything. Yet. Bramble nodded at Ash.

"Speak," he said to Alder.

"If we can't have the land as we should, no one will!" Alder shouted, in the deep voice of the grave. It made the words harsher, and everyone recoiled, ghosts and humans alike. Except the smaller ghost at his side, who shook his axe. Saker looked stunned, Acton thoughtful. The language lessons had worked well enough for him to understand Alder—their two languages were separated mostly by changes in pronunciation.

"You can make them speak!" Saker exclaimed.

"Kill them all," the small ghost said in the old tongue. Bramble bit her lip—that phrase brought back too many memories.

"When our land is regained, I will repair the compact," Saker said. Martine and Ash and Safred all shook their heads immediately. Saker turned to Ash. "You are lying."

"No," Ash said. "The compact is made of four spells, and needs four—four with power—to repair it. I can weave back the water strand, Safred the air, Martine the fire. We need you to stop the earth spirits. But you need *us*. You'll never do it alone."

Ash looked up at someone over Saker's shoulder, and Bramble saw his face freeze, then he nodded slightly at one of the ghosts, an attractive woman in modern dress. She bowed slightly, mockingly.

He turned back to the enchanter, ignoring her. "We must work together."

SAKER

SAKER STARED at the dark-haired enchanter. A man of his own blood, but working with the enemy. He had spoken with authority and conviction. Saker was sure he told the truth. He glanced up—the wind wraiths were closer. He shuddered at the thought of the compact broken, but to work with the enemy, to delay their revenge...His father glowered at him, but above his father's head were wind wraiths, high in the sky, and they were closer, just a little, than before. From the harbour below, smoke rose. He shuddered again, to think of fire spirits loosed upon his Travellers.

The ground beneath his feet seemed to tremble slightly, and the Well of Secrets caught her breath. "Now, Saker, enchanter," she said. "Or it all ends here."

The shrieking of the wind wraiths grew louder and the water in the stream—were shapes there again?

The tall dark-haired woman stepped forward. "You need to know us," she said. "I am Martine. This is Ash. Safred you have met."

She reminded him of his childhood, when everyone in his village had had that dark hair and pale skin. He bowed a little, trying to look formal, but feeling panic rise. If they were going to do it, let them do it now, before the wind wraiths broke through. They were advancing, inexorably, no longer in a single arrowhead but in several lines, as though they were approaching along rips in the spell. Attacking the weak points. His heart pounded hard in his chest. If they broke through, no agreement with him would stand. They would spare no one, including him. Including Zel. He glanced at her and she nodded encouragingly. She seemed to trust these people.

That gave him the courage to draw breath. "The compact spell ends just before the cliffs."

"So we repair it from here, back into the land," Ash said. He held out his hand and Saker hesitatingly took it.

He was used to grasping hands when he cast stones, but this was different. This was a kind of fellowship. Something he had never known. He had never cast a spell with someone before as an equal. Only as Freite's slave.

Martine took Ash's other hand and Safred completed the circle. She began to sing: "Spirit of air, come not within my land..."

Saker twitched and almost lost Ash's grip on his hand. It was an unbearable sound, like the voice his father had spoken in. A voice of power.

"Spirit of fire, come not within my land," Martine sang. Her voice, thankfully, was human.

"Spirit of water, come not within my land," Ash sang, also in the voice of the dead.

Saker felt weak in comparison to this young man. Not only an enchanter, but one who could make the dead speak, and spoke with their voice.

Ash squeezed his hand and Saker cleared his throat. The five notes were awkward, as they didn't quite fit the spell, so he had to concentrate to put words and notes together. "Spirit of earth, come not within my land," he sang, and knew his voice sounded thready beside theirs.

They closed their eyes, and there it was, the compact spell resting deep in the earth, woven out of the earth itself, it almost seemed, its layers distinct but closely adhering.

Ash squeezed Saker's hand again, and Saker gathered his strength and directed the song to the deep cracks in the lowest layer. He felt Ash follow him down to the third layer and sent his song into the fissures, which were growing. He sensed Martine and Safred doing the same to their levels. It was difficult, much more difficult than raising the dead, but there were no hissing spirits from beyond the grave to distract him. And to work a spell with others...to be in company with people like him, to use power to build and strengthen, that was a new thing, and it filled him with a kind of joy.

Saker had no sense of the passage of time, just of his growing weariness. The layer they had given him was the most damaged. Part of him resented it, but the part Freite had trained recognised that they were not suited—not strong in the right way—to knit the fabric of earth together into the spell. Each of the others, he could sense, was connected to something else, something greater than themselves. When he Saw Martine, she was surrounded by a nimbus of fire; Ash had a melody of running water twined around his spell song; Safred, a strangely empty presence, was a vessel, a pathway, for the power of the gods. They were here, through her, and Saker realised that they had inspired the compact in the beginning, had given their strength to the first compact spell, as they were giving Safred strength now. But the gods were not sending all their strength this time. Their attention was elsewhere.

The four of them sent their song out across the compact to the very edges of the Domains. They sang until their throats were raw, until none could draw more power from anywhere; and the fissures closed, slowly, until the world was whole again.

Finally, finally, Ash let his hand go and Saker opened his eyes.

MARTINE

THE WIND wraiths were disappearing, fleeing out to sea like tatters of mist before a gale. The waters of the stream were clear again. The fire wraiths had risen from the harbour in a ball like a second sun and now were gone. The ground no longer trembled beneath her feet.

They were safe.

Martine dropped Ash's hand and stood for a moment with him, coming back to the here and now. Saker stood dazed, hands at his sides. He seemed younger than he had, and much weaker, swaying with exhaustion. Safred merely looked pale.

"Horst," Thegan said softly. Martine turned to catch the warlord whispering to his archer. Thegan nodded towards Saker.

"My lord," Horst said urgently, "we need him alive! The Well of Secrets said—"

"Do what you are told," Thegan replied quietly.

Horst looked down at the bow in his hand, then up where the wind wraiths were scudding away across the sky, and his brows twitched. His eyes met Ash's, and Ash shook his head, pleadingly. Horst's hand opened, slowly, and the bow fell to the ground.

"You will obey me!" Thegan drew back his hand and felled Horst with one blow. Sorn's Leof tried to catch him but had been too far away; Horst came down against one of the many small boulders that dotted the headland.

Something woke in Martine's mind. Not Sight but the memory of Sight. The vision she had had when she was a girl, which Alder had beaten her for. The destruction of Cliffhaven by a warlord's men. By *this* man. He was much older, two decades older, but surely it was him.

She burned inside. This man had killed everyone she had ever loved. Her parents, Elva's parents, her brother, aunties, uncles, cousins... Everyone was gone when she had returned, and strangers lived in her dearest places. She was dizzy with rage and a grief that felt new-minted.

Leof knelt next to Horst and held his shoulders up. He was bleeding heavily from the nose and ears. Ash came and knelt next to them.

"You were right," Horst whispered to them both. "Shouldn't have trusted him." Then his head fell back and blood bubbled out of his ears.

Leof eased him back down to the ground. Another one of Thegan's sergeants arranged his sprawled limbs neatly, smoothing his hair down with a shaking hand.

"He won't obey you again, Thegan," Ash said bitterly. "Not ever."

Saker stepped forward. He held his hand above Horst's body and concentrated.

"This man was of our blood, too, although his blood was thin," he said. "Arise, sergeant."

Horst's ghost rose, hands empty. He stared at Thegan and moved to stand near Leof and Sorn. Saker turned slowly towards the parley group.

Now, Martine thought. If he can be swayed, it's now. She pushed Ash in the back and he took a step forward, put a hand out to Saker.

"There is something you don't know," he said. He held out his pouch of stones. "There is a new stone in the bag."

"What?" Saker said, thrown off his course. "New?"

"Evenness." Ash fished in the bag and brought out a small black stone. It was singing, a high simple song that Martine had never heard from any other stone. A single note, but with overtones and harmonies wreathed around it. It looked so innocent, lying there in his hand, she thought. How could it change anything?

"Change the stones, change the world," Saker whispered, staring at it.

Martine was aware that they were all staring at the new stone, ghosts and warlords and soldiers and councillors. The whole world seemed to be staring at Ash's hand, where the future lay.

"You're a stonecaster," Ash said, indicating the pouch at Saker's waist. "Can't you hear it sing?"

It was singing more loudly, and the other stones in his pouch sang, too. Saker nodded slowly, eyes fixed on the stone. "Evenness," he said. "It sings of fairness. Balance. Justice."

"Yes," Ash said. "Balance." He hesitated. "You were right—it is time for the world to change. But Balance needs *two* sides, not one. Acton's people as well as Travellers."

"Equal," Saker said. He raised burning eyes to Ash, as though the stone had sung him a vision of the future. "Balance means both sides equal."

They looked at each other carefully, and Martine was struck by their similarities: same age, height, powers. What could have pushed Saker to the extremes he had taken? She was filled with pride for Ash—he had said exactly the right things, exactly the right way, and now the world was about to change.

Saker turned slowly and faced the parley group.

"What do you want?" Ranny asked.

"Justice," Saker said. "Equality." He paused, as if thinking through something new to him. "All the laws that push my people into the dirt. The Generation Laws. The laws against owning property. The laws against Travellers being on town councils, or being village voices. The laws must be repealed!"

Saker's army started banging their weapons against each other in support. Flax's group joined in. Only Thegan and his soldiers stayed still.

Even Bramble was stamping now. Martine and Ash joined in, too. Saker was right about this, at least. The laws should change. She watched the warlords. They didn't look happy. Except Arvid. She smiled involuntarily. He had nothing to be ashamed of.

"We have no such laws," Arvid said to Saker.

"The laws will be repealed in Central Domain," Sorn said, in her soft voice. Thegan stepped forward but she stared up at him reprovingly. "They are not just, those laws, and should never have been made."

He stared back at her for a long moment, then turned aside, his fists clenched.

"I'll repeal the laws," Merroc said. "We all will." He looked around, and each warlord nodded, some more readily than others.

"Our land," Saker said, but his voice no longer had the flat tone of obsession, as it had before.

Martine's gaze shifted to a ghost dressed in the ancient style, who moved from behind Saker to Ash's side.

"Speak," Ash said readily, with a flick of a glance at Bramble. Martine

346

realised that this was Acton. *Acton*. They had done it, then. She felt dazed, staring at him. Acton, the invader.

"*Enough* land," he said in the grating voice of the dead. "This country was not fully settled when we came, but there were villages and towns. Give enough back to settle all who wish to be settled."

He hadn't identified himself. Why? The warlords looked at him closely. Thegan's eyes narrowed, as if assessing his identity, but Martine could see they never suspected who he truly was.

"I suppose," Merroc said grudgingly, "we could give you land—enough land to support you."

"Two or three villages in each Domain," Gos of said, nodding. "Safe havens for you and your kind."

"Good land," Acton put in. "Productive. From the warlords' own estates. Mixed in with everyone else, not fenced off, and separate."

He was enjoying this, Martine saw. Enjoying the game, enjoying hiding who he was, enjoying challenging the warlords. She saw him exchange a smile with Bramble and felt a sudden shock. Sympathy for Bramble overwhelmed her. It was hard enough to love a living warlord, but to love the dead...Martine shivered, imagining Arvid dead. She looked up to find him staring at her, his hazel eyes intent on her face, as though he saw something new there. She could feel her expression soften as she met his gaze, despite herself, and his whole face responded. It was only a moment, and then he turned back, but Martine knew that they had crossed some boundary and were in new territory. Love.

"Two villages in Central Domain," Thegan said, in the tone of one who had no choice, "and two in Cliff Domain. In good farming country. Your people will be safe there. You have my word."

Rage erupted through her. How dare he promise safety and deal only in treachery.

Saker had been looking at the ground, but at Thegan's words he looked up, a rage burning in him, too. " 'You have my word'?" he spat. "There were two villages of the old blood in Cliff Domain twenty-three years ago. Warlord's men destroyed them!"

Martine stepped forward, heart pounding, and pointed at Thegan, her whole arm extended so that even those at the back could see. "*You* destroyed them!"

Thegan simply nodded. "It was necessary," he said. He turned to the warlords. "The Ice King was gathering his troops, but I couldn't convince my father that we had to do the same. I *knew* he was going to attack. We had to prepare. So I sacrificed a couple of Traveller villages. I let my father believe the Ice King had attacked them, and he threw everything we had into preparation. And the next year, the king tried to invade. If we hadn't been prepared, the entire Eleven Domains might have been destroyed!"

The other warlords listened with suspicious eyes but nodded slightly, as if to say that they understood.

Martine was full of rage and grief, and Saker's face showed the same mix of emotions. The big ghost next to him was incandescent with fury. He was shouting, shouting and screaming silently with anger. She recognised him, finally. Alder. Of course. The Voice.

"There was a Saker, a young boy, the son of the Voice in Cliffhaven…" she whispered. "I was from Cliffhaven." Saker looked at her, startled. She stared into his eyes. "Saker, son of Alder—" she flicked a glance at his father— "I am Martine, daughter of Swift and Stickleback. I was away from Cliffhaven when…"

Saker swallowed visibly, his face a mixture of joy at finding her and anger at Thegan. He turned back to Thegan. "I was from Cliffhaven. Your men missed me!"

Martine's heart was skipping beats. Saker was Elva's cousin—Alder had been Elva's grandmother's brother.

"All this," Saker said, arms spread wide to encompass the whole ghost army, "is *your* doing."

As though that had been a signal, Alder charged forward, sword raised like a club.

Martine heard a sudden high buzzing, a terrible scraping like finger-nails down glass, like an animal in unbearable pain. It split through her skull and she dropped to her knees with the force of it. Ash was holding his head, too, and Bramble was swaying as if dizzy. Saker staggered a few steps, his face chalk white.

Everyone else was stunned into immobility. Except Leof. He ran forward followed by one of Thegan's sergeants, but Alder simply shouldered them aside and brought down his sword.

The blow was blocked, not by Thegan, but by Acton. Alder snarled and swung again, intent on getting to Thegan. What happened next was too fast for Martine to follow, but in a moment Alder was on the ground, his face in the dirt, and Acton's boot was on his back, his hands holding both swords.

The whining stopped. Martine climbed back to her feet slowly, head still ringing. Safred had fainted, and Sorn was ministering to her.

Alder bucked and threshed on the ground under Acton's foot, with Acton staring down at him with pity. Bramble, her face pale, squatted next to his head.

"You can't win, Alder," she said. "That's Acton."

SAKER

A LDER LAY still.

Saker looked at the ghost who had so easily vanquished his father. Knowledge of his identity wiped out any thought of the screaming from beyond the grave which had erupted when his father lifted his sword.

Acton. Evil incarnate. Invader. He moved only to defend his own, the warlord Thegan. He was dead, Saker reminded himself; Acton could not be killed again. His own tongue swelled in his mouth with rage, gagging him.

Acton moved back, slowly, and Alder got up and faced him, his shoulders hunched and wary. He was frightened.

Frightened. Saker had never seen his father frightened before. Come to that, he'd never seen anyone burlier than his father. Or better able to fight—although, now that he thought of it, Alder never had fought, except as a ghost, when he could not be hurt. His size meant that he only needed to threaten; and he was good at threats.

As though he saw him for the first time, Saker looked at his father. At the fear in his eyes, the servile tilt to the shoulders. He remembered Martine, now. She was the young woman his father had beaten so badly that her whole family had refused to ever speak to Alder again. His father, a beater of women. A coward in front of a stronger man. A bully.

His heart began to beat in long, slow strokes, and he cast around for Zel. Her clear eyes would help him understand all this. She was standing next to her brother, but her gaze was stony on Thegan. Something else they shared, Saker thought. Thegan had killed both their families.

Thegan bowed to Acton, his eyes wide. "My thanks, my lord," he said. Saker thought, now is the proof. The invader will clasp the murderer in his arms and praise him. Acton looked him up and down. Every warlord there, every warlord's officer, every attendant and council member, waited for his response.

350

Acton mimed spitting in the dust at Thegan's feet, and moved away.

Thegan paled.

"Speak," Ash said to Acton, with some satisfaction.

But Acton ignored Thegan and turned to Alder and Saker. "The dead should not kill the living," he said.

"Who heard them?" Safred asked, leaning on Sorn for support. "Who heard the crying from beyond death?"

Martine raised her hand. Then Ash, Bramble. Saker, finally, raised his own, and then others in the crowd of ghosts followed him. There weren't many—perhaps one in a hundred. Saker remembered the other times he had heard that sound: when he had raised the ghosts. It had started after the first battle at Spritford, he realised. After the dead had first killed the living.

He had thought it was the spirits of those he had killed shrieking for revenge. But...they were here. He had raised them all, and they stood before him. Who was it, then? Who was calling from beyond the burial caves?

The last sunlight disappeared, and they were left in the grey light of dusk.

Safred broke the silence, speaking to Martine and Ash. "We will deal with that later, I think," she said.

Safred turned back to him from the crowd. "Acton is here," she said, "to make reparation. Just as at a quickening. To acknowledge the wrongs that have been done in his name, and to offer sorrow for those wrongs."

A susurration went around the ghosts. Then one began to gently stamp her feet in approval. It was taken up immediately by the other ghosts, of both sides, so that they were surrounded by a circle of noise, so many ghosts stepping together that the rhythmic tread made the ground shake.

"Wait!" Saker cried. He flung up his hands, palms out, to quieten them. Gradually, the stamping died away. "Yes!" he said. "The warlord should acknowledge what was done. But I have acted to safeguard the future of your descendants. It's still undecided where they are to go."

"They're welcome in the Last Domain," Arvid offered.

Saker nodded to him, then addressed the ghosts: "Do you wish your descendants to live in the Last Domain, safe?"

Many of the ghosts began to stamp again, but Zel came forward, hotly. "No! That means they've finally won. They've got rid of us altogether!" She turned to Saker. "Can't you make another spell? Let them—" she pointed at the warlords, "let them change the laws and give us land, and you put a spell on them so that if they break their word and hurt us, the ghosts will rise again?"

Saker was uncertain. That was a very complex spell, and would he be left in peace to make it? He doubted that. He hesitated. "We cannot trust any warlord after what *he* did," he said, pointing at Thegan.

"But Thegan is no longer lord of Central Domain," Sorn said clearly. "I have renounced him, since he cannot give me heirs."

Thegan started towards her but Acton intercepted him and two of the other warlords moved to flank her, staring Thegan down. One of them, the younger one, smiled, and Saker saw a sudden resemblance to Thegan. Was this Gabra, his son, who held Cliff Domain for him?

"And I," Gabra said, "have discovered my true father is Masry, past warlord of Cliff Domain, and I will hold that Domain as his only son." He paused, as Thegan stared at him, face showing nothing. "Travellers will be safe in my Domain. The villages of Cliffhaven will be given back to them, complete, as they were taken, and the laws will be repealed."

Saker smiled at his father. Their villages regained! But his father only scowled at him and Saker realised, as if for the first time, that nothing would satisfy Alder but death, and more death. That he was so angry about his own death that he would kill the entire world. He thought, Father has never looked for others from Cliffhaven. Never tried to find out what happened to the others. Only him.

Thegan stood very still, and smiled at both Sorn and Gabra, as if at children, then turned to the other warlords. "These things," he said, "are not to be decided here. Do you want this man to hold you ransom? To threaten that if you do not treat his people well enough, he will raise another army? How well is 'well enough'? If one of them gets a stubbed toe because your roads are not smooth enough for them, will he blame you?"

They were frowning. Oh, he was so persuasive. So *reasonable*. Saker could see them listening to him, but didn't know what to say to make them realise that they were listening to one of the soul eaters in human flesh.

Then Ash stepped forward. "Right here, right now, we have seen this man strike down an innocent man," he said loudly. "Is this someone who should be *listened* to?"

The ghosts stamped their approval.

"Who are you to ask?" Thegan hissed.

Ash looked him straight in the eye. "I am the one who raised Acton's ghost. I am the one who allows him to speak. Don't you think it's time we heard from the real Lord of War?" The ghosts pounded their feet; the ground trembled. "Speak, Acton," Ash said. He looked around the waiting circle. "And remember, the dead cannot lie."

Acton turned, slowly, giving each ghost in the circle a chance to look at him. The moon was coming up, and it painted him silver, quicksilver.

"I am Acton, Lord of War," he announced in the ancient language, but in the same voice his father and Safred and Ash had used. The voice of the dead. The voice of power. A rustle went through the crowd. "But I am *not* a warlord!" Then he repeated himself in the common tongue. This time, there were exclamations from the parley group.

They gave way to a silence so intense that Saker felt the rocks themselves were listening.

"I opposed the warlord system," Acton proclaimed, first in one language, and then in the other. "I wanted everything to be run by councils, as it was in Turvite. And that is why they killed me, and hid my bones."

Saker was dumbstruck. That couldn't be true. But Ash said the dead couldn't lie. The ghosts stared, openmouthed; the warlords listened, their cheeks blanched, seeing their world crumbling. Ranny and the other Turvite councillors smiled.

But Owl came forward and shook his sword in Acton's face, and spat on the ground at his feet.

Acton's face changed, from challenge to compassion. "Yes," he said gently, in the old language. "I led the invasion. And I killed." He turned to the ghosts. "I am your killer. Lo, I proclaim it: it was I who took your

353

lives from you. I am here to offer reparation—blood for blood." He repeated it so everyone would understand.

"You have no blood to offer," Thegan said.

Acton turned slowly to look at him. Thegan backed a pace.

"If *you* had not destroyed Saker's village, Thegan," Safred said, "none of this would have happened. It seems to me that it is up to you to offer blood for blood."

Saker couldn't take in what Acton had said. Not responsible for the warlords? Did it make any difference? He'd said he *was* responsible for the invasion. Who was to blame? Who was *really* to blame? Saker spoke as if he were in a dream: "The blood must be offered freely."

"I offer nothing," Thegan said. "Anything you get from me you must take."

I will take it willingly, Saker thought. This was one sacrifice he was happy to cut himself. Only the past knew who was responsible for the warlord system. But Thegan, he knew for certain, was the killer of all he had held dear. He took a step forward and Thegan bent, whipped a knife from his boot and struck out at him. Lightning fast, lightning sharp. One of the officers lunged, Ash took a quick step and drew his own knife, but they were too late. As Thegan moved on him, Zel threw herself between them with a tumbler's litheness and the blade meant for Saker's heart sliced into Zel's neck. The two men each grabbed one of Thegan's arms, but he did not fight them. He simply turned his head to the blond officer and said, "You fool. You could have killed him more easily than I, and this would be over."

Saker made a wordless sound, feeling as if the knife had cut his heart open. He caught Zel as she fell, her blood pumping out in spurts from the wound. Safred came to stand next to them then, as if compelled, she sank down to her knees and placed her hand on Zel's chest. Saker looked up in sudden hope, but Safred shook her head. Zel's brother had dropped to the ground and buried his face in his hands.

Zel's blood slowed, and stopped. It was fast, Saker thought, fast and painless, and he clung to the thought to stop the tears, which were hard in his throat, from bursting out.

Saker lowered Zel gently to the ground and stood up, his eyes blank. His hand were stained red and he stared at them, then raised both so that he could smear his forehead and cheeks with streaks of her blood, willing her to rise and join him, willing it as he had never willed anything before.

She rose instantly and stood beside him, smiling at Thegan.

"This crime was committed on Turvite soil," Ranny said, hurrying her words to forestall him. "He will be punished. Hanged."

Saker turned his gaze towards her, not able to think, barely able to feel. He took Zel's cold hand and looked at Acton. "Blood is not enough," he said. He could hear that his voice was the voice of madness: flat, emotionless, empty. "You do not know how much pain you have caused. You offer blood, but you do not offer sorrow." He swung his hand in a wide arc and his heart seemed to swell in his chest. He felt as if he were going to die, and he welcomed the feeling. He wanted to die. Wanted to join her. Every ghost here had felt like that, had suffered as he was suffering. "Look at them!" he whispered. The silence was so intense that the words reached the whole plateau. "Look at them. Each of them was hurt. Each of them died. Each of them grieved." His voice gradually took on feeling, each sentence louder and darker. Anger was building in him, as thunder builds before a storm. He let it loose: "You cannot ask forgiveness when you do not know the evil you have done!"

He whirled on Ash, clutching him by the shoulders. "Make them speak!" he pleaded. "Make them all speak! Let them tell the true story of what has been done. Let it all be remembered."

The ghosts were listening hard. Saker let Ash go and went into the middle of the circle, turning so that he could see them all.

"You must be heard!" he shouted. "You must be listened to! Your deaths were an evil which should never have happened, but your stories can be told. Your stories can be *remembered*."

The ghosts, hesitantly, stamped their approval.

"Come," Saker said to Acton. "Come and hear."

Acton walked to stand beside him, and Ash took a step forward. Ash, his first ever real ally.

"Speak," Ash said quietly, fervently, turning on the spot so he could see every one of them. "Speak."

As one, they opened their mouths and spoke, in the terrible voices of the dead.

355

ASH

THE NOISE was so great, so huge, it sent Ash staggering to the ground. Saker, likewise, lost his footing. Acton held his arm to steady him. The voices were stabbing into his head. This wasn't what he had wanted; no one could hear anything in this.

"Quiet," Ash called out.

The silence then was like the ringing after your ears have been boxed. Ash needed advice, and there was only one person who could give it. Ash levered himself up and scanned the crowd for Doronit.

She saw him and came forward, smiling at him with malicious pleasure that he needed her.

"Doronit," he said. "Do you know a way to give them back their voices?"

She indicated her own mouth, and Ash flushed. "Speak," he said, expecting her to refuse to help him. But she was serious.

"All I know is what a wind wraith once told me," she said. "To give them back their voices, you must find yours."

"My voice *is* theirs," Ash said, feeling stupid, as if he should see an answer in her words. But the thought had flung open a door in his mind: Ash knew what to do, and it was something he could never have done before he met the River. He began to hum, the note he and Baluch had used to summon the water in the cavern—*Her* note—and then to sing the single word "speak."

He saw the others wince at the sound, and closed his eyes. This had nothing to do with them; and, in a way, nothing to do with the River. The ghosts spoke with the voice of the dead because they had left behind all human contact, all links. They were cold.

The way to his voice, to their voices, was through the simple warmth he could feel from Martine; the trust in Bramble's eyes; the memory of baby Ash sucking his finger on the day they had left Hidden Valley; Drema's gift of the felt coat; Baluch's comradeship. Even the fellowship of drumming for his parents, the three of them united in music. And the River's welcome, the River's acceptance.

He sang, thinking of these things, and felt a change in the sound, but it wasn't enough. The words themselves had to be new, he thought, as well as the voice. So instead of "speak" he began to craft a new song, a song about the most valuable thing he knew in this world, the baby Ash. A song about new life. It wasn't a song in the way his father's songs were. It didn't tell a story. It didn't have sentences. But into it he put all the words about life and love that he knew, from the three languages the ghosts held between them: the language of the old blood, of the landtaken, and of his own time. He repeated, mixed and merged the words over the notes and the music tied them together into something never heard before, never dreamt of before, building in strength and sweetness and joy and the fear in the heart of love.

His voice changed.

It wasn't trained, like his mother's or Flax's. It had cracks in it, and his breath control was terrible. But the notes rose purely, a full tenor that carried to the furthest edge of the plateau. He began to include all the words for "speak" and "story" he knew from the three languages, and he settled into a rhythm of calling, as the goatherds of the Sharp River call the goats home at evening, their voices rising and falling on the evening air.

"Speak your story; tell your truths; show your selves; speak and be satisfied; speak and be at rest," he sang, his voice fully human.

The ghosts were pressing in closer, the song drawing them, their lips working as they tried to talk, but the spell was incomplete.

Finally, Ash flung up his arms and cried *"Speak!"* on a long high note.

They spoke. It was still loud, but each voice was its own again. Acton moved from group to group, trying hard to listen, to hear, to understand.

Each of those alive was trying to listen, understanding somehow that Saker was right: in order to repair the wrong done, the wrong must first be understood, the pain given voice, the injustice exposed. But they could not possibly hear them all.

Safred was kneeling, her face upturned, transfigured by a kind of ecstasy as the words, the stories, the secrets, poured over her.

A pretty girl, with the mark of a cut throat, said to Sorn: *I were ugly, ugly as an unkind word, my gran used to say...*The small beaded ghost spoke to Acton: *I couldn't stop them. I didn't even realise the village was being attacked, until they burst the latch like it wasn't there...*A grey-haired man had found Bramble, whom he seemed to know, and told her: *It began on Sylvie's roof. My hands were cold...*Maryrose, Bramble's sister, spoke to Ranny, a half-smile on her face. *Before you were born and after the sun first shone, there was a girl.*

Zel and Flax, where were they? He found them finally, at the back of the crowd, listening to an older woman who strongly resembled Zel. Their mother? Zel spoke to both her and Flax: *Murder's an ugly word, don't never doubt that. But it's a solid one, like a stone in your hand.* Saker stood next to her, attentively.

He found Doronit. She'd been waiting for him: *It's true my parents were Travellers by blood, but they were as settled as can be by nature.* He listened to her story with horror and pity, and held her hand as her throat constricted with grief and she found it hard to go on. Understanding her, at last, he found a way to love her with a father's love, with sorrow. So much grief, all around him. So much anger, so many lives cut short.

Da came round the back of the milking shed in the middle of the morning, a girl said to Thegan's sergeant.

There were fishers on the bank, Cael said to Gabra, and Gabra's eyes were intent.

Ash found Acton listening to an older woman who smiled at him as though he were the centre of the world. She was dressed in ancient style. Was she his mother? *The women stay in the women's quarters. Yes, of course,* she said, ironically.

An old woman in animal skins grabbed his arm, the cold sliding through his muscles. *Listen to this one,* the River said sharply, so he focused on her bright eyes and listened hard. *My Aunty Lig was one of three sisters, as her mother had been, and her mother before her,* she started, and he took it all in, open-mouthed. The wrath of the Fire god! he realised, astonished, and wondered what the River would do if he rejected her. *I do not kill my lovers,* She said, amused. *They never leave me.*

Ash turned and noticed Baluch standing with a woman who carried a crutch; they both listened to a small man with a weak chin who faced them half-defiantly, half-ashamed: *I'd do it again. Even having to kill her, I'd do it again.*

What good was it? Where was the use? I had served, worked, been loyal—for what? Merroc knelt by a fair woman in her forties and, astonishingly, cried.

They were all listening, with Safred in the centre. So many stories.

In the end, we are animals, and all we can touch is flesh.

I always wanted to be beautiful, like my little sister, Osyth. She had that Traveller kind of beauty, dark and elegant and lithe.

There's no saying what will happen next. That's what I learnt, that summer, that winter, watching her change.

A stonecaster walked up to Ash, pouch hanging at his belt, a man with no hair at all and no eyebrows, with terrible burn marks down one side of him. He noted the pouch at Ash's belt and weighed his own pouch in his hand.

The desire to know the future gnaws at our bones, he said, and Ash listened.

BRAMBLE

THE STORIES flowed out of them like honey, like vinegar, like wine and water and vitriol.

So much grief. So much joy. So many questions unanswered. Safred knelt still through it all, drinking it in. Around the circle, the living humans also sank to their knees under the weight of the emotions pouring out around them. Most cried, or clutched their chests in shared pain, or sighed yearningly for those lost, long ago.

Some stories were longer than others, so that the voices fell out one by one until the last drifted to a close: *I wished the tanner was still alive so I could try his spell one more time...*" It was Osyth. Zel and Flax were next to her, listening hard, tears on their cheeks, and as she finished she reached out to them and they went to her as babies go to their mothers, with trust and love.

Acton touched Bramble gently on the shoulder, the cold sliding through her and settling her. Then he stepped forward to Safred and helped her up. She stumbled, white and unsteady, but her face was full of a kind of joy, of completion.

"I have them all," she said in wonder. "I was empty and now I'm full."

Baluch moved next to Acton, took the knife from his own belt, and poised it over his hand. Acton hesitated. He shot a look at Ash, as if to ask for guidance, and then squared his shoulders. She had seen him do that once before, when he spoke to the Moot as a young man. He had convinced his audience then; would he be able to now?

Saker waited; he looked exhausted. Bramble prayed that Acton would find the right words.

"I am Acton, Lord of War," Acton said, and in his own voice his words were strong, and her throat tightened. "I have heard you. I acknowledge the truth of your lives. And I say: What was done to you was wrong. What you have suffered should not have happened. What you have witnessed should never have occurred. What you have lost—" His voice faltered, as if he were remembering the many stories he had heard. "Those you have lost should have remained with you. And I say to you: Whatever I have done to make these things happen, I regret from the depth of my heart. From the centre of my soul, I am sorry."

Some wept softly, some looked to the ground, others away, as if his words had unlocked a part of themselves that had been separated for a long time.

Then Acton glanced at Baluch and he moved forward. "I am Baluch, second to the Lord of War," he said, his singer's voice reaching out like sunlight. A buzz of amazement went through the crowd.

"I was part of the landtaken and I regret my actions. I acknowledge my guilt and offer blood for blood in reparation." He hesitated. "I have killed others, of my own people, in defence of the Lake, and to those, too, I offer reparation. I offer myself as symbol of repentance."

He brought down the knife and cut the back of his hand, then held it out. Acton stood behind him, unmoving, his hand on Baluch's shoulder, so that they were offering tribute together.

One by one, they came and took blood. A few drank, but most simply touched.

One of the ghosts, the one Ash had called Doronit, hesitated for a while, until Ash went over to her.

"There's a new stone in this bag, remember," he said, showing her his stone pouch. "It says Evenness. Fairness. Say what you think."

She made a face at needing his help, but she spoke, "You think it means what?"

"I think the world is changing."

"The world is always changing, and rarely for the better," she said, with a shadow of charm. But she moved forward, and touched her hand to Baluch's, and smeared her face with his blood.

There were so many.

The whine started almost too low to hear. It crept into Bramble's head, slightly, very slightly, louder with each ghost that took blood. She shook her head to try to clear it, but the sound kept on, a high unpleasant vibration, like very loud screaming, very far away. She saw that Safred, Martine and Ash heard it too.

Baluch began to grow pale, and Ash and Martine rolled a rock over for him to sit on.

Bramble wasn't sure what she had expected—perhaps that as each ghost took the blood, it would fade, as ghosts did after a quickening. That didn't happen. They merely took their places back in the circle, and waited with inhuman patience.

The noise, now, was loud enough to give her a headache. Then, at the corner of her eye, she seemed to see movement, but when she turned her head there was nothing there. She walked over to Safred and Martine. Ash joined them, his hands at his ears.

"Can you hear that?" Bramble asked.

"It's the soul eaters..." Safred said, her eyes white-rimmed.

Bramble went cold. This—*this*—was what the gods had feared. This was the battle they had been fighting, against a myth, a story to frighten children: be good or the soul eaters will get you after death. If the soul eaters were here, in the land of the living, what would that mean?

"They came when we were at Obsidian Lake," Martine said, "but they faded once you were back."

Bramble looked over at Baluch. The noise had started, when? When Alder had tried to kill Thegan, when the soldiers' ghosts had tried to kill Saker, when the ghosts had bled a captive so they would not fade.

"The dead should not kill the living," she whispered. In the corner of her vision, shapes writhed. She let her eyes go out of focus, and saw them more clearly: distorted human shapes, elongated or swollen almost past recognition. Repulsive, hungry for life, for spirit, for everything that they were not.

Safred was nodding. "I think when the dead walk the land in solid bodies, and especially when the dead kill the living, the barrier between life and death grows thinner. If it grows thin enough, they will break through."

"What do they want?" Ash seemed paler than before, but he spoke forcefully.

"Life," Safred said.

Martine reeled, as if she had Seen something terrible. "They want to eat," she said. "Everything. All life. Not just humans. Everything."

"Once the ghosts are gone..." Bramble said. "The barrier will be strong again."

"Baluch will die, though," Martine whispered. She was ashen, and clung to Arvid's hand. "That one death might be enough to breach the wall."

"The ceremony's started," Arvid said. "Can we replace him before he dies? Can I give blood?"

As one, they shook their heads. Bramble wasn't sure why she was so certain, but she was. If this was going to work, it had to be Acton and Baluch, the ones who had begun it all.

"We just have to hope that the barrier can take one more death," Safred said.

When Baluch finally fainted, Acton sat on the rock, his friend's body lying across him. He supported Baluch's neck and laid the bleeding hand over his own, ready for the ghosts.

The whine had grown and the shapes filled half of Bramble's vision now, the writhing forms strangely overlaid on the real world, as though they were a thin curtain she could see through.

The ghosts came, and kept coming, in their thousands.

The leader of Saker's army, a ghost with beaded hair, approached last, when Baluch's blood had almost stopped flowing.

He came reluctantly, staring at Acton, and stood over Baluch but did not reach for him. His face was impossible to read, emotions changing on it rapidly.

Ash took pity on him. "Speak," he said gently.

"I swore revenge for the death of my wife," he said. "I thought she'd wait for me...but she hasn't. She's gone on."

"Perhaps she is waiting in the darkness beyond death," Ash said.

"I swore revenge," he repeated, as though it were the only truth he knew.

Acton smiled mirthlessly. "One more will finish him off. Take your blood and you'll kill the friend I held dearest in the world. Will that satisfy you?"

The man looked into his eyes and his face calmed. "I thought revenge would be sweet."

"So did I," Acton replied. "But it's like poisoned mead—sweet at first and then a spear in your vitals."

The ghost nodded and reached out to touch Baluch's hand; he

smeared the blood across his face. "I am Owl. I release you from your debt," he said.

A sigh went up from the ghosts and Acton laid Baluch down, tears ice white against the paleness of his face. He knelt for a moment beside the body, his hand on Baluch's chest. Bramble thought of their two baby heads crowding together over a bowl of soup, a thousand years and a lifetime away, and her throat was too tight to speak. She put a hand on Acton's cold shoulder.

Ash came forward to Baluch and hesitated, looking at Saker.

"No," Acton said. "Leave him be. No need to bring him back."

Ash nodded and touched Baluch's face, as if saying goodbye. The ghosts watched. Some even wept.

Now, Bramble thought. Now they'll fade. But they did not, and the shrieking of the soul eaters rose higher and higher in a triumphant scream.

SAKER

NO FORGIVENESS," Alder said flatly, staring at Owl in disgust. "Never."

Saker was huddled on a rock to one side. He raised his head, slowly, exhausted, the sound in his head driving him to madness. Of course his father would refuse. The chance to exercise power? He couldn't resist it. Hadn't he heard those stories? Hadn't he understood what they meant?

He went to his father. "We have a chance to find peace. For everyone. Justice for the future. Fairness."

Alder sneered at him. "They've cozened you, boy. They'll back out of it as soon as we're gone and you'll have done it all for nothing."

Saker felt emptied, calmer than he had ever felt in his whole life. Listening to the stories had changed him, shown him how much he shared with others. He was not a freak, an outcast. The stories had changed everyone there—he had seen it in their faces. Everyone except Lord Thegan. And his father. They were the same, Saker thought, men who saw others only as servants or enemies. He couldn't be angry with his father; but he could pity him. And he could control him.

"I raised you, Alder, son of Snipe, and I can cast you back into the darkness beyond death," he said.

"Hah!" Alder said. "Try it."

Saker cast a quick look at the sky, which was already lightening, the short summer night almost over.

"Alder, son of Snipe!" he called. "I seek justice. I seek balance. And in their name, I banish you to the darkness you came from."

His father turned, livid, his bull shoulders pulled up and his fists clenched, ready to strike Saker down as he had many time before.

Saker held out his own hand, palm up. "I strike you still!" he cried, a spell he had seen Freite use but never tried himself before.

Alder slowed and stopped like a man caught in treacle, then gathered his strength and tried to forge on against the spell.

His will against his father's. For a moment, Saker faltered. Then Zel came to his side, and Martine to his other like a mother, like his own mother whom she looked so much like.

He firmed his voice. "Alder, I cast you out—I cast you out of this company, into the arms of Lady Death!"

His father's ghost faded and was gone.

Now, Saker thought, the others can go on to rebirth. He took a long breath and looked around, waiting for the circle of ghosts to fade with the morning light.

But they did not.

The shapes at the corners of his eyes grew wilder and stronger.

BRAMBLE

THE SOUL eaters' constant whine was now an agonising shriek. Around them, others were beginning to hear it. Merroc and Ranny looked around as if searching for its origin. The ghosts moved uneasily and formed small groups again, instead of the united mass they had been.

"Something's wrong," Bramble said, barely able to see anything beyond the twisting shapes that blurred her vision. "The ghosts have to fade, and soon, or the barrier will breach. Safred, can you ask the gods?"

Safred's eyes glazed, as they had seen her do so many times before. This time, she shook her head. "They are not there. There is no space in me for them any more. I am filled." She paused, as if trying to decide whether she was glad or hurt, and then seemed to choose. "I will never hear them again," she said contentedly.

Bramble reached for the gods in her head, but they were so very far away, too far to hear clearly. "Can you cast, Martine?" she asked.

Saker came up and reluctantly she moved back to let him join their circle. She had hated him for so long...she could kill him now, and the ghosts would fade. This was her chance to take revenge, in a righteous cause. She drew her knife and looked across at Acton. He was staring at Saker with a deep compassion, and somehow that allowed her to let go of anger. Pity for Saker flowed through her, and a bemused understanding. She slid her belt knife back into its sheath, and the movement was like a sigh.

"I think," he said hesitantly, looking at the ground instead of meeting their eyes, "that they have lost their way. They are ready to go, but they don't know how. The spell has cut them off from the darkness beyond death, and they need to find a way back."

"Perhaps the soul eaters are concealing the way," she said slowly.

367

Saker blanched and looked wildly around at the twisting shapes. "Soul eaters?" His hands shook. "What have I done?"

"If you could banish me the way you did your father, could they follow me?" Acton asked.

"I don't think so. I sent him back to where he had been—which was not on the path to rebirth." The words came haltingly.

Then Maryrose came towards them, and they moved back to give her room. She looked at Ash.

"Say what you wish to say," he said.

"The door to rebirth opens at death," she said. "I have seen it, and did not go through. But if someone were to die and go through, we could follow, I think."

"Is that my job?" Saker asked. "To die? I could do that, I think."

That felt almost right to Bramble, but not quite. It was too easy, somehow.

"Ash," Martine said, "remember that song you sang us, in Hidden Valley, about the prey?"

Ash said the words aloud:

The gods' own prey is galloping, is riding up the hill
Her hands are wet with blood and tears and dread
She is rearing on the summit and her banner floats out still
Now the killer's hands must gather in the dead.

"The gods' own prey," Bramble said, thinking of Sebbi, speared upon the Ice King a thousand years ago. It was hard to think clearly, the noise was growing so loud. "That's me. The prey is the Kill, and I'm the Kill."

"The Kill Reborn," Martine said. "Are you ready to die?"

"I've died twice already—third time counts for all."

She wanted to laugh aloud. If she had any Sight—and she still wasn't sure about that—it was telling her loud and certain sure that this was the right thing to do. Acton looked at her sadly, but she smiled back with relief. No need to kill anyone. No need for anyone else to die.

The shapes grew stronger and across the plateau exclamations came thick and fast.

Swords were drawn and swiped at thin air, people tried to bat the shapes away from them, Friede picked up her crutch, swung it wildly and then stood stone still, realising she was hitting out at nothing solid. But the shapes grew stronger, fuller, as though they were drawing strength from the reactions. From the fear.

Bramble looked with blurred eyes at the shapes twisting just beyond death. "Now you won't have to wait at all for me," she said to Acton. "We can be reborn together, right now. And after all this, the gods owe us a good life!"

He laughed.

"I had a good life," he said. "But one with you will be better!"

Everyone else was solemn, but Bramble was filled with elation. She knelt and fished out the red scarf from her saddlebags, then hunted in the crowd of ghosts until she found a woman with a lance. She borrowed it and tied the scarf to the tip as it was in the Spring Chase.

It was almost sunrise. The grey light before dawn showed them all clearly: the warlords and their men, the Turviters, the wide circle of ghosts bedabbed with Baluch's blood. Bramble met the eyes of those she had known and nodded.

She stood holding the lance, ready — but something was missing.

"Wait," Martine said, her eyes blank with Sight. "Someone is coming."

Someone on horseback, galloping. Bramble could hear the hoofbeats, growing louder. They seemed, impossibly, to come from across the river. Closer now, but no horse in sight. Her heart started to beat in rhythm. She dropped the lance. As the sound seemed to pass through the circle of ghosts, a figure condensed out of the air, a figure that she knew, of course, who else? A gift from the gods — or may be he'd just decided to come back himself.

He came straight to her, trotting, his roan hide gleaming, his wise eyes welcoming her. She ran to him and threw her arms around his cold neck, until he butted her side and whinnied. Then she pulled back and looked him in the eye.

"I'm sorry," she said.

He butted her again, but this time impatiently, as if she were wasting time, so she swung up onto his back. He had only the old blanket she had used in Wooding. No saddle, no bridle, no bit. Her heart was singing. Acton came over to them and handed her the lance, the red scarf beginning to stir in the wind before dawn.

Then she touched the roan's neck and brought him over to Maryrose.

"Come up?" she asked, reaching a hand down. Maryrose eyed the horse dubiously, but grasped her hand. Acton helped her to mount behind Bramble, then stood with one hand on the roan's shoulder. Merrick came forward to stand at his other shoulder.

"What are you going to do?" Ash asked.

She looked up to where the cliff ended abruptly, far above the waves. "He's a jumper," she said. "We're going to jump."

Their faces were so solemn, she wanted to laugh, but she could feel tears prick her eyelids, too. Each of them, in turn, touched her leg in farewell: Ash, Martine, Safred, Leof, Sorn.

Even Saker. "Thank you," he said.

The twisting shapes were moving faster, the gestures clearer, more violent, the shrieking louder; those who could hear it clearly dropped to the ground clutching their heads, and others clapped hands uselessly to their ears.

They were trying to frighten her, she realised. Her death would only mend the Domains if she were not frightened. If she feared as she died, it would open the door to them, and they would burst into this world to destroy, a greater plague than ever the wind wraiths could be, because all of life was their enemy.

Then she let herself smile, the familiar pleasure she always felt before a chase rushing through her. She had never been on good terms with fear, and she wasn't going to start now, not with her love running beside her, not with the jump of her life before her.

She raised the lance above her head and the ghosts fell in behind her, Cael and Owl at their head.

She clicked her tongue to the roan.

He moved forward, gathering speed, cantering up the hill into the morning sun. Maryrose held on tightly. In the last yards he sped into a gallop and launched himself as he had from the edge of the chasm in Wooding, that vast, impossible leap that felt so much like flying. They went up into a fractured world of light and air, the red scarf streaming out behind her, and they were poised for a moment in space, waves beneath them, white water and cliffs beckoning, and she laughed as they fell.

ASH

ASH'S BREATH caught in his throat when he saw them outlined like shadows against the rising sun, and then saw the shadows fade in mid-air, dissipating as a water sprite shreds itself on the wind.

The rest of the ghost army followed, Cael leading the way, Flax and Zel next, more and more, faster and faster, as those behind realised what was happening and became urgent to move, to jump, to be released.

None of them looked back.

As each one jumped and faded, the shrill threat from the soul eaters grew a little less, the shapes moving across his vision retreating.

They were gone by the time the sun was fully up, ghosts and soul eaters alike, and Ash slowly became aware of the normal sounds of the headland. Cows lowed somewhere, waiting to be milked. The sea washed the rocks below. The dawn breeze wuthered gently through the rocks.

Ash looked around the headland, at the weapons discarded by the ghosts lying like a tribute pile around Baluch, at the humans left there. As he turned, he saw that they were surrounded by people: not just the parley group, but many more Turviters, and others, people who'd been on the Road by the look of them. The folk from the countryside who had run to Turvite for protection had finally arrived, including his parents. Rowan and Swallow walked towards him, smiling. He walked towards them stiffly, knowing that if he tried to run he'd fall down. His mother said his name, and there was a sob in the word, as if she'd been afraid for him. He fell into their embrace, exhausted but happy.

He turned to beckon Martine over, and saw that she was facing down a squad of the Moot staff from Turvite who wanted to arrest Saker. Saker wasn't resisting, but Martine held up a hand.

"Wait," she said. She took Saker and led him towards the cliff. Was she going to give him the option of jumping off? That didn't seem like her.

The crowd started shouting curses and threats at Saker.

Arvid walked towards them, looking troubled. Ash agreed with him. Saker had to be arrested. Of course. It was a waste, in a way, but...the River spoke sharply to him, more reprovingly than he had ever heard her.

We do not approve of waste, She said.

The ground around Saker's feet began to churn, just as the ground around the altar had churned.

"Martine!" Ash called, and raced towards her. She jumped back and took a few steps down the slope, but Saker stood still, staring at the earth without understanding. He looked so tired it was a miracle he was standing at all.

Then the delvers burst from the earth and surrounded him.

The crowd was silent. Some were running away, others were praying. Ranny, to Ash's admiration, walked forward. She stood next to Ash and Martine. Safred joined them, looking helpless.

"I can't stop them," she called to Saker apologetically.

He will be taken for healing, the River said to Ash. *And punishment.*

Then the ground flew up around Saker and he and the delvers disappeared, just as the altar had disappeared, as Cael had, leaving only ploughed earth behind.

Ash cleared his throat and turned to the crowd.

"He has been taken for punishment," he said. After a moment's silence, the crowd started cheering. It made Ash feel sick, which was stupid. These people had lost everything because of Saker, he told himself. Of course they want him punished. But he remembered the inhuman power that had destroyed the Weeping Caverns, and the cold, beautiful eyes of the water spirits, and shivered.

Sorn stepped forward and held up a hand and the crowd quieted, curious.

"Before witnesses on this last night, the spirit of Acton proclaimed that he had intended this land to be ruled by councils, not by warlords." She let the stir in the crowd die down before she went on, eyeing Thegan. "It is my purpose, as Lady of the Central Domain, to honour his wishes. The warlords' council is met here already. I suggest that it be made permanent, so that the Eleven Domains can become truly united, and that each Domain establish an advisory council such as exists already in the Last Domain, similar to the councils in the free towns. What say you?"

The crowd roared its approval and Sorn turned to the warlords with a smile. Thegan stepped forward to object, and Merroc waved him away.

"You have no voice in this council, Thegan. Your *nephew* is Lord of Cliff Domain, Sorn is Lady of Central. You have nothing, and you will not be listened to."

Ranny cleared her throat. "More than that, Lord Merroc. The officer Thegan is under charge of murder, of Horst the archer and Zel the Traveller. As we all witnessed."

Thegan smiled contemptuously at her. "Horst was my own man. You have no rights in his death."

He's going to get away with it, Ash thought. Again. Just like it's always been since the warlords took over. But this was not the same group of people who had climbed up the headland the day before.

"You will hang for Zel's death," Ranny said. "I promised that you would face justice, and I will not be forsworn."

Garham looked at the Moot staff and pointed to Thegan. "Arrest the officer and take him to the Moot Hall cells."

They surrounded Thegan and Boc held out his hand for Thegan's sword, which he surrendered reluctantly.

Ash moved over to Merroc and said, "If you don't support Turvite in his death, he'll have the Domains at war within a year." Merroc stiffened and nodded, once.

"I heard the stories," Merroc said. "If he has not been changed by them, he has the heart of a soul eater, and deserves to die."

"He carries three knives as well as his sword," Sorn said. Thegan shot her a glance of pure hatred; but he handed over the knives and went with Boc and his men, down the hill, head still high.

Eolbert offered his arm to Sorn, who took it after a brief look and smile to Leof. "Come, my lady. Let us go back to the Moot Hall out of this sun and discuss the best way to run this council of ours."

"Here is someone who can advise us," Sorn said, stopping next to a fat old lady in dusty clothes. "Vi, the Voice of Baluchston, is deep in the confidence of the Lake and wise in the ways of managing a free people."

Vi smiled at her approvingly. "As to that, lass, I don't know, but I wouldn't mind a chance to put my feet up."

Sorn laughed and offered Vi her other arm. They led the parley group and most of the Turviters down the hill towards the city. Arvid glanced back to Martine before he left, and she waved him away with a reassuring smile.

Ash stared out over a landscape which was coming back to life. Farmers were harvesting, wagons were back on the roads, boats on the river. Everywhere seemed alive but here, the plateau was enormous without the crowd. The trampled grass was already turning yellow under the sun.

Safred was standing in a daze of fatigue. Ash hoped that was all it was. He put a hand under her elbow and guided her towards the path, Martine taking her other arm. She moved slowly, as though she were wading through high water. His parents went ahead of them down the hill.

"What about you?" Martine asked him. "What are you going to do now?"

Ash paused, then took a deep breath and sang, in Flax's memory: "Up jumps the sun in the early, early morning…" His parents whirled around, his mother's face alight with a kind of joy he'd never seen there before. For a moment, he was full of regret for the life that he'd thought he'd wanted. He could have it now, if he chose. But the River and the music twined together in his mind, and he knew that Road was closed to him.

"I'm going to make music," he said. He looked his father in the eyes. "New music. Make it up and write it down. Bramble's story first."

His father seemed to understand but said nothing. His mother put a hand on his father's arm, and they turned and walked on.

Ash and Martine paused, looking back at the place where Bramble had seemed, for a moment, to fly.

"That will be a good song," Martine said.

Ash hoped so. He could hear it in his head, and feel the River listening with approval. They walked down to the city together as the music played for him, flute and drum and oud, twining together around the sweet notes of a horn, crying out her beauty and her courage. And her bloody-mindedness, too. He knew the refrain, already:

The road is long and the end is death
If we're lucky.

extras

orbit

meet the author

PAMELA FREEMAN is an award-winning writer for young people. She has a doctorate of creative arts from the University of Technology, Sydney, Australia, where she has also lectured in creative writing. She lives in Sydney with her husband and young son. To find out more about the author, visit www.castingstrilogy.com.

introducing

If you enjoyed
FULL CIRCLE,
look out for

HAND OF ISIS

by Jo Graham

Set in ancient Egypt, Hand of Isis *is the story of Charmian, a handmaiden, and her two sisters. It is a novel of lovers who transcend death, of gods who meddle in mortal affairs, and of women who guide empires.*

My mother was a Thracian slave girl who died when I was born, so I do not remember her. Doubtless I would have died too, as unwanted children will, had Iras' mother not intervened. Asetnefer was from Elephantine, where the Nile comes out of Nubia at the great gorges, and enters Egypt. Her own daughter was five months old when I was born, and she took me to her breast beside Iras, a pale scrap of a newborn beside my foster sister. She had attended at the birth, and took it hard when my mother died.

I do not know if they were exactly friends. I heard it said later

381

that Pharaoh had often called for them together, liking the contrast between them, the beauty of my mother's golden hair against Aset-nefer's ebony skin. Perhaps it was true, and perhaps not. Not every story told at court is true.

Whatever her reasons, Asetnefer nursed me as though I were a second child of her own, and she is the mother I remember, and Iras my twin. She had borne a son some years before Iras, but he had drowned when he was three years old, before my sister and I were born. It is this tragedy that colored our young lives more than anything else, I believe, though we did not mourn for him, having never known him. Asetnefer was careful with us. We should not play out of sight of people; we should not stray from her while she worked. She carried us both, one on each hip in a sling of cloth, Iras to the left and me to the right, until we grew too heavy and had to go on our feet like big children. She was freeborn, and there was doubtless some story of how she had come to be a slave in Alexandria by the sea, but I in my innocence never asked what it was.

And so the first thing I remember is this, the courtyards of the great palace at Alexandria, the slave quarters and the kitchens, the harbor and the market, and the Court of Birds where I was born. In the palace, as in all civilized places, the language of choice was Koine Greek, which educated people speak from one end of the world to the other, but in the slave quarters they spoke Egyptian. My eyes were the color of lapis, and my hair might glow bronze in the sun, but the amulet I wore about my neck was not that of Artemis, but a blue faience cat of Bastet.

In truth, that was not odd. There were golden-haired slaves from Epirus and the Black Sea, sharp Numidians and Sardinians, men from Greece fallen on hard times, mercenaries from Parthia and Italy. All the world met in Alexandria, and every language that is spoken was heard in the streets and in her slave quarters. A quarter of the people of the city were Jews, and it was said that there were more Jews in Alexandria than in Jerusalem. They had their own neighborhood, with shops and theaters and their own temples, but one could not even count the Jews who studied at the Museum and Library, or who taught there. A man might have a Greek name and blond hair, and yet keep the Jewish sabbath if it suited him. So it was of little importance that I looked Greek and acted Egyptian.

Iras, on the other hand, looked as Egyptian as possible and had the mind of a skeptic philosopher. From her earliest days she never ceased asking why. Why does the sea pile against the harbor mole? Why do the stars shine? What keeps us from flying off the ground? Her black hair lay smooth in the heavy braids that mine always escaped, and her skin was honey to my milk. We were as alike as night and day, parts of one thing, sides of the same coin.

The seas pile against the harbor mole because Isis set them to, and the stars are the distant fires of people camping in the sky. We could not fly because like young birds we had not learned yet, and when we did we should put off our bodies and our winged souls should cavort through the air, chasing and playing like swifts. The world was enchantment, and there should be no end it its magic, just as there was no end to the things that might hold Iras' curiosity. And that is who we were when we first met the Princess Cleopatra.

Knowing all that she became, it is often assumed that at that age she must have been willful and imperious. Nothing is further from the truth. To begin with, she was the fifth child and third daughter, and not reckoned of much account. Her mother was dead as well, and the new queen had already produced a fourth princess. There was little reason for anyone to take note of her, another Cleopatra in a dynasty full of them. I only noticed her because she was my age.

extras

In fact, she was exactly between me and Iras in age, born under the stars of winter in the same year, and when I met her I did not know who she was.

Iras and I were five years old, and enjoying a rare moment of freedom. Someone had called Asetnefer away with some question or another, and Iras and I were left to play under the eyes of half the other slave women of the household in the Court of Birds. There was a fountain there, with worn mosaics of birds around the base, and we were playing a splashing game, in which one of us would leap in to throw water on the other, who would try to avoid being soaked, waiting her turn to splash the other. Running from a handful of cold water, I noticed a girl watching us with something of a wistful expression on her face. She had soft brown hair falling down her back, wide brown eyes that seemed almost round, smudged with sooty lashes. She was wearing a plain white chiton and girdle, and she was my height precisely. I smiled at her.

At that she came out from the shadow of the balcony above and asked if she could play.

"If you can run fast enough," Iras said.

"I can run," she said, her chin coming up. Faster than a snake, she dipped in a full handful of water and dashed it on Iras.

Iras squealed, and the game was off again, a three-way game of soaking with no rules.

It lasted until Asetnefer returned. She called us to task immediately, upbraiding us for having our clothes wet, and then she saw the other girl and her face changed.

"Princess," she said gravely, "you should not be here rather than in the Royal Nursery. They will be searching for you and worrying if you have come to harm."

Cleopatra shrugged. "They never notice if I'm gone," she said. "There is Arsinoe and the new baby, and no one cares what becomes of me." She met Asetnefer's eyes squarely, like a grown-up, and there was no self-pity in her voice. "Why can't I stay here and play? Nothing bad will happen to me here."

"Pharaoh your father will care if something happens to you," Asetnefer said. "Though it's true you are safe enough here." A frown came between her eyes, and she glanced from the princess to Iras, who stood taller by half a head, then to me with my head to the side.

A princess, I thought with some surprise. She doesn't seem like a goddess on earth. At least not like what I think a goddess should be.

"Has he not arranged for tutors for you?" Asetnefer asked. "You are too old for the nursery."

She shrugged again. "I guess he forgot," she said.

"Perhaps he will remember," Asetnefer said. "I will take you back to the nursery now, before anyone worries. Girls! Iras! Charmian! Put dry clothes on and behave until I get back."

She did not return until the afternoon had changed into the cool shades of evening, and the birds sang in the lemon trees. Night came by the time Iras and I curled up in our cubicle in one bed, the sharp smell of meat roasted with coriander drifting in through the curtain door. Iras went straight to sleep, as she often did, but I was restless. I untangled myself from Iras' sleep weight, and went outside to sit with the women in the cool night air. Asetnefer sat alone by the fountain, her lovely head bent to the water as though something troubled her.

I came and stood beside her, saying nothing.

"You were born here," she said quietly, "on a night like this. A

extras

spring night, with the harvest coming in and all the land green, which is the gift of the Nile, the gift of Isis."

"I know," I said, having heard this story before, but not impatient with it.

"He is your father too," she said, and for a moment I did not know who she meant. "Ptolemy Auletes. Pharaoh. Just as he is Iras' father. You are sisters in blood and bone as well as milk sisters."

"I knew that too," I said, though I hadn't given much thought to my father. I had always known Iras was my real sister. To be told it as a great truth was no surprise.

"That makes her your sister too. Cleopatra. Born under the same stars, the scholars would say."

I digested this a minute. I supposed I didn't mind another sister. She had seemed like she could be as much fun as Iras, and if she was a goddess on earth, she was really a very small goddess.

"You will start lessons with her tomorrow," Asetnefer said. "You and Iras both. You will go to the palace library after breakfast." She looked at me sideways now, and I wondered what she saw. "Cleopatra is to have a tutor, and it is better if she has companions in her studies. She is too much alone, and her half-sister Arsinoe is barely two and much too young to begin reading and learning mathematics. You and Iras have been given to her to be her companions, to belong to her."

"Given by whom?" I asked.

"By your father," she said, "Pharaoh Ptolemy Auletes."